I0761509

FABLES, FOLKLORE & ANCIENT STORIES

WELSH

FOLK & FAIRY TALES

FLAME TREE PUBLISHING
6 Melbray Mews, Fulham,
London SW6 3NS, United Kingdom
www.flametreepublishing.com

26 28 30 29 27
1 3 5 7 9 10 8 6 4 2

ISBN: 978-1-83562-259-9

Cover and pattern art was created by Flame Tree Studio, with elements courtesy of Shutterstock.com/svekloid/Elka_Marina/ illustrationsbyLora. Additional interior decoration courtesy of Shutterstock.com/amingdesign.

Judith John (lists of Ancient Kings & Leaders) is a writer and editor specializing in literature and history. A former secondary school English Language and Literature teacher, she has subsequently worked as an editor on major educational projects, including *English A: Literature* for the Pearson International Baccalaureate series. Judith's major research interests include Romantic and Gothic literature, and Renaissance drama.

A Note to the Reader: It is important to remember that these fairy tales are very much a product of their time, the narrative often falling short of today's accepted language and societal standards. While an editorial decision has been made to publish these works unredacted, this should not be viewed as an uncritical reproduction.

The text in this book is compiled and edited, with a new introduction, from the following sources: *Welsh Fairy Tales* by William Elliot Griffis (1921), *Welsh Folk-lore, A Collection* by the Rev. Elias Owen (1887), *Welsh Fairytales and Other Stories*, Collected and Edited by P.H. Emerson (1894), *Celtic Fairytales* by Joseph Jacobs and John Dickson Batten (1892), *More Celtic Fairytales* by Joseph Jacobs (1894), *The Welsh Fairy Book* by W. Jenkyn Thomas (1908) and *A Relation of Apparitions of Spirits, in the County of Monmouth, and the Principality of Wales* by the Rev. Edmund Jones (1813).

A copy of the CIP data for this book is available
from the British Library.

Designed and created in the UK | Printed and bound in China

Represented in the EU for product safety and
compliance by Authorised Rep Compliance Ltd.,
Ground Floor, 71 Lower Baggot Street, Dublin, D02
P593, Ireland. Contact at www.arccompliance.com

COLLECTOR'S EDITIONS
FABLES, FOLKLORE
& ANCIENT STORIES
WELSH
FOLK & FAIRY TALES
Reading List & Glossary of Terms
with a New Introduction by
DR. DELYTH BADDER
FLAME TREE PUBLISHING

CONTENTS

FABLES, FOLKLORE & ANCIENT STORIES

WELSH

FOLK & FAIRY TALES

SERIES FOREWORD

Stretching back to the oral traditions of thousands of years ago, tales of heroes and disaster, creation and conquest have been told by many different civilizations, in ways unique to their landscape and language. Their impact sits deep within our own culture even though the detail in the stories themselves is a loose mix of historical record, the latest archaeological evidence, transformed narrative and the unwitting distortions of generations of storytellers.

Today the language of mythology lives around us: our mood is jovial, our countenance is saturnine, we are narcissistic and our modern life is hermetically sealed from others. The nuances of the ancient world form part of our daily routines and help us navigate the information overload of our interconnected lives.

The nature of a myth is that its stories are already known by most of those who hear or read them. Every era brings a new emphasis, but the fundamentals remain the same: a desire to understand and describe the events and relationships of the world. Many of the great stories are archetypes that help us find our own place, equipping us with tools for self-understanding, both individually and as part of a broader culture.

For Western societies it is Greek mythology that speaks to us most clearly. It greatly influenced the mythological heritage of the ancient Roman civilization and is the lens through which we still see the Celts, the Norse and many of the other great peoples and religions. The Greeks themselves inherited much from their neighbours, the Egyptians, an older culture that became weary with the mantle of civilization.

Of course, what we perceive now as mythology had its own origins in perceptions of the divine and the rituals of the sacred. The earliest civilizations, in the crucible of the Middle East, in the Sumer of the third millennium BCE, are the source to which many of the mythical archetypes can be traced. Over five thousand years ago, as humankind collected together in cities for the first time, developed writing and industrial-scale agriculture, started to irrigate the rivers and attempted to control rather than be at the mercy of its environment, humanity began to write down its tentative explanations of natural events, of floods and plagues, of disease.

Early stories tell of gods or god-like animals who are crafty and use their wits to survive, and it is not unreasonable to suggest that these were the first rulers of the gathering peoples of the earth, later elevated to god-like status with the distance of time. Such tales became more political as cities vied with each other for supremacy, creating new gods, new hierarchies for their pantheons. The older gods took on primordial roles and became the preserve of creation and destruction, leaving the new gods to deal with more current, everyday affairs. Empires rose and fell, with Babylon assuming the mantle from Sumeria in the 1800s BCE, in turn to be swept away by the Assyrians of the 1200s BCE; then the Assyrians and the Egyptians were subjugated by the Greeks, the Greeks by the Romans and so on, leading to the spread and assimilation of common themes, ideas and stories throughout the world.

The survival of history is dependent on the telling of good tales, but each one must have the 'feeling' of truth, otherwise it will be ignored. Around firesides, or embedded in a book or a computer, the myths and legends of the past are still the living materials of retold myth, not restricted to an exploration of historical origins. Now we have devices and global communications that give us unparalleled access to a diversity of traditions. We can find out about Indigenous American, Indian, Chinese and tribal African mythology in a way that was denied to our ancestors, we can find connections, plot the archaeology, religion and the mythologies of the world to build a comprehensive image of the human experience that is both humbling and fascinating.

The books in this series introduce the many cultures of ancient humankind to the modern reader. From the earliest migrations across the globe to settlements along rivers, from mountainous landscapes to vast steppes, from woodlands to deserts, humanity has adapted to its environments, nurturing languages and observations and expressing itself through records, mythmaking stories and living traditions. There is still so much to explore, but this is a great place to start.

Jake Jackson
General Editor

FABLES, FOLKLORE & ANCIENT STORIES

WELSH

FOLK & FAIRY TALES

INTRODUCTION
& FURTHER READING

INTRODUCTION TO WELSH FOLK & FAIRY TALES

Wales, like its neighbouring countries within the British Isles, is a land rich in lore and legend. Many of these tales have been shared for generations, reimagined and reshaped by each passing storyteller or author, before eventually making their home within the pages of this book. Here we'll come face to face with lake-dwelling monsters, faithful hounds, wailing ghouls and cunning devils, witches, fairies, conjurers, and tales deeply rooted in medieval myths.

But what can these tales tell us about the people of Wales and their identity, culture, language and beliefs? What monstrous motifs make these legends unique to the Land of Song? Does Wales even *have* its own mythology?

It appears Welsh fairy tales are not altogether what they may seem...

CELTIC WALES

Ask someone outside the Celtic nations how they perceive Celticity, and they may paint broad brushstrokes of fierce, redheaded tartan-clad warriors or ancient druids pontificating in oak trees. Pose that same question to a Welsh person and they might reply that being a Celt is part and parcel of their own national identity. But you may be surprised to learn that Celticity as we understand it today – that is, the Romantic Celt – is in fact a wholly modern construct.

Indeed, the very notion of being a modern 'Celt' was one concocted only in the eighteenth century by French chronologist Paul-Yves Pezron (1639–1706), who compared the common 'Keltoi' origins of Welsh and Breton, and Welsh linguist, geologist and antiquarian Edward Lhuyd (1660–1709), who ascertained that Gaelic (Irish, Scottish Gaelic and Manx) and Brittonic (Welsh, Cornish and Breton) languages were the offspring of the historical Celts.

While it may seem quite dissonant by today's standards, the Welsh were historically proud of their Roman heritage – that they were somehow culturally related to the Irish prior to Lhuyd's time would have been viewed as distasteful and even offensive. Whereas today our shared culture is widely celebrated, one need only look towards the ending of the Second Branch of Y *Mabinogi*, the story of Branwen, with its less than flattening portrayal of the Irish, to understand what might garner an appreciative laugh among medieval Welsh audiences! Edward Lhuyd and the scholarly disciples that followed in his tracks instead turned national identity on its head, and Celtic fever swept the country.

This obsession with Celticity does not appear to have abated, with the warring philosophies of 'Celtomania' and 'Celtoscepticism' cyclically vying for academic attention. In popular media, on the other hand, Celticity and Irishness / Scottishness are all too often broadly conflated, and the

Celtic nations presented as one homogenous whole. It is vitally important to remember that Wales, as with all the other nations, has its own distinct folkloric tradition, one which we will briefly summarize within the confines of this introductory chapter.

A WELSH MYTHOLOGY?

The quest for Welsh mythology will repeatedly bring you to the same four tales – or Branches, as they are known – of *Y Mabinogi*, found predominantly within the vellum manuscripts of the White Book of Rhydderch and the Red Book of Hergest, dated *c.* 1382 and the beginning of the fifteenth century respectively. Better yet, the gamut of surviving medieval stories now known as *Y Mabinogion* (a title which is believed to have arisen due to a scribe's transcribing error), translated and compiled by Lady Charlotte Guest (1812–95) between 1838 and 1849.

Here are legends of otherworldly pacts, decapitated giant talking heads, enchanted mists, cursed shapeshifters, and brides magically assembled from flowers – tales which are frequently and conveniently packaged as evidence of a 'Welsh mythology'.

A cursory internet search will tell you that Rhiannon, of the First and Third Branches, is a corruption of the Celtic horse goddess Epona rather than a complex and strong – if supernatural – female protagonist and calumniated wife figure, despite the fact that there is no surviving Epona myth on which to establish such a connection. With several examples such as this, *Y Mabinogi* is commonly exalted as written evidence of a surviving Welsh culture drenched in 'ancient' traditions and beliefs.

But while this contrived image of a mythical land moulded by resurrecting cauldrons, flawed deities and magnificent Arthurian quests is undoubtedly a boon for the tourist industry (which has historically struggled to establish its voice amid our Celtic cousins in Ireland and Scotland), there is in fact no provable evidence of an existing Welsh mythology, much less one that has survived to this day. Wales may be a land where legends of fire-breathing battling dragons, stone-throwing giants and the tricky *tylwyth teg* abound, yet the concept of Welsh mythology is, in its most simplistic form, itself a myth. But let's not let that get in the way of a good story.

To view these intrinsically complex medieval texts simply as 'Welsh myths', separate from their historical, societal and cultural place within the landscape in which they were written, would be to do them – and Wales, in fact – an inherent disservice. While academic study of these tales has thankfully moved on, the residue of reductive colonialist attitudes such as those by the likes of nineteenth-century English cultural critic Matthew Arnold (1822–88) still linger in certain circles today. Here, the medieval Welsh storyteller is viewed as nothing more than an ignorant 'peasant', plundering the Branches from an ancient and majestic spiritual tradition, which they could not possibly hope to comprehend, unwilling to accept that the Welsh people could – perish the thought! – be capable of their own original thought and artistic genius.

While the tales which make up the Four Branches were presumably originally intended to be orated, *Y Mabinogi* is evidence of the Welsh medieval literary tradition at its very finest, with running themes and societal conventions contemporaneous to the fourteenth- and fifteenth-century manuscripts in which they were transcribed, edited to entertain and enthral their prospective audiences. Court etiquette, kingship and allusions to Norman incursion are woven into tales of romance, heartbreak and revenge (with a magical salmon or two thrown in for good measure), making for one magical medieval soap opera.

But things are rarely black and white, and *Y Mabinogi* here is no exception. While there may be a lack of concrete evidence in support of a Welsh mythology, there are undoubtedly allusions in these texts to a pre-existing belief structure in some form. Euhemeristic characters bearing the names of pagan gods will occasionally appear in the text, some of which are congruent with names seen in extant Irish legend, such as Lleu Llaw Gyffes of the Fourth Branch and Lug Lámfota of the Irish Tuath Dé Danann (albeit presented in a different role), both of which have been connected with the Gaulish god Lugus.

And while we may speculate as to possible echoes of long-forgotten deities, *Y Mabinogi*'s legacy remains steadfast, as evidenced by some of the tales included in this book. Australian folklorist Joseph Jacobs's (1854–1916) 'Powel, Prince of Dyfed' is a retelling of the First Branch, while 'The Wooing of Olwen', by the same author, recounts the Arthurian adventure 'Culhwch ac Olwen', the characters' names anglicized and their actions moulded to fit a narrative perhaps more palatable as a Disneyfied fairy tale. There is certainly nothing wrong with these retellings, as loose as some may be – stories by their very nature evolve with time or are forgotten and perish.

And so while current academic thought might refute the Four Branches as definitive evidence of a Welsh mythology, popular consensus may well be forgiven for viewing them as such.

THE ORAL TRADITION

There is little surviving evidence today of a significant written tradition in Celtic Britain. The earliest written records of the Britons were made by the hands of their colonizers after the Roman occupation, with Caesar himself claiming druidic secrets were passed through oral tradition alone.

Within the medieval period, tales such as *Y Mabinogi* and epic poems were recounted to courts and the homes of noblemen by specially appointed storytellers known as *Cyfarwyddion* (singular *Cyfarwydd*). These stories were often recalled employing useful memory aids, such as *Trioedd Ynys Prydain* (*The Welsh Triads*), to remember for example three fierce warriors, or three powerful swineherds to namedrop at a moment's notice.

This strong oral tradition largely persisted in Wales through to the modern era, which saw families of the nineteenth and twentieth centuries congregating around a roaring hearth or at the communal *Noson Lawen* (Merry Evening) to share tales of local ghouls and goblins.

But while local folklore survived in spoken form through the generations, the movement to record these tales in writing and preserve extant Welsh manuscripts was frequently overlooked. Were it not for the travelling antiquaries and learned societies of the eighteenth century, and the clergymen scholars of the nineteenth and twentieth centuries, many of these legends and superstitions would have been lost to time. And so it is to the eighteenth century that we next turn our sights.

A WELSH ROMANCE

Welsh historian R.T. Jenkins (1881–1969) dubbed the eighteenth-century in Wales 'a century of revivals', noting that aside from the obvious Methodist Revival, similar cultural, educational and industrial resurgences were also busy transforming the Welsh landscape during those years. In terms of Welsh tradition, there occurred a seismic movement among scholars to rediscover (and, where necessary, reimagine) a perceived ancient and glorious heritage in the face of growing anglicization – one which travelling writers grumbled had all but disappeared in the wake of sixteenth-century Protestantism.

Sparked by the interest in druidism that had already gripped France, Scotland and England, eighteenth-century Welsh antiquarians decided they might like to have a punt at reclaiming their own druidic lineage. Inspired by Caesar's account of Ynys Môn (Anglesey) being the last bastion of druidic strongholds in Britain during the first century CE, antiquarians such as Henry Rowlands (1655–1723), began to espouse each prehistoric burial chamber and monolith as druidic places of worship.

A visionary Glamorganshire stonemason, antiquary, poet and master forger, Edward Williams (1747–1826), better known by his bardic name Iolo Morganwg, envisaged a Wales where bards existed as the direct cultural ancestors of druids, and set about concocting a neo-druidic doctrine partly based on his own

Unitarian beliefs. From Iolo, the *Gorsedd* of the Bards of the Isle of Britain – and with it a new national institution – was born, the first ceremony being held on Primrose Hill in London in 1792 before becoming intertwined with various *eisteddfodau* (Welsh cultural festivals) across the country soon after, cementing its legacy. A surprising number of Wales's existing lore and legends today can be traced back to Iolo's fertile imagination and, regardless of his countless forgeries and invented traditions, his contribution to Welsh culture cannot be understated.

Just as there had been a burgeoning movement to recognize the Welsh as 'Celtic', so too was the attention of Welsh societies drawn to preserving its folklore and traditions. These societies were first realized by members of London's Welsh communities (the so-called 'London Welsh'), such as the Society of Ancient Britons, the Honourable Society of Cymmrodorion, or the Gwyneddigion. Saint David's Day processions and highly successful *eisteddfodau* were financed and executed, meetings were held to discuss and debate aspects of Welsh history, literature and tradition, various publications were funded, and charity was provided to struggling Welsh families living in the city. Much of the texts published by these societies, while invaluable, were steeped in Romantic ideals, reimagining a Welsh cultural stronghold forged from ancient ritual and tradition.

A perfect example of this romanticism can be seen in William Elliot Griffis's (1843–1928) 'The Fairy Congress', which alludes to Wales's attachment to its 'most ancient and honorable [*sic*] instrument': the harp. But the simple harp once played across Wales of old had been replaced in the seventeenth century by the triple harp – today itself regarded as a bastion of Welsh musical tradition – and even then, by the eighteenth century, the popular pastime of singing Welsh verse to its accompaniment had near enough disappeared across most of the country.

From this renewed interest in Welsh tradition followed the notion that all contemporaneous folkloric customs were somehow conveniently rooted in 'ancient' and ambiguous pre-Christian or medieval social practices and culture. Tracing linear folkloric relationships such as this between the past and present would be considered unwise by today's scholarly standards. However, this practice was still espoused in later works, many of which were penned during the emergence of folklore as a recognized discipline and at the tail end of the Industrial Revolution. Here, the geographical, cultural and linguistic landscapes were rapidly transformed in the wake of mass immigration and increasing oppression from the British state. Eminent folklorists of the twentieth century, such as vice president of The Folklore Society and the first professor of Celtic at Oxford University, Sir John Rhŷs (1840–1915), continued with the ideals of his Romantic forefathers, viewing folklore study as a means of reconstructing a threatened age-old cultural heritage.

While the approaches of these authors may have inadvertently over-simplified and disregarded evolving and heterogeneous cultural narratives to varying degrees, it is important to remember that without their unwavering enthusiasm for the conservation of this folkloric material, many of these tales would now be lost.

A HISTORY OF THE GLORIOUS AND THE GRIMM

The term 'fairy tale' itself is difficult to classify – an eighteenth-century translation of the French *contes de fées*, its exact definition is subject to academic disagreement and yet liberally used as a 'catch-all' title within popular parlance.

In general terms, a fairy tale is regarded as a simple, fictional story containing magical or enchanting elements presented as a short narrative, with archetypal characters such as princes, princesses, wizards, witches and mythical beasts aplenty. The tale itself often comprises themes of morality, providing a means of escapism as well as cultural validation. They are not actually obliged to feature any fairies, and historically, were more often geared towards adult audiences rather than children. It is for these reasons that folklorists will often favour the alternative German term *Märchen* instead.

Just as there is an obvious crossover between fairy and folk tales (oral narratives of unknown origin preserved through generations), many of the stories presented in this book could in fact be more accurately recognized as legends – tales which are rooted in folk belief and exhibit some historical foundation. 'The Myddfai Legend', for example, as told by antiquarian and cleric Elias Owen (1833–99), recounts the invented supernatural 'origin story' of the Physicians of Myddfai, a lineage of skilled folkloric physicians said to have lived in the thirteenth century, their herbal recipes having survived in Welsh medieval manuscripts.

The most well-known examples of fairy tales are arguably those collected by the Brothers Grimm. Much like the eighteenth-century Romantic revival in Wales, Jacob (1785–1863) and Wilhelm (1786–1859) Grimm collated their tales in the name of German nationalism, with the desire to promote the language and revive a perceived forgotten culture. Often touted as the founding fathers of folklore, their seminal *Kinder- und Hausmärchen*

(*Children's and Household Tales*, 1812) proved immensely popular, despite being an academic exercise in its initial guise. Later editions by the brothers became increasingly embellished, with the addition of Christian motifs and redacted scenes of rape, sexuality and violence.

In a similar vein, the authors of the tales included in this book have endowed the original tales with their own biases and embellishments. Scholar William Jenkyn Thomas (1870–1959) compiled *The Welsh Fairy Book* (1907) as an educational tool for his pupils. Elias Owen collated *Welsh Folk-lore* (1896) for the purpose of a prize-winning essay, submitted in a competition at the 1887 National Eisteddfod. Peter Henry Emerson (1856–1936), an Australian photographer and non-Welsh speaker, collected the accounts for *Welsh Fairy-tales and Other Stories* (1894) while overwintering in Ynys Môn in 1891. The backgrounds of these various authors are often just as important as the tales themselves, aiding us in our interpretation and understanding of the narratives they choose to present.

WELSH FOLK BELIEF: A WHISTLESTOP TOUR

Fairies

Fairies in Wales – or the *tylwyth teg* (fair family) as they're often known – come in a myriad of shapes and sizes, many of which can be found lurking in this book. It should be noted, of course, that none of those qualities reflect the delicate and gentle winged Victorian variety. Welsh fairies are frequently depicted as rugged, cunning and even vicious spirits, bound to both earth and bodies of water, and often found walking among us, hidden in plain sight.

In 1880, American writer Wirt Sikes (1836–83) attempted to categorize the types of fairies that could be found in Wales in his seminal book, *British Goblins*. And while the nineteenth-century habit of trying to neatly classify each and every folkloric entity is nothing short of problematic, especially when considering the additional nuance that exists when translating these tales from another language, his supernatural line-up provides a useful, if generalized, starting point:

Ellyllon: elves
Coblynnau: mine fairies
Bwbachod: household fairies
Gwragedd Annwn: fairies of the lakes and streams
Gwyllion: mountain fairies

As one might expect, the above definitions do not always tally with those provided by other antiquarians and folklorists, depending on the region in which they were encountered. For example, the word *ellyll* today is perhaps colloquially more often used in the context of an evil spirit or demon, and *coblynnau* is arguably less often heard than the preferred vernacular *cnocwyr*. Furthermore, there exist several other terms to describe fairies in Wales, some of which we will encounter here, such as William Jenkyn Thomas's version of 'The Pwca of the Trwyn' – a lengthy discussion which falls far outside the remit of this introductory chapter.

Terminology aside, the relationship between fairies and the Welsh people is complex and ambiguous. While fairies are frequently portrayed as dangerous or mischievous, many of the tales depict a symbiotic co-existence, albeit one which often came bound with certain conditions: aiding witches and conjurers in their craft (as opposed to the hostile relationship suggested in Peter Henry Emerson's 'The Fairy of the Dell'), relying on community midwives to birth their offspring, and even completing household chores in return for sustenance. Acts of kindness to their kin or their animals would be rewarded while cruelty was met in kind, as we can see here in Elias Owen's 'A Cruel Man and a Fairy Dog'.

Tales of changelings, such as William Elliot Griffis's 'The Gors Goch Changeling Legend' and William Jenkyn Thomas's 'The Llanfabon Changeling' are dotted across the country, where bouncing human babes were swapped for sickly, mewling imps – a sinister theme which is likely to have arisen as a convenient explanation for babies born with congenital disorders or additional learning needs during times when medical understanding was rudimentary and fear of the supernatural rife. Time slips are frequently featured in these tales, usually with tragic consequences, as is the notion of mortal men marrying beautiful fairy women of the lake-dwelling variety – an example of the aforementioned *gwragedd Annwn* – and often at a hefty price (which is invariably paid).

Fairy lore in Wales is intertwined with themes of grief, lust, revenge, greed and enchantment, serving as morality tales and a stark warning to the curious, as well as a reflection of society's attitude towards those perceived as outsiders or 'other'. While the complexity of the Welsh fairy is impossible to unpack here, in these tales, we see a snippet of why these spirits of land and water remain stalwarts of the collective consciousness to this day.

Ghosts

Wales's ghostloric pantheon comprises a veritable feast of spectres, some of which will likely prove familiar. Household figures seen throughout the rest of Britain and Ireland are often wont to raise their undead heads – entities such as the ethereal *Ladi Wen* (White Lady), the mischievous poltergeist, or those spooks who are bound to return to relay an important message or disclose the location of some long-hidden treasure.

But Wales also boasts its own distinctive lore that separates it from its neighbouring countries. Bizarre and abstract apparitions, spectral animal shapeshifters, poetic howling ghouls and phantasmal death omens seem to lurk around each corner and haunt every stile. In Elias Owen's tale of the spirit of Llanfor Church, Gwynedd, the restless ghost is exorcised in the form of a fierce, mare-throwing pig. A horrifying screaming wraith with burning orbs for eyes prowls around Gloddaeth woods in Llandudno, Conwy. A grisly phantom procession is witnessed by lodging workmen at Penderlwyn Goch farm the night before one of the unfortunate party meets their untimely end. These tales represent only a scrap of the wonderfully diverse ghostlore Wales has to offer.

Mythical Beings

Whereas Wales's ghosts seem so numerous as to materialize on each dim path and in every remote farmhouse, so too its monsters. The most well-known – and indeed cherished – of these today is likely the famous national emblem: *Y Ddraig Goch* (the red dragon). While dragons were previously emblematic of Wales during the Middle Ages and later utilized by the House of Tudor, the red dragon was only officially adopted as the Welsh flag in 1959 having slowly gained popularity as a symbol of Wales again during the nineteenth century. A version of its earliest origin story taken from *Historia Brittonum*, written by Nennius c. 828 CE, is retold here by William Jenkyn Thomas for all to enjoy.

Next to the dragon, a demonic water spirit known as the Afanc is surely Wales's most popular – and undoubtedly curious – monster.

First described as a spear-throwing, cave-dwelling assailant in the medieval romance *Peredur fab Efrawg* (*Peredur son of Efrawg*), by the Early Modern period, it had evolved to appear as a monstrous lake creature, part-reptile, part-beaver. In this book, William Elliot Griffis reimagines the Afanc (referred to here as 'Afang', most probably due to the influence of earlier writers, who used variable spelling such as 'Avangk' or 'Afangc') as a hideous, big-eared fiend, its face ape-like with eyes 'as big as pumpkins'. Here, he recounts one of the more popular tales, where it is lulled to sleep on the lap of a beautiful maiden, only to be dragged from its watery lair by horned oxen – an account from Llyn yr Afanc (The Lake of the Afanc) in Betws-y-Coed, first recorded by Edward Lhuyd himself in 1693.

Giants feature prominently within the folklore of Wales, and tales of their excursions and misdeeds have been interwoven with innumerable place names and geological focal points across the country. Peter Henry Emerson's account of 'The Giant's Apron-Full' serves as an example of a popular legend surrounding the intricately carved Neolithic burial chamber, Barclodiad y Gawres, in Ynys Môn, whereby the cairn was said to have been formed from boulders carried in a giantess's apron, dropped to the ground when the apron strings snapped. Similar stories prevail across the country – for example, in Gwynedd alone, giant snapping apron strings account for Baich y Gawres in Rhinogydd, Bryn Diweddu in Beddgelert, Bwlch y Deufan in Aber, and Ffedogiad y Gawres in Llanaelhaearn to name but a few topographical landmarks.

From mermaids and demonic water horses, to hell hounds and even a werewolf or two, mythical beings are numerous within the Welsh tradition, their mark not only left in the fairy tales and legends that are still told of them, but also on the very landscape itself.

Witches, Cunning Folk and Magic

Should one have wished to rid themselves of some pesky spirit, recover a sum of money, place a protective charm on their livestock or household, or counteract a witch's curse, then in days gone by, one may well have approached a *dyn* or *dynes hysbys*, the Welsh term for a cunning man or woman, or a conjurer. This term has existed in print since at least the early eighteenth century, and denotes an occult practitioner with multiple purposes within their respective communities, providing charms, recovering lost possessions and laying ghosts – all for a nominal fee.

Huw Llwyd represents one of the most widely recognized of these cunning folk, a colourful character with both historic and folkloric roots. A sixteenth-century soldier, scholar, musician, bard, alchemist and folk magician, his name appears time and time again in folk tales concerning magical practitioners and the supernatural. Here, he appears in two tall tales retold by Elias Owen and William Jenkyn Thomas.

The historical relationship between Wales and its witches is inherently complex and beyond the scope of this chapter. In Welsh fairy tale, the folkloric witch often operates within the confines of a domestic setting, bewitching farm animals, causing butter to sour, and cursing those that cross their path, as is evident in several of the stories presented in this book. Shapeshifting elements are common, where the witch frequently adopts the guise of a hare, as documented by William Jenkyn Thomas in 'Goronwy Tudor and the Witches of Llanddona'.

It is important to note that many of the witches and conjurers mentioned in these stories, rather than being works of fiction, are based on historic characters. These people would often have lived on the margins of society, shunned, feared and even persecuted, often through no fault of their own – a stark reminder that fairy tales are often rooted in unpleasant truths.

HAPPILY EVER AFTER

But does it *really* matter if you're not exactly *au fait* with Welsh lore and legend? Will it hamper your enjoyment of these tales if you can't tell your Matholwch from your Manawydan, or your *bwbach* from your *bwci bo*? Of course not. While an understanding of the contexts in which these stories were written is vitally important in appreciating wider Welsh history and culture, their primary function is simply to enchant and entertain as they have done for centuries…

… although a happily ever after isn't always guaranteed.

Dr Delyth Badder

FURTHER READING

Badder, Delyth and Norman, Mark, *The Folklore of Wales: Ghosts* (Cardiff: Calon, 2023)

Baxter, Richard, *The Certainty of the World of Spirits. Fully Evidenced by the Unquestionable Histories of Apparitions, Operations, Witchcrafts, Voices, &c. Proving the Immortality of Souls, the Malice and Misery of the Devils, and the Damned, and the Blessedness of the Justified.* (London: T. Parkhurst at the Bible and Three Crowns in Cheapside; and J. Salusbury at the Rising Sun near the Royal Exchange in Cornhill, 1691)

Bromwich, Rachel, *Trioedd Ynys Prydein: The Triads of the Island of Britain* (Cardiff: University of Wales Press, 2014).

Davies, Jonathan Ceredig, *Folk-lore of West and Mid-Wales* (Aberystwyth: Welsh Gazette Offices, 1911)

Davies, Sioned (ed.), *The Mabinogion* (Oxford: Oxford University Press, 2018)

Jones, Edmund, *A Relation of Apparitions of Spirits, in the Principality of Wales; To Which is Added the Remarkable Account of the Apparition in Sunderland, With Other Notable Relations from England; Together with Observations About Them, And Instructions from Them: Designed to Confute and to Prevent the Infidelity of Denying the Being and Apparition of Spirits; Which Tends to Irreligion and Atheism* (Trevecca, 1780)

Jones, Thomas Gwynn, *Welsh Folklore and Folk-Custom* (London: Methuen & Co. Ltd, 1930)

Morgan, Prys, 'From a Death to a View: The Hunt for the Welsh Past in the Romantic Period', in: Hobsbawm, Eric and Ranger, Terence, *The Invention of Tradition* (Cambridge: Cambridge University Press, 2000), pp. 43–100

Owen, Elias, *Welsh Folk-Lore: A Collection of the Folk-Tales and Legends of North Wales, Being the Prize Essay of the National Eisteddfod, 1887* (Oswestry and Wrexham: Woodall, Minshall, & Co., 1896)

Owen, Trefor Meredith, *Welsh Folk Customs* (Llandysul: Gwasg Gomer, 1987)

Rhŷs, John, *Celtic Folklore: Welsh and Manx, Vol. I and Vol. II* (Oxford: Clarendon Press, 1901)

Roberts, Peter, *The Cambrian Popular Antiquities: or, an Account of Some Traditions, Customs, and Superstitions, of Wales; with Observations as to their Origin, &c.* (London: E. Williams, 1815)

Rodway, Simon, 'The Mabinogi and the Shadow of Celtic Mythology', in: *Studia Celtica*, 52(1), 2018, pp. 67–85

Rodway, Simon, 'The Where, Who, When and Why of Medieval Welsh Prose Texts: Some Methodological Considerations', in: *Studia Celtica*, 41(1), pp. 47–89

Sikes, Wirt, *British Goblins: Welsh Folk-Lore, Fairy Mythology, Legends and Traditions* (London: Sampson Low, Marston, Searle, & Rivington, 1880)

Sims-Williams, Patrick, 'Celtomania and Celtoscepticism', in: Sims-Williams, Patrick (ed.), *Cambrian Medieval Celtic Studies* (Aberystwyth: CMCS, 1998)

Starling, Mhara, *Welsh Fairies* (Minnesota: Llewellyn Books, 2024)

Thomas, William Jenkyn, *The Welsh Fairy Book* (Cardiff: University of Wales Press, 1996)

Thompson, Stith, *The Folktale* (Berkeley: University of California Press, 1977)

Wood, Juliette, 'Folk Narrative Research in Wales at the Beginning of the Twentieth Century: The Influence of John Rhŷs (1840–1916)', in *Folklore* 116(3), 2005, pp. 325–341

Dr Delyth Badder is a Welsh folklorist and Honorary Research Fellow at St Fagans National Museum of History, Cardiff. She is the co-author of *The Folklore of Wales: Ghosts* (Calon, 2023) and is a regular contributor to discussions on folklore in the media. Her primary research explores the appearance of spirits within the Welsh folkloric tradition. In 2024, she was honoured nationally by Gorsedd Cymru in recognition of her contribution to Welsh folklore study. She also works as a Medical Examiner for the NHS.

ANIMAL TALES

Llên y Milod, or the folklore of beasts, explores the relationships and belief structures that exist in Wales between man and animal. In this chapter, we see animals appear in fables and in superstition, as prognosticators and as protectors. We will meet the oldest creatures in existence in William Jenkyn Thomas's 'The Ancients of the World', and some of the most terrifying, such as the fierce *Gwyllgi* (Wild Dog). Common attributes of folkloric beasts such as shapeshifting are also exemplified in tales such as 'Cadwaladr and His Goat' and 'A Strange Otter'.

What is probably Wales's most famous fairy tale – the legend of Gelert – is also included here. The heartbreaking tale of Prince Llywelyn Fawr (Llywelyn the Great) and his faithful hound was the brainchild of pub landlord David Pritchard in 1793 as a highly successful means of attracting tourists to Beddgelert. That the 'grave' of his martyred hound remains a top tourist attraction speaks of the enduring legacy of folkloric animals within the collective consciousness today.

A CRUEL MAN AND A FAIRY DOG

The person from whom the following tale was derived was David Roberts, Tycerrig, Clocaenog, near Ruthin.

A fairy dog lost its master and wandered about here and there seeking him. A farmer saw the dog, and took it home with him, but he behaved very unkindly towards the wee thing, and gave it little to eat, and shouted at it, and altogether he showed a hard heart. One evening a little old man called at this farmer's house, and enquired if any stray dog was there. He gave a few particulars respecting the dog, and mentioned the day that it had been lost. The farmer answered in the affirmative, and the stranger said that the dog was his, and asked the farmer to give it up to him. This the farmer willingly did, for he placed no value on the dog. The little man was very glad to get possession of his lost dog, and on departing he placed a well-filled purse in the farmer's hand. Some time afterwards the farmer looked into the purse, intending to take a coin out of it, when to his surprise and annoyance he found therein nothing but leaves.

Roberts told the writer that the farmer got what he deserved, for he had been very cruel to the wee dog.

FABLE OF WHY THE HERON FREQUENTS THE BANKS OF RIVERS AND LAKES

The heron, the cat, and the bramble bought the tithe of a certain parish. The heron bought the hay, mowed it, harvested it, and cocked it, and intended carrying it the following day, but in the night a storm came on, and carried the hay away, and ever since then the heron frequents the banks of the rivers and lakes, looking for her hay that was carried away, and saying, "Pay me my tithe."

The cat bought the oats, cut them, and even threshed them, and left them in the barn, intending the following day to take them to the market for sale. But when she went into the barn, early the next morning, she found the floor covered with rats and mice, which had devoured the oats, and the cat flew at them and fought with them, and drove them from the barn, and this is why she is at enmity with rats and mice even to our day.

The bramble bought the wheat, and was more fortunate than the heron and cat, for the wheat was bagged, and taken to the market and sold, but sold on trust, and the bramble never got the money, and this is why it takes hold of everyone and says, "Pay me my tithe," for it forgot to whom the wheat had been sold.

THE MAGPIE

"**You know** the brook at the bottom of the hill. Well, my mother met with very bad luck there, a good many years ago, and it was in this way – she was going to Newtown fair, on our old horse, and she had a basket of eggs with her. But, just as she was going to leave the 'fould', a magpie flew before her. We begged of her not to go that day – that bad luck would attend her. She would not listen to us, but started off. However, she never got further than the brook, at the bottom of the hill, for, when she got there, the old mare made straight for the brook, and jerked the bridle out of mother's hand, and down went the mare's head to drink, and off went the basket, and poor mother too. All the eggs were broken, but I'm glad to say mother was not much the worse for her fall. But ever since then I know it is unlucky to see a magpie. "But sir," she added, "there is no bad luck for us today, for the *magpie flew from left to right*."

CROWS

One black crow, bad luck for me. Two black crows, good luck for me. Three black crows, a son shall be born in the family. Four black crows, a daughter shall be born in the family. Five black crows shall be a funeral in the family. Six black crows, if they fly head on, a sudden death. Seven black crows with their tails towards you, death within seven years.

There was a young man, not so very long ago, who had been to sea for years. He was married, but had no children. He was one of the most spirited men you ever saw. He used to complain of his dreams. He said, "All at once last Sunday I was up in the air, and I saw the vessel I was in going at great speed, making for a mountain, and I tried as hard as I could to keep her from the mountain. I don't believe I was asleep at all, I could see it so plainly. I went along in the air, looking at seven black crows all the time. I got dizzy, and the vessel seemed to lower on to the earth. The vessel lowered within a few hundred feet of the earth, and I saw what I thought were fairies. I thought I had been there for days; in truth, it seemed to me I had been up there for three days, and that I could hear the fairies with mournful sounds drawing a coffin. I watched and watched, and saw seven crows on the coffin. It seemed as if they were going to bury someone. Whilst the coffin was going the seven crows flew up and bursted, and the heavens were illuminated more strongly than by the sun. Then I lost sight of the fairies, but saw some big giants in white walking about, and there was a big throne with a roof to it. And all at once I was in total darkness, but I could hear things flapping about, flying through the air. Then I saw the moon rising and all the stars, and all sorts of objects flying through the air. And one came to me, and put his hand upon my shoulder, saying: 'Prepare to meet us tomorrow.' After that everything went dark again. The first thing I knew I was in a ship steering, and the seven black crows were in front of me. I had a great trouble to steer my vessel. And as I went on the vessel struck a steeple, and exploded, and I awoke. Whereupon I jumped out of bed, looking very pale."

I left him on the beach at 11.30, after he told me this, when he went home. When he got home he could see seven black crows on the house. Other people could see the crows, but could not count them. He saw them all perched head on. He went into the house, and said, "There is something in these crows, Jane; see them on the roof."

She cried out and ran out and looked, but could not see the seven. After that he didn't seem to be himself, though there was nothing the matter with him. A week afterwards, I went out on the Sunday morning after breakfast, and there was a seat on the beach, and on it sat this man, Johnny, and another man.

"Why, Johnny, you look very pale," I said.

"Do I?" he said.

"Yes! indeed you do," I replied.

"Well, I don't know, I have had such dreams."

"What will they have been, then?" I asked.

"That I was in a full-rigged ship, with all sails set; I was all alone, but could see nothing, only seven black crows. I counted them, but my wife could see nothing, but she could hear something."

That same day, when he went home, he said to his wife:

"Ah, Jane, there is something coming over me," and he fell down dead.

EVA'S LUCK

As **black-eyed**, black-haired Eva Sauvet was walking one day in Jersey she saw a lozenge-marked snake, whereupon she ran away frightened.

When she got home and told her mother, the old woman said:

"Well, child, next time you see the snake give it your handkerchief."

The next day Eva went out with beating heart, and ere long she saw the snake come gliding out from the bushes, so she threw down her handkerchief, for she was too frightened to hand it to the snake.

The snake's eyes gleamed and twinkled, and taking the handkerchief into his fangs, he made off to an old ruin, whither Eva followed.

But when they got to the ruin the snake disappeared, and Eva ran home to tell her mother.

Next day, Père Sauvet and some men went to the ruin, where Eva showed the hole where the snake had disappeared.

Old Père Sauvet lit a fire, and smoked the snake out, killing it with a stick as it glided over the stones.

After that they dug out the hole, when they found the handkerchief. Digging still further along, they came upon a hollow place, at the bottom of which they found a lot of gold.

CADWALADR AND HIS GOAT

Cadwaladr had a very handsome goat named Jenny, of which he was very proud. Now Jenny was a very well-behaved goat as a rule and gave no trouble, but one evening she would not let Cadwaladr catch her. She ran round and round the field, and though Cadwaladr was fleet of foot, do what he would, he could not get near her. Then she jumped over the hedge, like a hunter, into the next field. When Cadwaladr went after her, she jumped into the field beyond, and over the mountain wall towards the mountain.

Several times she allowed Cadwaladr to come close up to her and then darted away. The last time she rushed up to the top of a high precipice. Cadwaladr, who had been getting wilder and wilder as his breath became shorter, now picked up a great stone and threw it at the exasperating animal with all his force. The stone knocked her over the precipice and she fell bleating to her doom. Cadwaladr was now very sorry, and made his way to the foot of the crag: the goat was dying, and licked his hand. This so affected him that he burst into tears, and sitting on the ground took the goat's head on his arm. Suddenly the goat was transformed into a beautiful young woman. Looking joyfully at him with great brown eyes, she said, "Ah, Cadwaladr, have I at last found you? Come with me." He put his hand in hers and allowed her to conduct him away. As for the hand, it felt just like a hoof, but when Cadwaladr looked at it, it seemed like an ordinary hand though it was whiter and more shapely than any hand he had ever seen before.

The maiden led him on and on, and Cadwaladr had never listened to more agreeable conversation than hers. At last they came to the top of a very high mountain. It was now night and the moon was shining. Cadwaladr looked round and saw that they were surrounded by a countless flock of goats, and the din of a most unearthly bleating arose suddenly. One of the goats which was larger than all the rest bleated as loudly as all the rest put together. This one rushed at Cadwaladr and, butting him in the stomach, sent him toppling over, just as he had sent Jenny. Cadwaladr went rolling down the mountain side and did not stop until his head went crash against a great rock. He fainted away and he did not recover consciousness until the sun and the singing birds awakened him in the morning. But he saw no more of either his goat or the fairy she had turned into from that day to his death.

THE STRAY COW

In a secluded spot in the upland country behind Aberdovey is a small lake called Llyn Barfog, or the Lake of the Bearded One. Its waters are black and gloomy, no fish is ever seen to rise to the surface, and the fowls of the air fly high above it.

In times of old the neighbourhood of the lake was haunted by a band of elfin ladies. They were sometimes seen in the dusk of a summer evening, clad all in green, accompanied by their hounds and comely milk-white kine; but no one was favoured with more than a passing glimpse till an old farmer residing at Dyssyrnant, in the adjoining valley of Dyffryn Gwyn, had the good luck to catch one of the Gwartheg y Llyn, or kine of the lake, which had fallen in love with the cattle of his herd. From the day that he captured the elfin cow the farmer's fortune was made. Never was there such a cow, never such calves, never such milk and butter and cheese, and the fame of the Fuwch Gyfeiliorn, or the Stray Cow, spread through that central part of Wales known as Rhwng y Ddwy Afon, the Mesopotamia between the banks of the Mawddach and those of the Dovey. The farmer, who had been poor, became rich, the owner of vast flocks and herds, a very patriarch of the mountains.

But much wealth made him mad. Fearing that the elfin cow would become too old to be profitable, he thought that he had better fatten her for the market. Even when she was fattened she showed that she was different from earthly cattle, for never was such a fat beast seen as this cow grew to be. Killing day came, and the neighbours came from all about to see it slaughtered. The cow was tethered, no regard being paid to her mournful lowing and pleading eyes. The farmer counted up his gains from the sale, and the butcher raised his red right arm to strike the fatal blow. Just as the bludgeon was falling, a piercing cry awakened the echoes of the hills and made the welkin ring. The butcher's arm was paralysed and the bludgeon fell from his hand. Looking in the direction from which the shriek had come, the astonished assemblage beheld a female figure, clad in green, with uplifted arms, standing on one of the crags overhanging Llyn Barfog, and heard her calling with a voice loud as thunder:

"Come thou, Einion's Yellow One, Stray-horns, the Parti-coloured Lake Cow. And the hornless Dodyn, Arise, come home."

No sooner were these words uttered than the elfin cow and all her progeny to the third and fourth generation were in full flight towards the lake. Partly recovering from his astonishment, the farmer ran his hardest after them, but when, breathless and panting, he gained an eminence overlooking the water, he saw the elfin dame, with the cows and their calves formed in a circle round her, leisurely descending mid-lake. They disappeared beneath the dark surface, leaving only the yellow waterlily to mark the spot where they had vanished.

The farmer was reduced from wealth to poverty, but few felt pity for one who had shown himself so ungrateful as to propose slaying his benefactor.

A STRANGE OTTER

One day two friends went to hunt otters on the banks of the Pennant, in Merionethshire. When they were yet some distance from the river they saw some small creature of a red colour, running fast across the meadows in the direction of the stream. Off they ran after it, but before they could catch it the little animal hid itself beneath the roots of a tree, on the brink of a river. The two men thought it was an otter, but at the same time they could not understand why it was red. They thought they would like to catch such an extraordinary specimen alive, and one of them said to the other, "You go home to get a sack, while I watch." Now, there were two holes under the roots of the tree, and while one held the sack with its mouth open over one of them, the other pushed his stick into the other hole. Presently the creature went into the sack, and the two men set out for home, thinking they had achieved a great feat. Before they had proceeded the width of one field the inmate of the sack spoke in a sad voice, and said: "My mother is calling for me: oh, my mother is calling for me!" This gave the two hunters a great fright, and they at once threw down the sack. Great was their surprise when they saw a little man in a red dress running out of the sack towards the water. He disappeared from their sight in the bushes by the river. The two men were greatly terrified, and felt that it was more prudent to go home than meddle any further with the Fair Family.

WHY DEUNANT HAS THE FRONT DOOR IN THE BACK

The cattle of the farmer living at Deunant, close to Aberdaron, were grievously afflicted with the "short disease", which is the malady known in English as the black quarter. Naturally, he thought they were bewitched. Old Beti'r Bont, whose character was by no means above suspicion – she was thought to earn her living by stealing babies for the fairies – had called at Deunant when they were feathering geese and had begged much for one, but she had been refused, and the farmer concluded she was taking her revenge by harassing his stock. So he went to old Beti and told her that he would tie her hands and feet and throw her into a river unless she removed the charm. She vehemently denied possessing any magical powers, and repeated the Lord's Prayer correctly in proof of her innocence. The farmer was not altogether convinced even by this, and made her say, "Rhad Duw ar y da," "God's blessing be on the cattle." Now, if this is spoken over bewitched animals, they are always freed from their disease, but the farmer's stock was no better even after his invocation, and he was at his wits' end.

One night before going to bed he was standing a few steps in front of his house, meditating over his trouble. "I cannot imagine why the cattle do not get better," said he out loud to himself. "I will tell you," said a squeaky little voice close by him. The farmer turned in the direction of the sound and saw a tiny little man, looking very angrily at him. "It is," continued the mannikin, "because your family keeps on annoying mine so much." "How is that?" asked the farmer, surprised and puzzled. "They are always throwing the slops from your house down the chimney of my house," said the little man. "That cannot be," retorted the farmer, "there is no house within a mile of mine." "Put your foot on mine," said the small stranger, "and you will see that what I say is true." The farmer complying, put his foot on the other's foot, and he could clearly see that all the slops thrown out of his house went down the chimney of the other's house which stood far below in a street he had never seen before. Directly he took his foot off the other's, however, there was no sign of house or chimney. "Well, indeed, I am very sorry," said the farmer. "What can I do to make up for the annoyance which my family has caused you?" The tiny little man was satisfied by the farmer's apology, and he said: "You had better wall up the door on this side of your house and make another in the other side. If you do that, your slops will no longer be a nuisance to my family and myself." Having said this he vanished in the dusk of the night.

The farmer obeyed, and his cattle recovered. Ever after he was a most prosperous man, and nobody was so successful as he in rearing stock in all Lleyn. Unless they have pulled it down to build a new one, you can see his house with the front door in the back.

ST. BEUNO AND THE CURLEW

Boys who go bird-nesting often wonder why it is so hard to find the nest of the curlew. As a matter of fact it is the fault, as they would consider it, of St. Beuno. When he lived at Clynnog he used to go regularly on Sunday to preach at Llanddwyn, off the coast of Anglesey, walking on the sea with the book of sermons which he used to carry about with him. One Sunday, as he was coming back from Llanddwyn to Clynnog, treading the surface of the sea as if it had been dry land, he dropped his precious writings into the water, and failed to recover them. The saint was much worried, because even for saints the task of writing sermons is a troublesome one.

When he reached dry land he was much relieved to find his book on a stone out of the reach of the tide, with a curlew mounting guard over it. The pious bird had picked it up, and brought it to safety. Thereupon the holy man knelt down and prayed for the protection and favour of the Creator for the curlew. His prayer was heard, and ever since it has been extremely difficult to discover where the long-beaked bird lays its eggs.

A FAIRY DOG

Going home from Pentre Voelas Church, the good wife of Hafod y Gareg found a little dog in an exhausted state on the ground. She took it up tenderly and carried it home in her apron. This she did partly from natural kindliness of heart and partly from fear, because she remembered what had happened to her cousin of Bryn Heilyn. She had come across a strange little dog and treated it cruelly. The fairies had come to her as she was taking *glasdwr* (which is butter-milk diluted with water) to the hayfield. They seized her and inquired whether she would travel above wind, mid wind or below wind. She ought to have selected the middle course, which would have meant a pleasant voyage through the air at a moderate height, equally removed from the clouds and the earth. Above wind is a giddy and terrible passage through the thin ether between the worlds, and it was well that she did not choose it. But the course she made choice of, below wind, was almost as bad, because she was snatched through miry bog and swampy lea, through brambles and briars, until all her clothes were torn off her body, and she was brought back to her home scratched and bleeding all over.

The good wife of Hafod y Gareg had no desire for any such excursions, and she made a nice soft bed for the fairy dog in the pantry, and fed it well. The following day a company of fairies came to the farmhouse to make enquiries about it. She told them it was safe and sound, and that they were welcome to take it away. In gratitude for her kindness, they asked her which she would prefer, a clean or a dirty cow yard. Reflecting that you cannot have a clean cow yard unless your cows are very few in number, she gave the right answer, a dirty cow yard. She found two cows for every one she had possessed before, and their milk made the best butter in the whole neighbourhood.

THE ANCIENTS OF THE WORLD

There was once an Eagle living in the woods of Gwernabwy: he and his mate had young ones till the ninth generation and far beyond that; then the old mother Eagle died, leaving her husband a lonely widower, without anyone to console and cheer him in his old age. In the sadness of his heart he thought it would be well if he married an old widow of his own age. Hearing of the old Owl of Cwm Cawlyd, he took it into his head to make her his second wife, but before doing so, being anxious not to degrade his race, he determined to make enquiries about her.

He had an old friend, older than himself, the Stag of Rhedynfre, in Gwent. He went to him and asked the age of the old Owl. The Stag answered him thus:

"Seest thou, my friend, this oak by which I lie? It is now but a withered stump, without leaves or branches, but I remember seeing it an acorn on the top of the chief tree of this forest. An oak is three hundred years in growing, and after that three hundred years in its strength and prime, and after that three hundred years in returning unto earth. Upwards of sixty years of the last hundred of this oak are passed, and the Owl has been old since I first remember her. Nor does anyone of my kindred know her age. But I have a friend who is much older than I, the Salmon of Llyn Llifon. Go to him and ask him if he knows aught of the age and history of the old Owl."

The Eagle went to the Salmon, who answered him thus: "I have a year over my head for every gem on my skin and for every egg in my roe, but the Owl was old when first I remember her. But I have a friend who is much older than I, the Ousel of Cilgwri. Haply he knows more about the Owl than I do."

The Eagle went and found the Ousel sitting on a hard flint, and asked him if he knew aught of the age and history of the Owl. The Ousel answering, said: "Seest thou this flint on which I sit? I have seen it so large that it would have taken three hundred yoke of the largest oxen to move it, and it has never been worn away save by my cleaning my beak upon it once every night before going to sleep, and striking the tip of my wing against it after rising in the morning. Yet never have I known the Owl younger or older than she is today. But I have a friend who is much older than I, the Toad of Cors Fochno. Go to him and ask him if he knows aught of the age and history of the Owl."

The Eagle went to the Toad, who answered him thus:

"I never eat any food save the dust of the earth, and I never eat half enough to satisfy me. Seest thou the great hills around this bog? I have seen the place where they stand level ground. I have eaten all the earth they contain, though I eat so little for fear lest the mould of the earth should be consumed before my death. Yet never have I known the Owl anything else but an old grey hag who cried to-whit-to-whoo in the woods in the long winter nights, and scared children with her voice even as she does today."

Then the Eagle saw he could marry her without bringing disgrace or degradation on his tribe. And so it was from the courtship of the Eagle that it was known which were the oldest creatures in the world. They are the Eagle of Gwernabwy, the Stag of Rhedynfre, the Salmon of Llyn Llifon, the Ousel of Cilgwri, the Toad of Cors Fochno, and the Owl of Cwm Cawlyd, and the oldest of them all is the Owl.

NANSI LLWYD AND THE DOG OF DARKNESS

Nansi Llwyd was walking in the dusk of the evening towards Aberystruth, and she was in a very bad temper, for she was longing to get married, and according to all the omens she never would.

The previous night being All Hallow Eve, she and Gweno Dafydd and Sian Probert had been seeking to learn the future. Sian and Gweno were satisfied with the results of the *rhamanta* or divination, but Nansi was cruelly disappointed. What made it worse was that they had all made a great preparation for the test. Nansi had slept not long before on an oat-straw bed, Gweno had spent a night on a mattress made of the leaves of the mountain ash mixed with the seeds of spring fern, and Sian had a pillow of maiden hair on which she had laid her comely head. Nor had they confined themselves to one test. First of all they experimented with yarn. Taking a ball of yarn, Nansi and Gweno doubled the threads and tied tiny pieces of wood along them so as to form a little ladder. Then they went upstairs together and, opening the window, threw the ladder to the ground. Nansi began winding the yarn back, saying the while:

"I am winding, Who is holding?"

This she did three times, and no lover made his appearance, so that her chance of marriage for one year was lost. When Gweno performed the ceremony, on the other hand, Cadwaladr Rhys, a most desirable young man, appeared.

The water-in-basin test was still more unsatisfactory. Three basins were placed on the table, one filled with clear spring water, one with muddy water, and the other empty. The three girls were led blindfolded to the table, and told to place their hands on the basins. Gweno put her hand on the basin containing clear spring water, which showed that she was to marry a bachelor.

Sian touched the basin with the muddy water, which meant she was to wed a widower. Nansi's hand lighted on the empty basin. This meant that a single life was in store for her. Now, to remain unmarried for one year is not very serious, but lifelong maidenhood was a prospect which made Nansi feel first hot and then cold.

She consoled herself with the reflection that the water-in-basin test was not absolutely certain, and she decided to try the pullet's egg test. She took the first egg of a pullet, cut it through the middle, filled one half-shell with wheaten flour, added salt to the other, and then made a cake out of the egg, the flour and the salt. One-half of this cake she ate: the other half she placed in the foot of her left stocking under her pillow as she went to bed. Then she said her prayers, and lay down to sleep. Now she ought to have dreamt of some man coming to her bedside to offer her a drink of water: this man would be her future husband. But troubled as her dreams were, no human being figured in them, and she felt when she got up that all the sunshine had gone out of life. She became still more sad when she went to examine the movements of the snail she had placed under a basin early the day before. If it had been a right-minded snail it would have moved about and traced the initials of her future husband's name. But the slimy sluggard had remained motionless, and Nansi hurled it viciously out of the window. If it did not sustain serious injuries from the fall, it was not Nansi's fault. All this evidence that she was to be an old maid made Nansi very bad tempered, and she had not recovered when she took her walk.

Suddenly a horse came galloping down the road, and she was all but knocked down by the furious animal. She recognised the horse as that of Jenkin Pari, whom she had noticed going to market that morning, and she wondered how it had come to pass that the steed was bolting home at such a pace without its rider. As she proceeded on her way, thinking about the horse, she saw two large shining eyes, which drew nearer and nearer. Presently the body and limbs of a large spotted dog loomed into sight. Nansi had a mastiff with her, and she tried to set it on the strange hound. In vain: the mastiff crouched frightened at her feet and whined piteously. The great dog with the fiery eyes came right up to her, and Nansi, to protect herself, kicked at it as hard as she could with her right foot. Her foot was paralysed, and when a circle of fire surrounded the hound she had kicked, and it squatted on its haunches, setting up a loud, horrible unearthly howl, she fell senseless on the ground.

She was discovered, still unconscious, by old Antoni, Jenkin Pari's farm bailiff. He, seeing his master's horse standing trembling by the stable door, had set out in search of the farmer. He came across Nansi, and brought her to by dashing cold water on her face. Going further along the road he found Jenkin Pari lying in a dead faint on his back in the mud. Jenkin said when he came to himself that the horse had shied, reared and tumbled him off. Jenkin was none the worse for his fall, but Nansi's right leg was as black as coal until the day of her death. Had she not been in so bad a temper, she would have realised that it was the Gwyllgi, or Dog of Darkness, that had come along the road, and she would no more have touched it than she would have refused an offer of marriage.

THE PARTI-COLOURED COW

A parti-coloured cow once appeared on the high moorlands of Denbighshire. Everyone who was in want of milk went to her, and however big a vessel was taken, it was always filled with rich milk. However often she was milked, it made no difference.

This continued for a long time, and glad indeed were the people to avail themselves of her unfailing supply. At last a wicked witch determined to milk her dry. The hag took a riddle and milked and milked the parti-coloured cow until at last the milk ran dry. Immediately the cow went off to a lake near Cerrig y Drudion, bellowing horribly, and disappeared under its waters.

THE MARTYRED HOUND

Prince Llywelyn had a favourite greyhound named Gelert that had been given him by his father-in-law, King John of England. He was as gentle as a lamb at home, but a lion in the chase, so true and so brave that he had no equal in the whole of his master's dominion. He fed only at Llywelyn's board and sentinelled Llywelyn's bed.

One fine morning the Prince determined to go to the chase, and blew his horn in front of the castle. All his other hounds came to the call, but Gelert did not answer it. He blew a louder blast on his horn and shouted, "Come, Gelert, come," saying to his huntsman that it was strange that Gelert should be the last to hear his horn. But still the greyhound did not come, and the chase had to ride on without him.

Llywelyn enjoyed the chase of hart and hare through the vales of Snowdon but little that day, and the booty proved scant and small because Gelert was not there. Disappointed and displeased he turned back to his castle, and as he came to the gate whom should he see but Gelert bounding out to greet him. When the hound came near him the Prince was startled to see that he was smeared all over with gore, and that his lips and fangs were dripping with blood. Llywelyn gazed at him with fierce surprise, and the greyhound crouched and licked his feet, as if surprised or afraid at the way his master received his greeting.

Now, Llywelyn had a little son about two years old with whom Gelert used to play, and the thought that the hound seemed guilty of something or other made him hurry towards the child's nursery, Gelert following at his heels. Entering, he saw the floor and walls besprent with recent blood, and, worst of all, the child's cradle was overturned; the coverlet was torn and all was daubed with blood. Llywelyn called his son, but no voice replied: he searched for him, wild with terror, but nowhere could he find him. He jumped to the conclusion that Gelert had destroyed his boy, and shouting, "Hell-hound, thou hast devoured my child," the frantic father drew his sword and plunged it to the hilt in the greyhound's side, who fell with a deep groan, gazing piteously in his master's eyes. Gelert's dying groan was answered by a little child's cry from beneath the overturned cradle. There concealed beneath a tumbled heap which he had missed in his hurried search, Llywelyn found his little son unharmed and glowing from his rosy sleep. Just beside him lay the body of a great, gaunt wolf, all torn to pieces and stiff in death. Too late, Llywelyn realised what had happened while he was at the chase: Gelert had fought and slain the wolf which had come to destroy Llywelyn's heir.

In vain was all Llywelyn's grief: he could not bring his faithful hound to life again. So he buried him and raised a noble tomb over his bones, repenting his rashness with many tears. He could never bear the thought of the chase after this, and hung his horn and hunting spear at Gelert's grave. To this day the place is called Bedd Gelert, or the Grave of Gelert, and if you go there you will be shown the spot where the remains of the martyred hound lie.

WHY THE ROBIN'S BREAST IS RED

A Welsh boy was throwing stones one day at a robin redbreast. "My poor boy," said his grandmother to him, "have you not heard of the fiery pit and how this merciful bird takes cool dew on his little bill and lets it fall on sinful souls in torment? The marks of the fire that scorches him as he drops the water are to be seen on his red breast. Never throw a stone at a robin."

KINGDOMS, OTHERWORLDS & REALMS

It should come as no surprise that in a chapter dedicated to mythical kingdoms and enchanted otherworlds, Welsh medieval literature features prominently. Arthurian adventures spanning the length and breadth of Wales sit side-by-side with a retelling of the First Branch of *Y Mabinogi* by Joseph Jacobs.

Intrepid wanderers venture into fairy otherworlds, such as William Jenkyn Thomas's tale of 'Elidyr's Sojurn in Fairy-Land', first penned by medieval clergyman Gerald of Wales (*c.* 1146–1223) in 1188, and 'The Green Isles of the Ocean'. The risks of entering the realms of fairies are laid bare, with years lost in enchanted time slips, and harsh punishments doled out for rudely interrupting their merry festivities.

Sunken kingdoms and drowned villages feature heavily here, such as the legend of Cantre'r Gwaelod in today's Cardigan Bay, retold as 'The Drowning of the Bottom Hundred' by William Jenkyn Thomas, as well as 'Bala Lake' and 'Helig's Hollow', where themes surrounding neglected duties, wicked rulers and murder impart a moral underpinning to the tales.

THE WOOING OF OLWEN

Shortly after the birth of Kilhuch, the son of King Kilyth, his mother died. Before her death she charged the king that he should not take a wife again until he saw a briar with two blossoms upon her grave, and the king sent every morning to see if anything were growing thereon. After many years the briar appeared, and he took to wife the widow of King Doged. She foretold to her stepson, Kilhuch, that it was his destiny to marry a maiden named Olwen, or none other, and he, at his father's bidding, went to the court of his cousin, King Arthur, to ask as a boon the hand of the maiden. He rode upon a grey steed with shell-formed hoofs, having a bridle of linked gold, and a saddle also of gold. In his hand were two spears of silver, well-tempered, headed with steel, of an edge to wound the wind and cause blood to flow, and swifter than the fall of the dew-drop from the blade of reed grass upon the earth when the dew of June is at its heaviest. A gold-hilted sword was on his thigh, and the blade was of gold, having inlaid upon it a cross of the hue of the lightning of heaven. Two brindled, white-breasted greyhounds, with strong collars of rubies, sported round him, and his courser cast up four sods with its four hoofs like four swallows about his head. Upon the steed was a four-cornered cloth of purple, and an apple of gold was at each corner. Precious gold was upon the stirrups and shoes, and the blade of grass bent not beneath them, so light was the courser's tread as he went towards the gate of King Arthur's palace.

Arthur received him with great ceremony, and asked him to remain at the palace; but the youth replied that he came not to consume meat and drink, but to ask a boon of the king.

Then said Arthur, "Since thou wilt not remain here, chieftain, thou shalt receive the boon, whatsoever thy tongue may name, as far as the wind dries and the rain moistens, and the sun revolves, and the sea encircles, and the earth extends, save only my ships and my mantle, my sword, my lance, my shield, my dagger, and Guinevere my wife."

So Kilhuch craved of him the hand of Olwen, the daughter of Yspathaden Penkawr, and also asked the favour and aid of all Arthur's court.

Then said Arthur, "O chieftain, I have never heard of the maiden of whom thou speakest, nor of her kindred, but I will gladly send messengers in search of her."

And the youth said, "I will willingly grant from this night to that at the end of the year to do so."

Then Arthur sent messengers to every land within his dominions to seek for the maiden; and at the end of the year Arthur's messengers returned without having gained any knowledge or information concerning Olwen more than on the first day.

Then said Kilhuch, "Every one has received his boon, and I yet lack mine. I will depart and bear away thy honour with me."

Then said Kay, "Rash chieftain! Dost thou reproach Arthur? Go with us, and we will not part until thou dost either confess that the maiden exists not in the world, or until we obtain her."

Thereupon Kay rose up.

Kay had this peculiarity, that his breath lasted nine nights and nine days under water, and he could exist nine nights and nine days without sleep. A wound from Kay's sword no physician could heal. Very subtle was Kay. When it pleased him he could render himself as tall as the highest tree in the forest. And he had another peculiarity, so great was the heat of his nature, that, when it rained hardest, whatever he carried remained dry for a handbreadth above and a handbreadth below his hand; and when his companions were coldest, it was to them as fuel with which to light their fire.

And Arthur called Bedwyr, who never shrank from any enterprise upon which Kay was bound. None was equal to him in swiftness throughout this island except Arthur and Drych Ail Kibthar. And although he was one-handed, three warriors could not shed blood faster than he on the field of battle. Another property he had; his lance would produce a wound equal to those of nine opposing lances.

And Arthur called to Kynthelig the guide. "Go thou upon this expedition with the Chieftain." For as good a guide was he in a land which he had never seen as he was in his own.

He called Gwrhyr Gwalstawt Ieithoedd, because he knew all tongues.

He called Gwalchmai, the son of Gwyar, because he never returned home without achieving the adventure of which he went in quest. He was the best of footmen and the best of knights. He was nephew to Arthur, the son of his sister, and his cousin.

And Arthur called Menw, the son of Teirgwaeth, in order that if they went into a savage country, he might cast a charm and an illusion over them, so that none might see them whilst they could see every one.

They journeyed on till they came to a vast open plain, wherein they saw a great castle, which was the fairest in the world. But so far away was it that at night it seemed no nearer, and they scarcely reached it on the third day. When they came before the castle they beheld a vast flock of sheep, boundless and without end. They told their errand to the herdsman, who endeavoured to dissuade them, since none who had come thither on that quest had returned alive. They gave to him a gold ring, which he conveyed to his wife, telling her who the visitors were.

On the approach of the latter, she ran out with joy to greet them, and sought to throw her arms about their necks. But Kay, snatching a billet out of the pile, placed the log between her two hands, and she squeezed it so that it became a twisted coil.

"O woman," said Kay, "if thou hadst squeezed me thus, none could ever again have set their affections on me. Evil love were this."

They entered the house, and after meat she told them that the maiden Olwen came there every Saturday to wash.

They pledged their faith that they would not harm her, and a message was sent to her. So Olwen came, clothed in a robe of flame-coloured silk, and with a collar of ruddy gold, in which were emeralds and rubies, about her neck. More golden was her hair than the flower of the broom, and her skin was whiter than the foam of the wave, and fairer were her hands and her fingers than the blossoms of the wood anemone amidst the spray of the meadow fountain. Brighter were her glances than those of a falcon; her bosom was more snowy than the breast of the white swan, her cheek redder than the reddest roses. Whoso beheld was filled with her love. Four white trefoils sprang up wherever she trod, and therefore was she called Olwen.

Then Kilhuch, sitting beside her on a bench, told her his love, and she said that he would win her as his bride if he granted whatever her father asked.

Accordingly they went up to the castle and laid their request before him.

"Raise up the forks beneath my two eyebrows which have fallen over my eyes," said Yspathaden Penkawr, "that I may see the fashion of my son-in-law."

They did so, and he promised them an answer on the morrow. But as they were going forth, Yspathaden seized one of the three poisoned darts that lay beside him and threw it back after them.

And Bedwyr caught it and flung it back, wounding Yspathaden in the knee.

Then said he, "A cursed ungentle son-in-law, truly. I shall ever walk the worse for his rudeness. This poisoned iron pains me like the bite of a gad-fly. Cursed be the smith who forged it, and the anvil whereon it was wrought."

The knights rested in the house of Custennin the herdsman, but the next day at dawn they returned to the castle and renewed their request.

Yspathaden said it was necessary that he should consult Olwen's four great-grandmothers and her four great-grandsires.

The knights again withdrew, and as they were going he took the second dart and cast it after them.

But Menw caught it and flung it back, piercing Yspathaden's breast with it, so that it came out at the small of his back.

"A cursed ungentle son-in-law, truly," says he, "the hard iron pains me like the bite of a horse-leech. Cursed be the hearth whereon it was heated! Henceforth whenever I go up a hill, I shall have a scant in my breath and a pain in my chest."

On the third day the knights returned once more to the palace, and Yspathaden took the third dart and cast it at them.

But Kilhuch caught it and threw it vigorously, and wounded him through the eyeball, so that the dart came out at the back of his head.

"A cursed ungentle son-in-law, truly. As long as I remain alive my eyesight will be the worse. Whenever I go against the wind my eyes will water, and peradventure my head will burn, and I shall have a giddiness every new moon. Cursed be the fire in which it was forged. Like the bite of a mad dog is the stroke of this poisoned iron."

And they went to meat.

Said Yspathaden Penkawr, "Is it thou that seekest my daughter?"

"It is I," answered Kilhuch.

"I must have thy pledge that thou wilt not do towards me otherwise than is just, and when I have gotten that which I shall name, my daughter thou shalt have."

"I promise thee that willingly," said Kilhuch, "name what thou wilt."

"I will do so," said he.

"Throughout the world there is not a comb or scissors with which I can arrange my hair, on account of its rankness, except the comb and scissors that are between the two ears of Turch Truith, the son of Prince Tared. He will not give them of his own free will, and thou wilt not be able to compel him."

"It will be easy for me to compass this, although thou mayest think that it will not be easy."

"Though thou get this, there is yet that which thou wilt not get. It will not be possible to hunt Turch Truith without Drudwyn the whelp of Greid, the son of Eri, and know that throughout the world there is not a huntsman who can hunt with this dog, except Mabon the son of Modron. He was taken from his mother when three nights old, and it is not known where he now is, nor whether he is living or dead."

"It will be easy for me to compass this, although thou mayest think that it will not be easy."

"Though thou get this, there is yet that which thou wilt not get. Thou wilt not get Mabon, for it is not known where he is, unless thou find Eidoel, his kinsman in blood, the son of Aer. For it would be useless to seek for him. He is his cousin."

"It will be easy for me to compass this, although thou mayest think that it will not be easy. Horses shall I have, and chivalry; and my lord and kinsman Arthur will obtain for me all these things. And I shall gain thy daughter, and thou shalt lose thy life."

"Go forward. And thou shalt not be chargeable for food or raiment for my daughter while thou art seeking these things; and when thou hast compassed all these marvels, thou shalt have my daughter for wife."

Now, when they told Arthur how they had sped, Arthur said, "Which of these marvels will it be best for us to seek first?"

"It will be best," said they, "to seek Mabon the son of Modron; and he will not be found unless we first find Eidoel, the son of Aer, his kinsman."

Then Arthur rose up, and the warriors of the Islands of Britain with him; to seek for Eidoel; and they proceeded until they came before the castle of Glivi, where Eidoel was imprisoned.

Glivi stood on the summit of his castle, and said, "Arthur, what requirest thou of me, since nothing remains to me in this fortress, and I have neither joy nor pleasure in it; neither wheat nor oats?"

Said Arthur, "Not to injure thee came I hither, but to seek for the prisoner that is with thee."

"I will give thee my prisoner, though I had not thought to give him up to any one; and therewith shalt thou have my support and my aid."

His followers then said unto Arthur, "Lord, go thou home, thou canst not proceed with thy host in quest of such small adventures as these."

Then said Arthur, "It were well for thee, Gwrhyr Gwalstawt leithoedd, to go upon this quest, for thou knowest all languages, and art familiar with those of the birds and the beasts. Go, Eidoel, likewise with my men in search of thy cousin. And as for you, Kay and Bedwyr, I have hope of whatever adventure ye are in quest of, that ye will achieve it. Achieve ye this adventure for me."

These went forward until they came to the Ousel of Cilgwri, and Gwrhyr adjured her for the sake of Heaven, saying, "Tell me if thou knowest aught of Mabon, the son of Modron, who was taken when three nights old from between his mother and the wall."

And the Ousel answered, "When I first came here there was a smith's anvil in this place, and I was then a young bird, and from that time no work has been done upon it, save the pecking of my beak every evening, and now there is not so much as the size of a nut remaining thereof; yet the vengeance of Heaven be upon me if during all that time I have ever heard of the man for whom you inquire. Nevertheless, there is a race of animals who were formed before me, and I will be your guide to them."

So they proceeded to the place where was the Stag of Redynvre.

"Stag of Redynvre, behold we are come to thee, an embassy from Arthur, for we have not heard of any animal older than thou. Say, knowest thou aught of Mabon?"

The stag said, "When first I came hither, there was a plain all around me, without any trees save one oak sapling, which grew up to be an oak with an hundred branches. And that oak has since perished, so that now nothing remains of it but the withered stump; and from that day to this I have been here, yet have I never heard of the man for whom you inquire. Nevertheless, I will be your guide to the place where there is an animal which was formed before I was."

So they proceeded to the place where was the Owl of Cwm Cawlwyd, to inquire of him concerning Mabon.

And the owl said, "If I knew I would tell you. When first I came hither, the wide valley you see was a wooded glen. And a race of men came and rooted it up. And there grew there a second wood, and this wood is the third. My wings, are they not withered stumps? Yet all this time, even until today, I have never heard of the man for whom you inquire. Nevertheless, I will be the guide of

Arthur's embassy until you come to the place where is the oldest animal in this world, and the one who has travelled most, the eagle of Gwern Abwy."

When they came to the eagle, Gwrhyr asked it the same question; but it replied, "I have been here for a great space of time, and when I first came hither there was a rock here, from the top of which I pecked at the stars every evening, and now it is not so much as a span high. From that day to this I have been here, and I have never heard of the man for whom you inquire, except once when I went in search of food as far as Llyn Llyw. And when I came there, I struck my talons into a salmon, thinking he would serve me as food for a long time. But he drew me into the deep, and I was scarcely able to escape from him. After that I went with my whole kindred to attack him and to try to destroy him, but he sent messengers and made peace with me, and came and besought me to take fifty fish spears out of his back. Unless he knows something of him whom you seek, I cannot tell you who may. However, I will guide you to the place where he is."

So they went thither, and the eagle said, "Salmon of Llyn Llyw, I have come to thee with an embassy from Arthur to ask thee if thou knowest aught concerning Mabon, the son of Modron, who was taken away at three nights old from between his mother and the wall."

And the salmon answered, "As much as I know I will tell thee. With every tide I go along the river upwards, until I come near to the walls of Gloucester, and there have I found such wrong as I never found elsewhere; and to the end that ye may give credence thereto, let one of you go thither upon each of my two shoulders."

So Kay and Gwrhyr went upon his shoulders, and they proceeded till they came to the wall of the prison, and they heard a great wailing and lamenting from the dungeon.

Said Gwrhyr, "Who is it that laments in this house of stone?"

And the voice replied, "Alas, it is Mabon, the son of Modron, who is here imprisoned!"

Then they returned and told Arthur, who, summoning his warriors, attacked the castle.

And whilst the fight was going on, Kay and Bedwyr, mounting on the shoulders of the fish, broke into the dungeon, and brought away with them Mabon, the son of Modron.

Then Arthur summoned unto him all the warriors that were in the three islands of Britain and in the three islands adjacent; and he went as far as Esgeir Oervel in Ireland where the Boar Truith was with his seven young pigs. And the dogs were let loose upon him from all sides. But he wasted the fifth part of Ireland, and then set forth through the sea to Wales. Arthur and his hosts, and his horses, and his dogs followed hard after him. But ever and awhile the boar made a stand, and many a champion of Arthur's did he slay. Throughout all Wales did Arthur follow him, and one by one the young pigs were killed. At length, when he would fain have crossed the Severn and escaped into Cornwall, Mabon the son of Modron came up with him, and Arthur fell upon him together with the champions of Britain. On the one side Mabon the son of Modron spurred his steed and snatched his razor from him, whilst Kay came up with him on the other side and took from him the scissors. But before they could obtain the comb he had regained the ground with his feet, and from the moment that he reached the shore, neither dog nor man nor horse could overtake him until he came to Cornwall. There Arthur and his hosts followed in his track until they overtook him in Cornwall. Hard had been their trouble before, but it was child's play to what they met in seeking the comb. Win it they did, and the Boar Truith they hunted into the deep sea, and it was never known whither he went.

Then Kilhuch set forward, and as many as wished ill to Yspathaden Penkawr. And they took the marvels with them to his court. And Kaw of North Britain came and shaved his beard, skin and flesh clean off to the very bone from ear to ear.

"Art thou shaved, man?" said Kilhuch.

"I am shaved," answered he.

"Is thy daughter mine now?"

"She is thine, but therefore needst thou not thank me, but Arthur who hath accomplished this for thee. By my free will thou shouldst never have had her, for with her I lose my life."

Then Goreu the son of Custennin seized him by the hair of his head and dragged him after him to the keep, and cut off his head and placed it on a stake on the citadel.

Thereafter the hosts of Arthur dispersed themselves each man to his own country.

Thus did Kilhuch son of Kelython win to wife Olwen, the daughter of Yspathaden Penkawr.

POWEL, PRINCE OF DYFED

Powel, Prince of Dyfed, was lord of the seven Cantrevs of Dyfed; and once upon a time Powel was at Narberth, his chief palace, where a feast had been prepared for him, and with him was a great host of men. And after the first meal, Powel arose to walk, and he went to the top of a mound that was above the palace, and was called Gorseth Arberth.

"Lord," said one of the court, "it is peculiar to the mound that whosoever sits upon it cannot go thence without either receiving wounds or blows, or else seeing a wonder."

"I fear not to receive wounds and blows in the midst of such a host as this; but as to the wonder, gladly would I see it. I will go, therefore, and sit upon the mound."

And upon the mound he sat. And while he sat there, they saw a lady, on a pure white horse of large size, with a garment of shining gold around her, coming along the highway that led from the mound; and the horse seemed to move at a slow and even pace, and to be coming up towards the mound.

"My men," said Powel, "is there any among you who knows yonder lady?"

"There is not, lord," said they.

"Go one of you and meet her, that we may know who she is."

And one of them arose; and as he came upon the road to meet her she passed by, and he followed as fast as he could, being on foot; and the greater was his speed, the farther was she from him. And when he saw that it profited him nothing to follow her, he returned to Powel, and said unto him, "Lord, it is idle for any one in the world to follow her on foot."

"Verily," said Powel, "go unto the palace, and take the fleetest horse that thou seest, and go after her."

And he took a horse and went forward. And he came to an open level plain, and put spurs to his horse; and the more he urged his horse, the farther was she from him. Yet she held the same pace as at first. And his horse began to fail; and when his horse's feet failed him, he returned to the place where Powel was.

"Lord," said he, "it will avail nothing for any one to follow yonder lady. I know of no horse in these realms swifter than this, and it availed me not to pursue her."

"Of a truth," said Powel, "there must be some illusion here. Let us go towards the palace." So to the palace they went, and they spent that day. And the next day they arose, and that also they spent until it was time to go to meat. And after the first meal, "Verily," said Powel, "we will go, the same party as yesterday, to the top of the mound. Do thou," said he to one of his young men, "take the swiftest horse that thou knowest in the field." And thus did the young man. They went towards the mound, taking the horse with them. And as they were sitting down they beheld the lady on the same horse, and in the same apparel, coming along the same road. "Behold," said Powel, "here is the lady of yesterday. Make ready, youth, to learn who she is."

"My lord," said he "that will I gladly do." And thereupon the lady came opposite to them. So the youth mounted his horse; and before he had settled himself in his saddle, she passed by, and there was a clear space between them. But her speed was no greater than it had been the day before. Then he put his horse into an amble, and thought, that, notwithstanding the gentle pace at which his horse went, he should soon overtake her. But this availed him not: so he gave his horse the reins. And still he came no nearer to her than when he went at a foot's pace. The more he urged his horse, the farther was she from him. Yet she rode not faster than before. When he saw that it availed not to follow her, he returned to the place where Powel was. "Lord," said he, "the horse can no more than thou hast seen."

"I see indeed that it avails not that any one should follow her. And by Heaven," said he, "she must needs have an errand to some one in this plain, if her haste would allow her to declare it. Let us go back to the palace." And to the palace they went, and they spent that night in songs and feasting, as it pleased them.

The next day they amused themselves until it was time to go to meat. And when meat was ended, Powel said, "Where are the hosts that went yesterday and the day before to the top of the mound?"

"Behold, lord, we are here," said they.

"Let us go," said he, "to the mound to sit there. And do thou," said he to the page who tended his horse, "saddle my horse well, and hasten with him to the road, and bring also my spurs with thee." And the youth did thus. They went and sat upon the mound. And ere they had been there but a short time, they beheld the lady coming by the same road, and in the same manner, and at the same pace. "Young man," said Powel, "I see the lady coming: give me my horse." And no sooner had he mounted his horse than she passed him. And he turned after her, and followed her. And he let his horse go bounding playfully, and thought that at the second step or the third he should come up with her. But he came no nearer to her than at first. Then he urged his horse to his utmost speed, yet he found that it availed nothing to follow her. Then said Powel, "O maiden, for the sake of him who thou best lovest, stay for me."

"I will stay gladly," said she, "and it were better for thy horse hadst thou asked it long since." So the maiden stopped, and she threw back that part of her head-dress which covered her face. And she fixed her eyes upon him, and began to talk with him.

"Lady," asked he, "whence comest thou, and whereunto dost thou journey?"

"I journey on mine own errand," said she, "and right glad am I to see thee."

"My greeting be unto thee," said he. Then he thought that the beauty of all the maidens, and all the ladies that he had ever seen, was as nothing compared to her beauty. "Lady," he said, "wilt thou tell me aught concerning thy purpose?"

"I will tell thee," said she. "My chief quest was to seek thee."

"Behold," said Powel, "this is to me the most pleasing quest on which thou couldst have come. And wilt thou tell me who thou art?"

"I will tell thee, lord," said she. "I am Rhiannon, the daughter of Heveyth Hên, and they sought to give me to a husband against my will. But no husband would I have, and that because of my love for thee, neither will I yet have one unless thou reject me. And hither have I come to hear thy answer."

"By Heaven," said Powel, "behold this is my answer. If I might choose among all the ladies and damsels in the world, thee would I choose."

"Verily," said she, "if thou art thus minded, make a pledge to meet me ere I am given to another."

"The sooner I may do so, the more pleasing will it be unto me," said Powel, "and wheresoever thou wilt, there will I meet with thee."

"I will that thou meet me this day twelvemonth, at the palace of Heveyth. And I will cause a feast to be prepared, so that it be ready against thou come."

"Gladly," said he, "will I keep this tryst."

"Lord," said she, "remain in health, and be mindful that thou keep thy promise. And now I will go hence."

So they parted, and he went back to his hosts and to them of his household. And whatsoever questions they asked him respecting the damsel, he always turned the discourse upon other matters. And when a year from that time was gone, he caused a hundred knights to equip themselves, and to go with him to the palace of Heveyth Hên. And he came to the palace, and there was great joy concerning him, with much concourse of people, and great rejoicing, and vast preparations for his coming. And the whole court was placed under his orders.

And the hall was garnished, and they went to meat, and thus did they sit; Heveyth Hên was on one side of Powel, and Rhiannon on the other. And all the rest according to their rank. And they ate and feasted and talked, one with another; and at the beginning of the carousal after the meat, there entered a tall auburn-haired youth, of royal bearing, clothed in a garment of satin. And when he came into the hall he saluted Powel and his companions.

"The greeting of Heaven be unto thee, my soul," said Powel. "Come thou and sit down."

"Nay," said he, "a suitor am I; and I will do mine errand."

"Do so willingly," said Powel.

"Lord," said he, "my errand is unto thee; and it is to crave a boon of thee that I come."

"What boon soever thou mayest ask of me, as far as I am able, thou shalt have."

"Ah," said Rhiannon, "wherefore didst thou give that answer?"

"Has he not given it before the presence of these nobles?" asked the youth.

"My soul," said Powel, "what is the boon thou askest?"

"The lady whom best I love is to be thy bride this night; I come to ask her of thee, with the feast and the banquet that are in this place."

And Powel was silent because of the answer which he had given.

"Be silent as long as thou wilt," said Rhiannon. "Never did man make worse use of his wits than thou hast done."

"Lady," said he, "I knew not who he was."

"Behold, this is the man to whom they would have given me against my will," said she. "And he is Gwawl the son of Clud, a man of great power and wealth; and because of the word thou hast spoken, bestow me upon him, lest shame befall thee."

"Lady," said he, "I understand not thine answer. Never can I do as thou sayest."

"Bestow me upon him," said she, "and I will cause that I shall never be his."

"By what means will that be?" said Powel.

"In thy hand will I give thee a small bag," said she. "See that thou keep it well, and he will ask of thee the banquet and the feast, and the preparations, which are not in thy power. Unto the hosts and the household will I give the feast. And such will be thy answer respecting this. And as concerns myself, I will engage to become his bride this night twelvemonth. And at the end of the year be thou here," said she, "and bring this bag with thee and let thy hundred knights be in the orchard up yonder. And when he is in the midst of joy and feasting, come thou in by thyself, clad in ragged garments, and holding thy bag in thy hand, and ask nothing but a bagful of food: and I will cause that if all the meat and liquor that are in these seven cantrevs were put into it, it would be no fuller than before. And after a great deal has been put therein, he will ask thee whether thy bag will ever be full. Say thou then that it never will, until a man of noble birth and of great wealth arise and press the food in the bag with both his feet, saying, 'Enough has been put therein.' And I will cause him to go and tread down the food in the bag, and when he does so, turn thou the bag, so that he shall be up over his head in it, and then slip a knot upon the thongs of the bag. Let there be also a good bugle-horn about thy neck, and as soon as thou hast bound him in the bag, wind thy horn, and let it be a signal between thee and thy knights. And when they hear the sound of the horn, let them come down upon the palace."

"Lord," said Gwawl, "it is meet that I have an answer to my request."

"As much of that thou hast asked as it is in my power to give, thou shalt have," replied Powel.

"My soul," said Rhiannon unto him, "as for the feast and the banquet that are here, I have bestowed them upon the men of Dyved, and the household, and the warriors that are with us. These can I not suffer to be given to any. In a year from tonight a banquet shall be prepared for thee in this palace, that I may become thy bride."

So Gwawl went forth to his possessions, and Powel went also back to Dyved. And they both spent that year until it was the time for the feast at the palace of Heveyth Hên. Then Gwawl the son of Clud set out to the feast that was prepared for him, and he came to the palace and was received there with rejoicing. Powel also, the chief of Annuvyn, came to the orchard with his hundred knights, as Rhiannon had commanded him, having the bag with him. And Powel was clad in coarse and ragged garments, and wore large clumsy old shoes upon his feet. And when he knew that the carousal after the meat had begun, he went towards the hall, and when he came into the hall, he saluted Gwawl the son of Clud, and his company, both men and women.

"Heaven prosper thee!" said Gwawl, "and the greeting of Heaven be unto thee!"

"Lord," said he, "may Heaven reward thee! I have an errand unto thee."

"Welcome be thine errand, and, if thou ask of me that which is just, thou shalt have it gladly."

"It is fitting," answered he. "I crave but from want; and the boon that I ask is to have this small bag that thou seest filled with meat."

"A request within reason is this," said he, "and gladly shalt thou have it. Bring him food."

A great number of attendants arose, and began to fill the bag; but for all that they put into it, it was no fuller than at first.

"My soul," said Gwawl, "will thy bag be ever full?"

"It will not, I declare to Heaven," said he, "for all that may be put into it, unless one possessed of lands and domains and treasure shall arise, and tread down with both his feet the food which is within the bag, and shall say, 'Enough has been put herein.'"

Then said Rhiannon unto Gwawl the son of Clud, "Rise up quickly."

"I will willingly arise," said he. So he rose up, and put his two feet into the bag. And Powel turned up the sides of the bag, so that Gwawl was over his head in it. And he shut it up quickly, and slipped a knot upon the thongs, and blew his horn. And thereupon behold his household came down upon the palace. And they seized all the host that had come with Gwawl, and cast them into his own prison. And Powel threw off his rags, and his old shoes, and his tattered array. And as they came in, every one of Powel's knights struck a blow upon the bag, and asked, "What is here?"

"A badger," said they. And in this manner they played, each of them striking the bag, either with his foot or with a staff. And thus played they with the bag. Every one as he came in asked, "What game are you playing at thus?"

"The game of Badger in the Bag," said they. And then was the game of Badger in the Bag first played.

"Lord," said the man in the bag, "if thou wouldst but hear me, I merit not to be slain in a bag."

Said Heveyth Hên, "Lord, he speaks truth. It were fitting that thou listen to him; for he deserves not this."

"Verily," said Powel, "I will do thy counsel concerning him."

"Behold, this is my counsel then," said Rhiannon. "Thou art now in a position in which it behoves thee to satisfy suitors and minstrels: let him give unto them in thy stead, and take a pledge from him that he will never seek to revenge that which has been done to him. And this will be punishment enough."

"I will do this gladly," said the man in the bag.

"And gladly will I accept it," said Powel, "since it is the counsel of Heveyth and Rhiannon."

"Such, then, is our counsel," answered they.

"I accept it," said Powel.

"Seek thyself sureties."

"We will be for him," said Heveyth, "until his men be free to answer for him." And upon this he was let out of the bag, and his liege-men were liberated. "Demand now of Gwawl his sureties," said Heveyth; "we know which should be taken for him." And Heveyth numbered the sureties.

Said Gwawl, "Do thou thyself draw up the covenant."

"It will suffice me that it be as Rhiannon said," answered Powel. So unto that covenant were all the sureties pledged.

"Verily, lord," said Gwawl, "I am greatly hurt, and I have many bruises. I have need to be anointed; with thy leave I will go forth. I will leave nobles in my stead to answer for me in all that thou shalt require."

"Willingly," said Powel, "mayst thou do thus." So Gwawl went towards his own possessions.

And the hall was set in order for Powel and the men of his host, and for them also of the palace, and they went to the tables and sat down. And as they had sat that time twelvemonth, so sat they that night. And they ate and feasted, and spent the night in mirth and tranquillity.

And next morning, at the break of day, "My lord," said Rhiannon, "arise and begin to give thy gifts unto the minstrels. Refuse no one today that may claim thy bounty."

"Thus shall it be, gladly," said Powel, "both today and every day while the feast shall last." So Powel arose, and he caused silence to be proclaimed, and desired all the suitors and the minstrels to show and to point out what gifts were to their wish and desire. And this being done, the feast went on, and he denied no one while it lasted. And when the feast was ended, Powel said unto Heveyth, "My lord, with thy permission, I will set out for Dyved tomorrow."

"Certainly," said Heveyth. "May Heaven prosper thee! Fix also a time when Rhiannon may follow thee."

Said Powel, "We will go hence together."

"Willest thou this, lord?" said Heveyth.

"Yes," answered Powel.

And the next day they set forward towards Dyved, and journeyed to the palace of Narberth, where a feast was made ready for them. And there came to them great numbers of the chief men and the most noble ladies of the land, and of these there was none to whom Rhiannon did not give some rich gift, either a bracelet, or a ring, or a precious stone. And they ruled the land prosperously both that year and the next.

And in the fourth year a son was born to them, and women were brought to watch the babe at night. And the women slept, as did also Rhiannon. And when they awoke they looked where they had put the boy, and behold he was not there. And the women were frightened; and, having plotted together, they accused Rhiannon of having murdered her child before their eyes.

"For pity's sake," said Rhiannon, "the Lord God knows all things. Charge me not falsely. If you tell me this from fear, I assert before Heaven that I will defend you."

"Truly," said they, "we would not bring evil on ourselves for any one in the world."

"For pity's sake," said Rhiannon, "you will receive no evil by telling the truth." But for all her words, whether fair or harsh, she received but the same answer from the women.

And Powel the chief of Annuvyn arose, and his household and his hosts. And this occurrence could not be concealed; but the story went forth throughout the land, and all the nobles heard it. Then the nobles came to Powel, and besought him to put away his wife because of the great crime which she had done. But Powel answered them that they had no cause wherefore they might ask him to put away his wife.

So Rhiannon sent for the teachers and the wise men, and as she preferred doing penance to contending with the women, she took upon her a penance. And the penance that was imposed upon her was that she should remain in that palace of Narberth until the end of seven years, and that she should sit every day near unto a horse-block that was without the gate; and that she should relate the story to all who should come there whom she might suppose not to know it already; and that she should offer the guests and strangers, if they would permit her, to carry them upon her back into the palace. But it rarely happened that any would permit. And thus did she spend part of the year.

Now at that time Teirnyon Twryv Vliant was lord of Gwent Is Coed, and he was the best man in the world. And unto his house there belonged a mare than which neither mare nor horse in the kingdom was more beautiful. And on the night of every first of

May she foaled, and no one ever knew what became of the colt. And one night Teirnyon talked with his wife: "Wife," said he, "it is very simple of us that our mare should foal every year, and that we should have none of her colts."

"What can be done in the matter?" said she.

"This is the night of the first of May," said he. "The vengeance of Heaven be upon me, if I learn not what it is that takes away the colts." So he armed himself, and began to watch that night. Teirnyon heard a great tumult, and after the tumult behold a claw came through the window into the house, and it seized the colt by the mane. Then Teirnyon drew his sword, and struck off the arm at the elbow: so that portion of the arm, together with the colt, was in the house with him. And then, did he hear a tumult and wailing both at once. And he opened the door, and rushed out in the direction of the noise, and he could not see the cause of the tumult because of the darkness of the night; but he rushed after it and followed it. Then he remembered that he had left the door open, and he returned. And at the door behold there was an infant-boy in swaddling clothes, wrapped around in a mantle of satin. And he took up the boy, and behold he was very strong for the age that he was of.

Then he shut the door, and went into the chamber where his wife was. "Lady," said he, "art thou sleeping?"

"No, lord," said she: "I was asleep, but as thou camest in I did awake."

"Behold, here is a boy for thee, if thou wilt," said he, "since thou hast never had one."

"My lord," said she, "what adventure is this?"

"It was thus," said Teirnyon. And he told her how it all befell.

"Verily, lord," said she, "what sort of garments are there upon the boy?"

"A mantle of satin," said he.

"He is then a boy of gentle lineage," she replied.

And they caused the boy to be baptised, and the ceremony was performed there. And the name which they gave unto him was Goldenlocks, because what hair was upon his head was as yellow as gold. And they had the boy nursed in the court until he was a year old. And before the year was over he could walk stoutly; and he was larger than a boy of three years old, even one of great growth and size. And the boy was nursed the second year, and then he was as large as a child six years old. And before the end of the fourth year, he would bribe the grooms to allow him to take the horses to water.

"My lord," said his wife unto Teirnyon, "where is the colt which thou didst save on the night that thou didst find the boy?"

"I have commanded the grooms of the horses," said he, "that they take care of him."

"Would it not be well, lord," said she, "if thou wert to cause him to be broken in, and given to the boy, seeing that on the same night that thou didst find the boy, the colt was foaled, and thou didst save him?"

"I will not oppose thee in this matter," said Teirnyon. "I will allow thee to give him the colt."

"Lord," said she, "may Heaven reward thee! I will give it him." So the horse was given to the boy. Then she went to the grooms and those who tended the horses, and commanded them to be careful of the horse, so that he might be broken in by the time that the boy could ride him.

And while these things were going forward, they heard tidings of Rhiannon and her punishment. And Teirnyon Twryv Vliant, by reason of the pity that he felt on hearing this story of

Rhiannon and her punishment, inquired closely concerning it, until he had heard from many of those who came to his court. Then did Teirnyon, often lamenting the sad history, ponder with himself; and he looked steadfastly on the boy, and as he looked upon him, it seemed to him that he had never beheld so great a likeness between father and son as between the boy and Powel the chief of Annuvyn. Now the semblance of Powel was well known to him, for he had of yore been one of his followers. And thereupon he became grieved for the wrong that he did in keeping with him a boy whom he knew to be the son of another man. And the first time that he was alone with his wife he told her that it was not right that they should keep the boy with them, and suffer so excellent a lady as Rhiannon to be punished so greatly on his account, whereas the boy was the son of Powel the chief of Annuvyn. And Teirnyon's wife agreed with him that they should send the boy to Powel. "And three things, lord," said she, "shall we gain thereby – thanks and gifts for releasing Rhiannon from her punishment, and thanks from Powel for nursing his son and restoring him unto him; and, thirdly, if the boy is of gentle nature, he will be our foster-son, and he will do for us all the good in his power." So it was settled according to this counsel.

And no later than the next day was Teirnyon equipped and two other knights with him. And the boy, as a fourth in their company, went with them upon the horse which Teirnyon had given him. And they journeyed towards Narberth, and it was not long before they reached that place. And as they drew near to the palace, they beheld Rhiannon sitting beside the horse-block. And when they were opposite to her, "Chieftain," said she, "go not farther thus: I will bear every one of you into the palace. And this is my penance for slaying my own son, and devouring him."

"Oh, fair lady," said Teirnyon, "think not that I will be one to be carried upon thy back."

"Neither will I," said the boy.

"Truly, my soul," said Teirnyon, "we will not go." So they went forward to the palace, and there was great joy at their coming. And at the palace a feast was prepared because Powel was come back from the confines of Dyfed. And they went into the hall and washed, and Powel rejoiced to see Teirnyon. And in this order they sat: Teirnyon between Powel and Rhiannon, and Teirnyon's two companions on the other side of Powel, with the boy between them. And after meat they began to carouse and discourse. And Teirnyon's discourse was concerning the adventure of the mare and the boy, and how he and his wife had nursed and reared the child as their own. "Behold here is thy son, lady," said Teirnyon. "And whosoever told that lie concerning thee has done wrong. When I heard of thy sorrow, I was troubled and grieved. And I believe that there is none of this host who will not perceive that the boy is the son of Powel," said Teirnyon.

"There is none," said they all, "who is not certain thereof."

"I declare to Heaven," said Rhiannon, "that if this be true, there is indeed an end to my trouble."

"Lady," said Pendaran Dyfed, "well hast thou named thy son Pryderi (end of trouble), and well becomes him the name of Pryderi son of Powel chief of Annuvyn."

"Look you," said Rhiannon: "will not his own name become him better?"

"What name has he?" asked Pendaran Dyfed.

"Goldenlocks is the name that we gave him."

"Pryderi," said Pendaran, "shall his name be."

"It were more proper," said Powel, "that the boy should take his name from the word his mother spoke when she received the joyful tidings of him." And thus was it arranged.

"Teirnyon," said Powel, "Heaven reward thee that thou hast reared the boy up to this time, and, being of gentle lineage, it were fitting that he repay thee for it."

"My lord," said Teirnyon, "it was my wife who nursed him, and there is no one in the world so afflicted as she at parting with him. It were well that he should bear in mind what I and my wife have done for him."

"I call Heaven to witness," said Powel, "that while I live I will support thee and thy possessions as long as I am able to preserve my own. And when he shall have power, he will more fitly maintain them than I. And if this counsel be pleasing unto thee and to my nobles, it shall be, that, as thou hast reared him up to the present time, I will give him to be brought up by Pendaran Dyfed from henceforth. And you shall be companions, and shall both be foster-fathers unto him."

"This is good counsel," said they all. So the boy was given to Pendaran Dyfed, and the nobles of the land were sent with him. And Teirnyon Twryv Vliant and his companions set out for his country and his possessions, with love and gladness. And he went not without being offered the fairest jewels, and the fairest horses, and the choicest dogs; but he would take none of them.

Thereupon they all remained in their own dominions. And Pryderi the son of Powel the chief of Annuvyn was brought up carefully, as was fit, so that he became the fairest youth, and the most comely, and the best skilled in all good games, of any in the kingdom. And thus passed years and years until the end of Powel the chief of Annuvyn's life came, and he died.

THE DROWNING OF THE BOTTOM HUNDRED

I

In the beginning of the sixth century, Gwyddno Garanhir was King of Ceredigion. The most valuable portion of his dominions was the great plain of the Bottom Hundred, a vast tract of level land, stretching along that part of the sea coast which now belongs to the counties of Merioneth and Cardigan. This district was populous and fertile. It contained sixteen fortified towns, superior to all the towns and cities of the Cymry excepting Caer Lleon upon Usk. It contained also one of the three privileged ports of the Isle of Britain which was called the Port of Gwyddno, and had been known to the Phoenicians and Carthaginians when they visited the island for metal in the dim dawn of history. This lowland country was below the level of the sea, and the people of the Bottom Hundred had in very early times built an embankment of massy stone to protect it from the encroachment of that hungry element. This stony rampart had withstood the shock of the waves for centuries when Gwyddno began his reign. Watch-towers were erected along the embankment, and watchmen were appointed to guard against the first approaches of damage or decay. The whole of these towers and their companies of guards were ruled by a central castle, which commanded the seaport already mentioned, and wherein dwelt Prince Seithenyn, the son of Seithyn Saidi, who held the office of Lord High Commissioner of the Royal Embankment. Now, Seithenyn was one of the three immortal drunkards of the Isle of Britain. He left the embankment to his deputies, who left it to their assistants, who left it to itself.

One only was there who did his duty. He was Teithrin, the son of Tathral, who had the charge of a watch-tower where the embankment ended at the point of Mochras, in the high land of Ardudwy. Teithrin kept his portion of the embankment in good condition, and paced with daily care the limits of his charge. One day he happened to stray beyond them, and observed signs of neglect that filled him with dismay. This induced him to proceed till his wanderings brought him to the embankment's southern end, in the high land of Ceredigion. He met with abundant hospitality at the towers of his colleagues and at the castle of Seithenyn: he was supposed to be walking for his amusement. He was asked no questions, and he carefully abstained from asking any. He examined and observed in silence, and when he had completed his observations he hastened to Gwyddno's palace. It had been built of choice slate stone on the rocky banks of the Mawddach, just above the point where it entered the plain of the Bottom Hundred, and in it, among green woods and sparkling waters, Garanhir lived in festal munificence. On his arrival, he was informed by the porter that the knife was in the meat, and the drink in the horn; there was revelry in the great hall, and none might enter therein but the son of a king of a privileged country or a craftsman bringing his craft. The feast was to last so many days that Teithrin despaired of delivering his message, and went in search of the King's son, Elphin.

The young Prince was fishing in the Mawddach at a spot where the river, having quitted its native mountains and not yet entered the plain, ran in alternate streams and pools sparkling through a pastoral valley. He sat under an ancient ash, enjoying the calm brightness of an autumnal noon and the melody and beauty of the flying stream on which the shifting sunbeams fell chequering through the leaves. The monotonous music of the river and the profound stillness of the air had all but sent Elphin to sleep. He was startled into attention by a sudden rush of the wind through the trees, and he heard, or seemed to hear, in the gust that hurried by him, the words, "Beware of the oppression of Gwenhudiw!" The gust was momentary: the leaves ceased to rustle and the deep silence of nature returned.

Now, Gwenhudiw is the mermaid Shepherdess of Ocean: the waves are her sheep, and each ninth wave, which is always greater than the rest, is called her ram.

It was not the first time that the kingly house of Ceredigion had been warned against her oppression. Gwyddno had often heard the same mysterious words borne on the breeze. They had so haunted his memory and imagination that he had ceased to go down to the sea in ships, and dwelt inland, avoiding as far as he might the sight of the great waters. Elphin, too, had heard the prophecy before, but it had formed no part of his recent meditation. He could not, however, persuade himself that the words had not been actually spoken near him. He emerged from the shade of the trees that fringed the river, and looked round him from the rocky bank.

At this moment Teithrin discovered and approached him. Elphin knew him not and inquired his name.

"I am called," he answered, "Teithrin, the son of Tathral."

"And what seek you here?" said Elphin.

"I seek," answered Teithrin, "the Prince of the Bottom Hundred, Elphin, the son of Gwyddno Garanhir."

"You spoke," said Elphin, "as you approached?"

"Nay," said Teithrin, "I spoke never a word."

"Assuredly you did," said Elphin, "you repeated the words, 'Beware of the oppression of Gwenhudiw!'"

Teithrin again denied having spoken the words; but their mysterious impression made Elphin listen readily to his information about the decay of the royal embankment: and after their talk the Prince determined to accompany Teithrin on a visit of remonstrance to the Lord High Commissioner.

They crossed the centre of the enclosed country to the privileged Port of Gwyddno, near which stood the castle of Seithenyn. They walked towards the castle along a portion of the embankment, and Teithrin pointed out to the Prince its decayed condition.

The sea shone with the glory of the setting sun: the air was calm: and the white surf, tinged with the crimson of sunset, broke lightly on the sands below. Elphin turned his eyes from the dazzling splendour of the ocean to the green meadows of the plain: the trees that in the distance thickened into woods: the wreaths of smoke rising from among them, marking the solitary cottages or the populous towns: the massy barrier of mountains beyond, with the forest rising from their base: the precipices frowning over the forest: and the clouds resting on their summits reddened with the reflection of the west. Elphin gazed earnestly on the peopled plain, reposing in the calm of evening between the mountains and the sea, and thought, with deep feelings of secret pain, how much of life and human happiness was entrusted to the ruinous mound on which he stood.

II

The sun had sunk beneath the waves when they reached the castle of Seithenyn. The sound of the harp and the song saluted them as they approached it. As they entered the great hall, which was already blazing with torchlight, they found the whole household roaring the praises of the blue buffalo horn:

Fill high the blue horn, the blue buffalo horn: Fill high the long silver-rimmed buffalo horn: While the roof of the hall by our chorus is torn, Fill, fill to the brim the deep silver-rimmed horn.

Elphin and Teithrin stood some time on the floor of the hall before they attracted the attention of Seithenyn, who during the chorus was tossing and flourishing his golden goblet. The chorus had scarcely ended when he noticed them, and immediately shouted aloud, "You are welcome all four."

Elphin answered, "We thank you, we are but two."

"Two or four," said Seithenyn, "all is one. You are welcome all. When a stranger enters, the custom in other places is to begin by washing his feet. My custom is to begin by washing his throat. Seithenyn, the son of Seithyn Saidi, bids you welcome."

Elphin answered, "Elphin, the son of Gwyddno Garanhir, thanks you."

Seithenyn started up when he realized that he was in the presence of the son of the King, and with a bow intended to be gracious, invited the Prince to take his seat on his right hand. Teithrin remained at the end of the hall, on which Seithenyn shouted to him, "Come on, man, come on, sit and drink," and motioned him to seat himself next to Elphin.

"Prince Seithenyn," said Elphin, "I have visited you on a subject of deep moment. Reports have been brought to me that the embankment which has so long been entrusted to your care is in a state of dangerous decay."

"Decay," said Seithenyn, "is one thing and danger is another. Everything that is old must decay. That the embankment is old, I am free to confess; that it is somewhat rotten in parts, I will not altogether deny; that it is any the worse for that, I do most sturdily gainsay. It does its business well: it keeps out the water from the land. Cupbearer, fill."

"The stonework," said Teithrin, "is sapped and mined: the piles are rotten, broken and out of their places: the floodgates and sluices are leaky and creaky."

"Our ancestors were wiser than we," said Seithenyn; "they built the embankment in their wisdom: and if we should be so rash as to try to mend it, we should only mar it. This immortal work has stood for centuries and will stand for centuries more, if we let it alone. It is well: it works well: let well alone. Cupbearer, fill."

Elphin and Teithrin tried to reason with him, but all their words were met with the assurance that all was well with the embankment, and as every speech of the Lord High Commissioner ended with the command, "Cupbearer, fill," it was not long before he fell on sleep. The members of his household had been imitating the example of their chief, and the words of host and visitors had been punctuated by the heavy falls from their benches of men sent to sleep by the yellow mead. By the time their chief fell all except the cupbearers were lying flat on the floor.

Elphin and Teithrin were gazing in disgust upon this scene of drunken disorder, when a side door, at the upper end of the hall, to the left of Seithenyn's chair, opened, and a beautiful young girl entered the hall with her domestic bard and her attendant maidens.

It was Angharad, the daughter of Seithenyn. She gracefully saluted Prince Elphin, and he looked with delight at the beautiful lady, whose gentle and serious loveliness contrasted so strikingly with the fallen heroes of revelry that lay scattered at her feet.

"Stranger," she said, "this seems an unfitting place for you: let me conduct you where you will be more agreeably lodged."

"Still less should I deem it fitting for you, fair maiden," said Elphin.

She answered, "The pleasure of her father is the duty of Angharad."

Elphin paused to think what he should say in reply to this, and Angharad stood still, expecting that he would follow. In this interval of silence, there came a loud gust of wind blustering through the holes of the walls. "It bids fair to be a stormy night," said Elphin.

"We are used to storms," answered Angharad. "We are far from the mountains, between the lowlands and the sea, and the winds blow round us from all quarters."

There was another pause of deep silence; then there came another gust of wind, pealing like thunder through the holes. Amidst the fallen and sleeping revellers, the confused and littered hall, the low and wavering torches, Angharad, lovely always, shone with single and surpassing loveliness. The gust died away in murmurs and swelled again into thunder and died away in murmurs again: and, as it died away, mixed with the murmurs of ocean, a voice, that seemed one of the many voices of the wind, pronounced the ominous words, "Beware of the oppression of Gwenhudiw!"

They looked at each other, as if questioning whether all had heard alike.

"Did you not hear a voice?" said Angharad, after a pause.

"The same," said Elphin, "which has before seemed to say to me, 'Beware of the oppression of Gwenhudiw!'"

Teithrin hurried forth on the rampart: Angharad turned pale and leaned against a pillar of the hall. Elphin was amazed and awed, absorbed as his feelings were in her. The sleepers on the floor made an uneasy movement and uttered a cry.

Teithrin returned. "What saw you?" said Elphin. Teithrin answered, "A tempest is coming from the west. The moon has waned three days, and is half hidden in clouds, just visible above the mountains: the bank of clouds is black in the west: the scud is flying before them: and the white waves are rolling to the shore."

"This is the highest of the spring tides," said Angharad, "and they are very terrible in the storms from the west when the spray flies over the embankment and the breakers shake the tower which has its foot in the surf."

"Whence was the voice," said Elphin, "which we heard erewhile? Was it the cry of a sleeper in his drink, or an error of the fancy, or a warning voice from the elements?"

"It was surely nothing earthly," said Angharad, "nor was it an error of the fancy, for we all heard the words, 'Beware of the oppression of Gwenhudiw!' Often and often in the storms of the spring tides have I feared to see her roll her power over the fields of the Bottom Hundred."

"Pray Heaven she do not tonight," said Teithrin.

"Can there be such a danger?" said Elphin.

"I think," said Teithrin, "of the decay I have seen, and I fear the voice I have heard."

A long pause of deep silence ensued, during which they heard the peals of the wind, and the increasing sound of the rising sea, swelling ever into wilder and more menacing tumult, till, with one terrific impulse, the whole violence of the tempest seemed to burst upon the shore. Before long there came a tremendous crash. The tower, which had its foot in the sea, had long been sapped by the waves: and the storm hurled it into the surf, carrying with it a portion of the wall of the main building, and revealing through the chasm the white raging of the breakers beneath the blackness of the midnight storm. The wind rushed into the hall, putting out the torches within the line of its course, tossing the grey locks and loose mantle of the bard and the light white drapery and long black tresses of Angharad. With the crash of the falling tower and the shrieks of the women, the sleepers started from the floor, staring with drunken amazement, and Seithenyn rose staggering from his chair.

The Lord High Commissioner of the Royal Embankment leaned against a pillar and stared at the sea through the rifted wall with wild and vacant surprise. Then he looked at Elphin and Teithrin, at his daughter and at the members of his household, but the longer he looked, the less clearly he saw: and the longer he pondered, the less he understood. He felt the rush of the wind: he saw the white foam of the sea: his ears were dizzy with their mingled roar. He remained at length motionless, leaning against the pillar, and gazing on the breakers with fixed and glaring vacancy.

"The sleepers of the Bottom Hundred," said Elphin, "they who sleep in peace and security, trusting to the vigilance of Seithenyn, what will become of them?"

"Warn them with the beacon fire," said Teithrin, "if there be fuel on the summit of the landward tower."

"That, of course, has been neglected too," said Elphin. "Not so," said Angharad, "that has been my charge." Teithrin seized a torch and ascended the eastern tower, and in a few minutes the party in the hall beheld the breakers reddening with the reflected fire, and deeper and yet deeper crimson tinging the whirling foam and sheeting the massy darkness of the bursting waves.

An unusual tumult mingled with the roar of the waves. Teithrin rushed into the hall, exclaiming, "All is over! The mound is broken and the spring tide is rolling through the breach."

Another portion of the castle wall fell into the mining waves, and by the dim and thickly-clouded moonlight, and the red blaze of the beacon fire, they beheld a torrent pouring in from the sea upon the plain and rushing immediately beneath the castle walls, which, as well as the points of the embankment that formed the sides of the breach, continued to crumble away into the waters.

"Who has done this?" shouted Seithenyn. "Show me the enemy."

"There is no enemy but the sea," said Elphin, "to which you, in your drunken madness, have abandoned the land. Think, if you can think, of what is passing in the plain. The storm drowns the cries of your victims, but the curses of the perishing are upon you."

"Show me the enemy," shouted Seithenyn, drawing his sword furiously and flourishing it over his head.

"There is no enemy but the sea," said Elphin, "against which your sword avails not."

"Who dares to say so?" said Seithenyn. "Who dares to say that there is an enemy on earth against whom the sword of Seithenyn is unavailing? Thus, thus I prove the falsehood." And springing suddenly forward, he leaped into the torrent, flourishing his sword as he descended.

"Oh, my unhappy father!" sobbed Angharad, veiling her face with her arm on the shoulder of one of her female attendants.

"We must quit the castle," said Teithrin, "or we shall be buried in its ruins. We have but one path of safety, along the summit of the embankment, if there be not another breach between us and the high land, and if we can keep our footing in this storm. But let us go: the walls are melting away like snow."

Angharad, recovering from the first shock of Seithenyn's catastrophe, became awake to the imminent danger. The spirit of the Cymric female, vigilant and energetic in peril, disposed her and her attendant maidens to use their best exertions for their own preservation. Following the advice and example of Elphin and Teithrin, they armed themselves with spears, which they took down from the walls.

Teithrin led the way, striking the point of his spear firmly into the earth and leaning from it on the wind. Angharad followed in the same manner: Elphin followed Angharad; the attendant maidens followed Elphin: and the bard followed the female train. Behind them went the cupbearers, and behind them reeled those who were able and willing to move.

In front of them, as they marched, was the volumed blackness of the storm: the breakers burst white in the faint and scarcely perceptible moonlight: within the mound the waters rushed and rose: the red light of the beacon fire fell on them from behind: the surf rolled up the side of the embankment and broke almost at their feet: the spray flew above their heads, and it was only by thrusting their spears into the stony ground that they bore themselves up against the wind.

They had not proceeded far when the tide began to recede, the wind to abate somewhat of its violence, and the moon to look on them at intervals through the rifted clouds, disclosing the desolation of the flooded plain, silvering the angry surf, gleaming on the distant mountains and revealing a lengthened prospect of their solitary path that lay in its irregular line like a ribbon on the deep. Morning dawned before they reached safety; daylight showed fully how dreadful was the destruction. The foaming waves were covering the fertile plains which had been the habitation and support of a flourishing population. Of the inhabitants, only the party led by Teithrin from Seithenyn's castle and a few who saw the beacon fire in time to run to the high lands of Ardudwy and Eryri escaped destruction.

The nearest town to the submerged realm of Gwyddno is Aberdovey. If you stand on the beach there, you will sometimes hear in the long twilight evening chimes and peals of bells, sometimes near, sometimes distant, sounding low and sweet like a call to prayer, or as rejoicing for a victory. The sounds come from the bells of one of Gwyddno's drowned churches, and these are "The Bells of Aberdovey" that the song speaks about.

ELIDYR'S SOJOURN IN FAIRY-LAND

In that country of crosses, ruined chapels and rocking stones, caers and tumuli, cromlechs and camps, which is sometimes known as Dewisland, there once lived a boy named Elidyr whose father and mother wished him to become a priest. They accordingly sent him every day to the monks of St. David's to learn his letters, but the little rascal much preferred hoop and ball to book-learning; all that went in at one ear came out at the other, and as a scholar he therefore left much to be desired. His teachers, remembering that Solomon had said, "He that spareth his rod hateth his son, but he that loveth him chasteneth him betimes," showed their affection towards their pupil in the manner he advised. At first they corrected him lightly and infrequently, but Elidyr did not amend his ways, and before long not a lesson passed without chastisement. Not only were the stripes more frequent, but they also became more severe, till Elidyr could stand them no longer. So one day when he was twelve years old he ran away: he went on and on, and the further he got the happier he felt. Knowing that a search would be made for him, he looked diligently for a hiding place, but for a long time he could find no place where he could feel safe. At last he came to a river: under the hollow bank of this, there was a beautiful hiding place, where no pursuer would ever expect to find a runaway. Into this he crept and slept that night as soundly as the best little boy who ever tired himself out with lessons. The next day he realised that, glorious as his hiding place was as an escape from books and thwackings, it had its disadvantages: the chief was that there was nothing to eat and drink, and that is a very serious thing for a growing boy with a healthy appetite. It was not safe to go out even to look for hips and haws, because when he lifted his head above the river bank he saw men and women searching all over the countryside for him. He became hungrier and hungrier, and oh, how slowly the time passed! It was the longest day Elidyr had ever known: the sun simply crawled across the heavens, and it seemed to be an age before it dipped its red rim in the waters of St. Bride's Bay. He was no better off even when the sun did set, because night is worse than day when you cannot sleep, and it is very difficult to get even forty winks when you have an aching void inside you. Every time he woke up he felt hungrier, and he made up his mind to return home as soon as it was light enough for him to find his way.

Better two thrashings – for he knew that his father would lay on as well as the monks – than the wolf which was tearing his inside. When the shades of night were disappearing, he got up to start off, when to his intense surprise two little pigmies appeared to him and said, "Come with us, and we will lead you to a land full of sports and delights." Very curiously his hunger vanished that very minute, and with the hunger vanished the desire to return to those hateful lessons and thrashings. So he upped with him and offed with him with the two pigmies. They went first through an underground passage all in the dark, but soon they came out into a most beautiful country. There were purling streams, lush meadows and wooded hills, all as pleasant as can be.

The two little men led Elidyr to a magnificent palace. "What is this place?" asked the truant. "This is the palace of the King of Faery," answered his guides. They took him in, and there they found the King sitting on a splendid throne, with his courtiers in magnificent dresses all about him. He asked Elidyr who he was and whence he came. Elidyr told him, and the King said, "Thou shalt attend my son." The King then waved him away, and the King's son, who was about the same age as Elidyr, took him out of the court.

Then began a time of supreme happiness to Elidyr. He waited on the King's son and joined in all the games and sports of the little men. They were little, but they were not mis-shapen dwarfs, for all their limbs were well-proportioned.

They were fair of complexion, and their hair was thick and long, falling over their shoulders like that of women. They rode little horses about the size of greyhounds, and they never ate flesh nor fish, but lived on messes of milk flavoured with saffron. They took no oaths, but never spoke a lie, for there was nothing they detested so much as falsehood. They scoffed at men for their struggles, follies, vanities, fickleness, treacheries and lies. But they worshipped none, unless you might say they were worshippers of Truth. The country in which they lived was beautiful, as has already been described, but there was this that was curious about it. The sun never shone and clouds were always over the sky, so that even the days were obscure and the nights were pitch dark, for neither moon nor stars ever gave any light.

After a time Elidyr began to long for his mother, and he begged to be allowed to go and visit his old home. The King gave him permission, and the two little men who had brought him to the realm of Faery led him through the underground passage to the upper earth, and right up to his mother's cottage, keeping him invisible to all on the way. Imagine his mother's joy when he entered, for she had thought he was lost for ever. She plied him with questions, and he had to tell her everything about himself and the bourne from which he had returned. She begged him to stay with her, but he had given his word to go back, and soon he departed, after making his mother promise not to tell where he was or with whom. After this he often went to visit his mother, sometimes by the road by which he had first returned, sometimes by others. At first he was not allowed to go alone, but inasmuch as he always kept his promise to come back, he was subsequently permitted to go by himself.

Now one day when Elidyr was with his mother, he told her of the heavy yellow balls which the King's son and he used in their play. His mother knew that they must be made of gold, and she said to him, "Bring one of them with you next time you come." "It would not be right to do that," said the boy. "What is the harm?" asked his mother. "I have been told never to bring anything with me to earth," replied Elidyr, "Surely, out of the hundreds of balls which the King's son has, he would not miss just one," pleaded the mother, and the boy reluctantly consented. Some days after, when he thought no one was looking, he took up one of the golden balls, and started off to his mother's cottage, walking at first slowly, but increasing his pace as he drew nearer to the upper air. Just as he emerged out of the underground passage on to the earth, he thought he heard tiny footsteps pattering behind him, and he started to run. Turning his head round, he saw two little men running after him and looking very grim. He put his best foot forward and tore ahead; the little men raced after him, but Elidyr having the start reached the cottage first. When he reached the threshold, he stumbled and fell, and the golden ball rolled out of his hand right to the feet of his mother. At that moment the two little men jumped over him as he lay sprawling, seized the ball and rushed out of the house. As they passed Elidyr they spat at him and shouted, "Thief, traitor, false mortal," and other terms of reproach.

Full of grief and shame, he went sadly back to the river bank where the underground passage commenced, determined to go back to the land of the little men to tell them how sorry he was that he had listened to his mother's evil counsel, but he could find no trace of any opening. Again and again he searched, but never could he find any way back to that fair country. So after a time he went back to the monastery, and tried to deaden his longing for fairy-land by devotion to learning. In due time he became a monk. The story of his sojourn in Fairy-land gradually leaked out, and men used to come and ask him about the land of the little men, but he could never speak of the happy time he had spent there without shedding tears.

Now it happened that when Elidyr was old, David, the second Bishop of St. David's, came to visit the monastery and ask him about the manners and customs of the little men. Above all, he was curious to know what language they spoke, and Elidyr told him some of their words. When they asked for water they would say, "Udor udorurn," and when they wanted salt, they said, "Halgei udorum." Now the Bishop knew that the Greek for water is *νοωρ* and for salt *άλς*, and he thus discovered that the language of the fairies greatly resembles that of the ancient Greeks.

LOWRI DAFYDD EARNS A PURSE OF GOLD

Lowri Dafydd had just arrived at Hafodydd Brithion to nurse a sick woman, when a fine-looking man galloped up to the door on a noble grey horse and said in a loud voice, "Is Lowri Dafydd here?"

"Yes, sir," answered Lowri in a very meek voice.

"Then come with me at once," said the fine-looking man.

"But I have my duty to do here," remonstrated Lowri.

"Come with me 'at once'," repeated the fine-looking man; and he spoke in such a tone that Lowri had not the courage to say no.

She mounted behind him, and off they went, like the flight of a swallow, through Cwmllan, down Nant yr Aran, and over the Gader to Cwm Hafod Ruffydd, before the poor woman had time even to say, "Oh!"

When they reached Cwm Hafod Ruffydd, Lowri saw a magnificent mansion before her, splendidly lit up with such lamps as she had never seen before. They entered the court, and a crowd of servants in gorgeous liveries came to meet them.

"Lead her to the bed-chamber," said the fine-looking man; and Lowri was conducted through the great hall into a bed-chamber which surpassed in luxury and splendour anything she had ever dreamed of, let alone seen. There the mistress of the house, to whose aid she had been summoned, was awaiting her.

Lowri nursed her with her accustomed skill, and stayed with her until the lady was completely recovered. It was the pleasantest episode of Lowri's life; there was festivity day and night; dancing, singing and merriment went on ceaselessly. She was very sad when the time came for her to depart. The fine-looking man gave her a great, heavy purse, with the order not to open it until she reached her own house. Then he bade one of his servants escort her back the same way that she had come. When she reached home she opened the purse, and to her intense delight it was full of gold. She lived happily on these earnings to the end of her life.

WHY THE RED DRAGON IS THE EMBLEM OF WALES

After the Treachery of the Long Knives, King Vortigern called together his twelve wise men and asked them what he should do. They said to him: "Retire to the remote boundaries of your kingdom, and there build and fortify a city to defend yourself. The Saxon people you have received are treacherous, and they are seeking to subdue you by guile. Even during your life they will, if they can, seize upon all the countries which are subject to your power. How much more will they attempt it after your death?"

The King was pleased with this advice, and departing with his wise men travelled through many parts of his territories in search of a convenient place for building a citadel. Far and wide they travelled, but nowhere could they find a suitable place until they came to the mountains of Eryri, in Gwynedd. On the summit of one of these, which was then called Dinas Ffaraon, they discovered a fine place to build a fortress. The wise men said to the King: "Build here a city, for in this place you will be secure against the barbarians."

Then the King sent for artificers, carpenters and stonemasons, and collected all the materials for building; in the night, however, the whole of these disappeared, and by morning nothing remained of all that had been provided. Materials were procured from all parts a second time, but a second time they disappeared in the night. A third time everything was brought together for building, but by morning again not a trace of them remained. Vortigern called his wise men together and asked them the cause of this marvel. They replied: "You must find a child born without a father, put him to death, and sprinkle with his blood the ground on which the citadel is to be built, or you will never accomplish your purpose."

This did not appear such strange advice to King Vortigern as it does to us. In olden times there were very cruel practices in connection with building. Sometimes a human victim was sacrificed in order that his blood might be used as cement; at other times a living person was walled in a new building – often an innocent little child.

The King thought the advice of his wise men was good and sent messengers throughout Britain in search of a child born without a father. After having inquired in vain in all the provinces, they came to a field in Bassaleg, where a party of boys were playing at ball. Two of them were quarrelling, and one of them said to the other, "O boy without a father, no good will ever happen to you." The messengers concluded that this was the boy they were searching for; they had him led away and conducted him before Vortigern the King.

The next day the King, his wise men, his soldiers and retinue, his artificers, carpenters and stonemasons, assembled for the ceremony of putting the boy to death. Then the boy said to the King, "Why have your servants brought me hither?" "That you may be put to death," replied the King, "and that the ground on which my citadel is to stand may be sprinkled with your blood, without which I shall be unable to build it." "Who," said the boy, "instructed you to do this?" "My wise men," replied the King. "Order them hither," returned the boy.

This being done, he thus questioned the wise men: "By what means was it revealed to you that this citadel could not be built unless the spot were sprinkled with my blood? Speak without disguise, and declare who discovered me to you." Then turning to the King, "I will soon," said he, "unfold to you everything; but I desire to question your wise men and wish them to disclose to you what is hidden underneath this pavement." They could not do so and acknowledged their ignorance. Thereupon the boy said, "There is a pool; come and dig." They did so, and found a pool even as the boy had said. "Now," he continued, turning to the wise men again, "tell me what is in the pool." But they were ashamed and made no reply. "I," said the boy, "can discover it to you if the wise men cannot. There are two vases in the pool." They examined and found that it was so. Continuing his questions, "What is in the vases?" he asked. They were again silent. "There is a tent in them," said the boy; "separate them and you shall find it so."

This being done by the King's command, there was found in them a folded tent. The boy, going on with his questions, asked the wise men what was in it. But they knew not what to reply. "There are," said he, "two serpents, one white and one red; unfold the tent." They obeyed, and two sleeping serpents were discovered. "Consider attentively," said the boy, "what the serpents do." They began to struggle with each other, and the white one, raising himself up, threw down the other into the middle of the tent and sometimes drove him to the edge of it, and this was repeated thrice. At length the red one, apparently the weaker of the two, recovering his strength, expelled the white one from the tent, and the latter, being pursued through the pool by the red one, disappeared.

Then the boy asked the wise men what was signified by this wonderful omen, but they had again to confess their ignorance. "I will now," said he to the King, "unfold to you the meaning of this mystery. The pool is the emblem of this world, and the tent that of your kingdom; the two serpents are two dragons; the red serpent is your dragon, but the white serpent is the dragon of the Saxons, who occupy several provinces and districts of Britain, even almost from sea to sea. At length, however, our people shall rise and drive the Saxon race beyond the sea whence they have come; but do you depart from this place where you are not permitted to erect a citadel, you must seek another spot for laying your foundations."

Vortigern, perceiving the ignorance and deceit of the magicians, ordered them to be put to death, and their graves were dug in a neighbouring field. The boy's life was spared; he became known to fame afterwards as the great magician Myrddin Emrys (or Merlin, as he is called in English), and the mountain on which he proved his mighty power was called in after time Dinas Emrys instead of Dinas Ffaraon. He remained in the Dinas for a long time, until he was joined by Aurelius Ambrosius, who persuaded him to go away with him. When they were about to set out, Myrddin placed all his treasure in a golden cauldron and hid it in a cave. On the mouth of the cave he rolled a huge stone, which he covered up with earth and green turf, so that it was impossible for anyone to find it. This wealth he intended to be the property of some special person in a future generation. This heir is to be a youth with yellow hair and blue eyes, and when he comes to the Dinas a bell will ring to invite him into the cave, which will open out of its own accord as soon as his foot touches it.

EINION AND THE LADY OF THE GREENWOOD

Einion, the son of Gwalchmai, was one fine summer day walking in the woods of Trefeilir, when he beheld a slender, graceful lady. Her complexion surpassed every white and red in the morning dawn, and the mountain snow, and every beautiful colour in the blossoms of wood, field and hill. Feeling in his heart a vast love he saluted her, and, she returned the salutation, by which he perceived that his society was not disagreeable to her. He approached her in a courteous manner, and she also approached him. When he came near to her he saw that she had hoofs instead of feet, and would fain have fled. But she cast her glamour upon him and said, "Thou must follow me whithersoever I go." She had him in thrall, and he said he would go with her to the ends of the earth, but he requested of her permission first to go and bid farewell to his wife Angharad. This the Lady of the Greenwood agreed to, "but," said she, "I shall be with thee, invisible to all but to thyself."

So he went, and the goblin (for the Lady of the Greenwood was none other) went with him. When he saw Angharad his wife, she appeared an old hag, but he retained the recollection of days past and still felt true love for her, but he was not able to loose himself from the bond of his enchantment. "It is necessary for me," said he, "to part from thee for a time, I know not how long." They wept together and broke a gold ring between them: he kept one half and Angharad the other. They took their leave of each other, and he went with the Lady of the Greenwood and knew not whither: for a powerful spell was upon him, and he saw not any place or person or object under its true and proper appearance, excepting the half of the ring alone.

After being a long time, he knew not how long, with the Lady of the Greenwood, he looked one morning, as the sun was rising, upon the half of the ring, and he bethought him to place it in the most secret place he could find. He resolved to put it under his eyelid: as he was endeavouring to do so, he saw a man in white apparel and mounted on a snow-white horse coming towards him. The horseman asked him what he did there: Einion answered that he was cherishing the memory of his wife Angharad. "Post thou desire to see her? " asked the man in white. "I do," replied Einion, "above all things and all pleasures in the world." "If so," said the man in white, "get upon this horse behind me." That Einion did, and looking around he could not see any trace of the Lady of the Greenwood, except the track of hoofs of monstrous size, as if journeying towards the north. "What spell art thou under?" asked the man in white. Then Einion answered him and told everything, how it occurred betwixt him and the Lady of the Greenwood. "Take this white staff in thy hand, and wish for whatsoever thou desirest," said the man in white. Einion took it, and the first thing he wished was to see the Lady of the Greenwood, for he was not yet completely delivered from her spell. A hideous and uncanny beldam appeared to him, a thousand times more repulsive of aspect than the most frightful thing on earth. Einion uttered a cry of terror: the man in white cast his cloak over him, and in less than a twinkling Einion alighted on the hill of Trefeilir, by his own house, where he knew scarcely anyone, nor did anyone know him.

In the meantime, the goblin who had appeared to Einion as the Lady of the Greenwood had gone to Trefeilir in the form of an honourable and powerful nobleman, richly apparelled and wealthy. He placed a letter in Angharad's hand, in which it was stated that Einion had died in Norway more than nine years before. He cast his spell upon her, and she listened to his words of love. Soon, seeing that she should become a noble lady, higher than any in Wales, she named a day for her marriage with him. There was a great preparation of every elegant and sumptuous kind of apparel, and of meats and drinks, and of every excellence of song and instruments of music and festive entertainment.

Now, there was in Angharad's hall a very beautiful harp: when the goblin nobleman saw it, he wished to have it played, and the harpers who had assembled, the best in Wales, tried to put it in tune, but were not able. Just at this time Einion came into the house, and Angharad saw him as an old, decrepit, withered, grey-haired man, stooping with age, and dressed in rags. After the minstrels had failed to put the harp in tune, Einion took it in his hand and tuned it, and played on it an air which Angharad loved. She marvelled exceedingly, and asked him who he was. "I am Einion, the son of Gwalchmai," said he; "see, the bright gold is my token." And he gave her the ring. But she could not bring him to her recollection. Upon that he placed the white staff in Angharad's hand. Instantly the goblin, whom she had hitherto seen as a handsome and honourable nobleman, appeared to her as a monster, inconceivably hideous: she fainted from fear, and Einion supported her until she revived. When she opened her eyes, she saw neither the goblin nor any of the guests or minstrels, nothing except Einion and the harp and the banquet on the table, casting its savoury odour around. They sat down to eat, and exceeding great was their joy at the breaking of the spell which the goblin had cast over them.

THE GREEN ISLES OF THE OCEAN

The people of Pembrokeshire were for a long time puzzled to know where the fairies, or the Children of Rhys the Deep, as they are called in Little England beyond Wales, lived. They used to attend the markets at Milford Haven and other places regularly. They made their purchases without speaking, laid down their money and departed, always leaving the exact sum required, which they seemed to know without asking the price of anything. A certain Gruffydd ab Einion was wont to supply them with more corn than anybody else, and there was one special butcher at Milford Haven upon whom they bestowed their patronage exclusively. To ordinary eyes they were invisible, but some keen-sighted persons caught glimpses of them at the markets; no one, however, saw them coming or going, and great was the curiosity as to where they lived, for even fairies must make their home somewhere.

One day Gruffydd ab Einion was walking about St. David's churchyard, when he saw islands far out at sea where he had never observed land before. "Ah!" he said, "there are the Green Isles of Ocean, Gwerddonau Llion, about which the poets sing. I will go to see them." He started to go down to the seashore to get a nearer view, but the islands disappeared. He went back to the place where he had seen the vision; he could again see the islands quite distinctly, with houses dotted here and there among green fields. Now, Gruffydd was a very acute man; he cut the turf from which he espied the islands, and took it down to a boat. He stood upon it, and, setting sail, before long landed on the shore of one of the islands. The fairies welcomed him warmly and, after showing him all the wonders of their home, sent him back loaded with presents. They made him, however, leave behind the enchanted turf, and pointed out an underground passage by which he could come to visit them. He continued to be a great friend of Rhys the Deep's children as long as he lived, and the gold they presented him with made him the richest man in West Wales.

IANTO'S CHASE

Many, many years ago, there was a man in the hills of Breconshire whose proper name was Ifan Sion Watkin, but he was generally known as Ianto Coedcae, Ianto being a nickname for Ifan, and Coedcae being the name of the farm at which he lived.

Ianto was invited to the house of a friend on the borders of Glamorgan to celebrate a christening. He accepted the invitation gladly, expecting to have a jolly evening. Nor was he disappointed. There were plenty of good things to eat: there was an abundance of strong ale and old mead to drink: there was dancing and penillion were sung to the harp. The time passed so quickly that it was quite a shock to Ifan to hear the old clock in the corner striking twelve. He had urgent business to attend to at home next morning, and as he had a long way to go he began to make preparations for going.

His host looked out into the night. "Ianto," he said, "it is as dark as a cow's inside. Will you have a lantern to light you home?"

Ianto felt insulted. "Do you take me for a child?" he asked indignantly. "I have been out on nights so dark that I could not see my hand in front of me, and I have never failed to find my way home. A lantern for me? No, thank you."

After bidding good-night to the other guests, who having only a short distance to go were in no hurry to put an end to the festivities, and to his host and hostess, Ianto set off at a rattling pace for his home over the mountain. He had walked some time and covered the best portion of his journey when he thought he could hear at a great distance some sounds resembling music nearly in the direction he was going. As he advanced Ianto found himself approaching these sounds so near that he could plainly distinguish them as proceeding from a harp and some voices singing to it. He could even make out the tune, which was Ar Hyd y Nos – All Through the Night. Ianto laughed. "Jabox," he said, "that is a very appropriate tune." The remark he had made struck him as most apposite, and he laughed again right merrily.

He tried to discover who they were who were thus amusing themselves, but he could not do so on account of the darkness. As he knew there was no house within a great distance of that spot his curiosity was greatly excited. The music still continuing and seemingly but a short distance from the path, he thought there could be no harm in deviating a little out of his way in order to see what was going forward. Moreover, he thought that it would be a pity to pass so near such a merry party without giving them the opportunity of inviting him to join in their mirth. Accordingly he made an oblique cut in the direction of the music, and having gone fully as far as the place from which he was quite sure the sounds emanated when he left the path, he was not a little surprised to find that they were still at some distance from him.

"This is curious," said Ianto, and he was so puzzled that he scratched his head vigorously for a minute or two. This cleared his intellect, and he wondered why he had been so slow to realise the explanation of the difficulty. "There's dull I am," he said, "not to remember that sounds are heard at much greater distance by night than by day. That is how it is, of course."

Off he started again, but somehow or other the more he walked the less chance he saw of getting there. He stopped to think things over. The music at this time was quite a long way off and receding from him. "No," he said, "I will not give it up," and he quickened his pace lest he should lose the strain altogether. He had not gone more than ten yards when a strange thing happened. He tumbled up to his neck in a turf bog. When he had struggled out and tidied himself up as well as he could under the circumstances, the music struck up quite near him, and he heard his name called, "Ifan, Ifan."

This was the most respectful mode of addressing him, and he reflected, "Well, whoever they are, they must be well-bred people." Instead of giving up the chase, as he had fully intended to do after his accident, he became more desirous than ever of joining a company which was evidently as polite as it was harmonious. On he walked, and in a minute or two he heard himself called, "Ianto,

Ianto." This was not such a dignified appellation as "Ifan, Ifan," but he was in such a clever mood that he had no difficulty in arriving at the explanation. "There must be someone in the company who knows me intimately," he said, and he therefore concluded that the familiarity was excusable. The salutations, however, which seemed to alternate between "Ifan, Ifan," and "Ianto, Ianto," now became so indistinct that he could not always decide whether or not they proceeded from the grouse or the lapwings which he was continually disturbing among the heather.

At length, chagrined and mortified by his repeated disappointments and excessively fatigued, he determined to lie down on the ground till morning. But he had scarcely composed himself to sleep when the harp struck up again more brilliantly than ever, and seemed so near that he could plainly hear the words of the song that was being sung to it. Upon this he started up, absolutely determined, come what may, to achieve his quest. He tumbled into bogs, waded knee-deep through water, and scratched his legs in labouring through heather and gorse, but his blood was up and he did not mind. Suddenly he saw at a small distance from him a number of lights, which on a nearer approach he found to proceed from a house in which there appeared to be a large company assembled, enjoying a similar merrymaking to the one he had left, with music, with drink, and other good cheer. At the door a very bonny lass invited him in, seated him in a comfortable armchair by a roaring fire, and asked him whether he would have ale or mead. Ianto thought that ale would pick him up after his long walk rather than mead, and the maid bustled away to fetch it. But before it arrived, or he had time to take stock of the company around him, such was the effect of the fatigue he had undergone that he fell fast asleep.

He was awakened next morning by the sunbeams playing on his face. On opening his eyes and looking around him, he was more than astonished to find himself quite alone. The house and the convivial company had completely vanished, and not a vestige remained of what he had positively seen before going to sleep. Instead of being comfortably seated in a good armchair by a roaring fire, he found himself almost frozen with cold and lying on a bare rock on a point of one of the loftiest crags of Mynydd Pen Cyrn, a thousand feet in height, down which poor Ianto would have fallen headlong had he moved but a foot or two further.

BALA LAKE

Long, long ago, there was a fertile valley where now roll the waters of Bala Lake.

In a stately palace in the middle of the valley lived a cruel and unjust prince. "As a roaring lion and a ranging bear, so is a wicked ruler over the poor people." He feared not God, neither regarded man, and he so oppressed and vexed the five parishes of Penllyn that his name stank in the nostrils of the men of Meirion.

Those whom he afflicted cried to the Lord, and He sent a warning to the oppressor. As the wicked ruler walked in his garden he heard a voice saying, "Vengeance will come," but he laughed the warning to scorn. And he seemed to have reason, for he flourished exceedingly. He laid up treasure and took to wife a noble lady, who bore him a son.

To celebrate the birth of his first-born he prepared a splendid feast, and sent his servants to bid the highest in the land to it. Many made excuse, but many came, and they supped sumptuously. Every sort of meat and every sort of liquor was served that was ever seen elsewhere, and no vessel was placed upon the table that was not either of gold, or of silver, or of buffalo horn. Merry tales were told and mirthful songs were sung, and when it was more agreeable to them to dance than to listen to tales and songs, they danced to the strains of the harp.

About midnight there was an interval in the dancing and the harper was resting alone in a corner, when suddenly he heard a whisper in his ear, "Vengeance, vengeance." He turned at once, and saw a little bird hovering about him. Having arrested the harper's attention, the bird flew slowly to the door. The harper did not go after it, and the bird came back, sang plaintively a second time in his ear, "Vengeance, vengeance," after which it again flew off to the door, beckoning, as it were, to the harper to follow. This time the harper went after it, but after getting outside he hesitated. Once more the bird returned to him and piped, "Vengeance, vengeance," mournfully and sadly in his ear.

The harper now became afraid of refusing to follow, and proceeded to walk in the direction in which the bird invited him to advance. On they went, through thicket and through bog, the bird hovering the while in front of him and leading him along the easiest and safest paths. If he but stopped for a moment the bird would sing, "Vengeance, vengeance," and he felt constrained to continue his flight. At last he reached the top of a hill, some considerable distance from the palace. By this time he was fatigued and weary (for he was an old man), and he stopped to rest. He fully expected to hear the bird's warning note as before, but on this occasion, though he listened carefully, he could hear nothing but the murmuring of the little burn hard by. "How foolish I have been," he now thought to himself, "to allow myself to be led away in this fashion from the palace! They will be looking for me to play for the next dance and I must hurry back."

In his anxiety, however, to make haste, the old harper lost his way on the hill, and found himself forced to await the break of day.

When the sun's rim appeared above the Berwyn mountains, he turned his eye in the direction of the palace. He was astonished beyond measure to see no trace of it. The whole valley was one calm, large lake, and he could descry his harp floating on the face of the waters.

TUDUR AP EINION

Half-way up the ascent from Llangollen to Dinas Bran, or Bran's Fortress (the wicked man who called it Crow Castle ought to have been hanged, drawn and quartered), lies a hollow known by the name of Nant yr Ellyllon, the Elves' Dell. Once upon a time a young man, who was known as Tudur ap Einion Gloff, used to pasture his master's sheep in this hollow. One summer night Tudur was preparing to return to the lowlands with his woolly charge, when he suddenly saw, perched on a stone near him, a little man in moss breeches with a fiddle under his arm. He was the tiniest wee specimen of humanity imaginable. His coat was made of birch leaves, and he wore upon his head a helmet consisting of a gorse flower, while his feet were encased in shoes made of beetles' wings. He ran his fingers over his instrument, and the music made Tudur's hair stand on end. "Nos dawch, nos dawch," said the little man (this means in English, "Good night to you, good night to you.") "Ac i chwithau," replied Tudur, which is, being interpreted, "The same to you." Then continued the little man, "You are fond of dancing, Tudur: and if you but tarry awhile you shall behold some of the best dancers in Wales. I," added the little man, swelling his chest out, "I am a musician." "Where is your harp?" asked Tudur, "a Welshman cannot dance without a harp." "Harp?" repeated the wee being scornfully, "I can discourse better music for dancing upon my fiddle." "Is it a fiddle," rejoined Tudur, "that you call that stringed wooden spoon in your hand?" He had never seen such an instrument before. And now Tudur beheld through the dusk hundreds of pretty little sprites converging from all parts of the mountain towards the spot where they stood. Some were dressed in white and some in blue and some in pink, and some carried glow-worms in their hands as torches. So lightly did they tread that not a blade of grass nor any flower was crushed beneath their weight, and all made a curtsey or a bow to Tudur as they passed. Tudur was not to be outdone in politeness, and he doffed his cap and bowed to each in return.

Presently the little minstrel drew his bow across the strings of his instrument, and the music produced was so enchanting that Tudur stood transfixed to the spot. Then at the sound of the sweet melody the fairies, if fairies they were, ranged themselves in groups and began to dance, and as the minstrel quickened his bow the dancers went round and round. Now, of all the dancing Tudur had ever seen, none came near the dancing of the fairies. It was the very poetry of motion. Sian Lan was the best dancer within ten miles of Llangollen, and Tudur had often had a turn with her at the merry nights in Glyn Ceiriog, but Sian's dancing was clumsy and heavy compared with what he now saw. He felt an itching in his feet and could not help keeping time to the merry music, but he was afraid to join in the dance. He wanted to go to Heaven in good time, though he was in no particular hurry, and it occurred to him that it might not be the most direct route to Paradise to dance on a mountain at night in strange company, to, perhaps, the devil's fiddle. The music became faster and the dance wilder, and Tudur's whole body kept time.

"Dance away, Tudur," cried the little man. But Tudur was too wary. "Nay, nay," he said, "dance on, my little beauties, while I look on and admire." The music became sweeter and the dance more enticing than before. Tudur looked on, more absorbed than ever, and his feet and hands became more and more excited. At last, losing all control over himself, he went into the middle of the ring. "Now for it," he shouted, throwing his cap into the air. "Play away, fiddler."

No sooner were these words uttered than everything underwent a change. The gorse-blossom cap vanished from the minstrel's head, and a pair of goat's horns branched out instead. His face became as black as soot: a long tail grew out of his leafy coat and cloven hoofs replaced the beetle-wing pumps. Tudur's heart was heavy, but his heels were light. Horror was in his bosom, but irresistible motion was in his feet. The fairies changed into a variety of forms. Some became goats and some became dogs, some assumed the shape of foxes and others that of cats. It was the strangest crew that ever surrounded a human being. The dance became at last so furious that Tudur could not make out the forms of the dancers. They whirled round him with such rapidity that they resembled a wheel of fire. Tudur danced on and on. He could not stop, for the devil's music was too much for him, as the figure with the goat's horns poured it out of the strings of his fiddle with unceasing vigour. It went on thus throughout the night.

Next morning Tudur's master went up the mountain to see what had become of his sheep and his shepherd. He found the flock safe and sound, but was astonished to see Tudur spinning like mad in the middle of the hollow by himself. "Stop me, master, stop me," shouted Tudur to him. "Stop yourself," replied he. "What is the matter with you, in the name of Heaven?" At the word Tudur fell panting and exhausted at his master's feet, and it was long before he recovered his breath and his senses sufficiently to explain his strange conduct.

HELIG'S HOLLOW

Many ages ago, the fair and fertile tract of country stretching from the Gogarth (better known as the Great Orme) to Bangor, and from Llanfair Fechan to Ynys Seiriol (Puffin Island is another and an uglier name for this sea-girt knoll), was ruled by Helig ab Glannach, and was called Tyno Helig, or Helig's Hollow.

Helig had a daughter, Gwendud: she was as fair as Gwenhwyfar, the wife of Arthur, "when she appeared loveliest at the Offering on the day of the Nativity, or at the feast of Easter," but she had an evil heart, full of wickedness, cruelty and deceit.

She was loved and wooed by the son of one of the barons of Snowdon, and she loved him in return as much as she was capable of loving anyone other than Gwendud, the daughter of Helig. But she would not wed him because he had no golden collar.

Tathal (that was her suitor's name) tried for a long time to win this distinction fairly, but failed. Gwendud would not change her mind, so he determined to procure a collar by foul means.

Rhun, the son of Maelgwn Gwynedd, had led an expedition into Strathclyde, and after burning and slaying had brought back many prisoners to Caer Rhun, where he held them to ransom. The first captive whose liberty was bought by his kinsmen was a young chieftain who had won a golden collar in the wars against the Picts. Tathal went to him and offered his services as guide. After conducting him through the Perfeddwlad, he treacherously stabbed him and brought back his golden collar. His story was that they had been set upon by a band of robbers, headed by an outlaw noble, whom he had slain in fair fight. Gwendud now consented to wed him, and Helig made a great feast, bidding to it all his own kinsmen and those of the bridegroom.

A harper from Bangor was summoned to make music for the revel. The harper had the gift of second sight, and he asked the cupbearer to tell him if he saw anything out of the common when he went down to the cellar to draw the mead. The night was yet young when the cupbearer came in terror to the harper and said: "A stream of water is flowing into the cellar, and hundreds of little fishes are swimming in it."

"Let us fly for our lives," said the harper. The twain fled through the darkness towards the mountains. They were hardly out of the banqueting hall when they heard the sullen roar of a great flood. Soon they heard shrieks of terror, which made the blood run cold in their veins. Looking back they could dimly see the foam of mighty breakers racing towards them. Soon the water was lapping at their heels, and though they ran until their hearts almost burst within their bodies, they were more than once nearly overwhelmed by the vengeful deluge. At last they reached Rhiwgyfylchi, breathless and exhausted with fatigue, and there, safe from the pursuing waves, they waited for the morning. When the sun rose it disclosed an expanse of rippling water where Helig's Hollow had been. Nor has the sea ever given up its conquest.

Some men of Conway have, while fishing on July days when the water is very calm, seen the ruins of Helig's Palace deep down below the surface, but the sight is unlucky, for every man who has espied the drowned walls and towers has died very soon after.

OWEN GOES A-WOOING

Owen, one of the men-servants at Nannau, was going to see his sweetheart, who was a milkmaid at Dol y Clochydd. The night was very dark, and Owen lost his way. After wandering about for some time he fell into Llyn Cynnwch. He could not swim, and the water closed over him, and he sank down, down, down. As he descended his brain began to clear, and he found that the process of sinking was by no means as unpleasant as might have been expected. He breathed as freely as on land, and the further he went the clearer became the water. At last he alighted on a level spot at the bottom of the lake. He was surprised to find a beautiful country, with green fields and flowery hedges and leafy trees. Presently a short, fat old man came to him and asked him where he had come from. Owen explained how he had fallen into the lake on his way to see Siwsi, his sweetheart. "You are welcome," said the short, fat old man, and he conducted him to a beautiful mansion where there was a large company assembled, amusing themselves with all kinds of merriment and frolicking.

After he had been there for about an hour or two he went to the short, fat old man and said to him, "Would you be so kind, sir, as to show me the way to Dol y Clochydd? I am late as it is, and I am afraid Siwsi will give me up and go to bed unless I turn up soon." His host tried to induce him to stay, but Owen was anxious to go, and at last his petition was granted. The short, fat old man took him along a level path, which led right underneath the hearthstone of Dol y Clochydd. The stone lifted itself up when Owen came to it, and he found himself in the kitchen. Siwsi was sitting by the fire weeping for him. She was terribly frightened when she saw him, and he had much difficulty in proving to her that he was not a ghost, for instead of being an hour or two late, as he had imagined, he had been missing for over a month.

THE RICHEST MAN

In time long past there lived in a certain parish a great and wealthy lord. He had gold and silver, houses and land, and every honour which his country could give him.

One morning, after the cock had crowed three times, he heard a voice proclaiming three times, "This very night shall the richest man in this parish die." He was greatly troubled, and sent his servants in hot haste for the best of physicians far and near. He took to his bed, and the physicians watched unceasingly by his side, administering to him every medicine and every support of life which their study of the healing art had discovered.

The night came and wore away, although it appeared to the nobleman as long as a man's life. The dawn broke, and the nobleman and the physicians rejoiced exceedingly that he was still alive. While they rejoiced, lo, the church bell tolled the knell of someone dead. They sent to inquire who it was. The answer came that it was a poor old blind beggar-man, who was often to be seen sitting more than half-naked at the roadside asking for alms. The nobleman said, "The voice proclaimed that the greatest and richest man in the parish would die. The old beggar must have been a cheat and impostor. As he has neither children nor relatives, to me, the lord of this land, belongs by law the wealth which he must have been possessed of." So he sent his servants to search the hut in which the beggar had died. They found nothing but a truss of straw and a bolster of rushes, with the old man lying dead upon them: there was no food or drink or fire or clothes, and it was seen that the beggar had perished from hunger and cold.

"What then meant the voice?" asked the nobleman. And one of the physicians answered and said, "The blind beggar-man has laid up for himself treasures in Heaven, where neither moth nor rust doth corrupt, and where thieves do not break through and steal. Are these treasures not greater than the uncertain and deceitful riches of this world?"

The nobleman was changed from that hour: he relieved poverty and want, and endowed churches, hospitals and schools. On his death-bed he asked that he should be buried in the beggar-man's grave.

PENNARD CASTLE

Pennard Castle, in Gower, is now only a few ruined walls all but lost in the sand hills. Once it was the strong castle of a mighty warrior. He was summoned to the aid of a chief of Gwynedd, and his bravery and warlike skill turned the scale against the North Welsh-man's enemies. As a reward he was given the chief's beautiful daughter in marriage, and on his return to Gower high festival was held to celebrate the victory and the wedding.

At midnight the sentinel pacing round the castle wall thought he heard strange music coming from a grassy plot in the centre of the castle yard. He paused and felt a fear in his heart he could not explain. He called the porter; he also, listening intently, heard the strains. It was a clear moonlit night, and the two, approaching the grassy plot, saw a troop of fairies dancing to the music of little harps. Going into the banqueting hall they told their master that the Fair Family were sporting in the castle. The Lord of the Castle, maddened with wine, ordered his soldiers to drive them away.

Then someone said to him, "Have a care: if thou attackest the fairies, it will be thy undoing." The chieftain's rage was unbounded. "What care I," said he, "for man or spirit?" and starting up, he rushed on the moonlit spot, wildly brandishing his sword. But he clove the air in vain, and while he was fruitlessly wielding his weapon, a low voice pronounced his doom. "Since thou hast, without reason, broken in upon our innocent sport, thou shalt be without castle or feast," it said. While the judgment was yet being spoken, a cloud of sand came whirling round the walls, and faster and thicker the storm raged, until walls and towers were overwhelmed. And a mountain of sand was removed from Ireland that night.

AN ADVENTURE IN THE BIG BOG

A young harper of Bala was asked to play at a wedding in a farmhouse near Yspytty Ifan. When the joyous company broke up late at night he set off for home like the rest, but he had a much longer way to go than anyone else. When he was crossing the mountain a dense fog came on, and he lost his way. He was wandering about trying to find the path again, when he suddenly stepped into the Gors Fawr, "the big bog". The treacherous crust swayed for an instant under his tread, and then it broke. The soft mud oozed round his ankles, and he felt himself going further and further down. He tried to raise himself on his harp, but the only result of this was to plunge the beloved instrument into the bog, and he himself sank lower and lower. At last, with a desperate effort, he hurled himself full length upon the surface. The yielding crust caved under his body, and he clutched at the surface grass, but he only plucked the tufts from their roots. They gave him no hold. With every fresh effort to save himself he sank deeper. The gurgling slime sucked him down, down, down, and in the anguish of his soul he threw his head back in one last wild scream.

His cry was just dying away when the fog suddenly cleared, and a little man appeared on the brink of the bog. He threw a rope to the harper, who, after a great struggle, fastened it round his body under the arms. The little man pulled and pulled and gradually drew the harper out of the mire. He took him to a house blazing with light hard by, where there was singing and dancing and much revelry. The harper was given fine clean clothes, and after drinking a flagon of delicious mead he recovered sufficiently from the fright which the fall into the bog had given him to join in the festivity which was going on. There was a little lady there whom the company addressed as Olwen. She was the most beautiful little lady that the harper had ever seen and the best dancer. With her he danced hour after hour, and the only bitter in his cup of sweet was the thought that his beloved harp was in the slimy blackness of the Gors. When the whole company retired to rest he was put in a bed as soft as the softest down, and he thought he had reached a very heaven of delight.

But next morning he was awakened, not by a kiss from Olwen, but by the Plas Drain shepherd's dog licking his lips: he found himself lying by the wall of a sheepfold, and there was no trace of the house in which he had spent such a happy night. His clothes were all caked with bog mud, and his harp, which was in a clump of rushes at his feet, was black with the same defilement.

THE MEN OF ARDUDWY

The men of Ardudwy once upon a time found there were no maidens in their district for them to marry. In the Vale of Clwyd, on the other hand, there were so many maidens that husbands could not be found for all. There was a bitter feud, however, between the two districts, and the men of Ardudwy could not go a-wooing to the Vale in peace.

Those of the men of Ardudwy who wished to marry determined at last to steal wives for themselves, as they could not get them any other way, and taking advantage of the absence of the warriors of the Vale on an expedition they swooped down, and, snatching away the flower of the maidens, proceeded to carry them off to the mountains.

Messengers recalled the warriors of the Vale from their expedition, and a strong band of them started hot-foot in pursuit of the robbers. They overtook the fugitives near a lake among the mountains of Ffestiniog and summoned them to yield. The men of Ardudwy, though greatly outnumbered, scorned to surrender, and a fierce battle followed. All day long the noise of splintering spears, swords clashing on swords, and battleaxes crashing upon armour, rolled among the eternal mountains.

At first the men of the Vale rushed carelessly upon the men of Ardudwy, thinking that it was but a light task to overpower the little band, but so many of them fell that they drew off to order their attack better. They carefully marshalled the bravest of their number and charged; a desperate hand-to-hand struggle followed, but the men of Ardudwy, though they lost many good men, at last beat off the assault. They now feigned flight, but as the men of the Vale came on with wild cries and uproar, they wheeled round and cut down so many of them that they fled in disorder. They soon rallied, however, and delivered charge after charge. Time after time the men of Ardudwy flung them back, but they became fewer and fewer with each charge.

In the late afternoon there was a lull in the fray. Then the men of the Vale, gathering all their available force, delivered a last overwhelming charge on the weakened band. The men of Ardudwy sold their lives dearly, piling corpse upon corpse, but they were exhausted with wounds, their spears were shattered, and their swords were hacked and blunted. When the men of the Vale fell back to recover breath and strength, they found that there were only four of the defenders left alive. Though the number was so small, they did not close with them, but surrounded them and plied them with javelins and stones. Still the four of Ardudwy fought on while breath remained in their bodies; then one by one they sank down upon the pitiless storm of javelins, and at last there was nothing left of the gallant band but a heap of dead.

Even then, Death had not taken his full toll of victims. The maidens of the Vale had, ere their kindred came up, learned to love their captors. They had been stationed by them on the top of a precipice rising sheer and steep out of the lake, behind the position which was to be defended, and from here they had watched the long-drawn-out struggle. When the last of the men of Ardudwy fell, and the desperate fight was done, they plunged into the waters red with the blood of their lovers and kindred, like some great flight of white birds sweeping down from a wave-washed cliff down to the sea. The still waters leapt in foam: one loud shriek woke the air, and then silence reigned over all.

The lake was called after them Llyn y Morwynion, the Maidens' Lake, and not far from its margin great stones may still be seen marking the place where those who died in this great fight were buried.

TALES OF FAIRIES, TRICKS & TRANSFORMATION

As mentioned in the Introduction (see p. 20), the relationship between the *tylwyth teg* and the Welsh people is nuanced and ambiguous. Mischievous, cunning and often downright dangerous, tales of fairy trickery and transformation abound within Welsh lore. Here are sinister tales of babies swapped in their cribs as well as those of fairies and mortals working together. Fairy maidens are married to flawed mortal men, and farmers benefit from the enchantment of fairy beasts.

But while some fairy partnerships proved mutually beneficial, to break an agreement with the fairies was to risk punishment and even vengeance. In William Jenkyn Thomas's 'The Fairy Reward', Ianto finds himself out of pocket having divulged the supernatural source of his gold, and a midwife from the old county of Caernarfonshire loses an eye having failed to heed their instruction.

Conversely, humans – as well as the odd saint – will occasionally be the ones doing the outwitting. Examples may be seen in William Griffis's 'The Red Bandits of Montgomery' and William Jenkyn Thomas's 'St Collen and the King of Faery'.

THE PWCA OF THE TRWYN

A pranksome goblin once took up his abode at the Trwyn Farm, in the parish of Mynyddislwyn, and became known throughout the country as Pwca'r Trwyn, or the Pwca of the Trwyn. How he got there is not known. One story says that he once lived at Pant y Gaseg. Moses, one of farm servants of the Trwyn, came to Pant y Gaseg for a jug of barm, and the Pwca was heard to say, "The Pwca is going away now in this jug of barm, and he'll never come back," and he never was heard of at Pant y Gaseg again. Another story tells that a servant of Pant y Gaseg let fall a ball of yarn, and the Pwca said, "I am going in this ball, and I'll go to the Trwyn and never come back." Directly after this the ball was seen to roll down the hill-side and across the valley, ascending the hill on the other side and trundling along briskly across the mountain top of this new abode.

Anyhow, the Pwca came to the Trwyn, and though he remained invisible he became very friendly with Moses. He did all his work for him with great ease. For instance, he threshed a whole barnful of corn in a single night. Once, indeed, he gave him a good beating for doubting his word, but apart from that the two remained on the best possible terms for a long time. Moses went away, however, with David Morgan, the Jacobite, to join the Young Pretender, and never came back again.

After this the Pwca transferred his affections to Blodwen, one of the servant-girls, and very useful he proved to her. He did everything for her, washing, ironing, spinning and twisting wool – at the spinning wheel he was remarkably handy. No one was allowed to catch a sight of him, but he became very talkative, and often used to speak from out of an oven by the side of the hearth. He told Blodwen that it was very mean of her not to provide him with food and drink for helping her so much, and after this she used, with her master Job John Harri's permission, to place a bowl of fresh milk and a slice of white bread (the latter was a great luxury at that time) on the hearth every night for him before going to bed. By the morning the bread was eaten and the bowl empty. This fare made the Pwca light-hearted, and he used to make music o' nights with Job John Harri's fiddle, and very merry rollicking music it was.

One evening he revealed part of himself. The servant-girls were comparing their hands as to size and whiteness, when a voice from the ceiling was heard to say, "The Pwca's hand is the fairest and smallest." "Show it, then," said Blodwen, who used to speak quite freely to him. Immediately a hand appeared from the ceiling, small, fair, and beautifully formed, with a large gold ring on the little finger.

It was Blodwen's fault that the Pwca became troublesome. One night, in a spirit of mischief, she drank the milk and ate the bread that were usually provided for him, leaving him some stale crusts of barley bread and a bowlful of dirty water. It would have been better for her not to have done it. When she got up next morning he suddenly sprang from some corner, and, seizing her by the neck, began to beat her and kick her from one end of the house to the other, until she screamed for mercy.

After this the Pwca became freakish, and played all sorts of pranks. He began his games by knocking at the door, but when it was opened there was no one to be seen. Then he did all sorts of mischief about the house, and in the cowhouses and stable. He harassed the oxen when they ploughed and drew them after him everywhere, plough and all, nor could anyone prevent them.

The neighbours came to hear about these goings on, and one of them, Thomas Evans by name, said he would take a gun and shoot the Pwca. As Job John Harri was coming home one night from a journey the Pwca met him in the lane and said, "There is a man come to your house to shoot me, but you shall see how I will beat him." So Job went on to the house and found Thomas Evans there with his gun, breathing all manner of dire threats against the wicked sprite. Suddenly stones flew from all directions at Thomas and hurt him badly. The members of the household of the Trwyn got round him, thinking to protect him, but the stones still struck him. The curious part of the whole thing was that they never touched anyone else. At last Thomas Evans took his gun and ran home as fast as his legs could carry him, and never again did he talk of shooting the Pwca.

Job John Harri went to a fair, and night overtook him on the mountain as he was returning home. Somehow or other, though the path was quite familiar to him, he lost his way. Whether it was owing to the darkness or from some other cause (there are influences at fairs which cause many to stray from the right path) is uncertain; at any rate he wandered onwards in different directions over the mountain in much doubt and perplexity. At last he was brought to a full stop against a stone wall. As he was rubbing his forehead, which had got the worst of the collision with the wall, and considering the situation, a light suddenly arose upon the waste at a short distance to his right. "There is some one with a lantern," he said to himself, and he determined to follow in his wake. As he walked on he noticed that there were two very remarkable things about the light. One was that however fast or however slow he walked, the light kept at just the same distance from him. Again, it kept so near the ground that the arm which bore it must have belonged to a person of exceptionally short stature. Job concluded that it was a child carrying a lantern. He followed the light for several miles, when it suddenly stopped. Job had by this time come well nigh up to it, and was about to hail its bearer when the sound of a foaming torrent arose to his ears. Just then the bearer of the light took a flying leap and landed some thirty yards away. The light blazed forth brilliantly, and Job found himself on the brink of a frightful precipice. On the other side of the yawning chasm was a tiny little man, as naked as a new-born babe, with long hair and pointed ears, and a maliciously ugly expression on his face, peering down into the gorge (it was afterwards called Cwm Pwca). When he saw that Job had not fallen into the trap towards which he had led him, he uttered a loud shrill laugh and douted the light. Job was afraid to move, and remained on the spot, stiff with terror, until daylight appeared, when he made his way home. After that the Pwca was never heard or seen at the Trwyn.

THE FAIRY CONGRESS

One can hardly think of Wales without a harp. The music of this most ancient and honourable instrument, which emits sweet sounds, when heard in a foreign land makes Welsh folks homesick for the old country and the music of the harp. Its strings can wail with woe, ripple with merriment, sound out the notes of war and peace, and lift the soul in heavenly melody.

Usually a player on the harp opened the Eisteddfod, as the Welsh literary congress is called, but this time they had engaged for the fairies a funny little fellow to start the programme with a solo on his violin.

The figure of this musician, at the congress of Welsh fairies, was the most comical of any in the company. The saying that he was popular with all the mountain spirits was shown to be true, the moment he began to scrape his fiddle, for then they all crowded around him.

"Did you ever see such a tiny specimen?" asked Queen Mab of Puck.

The little fiddler came forward and drawing his instrument from under his arm, proceeded to scrape the strings. He had on a pair of moss trousers, and his coat was a yellow gorse flower. His feet were clad in shoes made of beetles' wings, which always kept bright, as if polished with a brush.

When one looked at the fiddle, he could see that it was only a wooden spoon, with strings across the bowl. But the moment he drew the bow from one side to the other, all the elves, from every part of the hills, came tripping along to hear the music, and at once began dancing.

Some of these elves were dressed in pink, some in blue, others in yellow, and many had glow-worms in their hands. Their tread was so light that the flower stems never bent, nor was a petal crushed, when they walked over the turf. All, as they came near, bowed or dropped a curtsey. Then the little musician took off his cap to each, and bowed in return.

There was too much business before the meeting for dancing to be kept up very long, but when the violin solo was over, at a sign given by the fiddler, the dancers took seats wherever they could find them, on the grass, or gorse, or heather, or on the stones. After order had been secured, the chairman of the meeting read regrets from those who had been invited but could not be present.

The first note was from the mermaids, who lived near the Green Isles of the Ocean. They asked to be excused from travelling inland and climbing rocks. In the present delicate state of their health this would be too fatiguing. Poor things!

It was unanimously voted that they be excused.

Queen Mab was dressed, as befitted the occasion, like a Welsh lady, not wearing a crown, but a high peaked hat, pointed at the top and about half a yard high. It was black and was held on by fastenings of scalloped lace, that came down around her neck.

The lake fairies, or Elfin Maids, were out in full force. These lived at the bottom of the many ponds and pools in Wales. Many stories are told of the wonderful things they did with boats and cattle.

Nowadays, when they milk cows by electric machinery and use steam launches on the water, most of the water sprites of all kinds have been driven away, for they do not like the smell of kerosene or gasoline. It is for these reasons that, in our day, they are not often seen. In fact, cows from the creameries can wade out into the water and even stand in it, while lashing their tails to keep off the flies, without any danger, as in old times, of being pulled down by the Elfin Maids.

The little Red Men, that could hide under a thimble, and have plenty of room to spare, were all out. The elves and nixies and sprites, of all colours and many forms, were on hand.

The pigmies who guard the palace of the king of the world underground, came in their gay dresses. There were three of them, and they brought in their hands balls of gold, with which to play tenpins, but they were not allowed to have any games while the meeting was going on.

In fact, just when these little fellows from down under the earth were showing off their gay clothes and their treasures from the caves, one mischievous fairy maid sidled up to their chief and whispered in his ear:

"Better put away your gold, for this is in modern Wales, where they have pawn shops. Three golden balls, two above the one below, which you often see nowadays, mean that two to one you will never get it again. These hang out as the sign of a pawnbroker's shop, and what you put in does not, as a rule, come out. I am afraid that some of the Cymric fairies from Cornwall, or Montgomery, or Cheshire, might think you were after business, and you understand that no advertising is allowed here."

In a moment, each of the three leaders thrust his ball into his bosom. It made his coat bulge out, and at this, some of the fairies wondered, but all they thought of was that this spoiled a handsome fellow's figure. Or was it some new idea? To tell the truth, they were vexed at not keeping up with the new fashions, for they knew nothing of this latest fad among such fine young gallants.

Much of the chat and gossip, before and after the meeting, was between the fairies who live in the air, or on mountains, and those down in the earth, or deep in the sea. They swapped news, gossip and scandal at a great rate.

There were a dozen or two fine-looking creatures who had high brows, who said they were Coeds. This did not mean that these fairies had ever been through college. "Certainly the college never went through them," said one very homely fairy, who was spiteful and jealous. The simple fact was that the one they called Betty, the Co-ed, and others from that Welsh village, called Bryn Mawr, and another from Flint, and another from Yale, and still others from Brimbo and from Co-ed Poeth, had come from places so named and down on the map of Wales, though they were no real Co-ed girls there, that could talk French, or English, or read Latin. In fact, Co-ed simply meant that they were from the woods and lived among the trees; for Coed in Welsh means a forest.

The fairy police were further instructed not to admit, and, if such were found, to put out the following bad characters, for this was a perfectly respectable meeting. These naughty folks were:

The Old Hag of the Mist. The Invisible Hag that moans dolefully in the night. The Tolaeth, a creature never seen, but that groans, sings, saws, or stamps noisily. The Dogs of the Sky. All witches, of every sort and kind. All peddlers of horseshoes, crosses, charms, or amulets. All mortals with brains fuddled by liquor.

All who had on shoes which water would not run under. All fairies that were accustomed to turn mortals into cheese. Every one of these, who might want to get in, were to be refused admittance.

Another circle of rather exclusive fairies, who always kept away from the blacksmiths, hardware stores, smelting furnaces and mines, had formed an anti-iron society. These were a kind of a Welsh "Four Hundred", or élite, who would have nothing to do with anyone who had an iron tool, or weapon, or ornament in his hand, or on his dress, or who used iron in any form, or for any use. They frowned upon the idea of Cymric

Land becoming rich by mining, and smelting, and selling iron. They did not even approve of the idea that any imps and dwarfs of the iron mines should be admitted to the meeting.

One clique of fairies, that looked like elves were in bad humour, almost to moping. When one of these got up to speak, it seemed as if he would never sit down. He tired all the lively fairies by long-winded reminiscences, of druids, and mistletoe, and by telling every one how much better the old times were than the present.

President Puck, who always liked things short, and was himself as lively as quicksilver, many times called these long-winded fellows to order; but they kept meandering on, until daybreak, when it was time to adjourn, lest the sunshine should spoil them all, and change them into slate or stone.

It was hard to tell just how much business was disposed of at this session, or whether one ever came to the point, although there was a great deal of oratory and music. Much of what was said was in poetry, or in verses, or rhymes, of three lines each. What they talked about was mainly in protest against the smoke of factories and collieries, and because there was so much soot, and so little soap, in the land.

But what did they do at the fairy congress?

The truth is, that nobody today knows what was done in this session of the fairies, for the proceedings were kept secret. The only one who knows was an old Welshman whom the story-teller used to meet once in a while. He is the one mortal who knows anything about this meeting, and he won't tell; or at least he won't talk in anything but Welsh. So we have to find out the gist of the matter by noticing, in the stories which we have just read, what the fairies did.

THE MYDDVAI LEGEND

A **widow, who had** an only son, was obliged, in consequence of the large flocks she possessed, to send, under the care of her son, a portion of her cattle to graze on the Black Mountain near a small lake called Llyn-y-Van-Bach.

One day the son perceived, to his great astonishment, a most beautiful creature with flowing hair sitting on the unruffled surface of the lake combing her tresses, the water serving as a mirror. Suddenly she beheld the young man standing on the brink of the lake with his eyes riveted on her, and unconsciously offering to herself the provision of barley bread and cheese with which he had been provided when he left his home.

Bewildered by a feeling of love and admiration for the object before him, he continued to hold out his hand towards the lady, who imperceptibly glided near to him, but gently refused the offer of his provisions. He attempted to touch her, but she eluded his grasp, saying:

Cras dy fara; Nid hawdd fy nala.

Hard baked is thy bread; It is not easy to catch me.

She immediately dived under the water and disappeared, leaving the love-stricken youth to return home a prey to disappointment and regret that he had been unable to make further acquaintance with the lovely maiden with whom he had desperately fallen in love.

On his return home he communicated to his mother the extraordinary vision. She advised him to take some unbaked dough the next time in his pocket, as there must have been some spell connected with the hard baked bread, or "Bara Cras", which prevented his catching the lady.

Next morning, before the sun was up, the young man was at the lake, not for the purpose of looking after the cattle, but that he might again witness the enchanting vision of the previous day. In vain did he glance over the surface of the lake; nothing met his view, save the ripples occasioned by a stiff breeze, and a dark cloud hung heavily on the summit of the Van.

Hours passed on, the wind was hushed, the overhanging clouds had vanished, when the youth was startled by seeing some of his mother's cattle on the precipitous side of the acclivity, nearly on the opposite side of the lake. As he was hastening away to rescue them from their perilous position, the object of his search again appeared to him, and seemed much more beautiful than when he first beheld her. His hand was again held out to her, full of unbaked bread, which he offered to her with an urgent proffer of his heart also, and vows of eternal attachment, all of which were refused by her, saying:

Llaith dy fara! Ti ni fynna.

Unbaked is thy bread! I will not have thee.

But the smiles that played upon her features as the lady vanished beneath the waters forbade him to despair, and cheered him on his way home. His aged parent was acquainted with his ill success, and she suggested that his bread should the next time be but slightly baked, as most likely to please the mysterious being.

Impelled by love, the youth left his mother's home early next morning. He was soon near the margin of the lake impatiently awaiting the reappearance of the lady. The sheep and goats browsed on the precipitous sides of the Van, the cattle strayed amongst the rocks, rain and sunshine came and passed away, unheeded by the youth who was wrapped up in looking for the appearance of her who had stolen his heart. The sun was verging towards the west, and the young man casting a sad look over the waters ere departing homewards was astonished to see several cows walking along its surface, and, what was more pleasing to his sight, the maiden reappeared, even lovelier than ever. She approached the land and he rushed to meet her in the water. A smile encouraged him to seize her hand, and she accepted the moderately baked bread he offered her, and after some persuasion she consented to become his wife, on condition that they should live together until she received from him three blows without a cause,

Tri ergyd diachos,
Three causeless blows,

when, should he ever happen to strike her three such blows, she would leave him for ever. These conditions were readily and joyfully accepted.

Thus the Lady of the Lake became engaged to the young man, and having loosed her hand for a moment she darted away and dived into the lake. The grief of the lover at this disappearance of his affianced was such that he determined to cast himself headlong into its unfathomed depths, and thus end his life. As he was on the point of committing this rash act, there emerged out of the lake two most beautiful ladies, accompanied by a hoary headed man of noble mien and extraordinary stature, but having otherwise all the force and strength of youth. This man addressed the youth, saying that, as he proposed to marry one of his daughters, he consented to the union, provided the young man could distinguish which of the two ladies before him was the object of his affections. This was no easy task, as the maidens were perfect counterparts of each other.

Whilst the young man narrowly scanned the two ladies and failed to perceive the least difference betwixt the two, one of them thrust her foot a slight degree forward. The motion, simple as it was, did not escape the observation of the youth, and he discovered a trifling variation in the mode in which their sandals were tied. This at once put an end to the dilemma, for he had on previous occasions noticed the peculiarity of her shoe-tie, and he boldly took hold of her hand.

"Thou hast chosen rightly," said the Father, "be to her a kind and faithful husband, and I will give her, as a dowry, as many sheep, cattle, goats, and horses, as she can count of each without heaving or drawing in her breath. But remember, that if you prove unkind to her at any time and strike her three times without a cause, she shall return to me, and shall bring all her stock with her."

Such was the marriage settlement, to which the young man gladly assented, and the bride was desired to count the number of sheep she was to have. She immediately adopted the mode of counting by fives, thus: – One, two, three, four, five, – one, two, three, four, five; as many times as possible in rapid succession, till her breath was exhausted. The same process of reckoning had to determine the number of goats, cattle, and horses, respectively; and in an instant the full number of each came out of the lake, when called upon by the father.

The young couple were then married, and went to reside at a farm called Esgair Llaethdy, near Myddvai, where they lived in prosperity and happiness for several years, and became the parents of three beautiful sons.

Once upon a time there was a christening in the neighbourhood to which the parents were invited. When the day arrived the wife appeared reluctant to attend the christening, alleging that the distance was too great for her to walk. Her husband told her to fetch one of the horses from the field. "I will," said she, "if you will bring me my gloves which I left in our house." He went for the gloves, and finding she had not gone for the horse, he playfully slapped her shoulder with one of them, saying "*Dôs, dôs*, go, go," when she reminded him of the terms on which she consented to marry him, and warned him to be more cautious in the future, as he had now given her one causeless blow.

On another occasion when they were together at a wedding and the assembled guests were greatly enjoying themselves the wife burst into tears and sobbed most piteously. Her husband touched her on the shoulder and inquired the cause of her weeping; she said, "Now people are entering into trouble, and your troubles are likely to commence, as you have the second time stricken me without a cause."

Years passed on, and their children had grown up, and were particularly clever young men. Amidst so many worldly blessings the husband almost forgot that only one causeless blow would destroy his prosperity. Still he was watchful lest any trivial occurrence should take place which his wife must regard as a breach of their marriage contract. She told him that her affection for him was unabated, and warned him to be careful lest through inadvertence he might give the last and only blow which, by an unalterable destiny, over which she had no control, would separate them for ever.

One day it happened that they went to a funeral together, where, in the midst of mourning and grief at the house of the deceased, she appeared in the gayest of spirits, and indulged in inconsiderate fits of laughter, which so shocked her husband that he touched her, saying – "Hush! hush! don't laugh." She said that she laughed because people when they die go out of trouble, and rising up, she went out of the house, saying, "The last blow has been struck, our marriage contract is broken, and at an end. Farewell!" Then she started off towards Esgair Llaethdy, where she called her cattle and other stock together, each by name, not forgetting, the "little black calf" which had been slaughtered and was suspended on the hook, and away went the calf and all the stock, with the Lady across Myddvai Mountain, and disappeared beneath the waters of the lake whence the Lady had come. The four oxen that were ploughing departed, drawing after them the plough, which made a furrow in the ground, and which remains as a testimony of the truth of this story.

She is said to have appeared to her sons, and accosting Rhiwallon, her firstborn, to have informed him that he was to be a benefactor to mankind, through healing all manner of their diseases, and she furnished him with prescriptions and instructions for the preservation of health. Then, promising to meet him when her counsel was most needed, she vanished. On several other occasions she met her sons, and pointed out to them plants and herbs, and revealed to them their medicinal qualities or virtues.

So ends the Myddvai Legend.

THE LLANFABON CHANGELING

At a farmhouse called Berth Gron, in the parish of Llanfabon, there once lived a young widow. She had a little boy whom she loved more than her own eyes. He was her only comfort, and she was afraid of letting the sun shine on him, as the saying goes. Pryderi – that was the name she had given him – was about three years old, and a fine child for his age.

At this time the parish of Llanfabon was full of fairies. On nights when the moon was bright, they often used to keep the hard-working farmers awake with their music until the cock crew in the morning. On nights when the moon was dark, they delighted in luring men into desolate bogs by displaying false lights. Even in the daytime they would play tricks on people if they were not very careful.

The widow knew that the Fair Family were very fond of stealing babies out of their cradles, and you can imagine how careful she was of her little treasure. She hated leaving him out of her sight by night or day: if ever she had to do so, she was miserable until she returned to him and found him safe and sound.

One day when he was lying asleep in his cradle, she heard the cows in the byre lowing piteously as if they were in great pain. As there was nobody in the house but herself to look after her precious boy, she was afraid at first of going out to see what was amiss. The lowing, however, became more and more agonized, and she became frightened. Not being able to stand it any longer, she rushed out, forgetting in her fright to place the tongs crossways on the cradle.

When she got to the cow house, she was amazed to find that there was nothing whatever the matter with the cattle: they were chewing their cud placidly, and they turned their great meek eyes in mild surprise upon her, evidently wondering why she had burst in upon them so unceremoniously. Realising that she had been the victim of some deception, she ran back to the house as fast as her feet could carry her, and to the cradle. She was afraid of finding it empty, but bending over it she found a little boy in it who greeted her with "Mother." She looked hard at him: he was very like Pryderi, and yet there was a something about him which made her think that he was different from him. At last she said doubtingly, "You are not my child."

"I am truly," said the little one. "What do you mean, mother?"

But something kept whispering to her constantly that he was not her child, and as time went on she became convinced that she was right. The little boy after a while became cross and fretful, unlike Pryderi, who was always as good as gold. In a whole year he never grew at all.

Pryderi, on the other hand, was a very growing child. Besides, the little fellow seemed to get uglier every day, whereas Pryderi had been getting prettier and prettier: at least his mother thought so. She did not know what to do.

Now, there was in the parish of Llanfabon a man who had the reputation of being well-informed on matters which are dark to most people. This reputation he had gained by living at a place called the Castle of the Night. This castle had been built of stones from Llanfabon Church, and was haunted. Many men had tried to live there, but had been compelled to leave because ghosts plagued them so. That this man was able to dwell there in seeming peace and comfort was proof positive, in the eyes of the people of Llanfabon, that he had some control at least over the powers of darkness.

The widow went to this wise man and laid her trouble before him. After hearing her story he said to her, "If you follow my directions faithfully and minutely, I think I shall be able to help you. At noon tomorrow take an eggshell and prepare to brew some beer in it. See that the boy watches what you are doing, but take care not to tell him to pay attention. He will ask you what you are doing. You are to say, 'I am brewing beer for the harvestmen.' Listen carefully to what he says when he hears that, but pretend not to catch it. After you have put him to bed tomorrow night, come and tell me all about it."

The widow returned home, and the next day at noon she followed the cunning man's advice. She took an eggshell and got everything ready for brewing beer. The boy stood by her, watching her as an oat watches a mouse. Presently, he asked, "What are you doing, mother?" She said, "I am brewing beer for the harvestmen, my boy." Then the boy said quietly to himself:

"I am very old this day, I was living before my birth, I remember yonder oak An acorn in the earth, But I never saw, the egg of a hen Brewing beer for harvestmen."

The widow heard what he said, but pretended not to have caught it, and asked, "What did you say, my son?" He said, "Nothing, mother." She then turned round and saw that he was very cross, and the angry expression on his face made him very repulsive to look upon.

After she had put him to bed that night, the widow went to the Castle of the Night, as she had been ordered. As soon as she entered, the wise man asked, "Were you able to catch what he said?"

"He spoke very quietly to himself," answered the widow, "but I am quite sure that what he said was:

'I am very old this day, I was living before my birth, I remember yonder oak An acorn in the earth, But I never saw the egg of a hen Brewing beer for harvestmen.'"

"It is well," said the wise man. "If you follow my directions faithfully and minutely, I think I shall be able to help you. The moon will be full in four days, and you must go at midnight to where the four roads meet above the Ford of the Bell. Hide yourself somewhere where you can see everything that comes along any of the roads without being seen yourself. Whatever happens, do not stir or utter a sound. If you do, my plans will be frustrated and your own life will be in danger. Come to me the day after and tell me what you see."

By midnight on the appointed day the widow had concealed herself carefully behind a large bush near the cross-roads above the Ford of the Bell, where she could see everything that came along any of the four roads without being seen herself. For a long time there was nothing to be seen or heard: the moon shone brightly, and the melancholy silence of midnight lay over all. Before long dark clouds obscured the moon, and at last the anxious widow heard the faint sounds of music in the far distance. The strains came nearer and nearer, and she listened with rapt attention. Before long the melody was close at hand, and she saw a procession of fairies coming along one of the roads. Soon the vanguard of the procession came up, and she saw that there were hundreds of fairies marching along. They were singing the sweetest songs she had ever heard, and she felt that she could listen to them for ever. Just as the middle of the procession came opposite her hiding place, the moon emerged from behind a black cloud, and in the clear, cold light which then flooded the earth she beheld a sight which turned her pleasure into bitter pain and made her heart beat almost out of her body. Walking between two fairies was her own dear little boy. She nearly forgot herself altogether, and was on the point of springing into the midst of the fairies to snatch her darling from them. But she remembered in time that the wise man had warned her that his plans would be upset and her own life in danger if she carried out her intention, and controlling herself by a supreme effort she neither stirred nor uttered a sound. When the long procession had wound itself past and the music had died away in the distance, she issued from her concealment and went home to bed, but her heart was so full of longing for her lost child that she never slept a wink all night.

On the morrow she went to the wise man early. He was expecting her, and as she entered he perceived by her looks that she had seen something to disturb her. She told him what she had witnessed at the cross-roads, and he again said, "It is well. If you will follow my directions faithfully and minutely, I think I shall be able to help you."

He then brought out a great book, bound in calf-skin, opened it, and pored long over it. After much deliberation he said, "You must find a black hen without a single white feather, or one of any other colour than black. Do you burn peat or wood?"

"I burn peat," said the widow.

"After you have found the hen," resumed the wise man, "you must light a wood fire and bake the hen before it, with its feathers and all intact. After you have placed it to bake before the fire, close every passage and hole in the wall, leaving only the chimney open. After that, avoid looking at the boy, but watch the hen baking, and do not take your eyes off it until the last feather has fallen off it."

Strange as the directions of the wise man appeared, she determined to follow them as faithfully and minutely as she had the previous directions. But oh, the weary tramp she had before she could find a black hen without a single white feather or one of any other colour than black. She tried every farm in the parish of Llanfabon in vain, and she was nearly driven to the conclusion that if this breed of hens had ever existed on the earth it had become extinct. It was weeks before she secured the right hen, and it was at a farm miles away from Llanfabon that she was successful in her search.

Her repeated disappointments were all the more bitter because she was forced to hide her disgust with the little fellow who was there instead of her boy. When he addressed her as "Mother," it was almost more than she could bear, but she was just able to make no difference in her behaviour towards him, though he seemed to be getting smaller, crosser and uglier every day.

Having found the black hen, she built up a wood fire, and when it was burning brightly she wrung the hen's neck and placed it as it was, feathers and all, in front of the fire. She then closed every passage and hole in the walls, leaving only the chimney open, and sat in front of the fire to watch the hen baking. The little fellow called to her several times, but though she answered him she was careful not to look at him. After a bit she fell into a swoon. When she came out of it she saw that all the feathers had fallen off the hen, and looking round the house she saw that the changeling had disappeared. Then she heard the strains of music outside the house, and they were the same as those she had heard at the cross-roads. All of a sudden the music ceased, and she heard a little boy's voice calling, "Mother." She rushed out, and lo! and behold, who should be standing within a few paces of the threshold but her own dear little boy.

She snatched him up in her arms and almost smothered him with kisses. She laughed and wept in turn, and her joy was greater than words can tell. When asked where he had been all this long while, the little boy had no account to give of himself except that he had been listening to lovely music. He was pale and wan and thin, but under his mother's loving care he soon became his bonny self again, and mother and son lived happily ever afterwards.

THE GORS GOCH CHANGELING LEGEND

There was once a happy family living in a place called Gors Goch. One night, as usual, they went to bed, but they could not sleep a single wink, because of the noise outside the house. At last the master of the house got up, and trembling, enquired "What was there, and what was wanted." A clear sweet voice answered him thus, "We want a warm place where we can tidy the children." The door was opened when there entered half full the house of the *tylwyth têg*, and they began forthwith washing their children. And when they had finished, they commenced singing, and the singing was entrancing. The dancing and the singing were both excellent. On going away they left behind them money not a little for the use of the house. And afterwards they came pretty often to the house, and received a hearty welcome in consequence of the large presents which they left behind them on the hob. But at last a sad affair took place which was no less than an exchange of children. The Gors Goch baby was a dumpy child, a sweet, pretty, affectionate little dear, but the child which was left in its stead was a sickly, thin, shapeless, ugly being, which did nothing but cry and eat, and although it ate ravenously like a mastiff, it did not grow. At last the wife of Gors Goch died of a broken heart, and so also did all her children, but the father lived a long life and became a rich man, because his new heir's family brought him abundance of gold and silver.

THE TOUCH OF CLAY

Long, long ago before the Cymry came into the beautiful land of Wales, there were dark-skinned people living in caves.

In these early times there were a great many fairies of all sorts, but of very different kinds of behaviour, good and bad.

It was in this age of the world that fairies got an idea riveted into their heads which nothing, not even hammers, chisels or crowbars, can pry up. Neither horse power, nor hydraulic force nor sixteen-inch bombs, nor cannon balls, nor torpedoes can drive it out.

It is a settled matter of opinion in Fairy-Land that, compared with fairies, human beings are very stupid. The fairies think that mortals are dull-witted and awfully slow, when compared to the smarter and more nimble fairies, that are always up to date in doing things.

Perhaps the following story will help explain why this is.

These ancient folks who lived in caves could not possibly know some things that are like A B C to the fairies of today. For the Welsh fairies, King Puck and Queen Mab, know all about what is in the telegraphs, submarine cables and wireless telegraphy of today. Puck would laugh if you should say that a telephone was any new thing to him. Long ago, in Shakespeare's time, he boasted that he could "put a girdle round the earth in forty minutes." Men have been trying ever since to catch up with him, but they have not gone ahead of him yet.

If, only three hundred years ago, this were the case, what must have been Puck's fun, when he saw men in the early days, working so hard to make even a clay cup or saucer. These people who slept and ate in cave boarding-houses knew nothing of metals, or how to make iron or brass tools, wire, or machines, or how to touch a button and light up a whole room, which even a baby can now do.

There is one thing that we, who have travelled in many fairy lands, have often noticed and told our friends, the little folks, and that is this:

All the fairies we ever knew are very slow to change either their opinions, or their ways, or their fashions. Like many mortals, they think a great deal of their own notions. They imagine that the only way to do a thing is in that which they say is the right one.

So it came to pass that even when the Cymric folk gave up wearing the skins of animals, and put on pretty clothes woven on a loom, and ate out of dishes instead of clam shells, there were still some fairies that kept to the notions and fashions of the cave days. To one of these came trouble because of this failing.

Now there was once a pretty nymph, who lived in the Red Lake, to which a young and handsome farmer used to come to catch fish. One misty day, when the lad could see only a few feet before him, a wind cleared the air and blew away the fog. Then he saw near him a little old man, standing on a ladder. He was hard at work in putting a thatched roof on a hut which he had built.

A few minutes later, as the mist rose and the breezes blew, the farmer could see no house, but only the ripplings of water on the lake's surface.

Although he went fishing often, he never again saw anything unusual during the whole summer.

On one hot day in the early autumn, while he stopped to let his horse drink, he looked and saw a very lovely face on the water. Wondering to whom it might belong, there rose up before him the head and shoulders of a most beautiful woman. She was so pretty that he had two tumbles. He fell off his horse and he fell in love with her at one and the same time.

Rushing towards the lovely vision, he put out his arms at that spot where he had seen her, but only to embrace empty air. Then he remembered that love is blind. So he rubbed his eyes, to see if he could discern anything. Yet though he peered down into the water, and up over the hills, he could not see her anywhere.

But he soon found out to his joy that his eyes were all right, for in another place, the face, flower-crowned hair, and her reflection in the water came again. Then his desire to possess the damsel was doubled. But again, she disappeared, to rise again somewhere else.

Five times he was thus tantalized and disappointed. She rose up, and quickly disappeared.

It seemed as though she meant only to tease him. So he rode home sorrowing, and scarcely slept that night.

Early morning found the lovelorn youth again at the lake side, but for hours he watched in vain. He had left his home too excited to have eaten his usual breakfast, which greatly surprised his housekeeper. Now he pulled out some sweet apples, which a neighbour had given him, and began to munch them, while still keeping watch on the waters.

No sooner had the aroma of the apples fallen on the air than the pretty lady of the lake bobbed up from beneath the surface, and this time quite near him. She seemed to have lost all fear, for she asked him to throw her one of the apples.

"Please come, pretty maid, and get it yourself," cried the farmer. Then he held up the red apple, turning it round and round before her, to tempt her by showing its glossy surface and rich colour.

Apparently not afraid, she came up close to him and took the apple from his left hand. At once, he slipped his strong right arm around her waist, and hugged her tight. At this, she screamed loudly.

Then there appeared in the middle of the lake the old man he had seen thatching the roof by the lake shore. This time, besides his long snowy beard, he had on his head a crown of water lilies.

"Mortal," said the venerable person. "That is my daughter you are clasping. What do you wish to do with her?"

At once, the farmer broke out in passionate appeal to the old man that she might become his wife. He promised to love her always, treat her well, and never be rough or cruel to her.

The old father listened attentively. He was finally convinced that the farmer would make a good husband for his lovely daughter. Yet he was very sorry to lose her, and he solemnly laid one condition upon his future son-in-law.

He was never under any pretence, or in any way, to strike her with clay, or with anything made or baked from clay. Any blow with that from which men made pots and pans, and jars and dishes, or in fact, with earth of any sort, would mean the instant loss of his wife. Even if children were born in their home, the mother would leave them, and return to Fairy-Land under the lake, and be for ever subject to the law of the fairies, as before her marriage.

The farmer was very much in love with his pretty prize, and as promises are easily made, he took oath that no clay should ever touch her.

They were married and lived very happily together. Years passed and the man was still a good husband and lover. He kept up the habit which he had learned from a sailor friend. Every night, when far from home and out on the sea, he and his mates used to drink this toast: "Sweethearts and wives: may every sweetheart become a wife and every wife remain a sweetheart, and every husband continue a lover."

So he proved that though a husband he was still a lover, by always doing what she asked him and more. When the children were born and grew up, their father told them about their mother's likes and dislikes, her tastes and her wishes, and warned them always to be careful. So it was altogether a very happy family.

One day, the wife and mother said to her husband that she had a great longing for apples. She would like to taste some like those which he long ago gave her. At once, the good man dropped what he was doing and hurried off to his neighbour, who had first presented him with a trayful of these apples.

The farmer not only got the fruit, but he also determined that he would plant a tree and thus have apples for his wife whenever she wanted them. So he bought a fine young sapling to set in his orchard, for the children to play under and to keep his pantry full of the fine red-cheeked fruit. At this his wife was delighted.

So happy enough – in fact, too merry to think of anything else, they, both husband and wife, proceeded to set the sapling in the ground. She held the tree, while he dug down to make the hole deep enough to make sure of its growing.

But farmers are sometimes very superstitious. They even believe in luck, though not in Puck. Some of them have faith in what the almanac and the patent medicine may say, and in planting potatoes according to the moon, but they scout the idea of there being any fairies.

With the farmer, this had become a fixed state of mind and now it brought him to grief, as we shall see. For though he remembered what his wife liked and disliked, and recalled what her father had told him, he had forgotten that she was a fairy.

With this farmer and other Welsh mortals, it had become a habit, when planting a young tree, to throw the last shovelful of earth over the left shoulder. This was for good luck. The farmer was afraid to break such a good custom, as he thought it to be.

So merrily he went to work, forgetting everything in his adherence to habit. He became so absorbed in his job that he did not look where his spadeful went, and it struck his dear wife full in the breast.

At that moment, she cried out bitterly, not in pain, but in sorrow. Then she started to run towards the lake. At the shore, she called out, "Good-by, dear, dear husband." Then, leaping into the water, she was never seen again and all his tears and those of the children never brought her back.

THE WELSH FAIRIES HOLD A MEETING

In the ancient Cymric gatherings, the Druids, poets, prophets, seers and singers all had a part. The one most honoured as the president of the meeting was crowned and garlanded. Then he was led in honour and sat in the chair of state. They called this great occasion an Eisteddfod, or sitting, after the Cymric word, meaning a chair.

All over the world, the Welsh folks, who do so passionately love music poetry and their own grand language, hold the Eisteddfod at regular intervals. Thus they renew their love for the Fatherland and what they received long ago from their ancestors.

Now it happens that the fairies in every land usually follow the customs of the mortals among whom they live. The Swiss, the Dutch, the Belgian, the Japanese and Korean fairies, as we all know, although they are much alike in many things are as different from each other as the countries in which they live and play. So, when the Welsh fairies all met together, they resolved to have songs and harp music and make the piper play his tunes just as in the Eisteddfod.

The Cymric fairies of our days have had many troubles to complain of. They were disgusted with so much coal smoke, the poisoning of the air by chemical fumes, and the blackening of the landscape from so many factory chimneys. They had other grievances also.

So the Queen Mab, who had a Welsh name, and another fairy, called Pwca, or in English King Puck, sent out invitations into every part of Wales, for a gathering on the hills, near the great rock called Dina's Seat. This is a rocky chair formed by nature. They also included in their call those parts of western and southern England, such as are still Welsh and spiritually almost a part of Wales. In fact, Cornwall was the old land, in which the Cymry had first landed when coming from over the sea.

The meeting was to be held on a moonlight night, and far away from any houses, lest the merry-making, dancing and singing of the fairies should keep the farmers awake. This was something of which the yokels, or men of the plough, often complained. They could not sleep while the fairies were having their parties.

Now among the Welsh fairies of every sort, size, dress and behaviour, some were good, others were bad, but most of them were only full of fun and mischief. Chief of these was the lively little fellow, Puck, who lived in Cwm Pwcca, that is, Puck Valley, in Breconshire.

Now it had been an old custom, which had come down from the days of the cave men, that when anyone died, the people, friends and relatives sat up all night with the corpse. The custom arose, at first, with the idea of protection against wild beasts and later from insult by enemies. This was called a wake. The watchers wept and wailed at first, and then fell to eating and drinking. Sometimes, they got to be very lively. The young folks even looked on a wake, after the first hour or two, as fine fun. Strong liquor was too plentiful and it often happened that quarrels broke out. When heads were thus fuddled, men saw, or thought they saw, many uncanny things, like leather birds, cave eagles, and the like.

But all these fantastic things and creatures, such as foolish people talk about, and with which they frighten children, such as corpse candles, demons and imps, were ruled out and not invited to the fairy meeting. Some other objects, which ignorant folks believed in, were not to be allowed in the company. The door-keeper was notified not to admit the eagles of darkness, that live in a cave which is never lighted up; or the weird, featherless bird of leather, from the Land of Illusion and Phantasy, that brushes its wing against windows when a funeral is soon to take place; or the greedy dog with silver eyes. None of these would be permitted to show themselves, even if they came and tried to get in. Some other creatures, not recognized in the good society of Fairy-Land, were also barred out.

To this gathering, only the bright and lively fairies were welcome. Some of the best-natured among the big creatures, and especially giants and dragons, might pay a visit, if they wanted to do so; but all the bad ones, such as lake hags, wraiths, sellers of liquids for wakes, who made men drunk, and all who, under the guise of fairies, were only agents for undertakers, were ruled out. The Night Dogs of the Wicked Hunter Annum, the monster Afang, Cadwallader's Goats, and various, cruel goblins and ogres, living in the ponds, and that pulled cattle down to eat them up, and the immodest mermaids, whose bad behaviour was so well known, were crossed off the list of invitations.

No ugly brats, such as wicked fairies were in the habit of putting in the cradles of mortal mothers, when they stole away their babies, were allowed to be present, even if they should come with their mothers. This was to be a perfectly respectable company, and no bawling, squealing, crying, or blubbering was to be permitted.

When they had all gathered together, at the evening hour, there was seen, in the moonlight, the funniest lot of creatures that one could imagine, but all were neatly dressed and well behaved.

Quite a large number of the famous Fair Family, that moved only in the best society of Fairy Land, fathers, mothers, cousins, uncles and aunts, were on hand. In fact, some of them had thought it was to be a wake, and were ready for whatever might turn up, whether solemn or frivolous. These were dressed in varied costume.

Queen Mab, who, above all else, was a Welsh fairy, and whose name, as everybody knows who talks Cymric, suggested her extreme youth and lively disposition, was present in all her glory.

When they saw her, several learned fairies, who had come from a distance, fell at once into conversation on this subject. One remarked: "How would the Queen like to add another syllable to her name? Then we should call her Mab-gath (which means Kitten, or Little Puss)."

"Well not so bad, however; because many mortal daddies, who have a daughter, call her Puss. It is a term of affection with them and the little girls never seem to be offended."

"Oh! Suppose that in talking to each other we call our Queen Mab-gath, what then?" asked another, with a roguish twinkle in the eye.

"It depends on how you use it," said a wise one dryly. This fairy was a stickler for the correct use of every word. "If you meant 'babyish', or 'childish', she, or her friends might demur; but, if you use the term 'love of children', what better name for a fairy queen?"

"None. There could not be any," they shouted, all at once, "but let us ask our old friend the harper."

Now such a thing as inquiring into each other's ages was not common in FairyLand. Very few ever asked such a question, for it was not thought to be polite. For, though we hear of ugly fairy brats being put into the cradles, in place of pretty children, no one ever heard either of fairies being born or of dying, or having clocks, or watches, or looking to see what time it was. Nor did doctors, or the census clerks, or directory people ever trouble the fairy ladies to ask their age.

Occasionally, however, there was one fairy, so wise, so learned, and so able to tell what was going to happen tomorrow, or next year, that the other fairies looked up to such an one with respect and awe.

Yet these honourables would hardly know what you were talking about if you asked any of them how old they might be, or spoke of "old" or "young". If, by any chance, a fairy did use the world "old" in talking of their number, it would be for honour or dignity, and they would mean it for a compliment.

The fact was that many of the most lively fairies showed their frivolous disposition at once. These were of the kind that, like kittens, cubs, or babies, wanted to play all the time, yes, every moment. Already, hundreds of them were tripping from flower to flower, riding on the backs of fireflies, or harnessing night moths, or any winged creatures they could saddle, for flight through the air. Or they were waltzing with glow-worms, or playing "ring around the rosie", or dancing in circles. They could not keep still one moment.

In fact, when a great crowd of the frolicsome creatures got singing together, they made such a noise that a squad of fairy policemen, dressed in club moss and armed with pistils, was sent to warn them not to raise their voices too high, lest the farmers, especially those that were kind to the fairies, should be awakened, and feel in bad humour.

So the knot of learned fairies had a quiet time to talk and, when able to hear their own words, the harper, who was very learned, answered their questions about Queen Mab as follows:

"Well, you know the famous children's story book, in which mortals read about us, and which they say they enjoy so much, is named Mabinogion, that is, The Young Folks' Treasury of Cymric Stories."

"It is well named," said another fairy savant, "since Queen Mab is the only fairy that waits on men. She inspires their dreams, when these are born in their brains."

The talk now turned on Puck, who was to be the president of the meeting. They were expected to show much dignity in his presence, but some feared he would, as usual, play his pranks. Before he arrived in his chariot, which was drawn by dragonflies, some of his neighbours that lived in the valley nearby chatted about him, until the gossip became quite personal. Just for the fun of it, and the amusement of the crowd, they wanted Puck to give an exhibition, off-hand, of all his very varied accomplishments for he could beat all rivals in his special variety, or as musicians say, his repertoire.

"No. 'Twould be too much like a Merry Andrew's or a Buffoon's sideshow, where the freaks of all sorts are gathered, such as they have at those county fairs which the mortals get up, to which are gathered great crowds. The charge of admission is a sixpence. I vote 'no.'"

"Well, for the very reason that Puck can beat the rest of us at spells and transformations, I should like to see him do for us as many stunts as he can. I've heard from a mortal, named Shakespeare, that, in one performance, Puck could be a horse, a hound, a hog, a bear without any head, and even kindle himself into a fire; while his vocal powers, as we know, are endless. He can neigh, bark, grunt, roar, and even burn up things. Now, I should like to see the fairy that could beat him at tricks. It was Puck himself who told the world that he was in the habit of doing all these things, and I want to see whether he was boasting."

"Tut, tut, don't talk that way about our king," said a fourth fairy.

All this was only chaff and fun, for all the fairies were in good humour. They were only talking to fill up the interval until the music began.

Now the canny Welsh fairies had learned the trick of catching farthings, pennies and sixpences from the folks who have more curiosity in them than even fairies do. These human beings, cunning fellows that they are, let the curtain fall on a show just at the most interesting part. Then they tell you to come next day and find out what is to happen. Or, as they say in a story paper, "to be continued in our next."

Or, worse than all, the story teller stops at some very exciting episode, and then passes the hat or collection-box around, to get the copper or silver of his listeners, before he will go on.

This time, however, it was Puck himself who came forward and declared that, unless every one of the fairies would promise to attend the next meeting, there should be no music. Now a meeting of the Welshery, whether fairies or human, without music was a thing not to be thought of. So, although at first some fairies grumbled and held back, and were quite sulky about it, even muttering other grumpy words, they at last all agreed, and Puck sent for the fiddler to make music for the dance.

THE RED BANDITS OF MONTGOMERY

When chimneys were first added to houses in Wales, and the style of house-building changed, from round to square, many old people found fault with the new fashion of letting the smoke out.

They declared they caught colds and sneezed oftener than in the times gone by. The chimneys, they said, cost too much money, and were useless extravagances. They got along well enough, in the good old days, when the smoke had its own way of getting out. Then, it took plenty of time to pass through the doors and wind holes, for no one person or thing was in a hurry when they were young. Moreover, when the fireplace was in the middle of the floor, the whole family sat around it and had a sociable time.

It was true, as they confessed, when argued with, that the smell of the cooking used to linger too long. The soot also hung in long streamers from the rafters, and stuck to the house, like old friends.

But the greatest and most practical objection of the old folks to the chimneys was that robbers used them to climb down at night and steal people's money when they were asleep. So, many householders used to set old scythe blades across the new smoke holes, to keep out the thieves, or to slice them up if they persisted.

In Montgomery, which is one of the Welsh shires, there was an epidemic of robbery, and the doings of the Red Bandits are famous in history.

Now there was a young widow, whose husband had been killed by the footpads, or road robbers. She was left alone in the world, with a little boy baby in the cradle and only one cow in the byre. She had hard work to pay her rent, but as there were three or four scythes set in the chimney, and the cow stable had a good lock on it, she thought she was safe from burglars or common thieves.

But the Reds picked out the most expert chimney-climber in their gang, and he one night slipped down into the widow's cottage, without making any noise or cutting off his nose, toes, or fingers. Then, robbing the widow of her rent money, he picked the lock of the byre and drove off the cow. In the morning, the poor woman found both doors open, but there was no money and no cow.

While she was crying over her loss, and wringing her hands, because of her poverty, she heard a knock at the door.

"Come in," said the widow.

There entered an old lady with a kindly face. She was very tall and well dressed. Her cloak, her gloves, and shoes, and the ruffles under her high-peaked Welsh head dress, were all green. The widow thought she looked like an animated leek. In her right hand was a long staff, and in her left, under her cloak, she held a little bag, that was green also.

"Why do you weep?" asked the visitor.

Then the widow told her tale of woe – the story of the loss of her husband, and how a Red robber, in spite of the scythe blades set in the chimney, had come down and taken away both her money and her cow.

Now, although she had sold all her butter and cream, she could neither pay her rent, nor have any buttermilk with her rye bread and flummery.

"Dry your tears and take comfort," said the tall lady in the green peaked hat. "Here is money enough to pay your rent and buy another cow." With that, she sat down at the round table near the peat fire. Opening her bag, the shining gold coins slid out and formed a little heap on the table.

"There, you can have all this, if you will give me all I want."

At first, the widow's eyes opened wide, and then she glanced at the cradle, where her baby was sleeping. Then she wondered, though she said nothing.

But the next moment, she was laughing at herself, and looking around at her poor cottage. She tried to guess what there was in it that the old lady could possibly want.

"You can have anything I have. Name it," she said cheerfully to her visitor.

But only a moment more, and all her fears returned at the thought that the visitor might ask for her boy.

The old lady spoke again and said:

"I want to help you all I can, but what I came here for is to get the little boy in the cradle."

The widow now saw that the old woman was a fairy, and that if her visitor got hold of her son, she would never see her child again.

So she begged piteously of the old lady, to take anything and everything, except her one child.

"No, I want that boy, and, if you want the gold, you must let me take him."

"Is there anything else that I can do for you, so that I may get the money?" asked the widow.

"Well, I'll make it easier for you. There are two things I must tell you to cheer you."

"What are they?" asked the widow, eagerly.

"One is that by our fairy law, I cannot take your boy until three days have passed. Then, I shall come again, and you shall have the gold; but only on the one condition I have stated."

"And the next?" almost gasped the widow.

"If you can guess my name, you will doubly win; for then, I shall give you the gold and you can keep your boy."

Without waiting for another word, the lady in green scooped up her money, put it back in the bag, and moved off and out the door.

The poor woman, at once a widow and mother, and now stripped of her property, fearing to lose her boy, brooded all night over her troubles and never slept a wink.

In the morning, she rose up, left her baby with a neighbour, and went to visit some relatives in the next village, which was several miles distant. She told her story, but her kinsfolk were too poor to help her. So, all disconsolate, she turned her face homewards.

On her way back she had to pass through the woods, where, on one side, was a clearing. In the middle of this open space was a ring of grass. In the ring a little fairy lady was tripping around and singing to herself.

Creeping up silently, the anxious mother heard to her joy a rhymed couplet and caught the sound of a name, several times repeated. It sounded like "Silly Doot".

Hurrying home and perfectly sure that she knew the secret that would save her boy, she set cheerily about her regular work and daily tasks. In fact, she slept soundly that night.

Next day, in came the lady in green as before, with her bag of money. Taking her seat at the round table, near the fire, she poured out the gold. Then jingling the coins in the pile, she said:

"Now give up your boy, or guess my name, if you want me to help you."

The young widow, feeling sure that she had the old fairy in a trap, thought she would have some fun first.

"How many guesses am I allowed?" she asked.

"All you want, and as many as you please," answered the green lady, smiling.

The widow rattled off a string of names, English, Welsh and Biblical; but every time the fairy shook her head. Her eyes began to gleam, as if she felt certain of getting the boy. She even moved her chair around to the side nearest the cradle.

"One more guess," cried the widow. "Can it be Silly Doot?"

At this sound, the fairy turned red with rage. At the same moment, the door opened wide and a blast of wind made the hearth fire flare up. Leaving her gold behind her, the old woman flew up the chimney, and disappeared over the housetops.

The widow scooped up the gold, bought two cows, furnished her cottage with new chairs and fresh flowers, and put the rest of the coins away under one of the flagstones at the hearth. When her boy grew up, she gave him a good education, and he became one of the fearless judges, who, with the aid of Baron Owen, rooted out of their lair the Red Bandits that had robbed his mother. Since that day, there has been little crime in Wales – the best-governed part of the kingdom.

THE YSTRAD LEGEND

"**In a meadow belonging** to Ystrad, bounded by the river which falls from Cwellyn Lake, they say the Fairies used to assemble, and dance on fair moon-light-nights. One evening a young man, who was the heir and occupier of this farm, hid himself in a thicket close to the spot where they used to gambol; presently they appeared, and when in their merry mood, out he bounced from his covert and seized one of their females; the rest of the company dispersed themselves, and disappeared in an instant. Disregarding her struggles and screams, he hauled her to his home, where he treated her so very kindly that she became content to live with him as his maidservant; but he could not prevail upon her to tell him her name. Some time after, happening again to see the Fairies upon the same spot, he heard one of them saying, 'The last time we met here, our sister Penelope was snatched away from us by one of the mortals!' Rejoiced at knowing the name of his incognita, he returned home; and as she was very beautiful, and extremely active, he proposed to marry her, which she would not for a long time consent to; at last, however, she complied, but on this condition, 'That if ever he should strike her with iron, she would leave him, and never return to him again.' They lived happily for many years together, and he had by her a son, and a daughter; and by her industry and prudent management as a housewife he became one of the richest men in the country. He farmed, besides his own freehold, all the lands on the north side of Nant-y-Bettws to the top of Snowdon, and all Cwmbrwynog in Llanberis; an extent of about five thousand acres or upwards.

Unfortunately, one day Penelope followed her husband into the field to catch a horse; and he, being in a rage at the animal as he ran away from him, threw at him the bridle that was in his hand, which unluckily fell on poor Penelope. She disappeared in an instant, and he never saw her afterwards, but heard her voice in the window of his room one night after, requesting him to take care of the children, in these words: –

Rhag bod anwyd ar fy mab,
Yn rhodd rhowch arno gôb ei dad,
Rhag bod anwyd ar liw'r cann,
Rhoddwch arni bais ei mam.

That is –

Oh! lest my son should suffer cold,
Him in his father's coat infold,
Lest cold should seize my darling fair,
For her, her mother's robe prepare.

These children and their descendants, they say, were called Pellings; a word corrupted from their mother's name, Penelope.

A BRYNEGLWYS MAN INVEIGLED BY THE FAIRIES

Two waggoners were sent from Bryneglwys for coals to the works over the hill beyond Minera. On their way they came upon a company of Fairies dancing with all their might. The men stopped to witness their movements, and the Fairies invited them to join in the dance. One of the men stoutly refused to do so, but the other was induced to dance awhile with them. His companion looked on for a short time at the antics of his friend, and then shouted out that he would wait no longer, and desired the man to give up and come away. He, however, turned a deaf ear to the request, and no words could induce him to forego his dance. At last his companion said that he was going, and requested his friend to follow him. Taking the two waggons under his care he proceeded towards the coal pits, expecting every moment to be overtaken by his friend; but he was disappointed, for he never appeared. The waggons and their loads were taken to Bryneglwys, and the man thought that perhaps his companion, having stopped too long in the dance, had turned homewards instead of following him to the coal pit. But on enquiry no one had heard or seen the missing waggoner. One day his companion met a Fairy on the mountain and inquired after his missing friend. The Fairy told him to go to a certain place, which he named, at a certain time, and that he should there see his friend. The man went, and there saw his companion just as he had left him, and the first words that he uttered were, "Have the waggons gone far?" The poor man never dreamt that months and months had passed away since they had started together for coal.

A MAN WHO SPENT TWELVE MONTHS AND A DAY WITH THE FAIRIES

A **young man**, a farm labourer, and his sweetheart were sauntering along one evening in an unfrequented part of the mountain, when there appeared suddenly before them two Fairies, who proceeded to make a circle. This being done, a large company of Fairies accompanied by musicians appeared, and commenced dancing over the ring; their motions and music were entrancing, and the man, an expert dancer, by some irresistible power was obliged to throw himself into the midst of the dancers and join them in their gambols. The woman looked on enjoying the sight for several hours, expecting every minute that her lover would give up the dance and join her, but no, on and on went the dance, round and round went her lover, until at last daylight appeared, and then suddenly the music ceased and the Fairy band vanished; and with them her lover. In great dismay, the young woman shouted the name of her sweetheart, but all in vain, he came not to her. The sun had now risen, and, almost broken-hearted, she returned home and related the events of the previous night. She was advised to consult a man who was an adept in the black art. She did so, and the conjuror told her to go to the same place at the same time of the night one year and one day from the time that her lover had disappeared and that she should then and there see him. She was further instructed how to act. The conjuror warned her from going into the ring, but told her to seize her lover by the arm as he danced round, and to jerk him out of the enchanted circle. Twelve months and a day passed away, and the faithful girl was on the spot where she lost her lover. At the very moment that they had in the first instance appeared the Fairies again came to view, and everything that she had witnessed previously was repeated. With the Fairy band was her lover dancing merrily in their midst. The young woman ran round and round the circle close to the young man, carefully avoiding the circle, and at last she succeeded in taking hold of him and desired him to come away with her. "Oh," said he, "do let me alone a little longer, and then I will come with you." "You have already been long enough," said she. His answer was, "It is so delightful, let me dance on only a few minutes longer." She saw that he was under a spell, and grasping the young man's arm with all her might she followed him round and round the circle, and an opportunity offering she jerked him out of the circle. He was greatly annoyed at her conduct, and when told that he had been with the Fairies a year and a day he would not believe her, and affirmed that he had been dancing only a few minutes; however, he went away with the faithful girl, and when he had reached the farm, his friends had the greatest difficulty in persuading him that he had been so long from home.

THE SON OF LLECH Y DERWYDD AND THE FAIRIES

The son of Llech y Derwydd was the only son of his parents and heir to the farm. He was very dear to his father and mother, yea, he was as the very light of their eyes. The son and the head servant man were bosom friends, they were like two brothers, or rather twins. As they were such close friends the farmer's wife was in the habit of clothing them exactly alike. The two friends fell in love with two young handsome women who were highly respected in the neighbourhood. This event gave the old people great satisfaction, and ere long the two couples were joined in holy wedlock, and great was the merry-making on the occasion. The servant man obtained a convenient place to live in on the grounds of Llech y Derwydd. About six months after the marriage of the son, he and the servant man went out to hunt. The servant penetrated to a ravine filled with brushwood to look for game, and presently returned to his friend, but by the time he came back the son was nowhere to be seen. He continued awhile looking about for his absent friend, shouting and whistling to attract his attention, but there was no answer to his calls. By and by he went home to Llech y Derwydd, expecting to find him there, but no one knew anything about him. Great was the grief of the family throughout the night, but it was even greater the next day. They went to inspect the place where the son had last been seen. His mother and his wife wept bitterly, but the father had greater control over himself, still he appeared as half mad. They inspected the place where the servant man had last seen his friend, and, to their great surprise and sorrow, observed a Fairy ring close by the spot, and the servant recollected that he had heard seductive music somewhere about the time that he parted with his friend. They came to the conclusion at once that the man had been so unfortunate as to enter the Fairy ring, and they conjectured that he had been transported no one knew where. Weary weeks and months passed away, and a son was born to the absent man. The little one grew up the very image of his father, and very precious was he to his grandfather and grandmother. In fact, he was everything to them. He grew up to man's estate and married a pretty girl in the neighbourhood, but her people had not the reputation of being kind-hearted. The old folks died, and also their daughter-in-law.

One windy afternoon in the month of October, the family of Llech y Derwydd saw a tall thin old man with beard and hair as white as snow, approaching slowly, very slowly, towards the house. The servant girls stared mockingly through the window at him, and their mistress laughed unfeelingly at the old man and lifted the children up, one after the other, to get a sight of him as he neared the house. He came to the door, and entered the house boldly enough, and inquired after his parents. The mistress answered him in a surly and unusually contemptuous manner, and wished to know, "What the drunken old man wanted there," for they thought he must have been drinking or he would never have spoken in the way he did. The old man looked at everything in the house with surprise and bewilderment, but the little children about the floor took his attention more than anything else. His looks betrayed sorrow and deep disappointment. He related his whole history, that yesterday he had gone out to hunt, and that he had now returned. The mistress told him that she had heard a story about her husband's father, which occurred before she was born, that he had been lost whilst hunting, but that her father had told her that the story was not true, but that he had been killed. The woman became uneasy and angry that the old man did not depart. The old man was roused and said that the house was his, and that he would have his rights. He went to inspect his possessions, and shortly afterwards directed his steps to the servant's house. To his surprise he saw that things there were greatly changed. After conversing awhile with an aged man who sat by the fire, they carefully looked each other in the face, and the old man by the fire related the sad history of his lost friend, the son of Llech y Derwydd. They conversed together deliberately on the events of their youth, but all seemed like a dream. However, the old man in the corner came to the conclusion that his visitor was his dear friend, the son of Llech y Derwydd, returned from the land of the Fairies after having spent there half a hundred years. The old man with the white beard believed the story related by his friend, and long was the talk and many were the questions which the one gave to the other. The visitor was informed that the master of Llech y Derwydd was from home that day, and he was persuaded to eat some food; but, to the horror of all, when he had done so, he instantly fell down dead.

A YOUNG MAN MARRIES A FAIRY LADY IN FAIRY LAND, AND BRINGS HER TO LIVE WITH HIM AMONG HIS OWN PEOPLE

"**Once on a** time a shepherd boy had gone up the mountain. That day, like many a day before and after, was exceedingly misty. Now, though he was well acquainted with the place, he lost his way, and walked backwards and forwards for many a long hour. At last he got into a low rushy spot, where he saw before him many circular rings. He at once recalled the place, and began to fear the worst. He had heard, many hundreds of times, of the bitter experiences in those rings of many a shepherd who had happened to chance on the dancing-place or the circles of the Fair Family. He hastened away as fast as ever he could, lest he should be ruined like the rest; but though he exerted himself to the point of perspiring, and losing his breath, there he was, and there he continued to be, a long time. At last he was met by a little fat old man with merry blue eyes, who asked him what he was doing. He answered that he was trying to find his way homeward. 'Oh,' said he, 'come after me, and do not utter a word until I bid thee.' This he did, following him on and on until they came to an oval stone, and the little old fat man lifted it, after tapping the middle of it three times with his walking stick. There was there a narrow path with stairs to be seen here and there, and a sort of whitish light, inclining to grey and blue, was to be seen radiating from the stones. 'Follow me fearlessly,' said the fat man, 'no harm will be done thee.' So on the poor youth went, as reluctantly as a dog to be hanged; but presently a fine-wooded, fertile country spread itself out before them, with well-arranged mansions dotting it over, while every kind of apparent magnificence met the eye, and seemed to smile in its landscape; the bright waters of its rivers meandered in twisted streams, and its hills were covered with the luxuriant verdure of their grassy growth, and the mountains with a glossy fleece of smooth pasture. By the time they had reached the stout gentleman's mansion, the young man's senses had been bewildered by the sweet cadence of the music which the birds poured forth from the groves, then there was gold there to dazzle his eyes and silver flashing on his sight. He saw there all kinds of musical instruments and all sorts of things for playing, but he could discern no inhabitant in the whole place; and when he sat down to eat, the dishes on the table came to their places of themselves and disappeared when one had done with them. This puzzled him beyond measure; moreover, he heard people talking together around him, but for the life of him he could see no one but his old friend. At length the fat man said to him, 'Thou canst now talk as much as it may please thee;' but when he attempted to move his tongue it would no more stir than if it had been a lump of ice, which greatly frightened him. At this point, a fine old lady, with health and benevolence beaming in her face, came to them and slightly smiled at the shepherd. The mother was followed by her three daughters, who were remarkably beautiful. They gazed with somewhat playful looks at him, and at length began to talk to him, but his tongue would not wag. Then one of the girls came to him, and, playing with his yellow and curly locks, gave him a smart kiss on his ruddy lips. This loosened the string that bound his tongue, and he began to talk freely and eloquently. There he was, under the charm of that kiss, in the bliss of happiness, and there he remained a year and a day without knowing that he had passed more than a day among them, for he had got into a country where there was no reckoning of time. But by and by he began to feel somewhat of a longing to visit his old home, and asked the stout man if he might go. 'Stay a little yet,' said he, 'and thou shalt go for a while.' That passed, he stayed on; but Olwen, for that was the name of the damsel that had kissed him, was very unwilling that he should depart. She looked sad every time he talked of going away, nor was he himself without feeling a sort of a cold thrill passing through him at the thought of leaving her. On condition, however, of returning, he obtained leave to go, provided with plenty of gold and silver, of trinkets and gems. When he reached home, nobody knew who he was; it had been the belief that he had been killed by another shepherd, who found it necessary to betake himself hastily far away to America, lest he should be hanged without delay. But here is Einion Las at home, and everybody wonders especially to see that the shepherd had got to look like a wealthy man; his manners, his dress, his language, and the treasure he had with him, all conspired to give him the air of a gentleman. He went back one Thursday night, the first of the moon that month, as suddenly as he had left the first time, and nobody knew whither. There was great joy in the country below when Einion returned thither, and nobody was more rejoiced at it than Olwen, his beloved. The two were right impatient to get married, but it was necessary to do that quietly, for the family below hated nothing more than fuss and noise; so, in a sort of a half-secret fashion, they were wedded. Einion was very desirous to go once more among his own people, accompanied, to be sure, by his wife. After he had been long entreating the old man for leave, they set out on two white ponies, that were, in fact, more like snow than anything else in point of colour; so he arrived with his consort in his old home, and it was the opinion of all that Einion's wife was the handsomest person they had anywhere seen. Whilst at home, a son was born to them, to whom they gave the name of Taliesin. Einion was now in the enjoyment of high repute, and his wife received proper respect. Their wealth was immense, and soon they acquired a large estate; but it was not long till people began to inquire after the pedigree of Einion's wife – the country was of opinion that it was not the right thing to be without a pedigree. Einion was questioned about it, without his giving any satisfactory answer, and one came to the conclusion that she was one of the Fair Family (tylwyth têg). 'Certainly,' replied Einion, 'there can be no doubt that she comes from a very fair family, for she has two sisters who are as fair as she, and if you saw them together, you would admit that name to be a capital one.' This, then, is the reason why the remarkable family in the land of charm and phantasy (Hud a Lledrith) are called the Fair Family."

A MAN CARRIED THROUGH THE AIR BY THE FAIRIES

"**One Edward Jones,** or 'Ned the Jockey', as he was familiarly called, resided, within the memory of the writer, in one of the roadside cottages a short distance from Llanidloes, on the Newtown road. While returning home late one evening, it was his fate to fall in with a troop of Fairies, who were not pleased to have their gambols disturbed by a mortal. Requesting him to depart, they politely offered him the choice of three means of locomotion, viz., being carried off by a 'high wind, middle wind, or low wind.' The jockey soon made up his mind, and elected to make his trip through the air by the assistance of a high wind. No sooner had he given his decision than he found himself whisked high up into the air and his senses completely bewildered by the rapidity of his flight; he did not recover himself till he came in contact with the earth, being suddenly dropped in the middle of a garden near Ty Gough, on the Bryndu road, many miles distant from the spot whence he started on his aerial journey. Ned, when relating this story, would vouch for its genuineness in the most solemn manner, and the person who narrated it to the writer brought forward as a proof of its truth, 'that there was not the slightest trace of any person going into the garden while Ned was found in the middle of it.'"

THE FAIRIES OF CARAGONAN

Once upon a time a lot of fairies lived in Mona.

One day the queen fairy's daughter, who was now fifteen years of age, told her mother she wished to go out and see the world.

The queen consented, allowing her to go for a day, and to change from a fairy to a bird, or from a bird to a fairy, as she wished.

When she returned one night she said:

"I've been to a gentleman's house, and as I stood listening, I heard the gentleman was witched: he was very ill, and crying out with pain."

"Oh, I must look into that," said the queen.

So the next day she went through her process and found that he was bewitched by an old witch. So the following day she set out with six other fairies, and when they came to the gentleman's house she found he was very ill.

Going into the room, bearing a small blue pot they had brought with them, the queen asked him:

"Would you like to be cured?"

"Oh, bless you; yes, indeed."

Whereupon the queen put the little blue pot of perfume on the centre of the table, and lit it, when the room was instantly filled with the most delicious odour.

Whilst the perfume was burning, the six fairies formed in line behind her, and she leading, they walked round the table three times, chanting in chorus:

"Round and round three times three,
We have come to cure thee."

At the end of the third round she touched the burning perfume with her wand, and then touched the gentleman on the head, saying:

"Be thou made whole."

No sooner had she said the words than he jumped up hale and hearty, and said:

"Oh, dear queen, what shall I do for you? I'll do anything you wish."

"Money I do not wish for," said the queen, "but there's a little plot of ground on the sea-cliff I want you to lend me, for I wish to make a ring there, and the grass will die when I make the ring. Then I want you to build three walls round the ring, but leave the sea-side open, so that we may be able to come and go easily."

"With the greatest of pleasure," said the gentleman; and he built the three stone walls at once, at the spot indicated.

II

Near the gentleman lived the old witch, and she had the power of turning at will into a hare. The gentleman was a great hare hunter, but the hounds could never catch this hare; it always disappeared in a mill, running between the wings and jumping in at an open window, though they stationed two men and a dog at the spot, when it immediately turned into the old witch. And the old miller never suspected, for the old woman used to take him a peck of corn to grind a few days before any hunt, telling him she would call for it on the afternoon of the day of the hunt. So that when she arrived she was expected.

One day she had been taunting the gentleman as he returned from a hunt, that he could never catch the hare, and he struck her with his whip, saying "Get away, you witchcraft!"

Whereupon she witched him, and he fell ill, and was cured as we have seen.

When he got well he watched the old witch, and saw she often visited the house of an old miser who lived nearby with his beautiful niece. Now all the people in the village touched their hats most respectfully to this old miser, for they knew he had dealings with the witch, and they were as much afraid of him as of her; but everyone loved the miser's kind and beautiful niece.

III

When the fairies got home the queen told her daughter:

"I have no power over the old witch for twelve months from today, and then I have no power over her life. She must lose that by the arm of a man."

So the next day the daughter was sent out again to see whether she could find a person suited to that purpose.

In the village lived a small crofter, who was afraid of nothing; he was the boldest man thereabouts; and one day he passed the miser without saluting him. The old fellow went off at once and told the witch.

"Oh, I'll settle his cows tonight!" said she, and they were taken sick, and gave no milk that night.

The fairy's daughter arrived at his croft-yard after the cows were taken ill, and she heard him say to his son, a bright lad:

"It must be the old witch!"

When she heard this, she sent him to the queen.

So next day the fairy queen took six fairies and went to the croft, taking her blue pot of perfume. When she got there she asked the crofter if he would like his cows cured?

"God bless you, yes!" he said.

The queen made him bring a round table into the yard, whereon she placed the blue pot of perfume, and having lit it, as before, they formed in line and walked round thrice, chanting the words:

"Round and round three times three,
We have come to cure thee."

Then she dipped the end of her wand into the perfume, and touched the cows on the forehead, saying to each one:

"Be thou whole."

Whereupon they jumped up cured.

The little farmer was overjoyed, and cried:

"Oh, what can I do for you? What can I do for you?"

"Money I care not for," said the queen, "all I want is your son to avenge you and me."

The lad jumped up and said:

"What I can do I'll do it for you, my lady fairy."

She told him to be at the walled plot the following day at noon, and left.

IV

The next day at noon, the queen and her daughter and three hundred other fairies came up the cliff to the green grass plot, and they carried a pole, and a tape, and a mirror. When they reached the plot they planted the pole in the ground, and hung the mirror on the pole. The queen took the tape, which measured ten yards and was fastened to the top of the pole, and walked round in a circle, and wherever she set her feet the grass withered and died. Then the fairies followed up behind the queen, and each fairy carried a harebell in her left-hand, and a little blue cup of burning perfume in her right. When they had formed up the queen called the lad to her side, and told him to walk by her throughout. They then started off, all singing in chorus:

"Round and round three times three,
Tell me what you see."

When they finished the first round, the queen and lad stopped before the mirror, and she asked the lad what he saw.

"I see, I see, the mirror tells me,
It is the witch that I see,"

said the lad. So they marched round again, singing the same words as before, and when they stopped a second time before the mirror the queen again asked him what he saw.

"I see, I see, the mirror tells me,
It is a hare that I see,"

said the lad.

A third time the ceremony and question were repeated.

"I see, I see, the mirror tells me,
The hares run up the hill to the mill."

"Now," said the queen, "there is to be a hare-hunting this day week; be at the mill at noon, and I will meet you there."

And then the fairies, pole, mirror, and all, vanished and only the empty ring on the green was left.

V

Upon the appointed day the lad went to his tryst, and at noon the Fairy Queen appeared, and gave him a sling, and a smooth pebble from the beach, saying:

"I have blessed your arms, and I have blessed the sling and the stone.

"Now as the clock strikes three,
Go up the hill near the mill,
And in the ring stand still
Till you hear the click of the mill.
Then with thy arm, with power and might,
You shall strike and smite
The devil of a witch called Jezabel light,
And you shall see an awful sight."

The lad did as he was bidden, and presently he heard the huntsman's horn and the hue and cry, and saw the hare running down the opposite hill-side, where the hounds seemed to gain on her, but as she breasted the hill on which he stood she gained on them. As she came towards the mill he threw his stone, and it lodged in her skull, and when he ran up he found he had killed the old witch. As the huntsmen came up they crowded round him, and praised him; and then they fastened the witch's body to a horse by ropes, and dragged her to the bottom of the valley, where they buried her in a ditch. That night, when the miser heard of her death, he dropped down dead on the spot.

As the lad was going home the queen appeared to him, and told him to be at the ring the following day at noon.

VI

Next day all the fairies came with the pole and mirror, each carrying a harebell in her left-hand, and a blue cup of burning perfume in her right, and they formed up as before, the lad walking beside the queen. They marched round and repeated the old words, when the queen stopped before the mirror, and said:

"What do you see?"

"I see, I see, the mirror tells me,
It is an old plate-cupboard that I see."

A second time they went round, and the question was repeated.

"I see, I see, the mirror tells me,
The back is turned to me."

A third time was the ceremony fulfilled, and the lad answered:

"I see, I see, the mirror tells me,
A spring-door is open to me."

"Buy that plate-cupboard at the miser's sale," said the queen, and she and her companions disappeared as before.

VII

Upon the day of the sale all the things were brought out in the road, and the plate-cupboard was put up, the lad recognizing it and bidding up for it till it was sold to him. When he had paid for it he took it home in a cart, and when he got in and examined it, he found the secret drawer behind was full of gold. The following week the house and land, thirty acres, was put up for sale, and the lad bought both, and married the miser's niece, and they lived happily till they died.

OLD GWILYM

Old Gwilym Evans started off one fine morning to walk across the Eagle Hills to a distant town, bent upon buying some cheese. On his way, in a lonely part of the hills, he found a golden guinea, which he quickly put into his pocket.

When he got to the town, instead of buying his provisions, he went into an alehouse, and sat drinking and singing with some sweet-voiced quarrymen until dark, when he thought it was time to go home. Whilst he was drinking, an old woman with a basket came in, and sat beside him, but she left before him. After the parting glass he got up and reeled through the town, quite forgetting to buy his cheese; and as he got amongst the hills they seemed to dance up and down before him, and he seemed to be walking on air. When he got near the lonely spot where he had found the money he heard some sweet music, and a number of fairies crossed his path and began dancing all round him, and then as he looked up he saw some brightly lit houses before him on the hill; and he scratched his head, for he never remembered having seen houses thereabouts before. And as he was thinking, and watching the fairies, one came and begged him to come into the house and sit down.

So he followed her in, and found the house was all gold inside it, and brightly lit, and the fairies were dancing and singing, and they brought him anything he wanted for supper, and then they put him to bed.

Gwilym slept heavily, and when he awoke turned round, for he felt very cold, and his body seemed covered with prickles; so he sat up and rubbed his eyes, and found that he was quite naked and lying in a bunch of gorse.

When he found himself in this plight he hurried home, and told his wife, and she was very angry with him for spending all the money and bringing no cheese home, and then he told her his adventures.

"Oh, you bad man!" she said, "the fairies gave you money and you spent it wrongly, so they were sure to take their revenge."

THE FAIRIES' MINT

Once upon a time there was a miller, who lived in Anglesey. One day he noticed that some of his sacks had been moved during the night. The following day he felt sure that some of his grain had been disturbed, and, lastly, he was sure someone had been working his mill in the night during his absence. He confided his suspicions to a friend, and they determined to go the next night and watch the mill. The following night, at about midnight, as they approached the mill, that stood on a bare stony hill, they were surprised to find the mill all lit up and at work, the great sails turning in the black night. Creeping up softly to a small window, the miller looked in, and saw a crowd of little men carrying small bags, and emptying them into the millstones. He could not see, however, what was in the bags, so he crept to another window, when he saw golden coins coming from the mill, from the place where the flour usually ran out.

Immediately the miller went to the mill door, and, putting his key into the lock, he unlocked the door; and as he did so the lights went out suddenly, and the mill stopped working. As he and his friend went into the dark mill they could hear sounds of people running about, but by the time they lit up the mill again there was nobody to be seen, but scattered all about the millstones and on the floor were cockleshells.

After that, many persons who passed the mill at midnight said they saw the mill lit up and working; but the old miller left the fairies alone to coin their money.

RHYS AND LLYWELYN

Two farm servants named Rhys and Llywelyn were one fine evening at twilight returning home to Llwyn y Ffynon from the mountain, where they had been cutting peat. They were walking through a wood when Rhys suddenly said, "Stop: listen to that enchanting music: that's a tune I've danced to a hundred times and I can't resist it now. I must find the musicians and have my dance: if you don't want to stop, you can go and have your supper and I'll be with you presently."

"Music and dancing indeed," replied Llywelyn, "I hear no music and how should you? Come, come, no nonsense, come home with me."

He might have spared his breath to cool the porridge which was awaiting him at Llwyn y Ffynon, for Rhys plunged into the trees, leaving Llywelyn to pursue his homeward journey alone. As he was walking along, he thought that all Rhys's talk about music must have been just an excuse for going to the alehouse, which was five miles away; so he ate his supper and retired to rest in the stable loft without any anxiety about his companion. Nor was he troubled about him when he woke up in the middle of the night and found himself alone, reflecting that under the influence of the ale Rhys would probably go a-wooing and return before morning as he had often done before.

When morning came, however, there was no Rhys, and when questioned by his master, Llywelyn said that he had gone off suddenly the night before, presumably to the alehouse. As there was a heavy day's work to be gone through, a messenger was sent to the alehouse to inquire about Rhys, but came back with the information that Rhys had not been there at all. By-and-by, his master thought it advisable to question Llywelyn more closely as to where, how and why Rhys had left him. Llywelyn stated that as they were walking through the wood, Rhys had suddenly heard music and left him, as he said, to join the dance.

"Did you hear the music?" inquired his master, and when Llywelyn replied that he had not, his account of his fellow servant's disappearance was considered very unsatisfactory.

A search was made for the lost Rhys, but not a trace of him could be found. There had been no dance in the whole country round: not a sound of music had reached the ear of anyone: and suspicion gradually fell on Llywelyn. It was supposed that he must have quarrelled with Rhys on the way home and murdered him, and he was arrested and put in prison. He protested his innocence, but as he could give no account of his companion's disappearance except that, at the sound of music which no one had heard, he had suddenly gone off to a dance which had not taken place, he was generally thought to be guilty, and he was kept in prison until the dead body could be found and his guilt could be brought home to him.

Things remained thus for nearly a year, when a newcomer into the neighbourhood, who had some experience of fairy ways and customs, suggested that he and a company of neighbours should go with Llywelyn to the place where he had parted from Rhys. This was agreed to and they came to a fairy ring.

"This is the very spot," said Llywelyn, "and hush, I hear music; melodious harps I hear."

The whole company listened, but could hear nothing, and told Llywelyn so.

"Put your foot on mine, David," said Llywelyn, whose foot was now upon the outward edge of the fairy circle, to one of the company. David put his foot on Llywelyn's, and so did they all, one after another: and then they heard the sound of many harps in full concert, and saw within the circle a number of little figures enjoying themselves vastly. They were dancing round and round the ring with hands joined, and among them was Rhys, footing it with the best of them.

As he came whirling by, Llywelyn seized hold of his smock frock and switched him out of the circle, taking great care not to overstep the edge of the ring.

"Let me finish my dance," said Rhys, "I never enjoyed a dance like this before, and I have not been above five minutes at it. Let me return to the dance."

"Five minutes, indeed," said the enraged Llywelyn, "you've been there long enough to come near getting me hanged, anyhow. I've been accused of murdering you, and you must clear my character. Come, answer for yourself and account for your conduct." And he restrained him by main force.

But to all the questions with which he was plied, he could only reply that he had been dancing for about five minutes. Of the people with whom he was, he could give no account whatever, except that they danced exquisitely. They were strangers to him, he said. He had not eaten or drunk or slept, and he was in the same clothes as when he disappeared. He became sad, sullen and silent, took to his bed and before long died.

THE ADVENTURES OF THREE FARMERS

Three men who once went to Beddgelert Fair had strange adventures before they reached home.

One of them was the farmer of the Gilwern. On his *way* home he came across the Fair Family dancing. He looked on for hours, and the music was so sweet that he felt certain that even in Heaven he would not hear sweeter. But he forgot himself while listening and went too near. When they noticed him the little people threw a kind of dust in his eyes, and while he was wiping it away they betook themselves somewhere out of his sight, so that he neither saw nor heard anything more of them.

This was what befell the second, the farmer of the Ffridd. He also saw a company of fairies engaged in their revels, and while he was watching them he fell asleep. As he slept they bound him so tightly that he could not have stirred, and then they covered him over with a veil of gossamer, so that nobody could see him in case he called for help. As he did not return home his family made a minute search for him, in vain. However, about the same time the following night the fairies came and liberated him, and he shortly woke up after sleeping a whole night and a day. After awaking he had no idea where on earth he was; he wandered about on the slopes of the Gader and near the Gors Fawr until the cock crew, when he found where he was, namely, less than a quarter of a mile from his home.

The third was the farmer of Drws y Coed. He was going home along the old road over the Gader, and when he was near the top he saw a fine, handsome house, in which there was a rare merrymaking. He knew very well that there was no such building anywhere on his way, and it made him think that he had mistaken his road and gone astray. He therefore resolved to turn into the house to ask for a night's lodging. His request was readily granted, and when he entered he thought that a wedding feast (*neithior*) was being celebrated, such was the jollity, the singing and the dancing. The house was full of young men and women and children, all disporting as merrily as could be. Presently the company began to disperse one by one, and he asked if he might go to bed. He was led into a beautiful bed-chamber, where there was a bed of the softest down covered with bed-clothes as white as snow. He at once undressed, went into bed, and slept quietly enough until the morning. He opened his eyes and found he was sleeping on the open bogland, with a clump of rushes as his pillow and the blue sky as his coverlet.

THE FAIRY HARP

A company of fairies who lived in the recesses of Cader Idris were in the habit of going about from cottage to cottage in that part of the country to test the dispositions of the cottagers. Those who gave the fairies an ungracious welcome were subject to bad luck during the rest of their lives; but those who were good to the little folk who visited them in disguise received substantial favours from them.

Old Morgan ap Rhys was sitting one night by himself in his own chimney corner, solacing his loneliness with his pipe and some Llangollen ale. The generous liquor made Morgan very light-hearted, and he began to sing – at least he was under the impression that he was singing. His voice, however, was anything but sweet, and a bard whom he had offended – it is a very dangerous thing to fall foul of the bards in Wales, because they often have such bitter tongues – had likened his singing to the lowing of an old cow or the yelping of a blind dog which has lost its way to the cow yard. His singing, however, gave Morgan himself much satisfaction, and this particular evening he was especially pleased with the harmony he was producing. The only thing which marred his sense of contentment was the absence of an audience. Just as he was coming to the climax of his song, he heard a knock at the door. Delighted with the thought that there was someone to listen to him, Morgan sang with all the fervour he was capable of, and his top note was, in his opinion, a thing of beauty and a joy for ever. When he had quite finished, he again heard a knock at the door, and shouted out, "What is the door for but to come in by? Come in, whoever you are." Morgan's manners, you will see, were not very polished.

The door opened and in came three travellers, travel-stained and weary-looking. Now these were fairies from Cader Idris disguised in this manner to see how Morgan treated strangers, but he never suspected they were other than they appeared. "Good sir," said one of the travellers, "we are worn and tired, but all we seek is a bite of food to put in our wallets, and then we will go on our way."

"Brensiach," said Morgan, "is that all you want? Welt, there, look you, is the loaf and the cheese, and the knife lies by them, and you cut what you like. Eat your heartiest and fill your wallets, for never shall it be said that Morgan ap Rhys denied bread and cheese to strangers that came into his house." The travellers proceeded to help themselves, and Morgan, determined not to fail in hospitality, sang to them while they ate, moistening his throat occasionally with Llangollen ale when it became dry.

The fairy travellers, after they had availed themselves sufficiently, got up to go and said, "Good sir, we thank you for our entertainment. Since you have been so generous we will show that we are grateful. It is in our power to grant you any one wish you may have: tell us what that wish may be."

"Well, indeed," said Morgan, "the wish of my heart is to have a harp that will play under my fingers, no matter how ill I strike it: a harp that will play lively tunes, look you – no melancholy music for me. But surely it's making fun of me you are."

But that was not the case: he had hardly finished speaking when, to his astonishment, there on the hearth before him stood a splendid harp. He looked round and found his guests had vanished. "That's the most extraordinary thing I have ever seen in my life," said Morgan, "they must have been fairies," and he was so flabbergasted that he felt constrained to drink some more ale. This allayed to some extent his bewilderment, and he proceeded to try the instrument he had been so mysteriously presented with. As soon as his fingers touched the strings, the harp began to play a mad and capering tune. Just then there was a sound of footsteps, and in came his wife with some friends. No sooner did they hear the strains of the harp than they began dancing, and as long as Morgan's fingers were on the strings, they kept footing it like mad creatures.

The news that Morgan had come into possession of a harp with some mysterious power spread like wildfire over the whole country, and many were the visitors who came to see him and it. Every time he played it everyone felt irresistibly impelled to dance, and could not leave off until Morgan stopped. Even lame people capered away, and a one-legged man who visited him danced as merrily as any biped.

One day, among the company who had come to see if the stories about the harp were true, was the bard who had made such unpleasant remarks about Morgan's singing. Morgan determined to pay him out, and instead of stopping as usual after the dance had been going on for a few minutes, he kept on playing. He played on and on until the dancers were exhausted and shouted to him to stop. But Morgan was finding the scene much too amusing to want to stop. He laughed until his sides ached and the tears rolled down his cheeks at the antics of his visitors, and especially at those of the bard. The longer he played the madder became the dance: the dancers spun round and round, wildly knocking over the furniture, and some of them bounded up against the roof of the cottage till their heads cracked again. Morgan did not stop until the bard had broken his legs and the rest had been jolted almost to pieces. By that time his revenge was satisfied, and his sides and jaws were so tired with laughing that he had to take his fingers away from the strings.

But this was the last time he was to have the chance of venting his spite on his enemies. By next morning the harp had disappeared, and was never seen again. The fairies, evidently displeased with the evil use to which their gift had been put, must have taken it away in the night. And this is a warning to all who abuse the gifts of the fairies.

GUTO BACH AND THE FAIRIES

Gruffydd was the name given at baptism to a little boy who once lived at Llangybi, but everyone called him Guto Bach. One day, after he had been up to the mountain to see his father's sheep, he brought home a number of pieces, the size of crowns, with letters stamped on them and resembling real crown pieces exactly, only that they were made of white paper instead of silver. His mother asked him where he had got them. "I played with some little children on the mountain," said little Guto, "and they gave them to me." "Whose children?" asked the mother. "I don't know," he replied; "they are very nice children, much nicer than I am." But his mother knew they were fairies, and told him he must never go on the mountain again by himself, because no good ever came of playing with strange children.

But Guto was longing to have another game with the little children. One day he disobeyed his mother and slipped away to the mountain. He did not come back, and though every search was made for him, no trace of Guto Bach could be found anywhere. Two years after, however, what should his mother see on opening the door in the morning but little Guto sitting on the threshold with a bundle under his arm. He was the very same size and dressed in the same little clothes as on the day of his disappearance, and he did not look a day older. "My child," said the astonished and delighted mother, "where have you been this long, long while?" "Mother," said Guto, "I have not been long away; it was only yesterday that I went to play with the little children. Look what pretty clothes they have given me." The mother opened the bundle; it contained a dress of very white paper without seam or sewing. As it had been given to him by the fairies she burnt it, and Guto's long disappearance made her more sure that no good could come of playing with strange children.

But she was wrong all the same. Guto Bach's friendship with the little children, as he still thought they were, proved to be very advantageous. Shortly after his reappearance his father and mother suffered a very great loss. They had invested all their savings and all the money they could raise in a ship sailing from Pwllheli, which had been making very profitable voyages and bringing great wealth to those who had shares in her. The vessel went down in a storm, and ruin stared Guto's parents in the face. Now there was on Pentyrch, the hill above Llangybi, a great rock under which there was said to be a great treasure of gold hidden. Many men had tried to move the rocks but had failed because they were undeserving. Guto's father determined to make another effort to dislodge the stone, in the hope that the treasure underneath it would recoup his losses. His neighbours sympathized with him, and brought all the horses of the parish to help him. But the rock was so heavy and fixed so fast in the ground that the combined efforts of all the men and horses of Llangybi were unavailing. Guto's father's hopes had been high: whatever the others might have been who had attempted to reach the treasure, he at least, he thought, was deserving. The disappointment, therefore, was all the harder to bear.

Seeing his parents' grief, Guto remembered that the little children with whom he had played had plenty of gold and silver, and he made up his mind to ask them to help his father and mother in their distress. He went again to the mountain and found the little children playing as before. He told them his trouble, and asked them whether they could spare him some of their money. "No," they said, "there is plenty of gold and silver waiting for you under the rock on Pentyrch." "But," remonstrated little Guto, "it would not budge for all the men and horses of Llangybi." "We are aware of that," said the little children, "but do you try to move it and see what will happen."

Guto went home and told his parents what the little children had said to him. They laughed at the idea that little Guto would succeed where the full strength of Llangybi parish had failed. But they were in such a desperate plight that they allowed Guto to do as the fairies had directed. They took him to the rock. He put his little hand on it, and the great mass trembled. He gave it a shove, and the huge stone crashed down the hill. Underneath it there was found enough gold and silver not only to replace all their losses, but to make Guto and his parents the richest people in Carnarvonshire.

THE FAIRY WALKING STICK

A farmer was rounding up his sheep in Cwmllan when he heard the sound of weeping. As a general rule, only human beings weep noisily, and as the farmer had not observed any human beings in the vicinity he was considerably surprised. He went in the direction from which the sound came. For some time he could not discover who was causing it, but after a bit he saw a wee little lass lying on a narrow ledge of rock on the face of a great precipice, and sobbing as if her heart would break. He went to her rescue, and with great difficulty extricated her from her dangerous position. No sooner had he brought her to safety than a little old man appeared. "I thank thee," said he, "for thy kindness to my daughter. Accept this in remembrance of thy good deed," handing a walking-stick to the farmer. The farmer took it, and the moment it was in his hand both the wee lass and the little old man disappeared from his sight.

The year after this every sheep in the farmer's possession had two ewe-lambs, and this continued for many years. His flocks during all this time were singularly free from accident and disease. Sheep-stealers were always frustrated in their evil designs upon them: birds of prey never ventured near them to pick out the eyes of the young lambs: even when a murrain devastated other flocks, these were untainted: when they were buried under snow-drifts in winter, and had to be dug out, they seemed better rather than worse for their experiences: and their wool was finer and more plentiful than that of any other sheep in the country. The farmer became rich, and all envied him.

One night, shortly after the sheep had been brought down from the mountains for the winter, the farmer went to a village some distance away to match his blue gamecock against a black fighter which was carrying all before it. It was late before the farmer started home, and a great storm arose. The wind howled, and the rain came down in sheets, and a horror of great darkness fell upon the land. On his way home the farmer had to cross a stream on some stepping stones. When he came to it the river was swollen, and sweeping all before it in a swift current. As he was feeling for the stones with the walking stick given him by the little old man, it somehow or other slipped from his hand and was swept away by the raging torrent, and he had a narrow escape of being carried away himself.

He reached home, and as soon as day came went out to search for the stick, and at the same time to see what damage had been done by the flood. He found that nearly all his sheep had been swept away by it. His wealth had gone as it came – with the walking stick.

DICK THE FIDDLER'S MONEY

Dick the Fiddler used to spend on drink all the money he earned by playing at merrymakings, weddings and fairs. After a week's fuddle at Darowen he was one night wending his way home to his wife and children. He had to go through Fairy Green Lane, just above the farm-stead of Cefn Cloddiau, and when he came to it he felt nervous. To banish fear he tuned his beloved instrument, and as he walked along he played his favourite air, "The Crow's Black Wing". When he passed the greensward where the fairies used to revel he felt his fiddle suddenly becoming very heavy, and he heard a rattling and a tinkling inside it. This continued until he reached Llwybr Scriw Riw, his home. When he entered the cottage he had to listen to harsher music than he was wont to extract from his fiddle, to wit, the angry voice of his wife, who, justly angered at his absence, began to lecture and scold him. He was called names which he richly deserved: idler, fool, drunken sot, and so forth. "How is it possible," asked his wife, "for me to beg enough for myself and half a houseful of children nearly naked, while you go about the country spending on drink the little money you earn? The landlord came here this morning, and said that if you do not pay him the rent which has long been overdue he will turn us all out, and what are we to do then? I am sure you have spent all your earnings as usual on beer, and that you haven't got a ha'penny in your pocket." "Hush, hush, my good woman," said Dick, "see what's in my old fiddle." She obeyed, shook it, and out tumbled a number of bright new five-shilling pieces, more than enough to pay the rent. She promptly put the money away in a safe place, and asked him how he had come into possession of it, and he told her.

The following day he went to Llanidloes to pay his rent. His landlord was more than surprised to find that Dick had come, not to beg for mercy, as he had done several times before, but to discharge his debt. He gave him a receipt, and thirsty Dick betook himself to the "Unicorn" to sample Betty Brunt's ale before returning home. He had not consumed more than a trifle of half-a-dozen glasses when in came his landlord in a state of great excitement. "Where did you get the money you gave me?" he asked. "Why, what's the matter with it?" asked Dick. "It has turned into cockleshells," said the landlord. "Well, it was all right when I gave it you, and here is the receipt," said Dick, flourishing the document triumphantly. "Somebody must have bewitched the coins." He vouchsafed no further explanation, and even when he was gloriously drunk, as he finished up the evening by becoming, no one was able to pump any information out of him as to the origin of the money he had given the landlord.

FAIRY OINTMENT

The old couple who lived at the Garth Dorwen went to Carnarvon to hire a servant maid at the Allhallows' Fair. They went to the spot where the young men and women who wanted places were accustomed to station themselves, and saw a lass with golden hair, standing a little apart from all the others. They asked her if she wanted a place: she replied that she did, and she hired herself at once and came to her place at the time fixed. Her name, she said, was Eilian.

In those days it was customary to spin after supper during the long winter months. Now Eilian, on nights when the moon was shining, would take her wheel down to the meadow, and the Fair Family used to come to help her. On these occasions an enormous amount of spinning was done, and great was the joy of the old couple at having secured such a maid-servant.

But their fortune was too good to last: in the spring when the days grew long Eilian disappeared. Everyone thought that she had gone with the Fair Family, and for once everyone was right. Now this is how it was found out for certain that Eilian was with the fairies. The old woman of Garth Dorwen was by way of being a nurse, and some time after Eilian's disappearance, on a night when the moon was full and there was a little rain falling through a thin mist, a gentleman on horseback came to fetch her. So she rode off behind the stranger on his horse and came to Rhos y Cowrt. The two dismounted and entered a great cave, and through a door at the far end of it passed into a bed-chamber, where a lady lay in her bed: it was the finest place the old woman had ever seen in her life.

The old woman saw and heard nobody there but the gentleman who had fetched her, the mother and the baby. This was curious, because she found dainty food prepared for the mother, and everything she wanted was procured by some invisible power. The mystery was not solved until one morning the husband gave her a bottle of ointment to anoint the baby's eyes with. "Take care," he said, "that you do not touch your own eyes with it, or evil will befall you." The old woman promised to be careful, but somehow or other, after putting the bottle by, her left eye began to itch, and without thinking what she was doing she rubbed it with the same finger that she had used for the baby's eyes. And now a strange thing happened: with the right eye she saw everything as before, gorgeous and luxurious as the heart could wish, but with the left eye she saw a damp, miserable cave, and lying on some rushes and withered ferns, with big stones all round her, was her former servant girl, Eilian. In the course of the day she saw a great deal more. There were small men and small women going in and out, their movements being as light as the morning breeze. They prepared dainties with the utmost skill and rapidity, and served Eilian with a kindness and affection that was truly remarkable.

In the evening the old woman said, "You have had a great many visitors today, Eilian."

"Yes," was the reply, "but how do you know me?" Then the old woman explained that she had accidentally rubbed her left eye with the baby's ointment.

"Take care that my husband does not find out that you recognise me," said Eilian, and she told the old woman her story. She had been helped with her spinning by the fairies on condition that she married one of them. "I never meant to carry out the agreement," she added, "and I used to draw a knife whenever they pestered me too much about it on the meadow. That made them vanish immediately. And for fear they should carry me off when I was asleep, I placed a long stick of mountain ash regularly across my bed, for no fairy dare touch or cross a branch of the rowan tree. That kept me safe so long that I grew careless, and the day we sheared the sheep I was so tired that I forgot to protect my bed. That very night I was whisked off to Fairyland."

The old woman was very cautious after Eilian's warning, and gave the fairy husband no inkling that her left eye had any different power of vision from the right. Her time came to an end without mishap, and she was taken home on horseback just as she had come, and she was given a fine sum of money for her services.

Some time after the old woman was late in getting to market. When she arrived a friend said to her, "The fairies must be here today; the noise is swelling and prices are rising." Sure enough the fairies were there, but they were invisible to all eyes except the old woman's left eye. She saw Eilian's husband stealing something from a stall close by her: she went up to him and, forgetting the warning, said, "Good morning, master, how is Eilian?" "She is quite well," replied the fairy, "but with what eye do you see me?" "With this," said the old woman, pointing to her left. The fairy immediately put out her eye with a bulrush, and her right eye had to do the work of two all the rest of her life.

EINION AND THE FAIR FAMILY

Once on a time a shepherd went up a mountain to look after his sheep. A thick mist came on, and he lost his way, and walked backwards and forwards for many a long hour. At last he got into a low rushy place, where he saw before him many circular rings. He knew at once that they were the circles in which the Fair Family danced, and remembering how many a shepherd who had chanced on these rings had disappeared from mortal eyes, he determined to run away as fast as he could. As he was racing off he was met by an old fat little man. "Stop," said the old man, and there was something in this voice which made Einion (that was the shepherd's name) obey. "What art thou doing?" "I am running home," said the shepherd. "Come after me," said the old man, "and do not utter a word until I bid thee." The shepherd could not choose but obey, and he followed his guide on and on until they came to an oval stone. The old man tapped the stone three times with his walking stick, and the stone rose of its own accord, disclosing a narrow passage leading into the earth. "Follow me fearlessly," said the fat man; "no harm will be done thee." On the youth went, as reluctantly as a dog to be hanged. It was dark in the passage, though a sort of whitish light radiated from the stones which formed the roof: at last the tunnel opened into a fine wooded fertile country. Birds sang in the groves, and streams of clear water, flowing through meadows carpeted with bright flowers, made music as sweet as that of the feathered tribe. Dotting the landscape were splendid mansions, and into one of these Einion was led by the little man. Both sat down to eat at a table of silver: golden dishes containing the most delicious meats and golden goblets full of exquisite wine came to their places of themselves and disappeared of themselves when done with. This puzzled the shepherd beyond measure: moreover, he heard people talking together around him, but for the life of him he could see no one but his aged friend. At length the fat man said to him, "Thou canst now talk as much as it may please thee." Einion tried to speak, but he found that his tongue would no more stir than if it had been a lump of ice. Three beautiful maidens came in: they looked archly at him and began to talk to him, but still his tongue would not wag. Then one of the maidens came to him, and playing with his fair curling hair, gave him a kiss on his ruddy lips. This loosened the string that bound his tongue, and Einion began to talk freely, and he had much to say, especially to the maiden who had kissed him.

He remained a year and a day with the little man and his daughters without knowing that he had passed more than a day among them, for he was so happy. But by-and-by he began to feel somewhat of a longing to visit his old home, and he asked his fat host if he might go. "Stay a little yet," said he, "and thou shalt go for a while." He asked a second time after some while, and was again refused permission. Mererid (that was what the damsel who kissed him was called) looked very sad when he talked of going away; nor was he himself without feeling a sort of a cold thrill passing through him at the thought of leaving her. The longing for home, however, would not leave him, and he asked a third time to be allowed to go to earth. This time, on condition that he returned on the first night of the new moon, he obtained leave to go.

Everyone was delighted to see him, for it was thought that he had been killed. Another shepherd had been suspected of murdering him, and had been compelled to run away to Merthyr Tydfil (that was where all persons fled to at that time when they wished to avoid punishment) lest he should be hanged. Einion would not tell anyone where he had been, and on the appointed night he went back to Fairyland. Mererid was rejoiced at his return, and before long the twain were wedded, and lived very happily. Einion, however, could not rest contented with his life in Fairyland, and entreated the old man for leave to take his wife with him and dwell on earth. At last the old man consented and gave him much silver and gold, and many precious gems to take with him. So Einion and his bride set out on two ponies whiter than snow and arrived at his old home. With the treasure which they had brought with them they acquired an immense estate, and no couple in the country were more honoured than they. But it was not long before people began to inquire about the pedigree of Einion's wife, and as he would not tell them who she was, they came to the conclusion that she was one of the Fair Family. "Certainly," said Einion, when asked whether this were so, "there can be no doubt that she comes from a very fair family:

for she has two sisters who are almost as fair as she is, and if you saw them together, you would admit that this name is a most fitting one."

ST COLLEN AND THE KING OF FAERY

St Collen was so distressed with the wickedness of the people that he withdrew to a mountain and made himself a cell under the shelter of a rock in a remote and secluded spot.

One day when he was in his cell he heard two men conversing about Gwyn ab Nudd, and saying that he was King of Annwn and of the fairies. Collen put his head out of the cell and said to them, "Hold your tongues quickly, those are but Devils." "Hold thou thy tongue," said they, "thou shalt receive a reproof from him." And Collen shut his cell as before. Soon after he heard a knocking at the door of his cell, and someone inquired if he were within. Then said Collen: "I am. Who is it that asks?" "It is I, a messenger from Gwyn ab Nudd, King of Annwn and of the fairies, to command thee to go and speak with him on the top of the hill at noon."

But Collen did not go. And the next day, behold, the same messenger came, ordering Collen to go and speak with the King on the top of the hill at noon.

But Collen did not go. And the third day behold the same messenger came, ordering Collen to go and speak with the King on the top of the hill at noon. "And if thou dost not go, Collen, thou wilt be the worse for it."

Then Collen, being afraid, arose and prepared some holy water, and put it in a flask at his side and went to the top of the hill. And when he came there he saw the fairest castle he had ever beheld, and around it the best-appointed troops, and numbers of minstrels, and every kind of music of voice and instrument, and steeds with youths upon them the comeliest in the world, and maidens of elegant aspect, sprightly, light of foot, of graceful apparel and in the bloom of youth: and every magnificence becoming the court of a great king. A courteous man on the top of the castle bade him enter, saying that the King was waiting for him to come to meat. Collen went into the castle, and when he entered the King was sitting in a golden chair. He welcomed Collen honourably, and desired him to eat, assuring him that besides what he saw he should have the most luxurious of every dainty and delicacy that the mind could desire, and should be supplied with every drink and liquor that his heart could wish: and that there should be in readiness for him every luxury of courtesy and service, of banquet and of honourable entertainment, of rank and of presents: and every respect and welcome due to a man of wisdom. "I will not eat," said Collen.

"Didst thou ever see men of better equipment than those in red and blue?" asked the King.

"Their equipment is good enough," said Collen, "for such equipment as it is."

"What kind of equipment is that?" said the King. Then said Collen: "The red on the one part signifies burning, and the blue on the other signifies coldness." With that Collen drew out his flask, and threw the holy water on their heads, whereupon they vanished from his sight, so that there was neither castle, nor troops, nor men, nor maidens, nor music, nor song, nor steeds, nor youths, nor banquet, nor the appearance of anything whatever but the green hillock.

THE FAIRY REWARD

Ianto Llywelyn lived by himself in a cottage at Llanfihangel. One night after he had gone to bed he heard a noise outside the door of the house. He opened his window and said, "Who is there? And what do you want?" He was answered by a small silvery voice, "It is room we want to dress our children." Ianto went down and opened the door: a dozen small beings entered carrying tiny babies in their arms, and began to search for an earthen pitcher with water; they remained in the cottage for some hours, washing the infants and adorning themselves. Just before the cock crew in the morning they went away, leaving some money on the hearth as a reward for the kindness they had received.

After this lanto used to keep his fire of coal balls burning all night long, leaving a vessel of water on the hearth, and bread with its accompaniments on the table, taking care, also, to remove everything made of iron before going to bed. The fairies often visited his cottage at night, and after each visit he found money left for him on the hearth. lanto gave up working, and lived very comfortably on the money which he received in return for his hospitality from the Fair Family. His income from this source was more than enough to keep himself in comfort, so lanto married a wife.

Betsi – that was the name of her whom lanto thus honoured – did not bother about the way in which he got his money before she married him, but after the knot had been tied she became very curious. lanto refused to tell her, and this of course made her more inquisitive than ever. "I don't believe you get it honestly," she said. lanto denied by wood, field and mountain that there was anything dishonest about his means of livelihood. She gave him no peace, however. "Nine shames on you," she said, "for having a bad secret from your own dear wife." "But," remonstrated Ianto, "if I tell you, Betsi *bach*, I'll never get any more money." "Ah," she said (she had already had her doubts about Ianto's nightly preparations of fire and hot water), "then it's the fairies." "Drato," said he, "yes, the fairies it is." With that he thrust his hands down in his breeches pocket in a sullen manner and left the house. He had seven shillings in his pockets up to that minute. When he went feeling for them, thinking that a glass of beer and a pipe of tobacco at the inn would not be amiss after such a matrimonial squabble, he found they were gone. In place of them were some pieces of paper, no good even to light his pipe. From that day the fairies brought him no more money, and he had once more to eat his bread in the sweat of his face, which is a more scriptural but less pleasant method of earning a living than gathering up fairy money.

THE SUPERNATURAL

Reader, beware! Here lurk some of Wales's most terrifying spirits. From shapeshifting spectres to phantom balls of fire, disembodied voices to the devil himself, many of Wales's unique ghostly motifs can be found within these pages.

In Wales, the folkloric figure of the devil shares many of the same attributes as it does in the rest of Britain. Often regarded as a somewhat laughable and dimwitted character (as exemplified by William Jenkyn Thomas's retelling of 'The Devil's Bridge' or Elias Owen's 'Satan Outwitted'), many of these tales also serve as warnings to those who would risk punishment for their sins, such as breaking the Sabbath or being a drunkard.

Similarly, the wraiths and ghouls that haunt the Welsh landscape often serve their own folkloric purpose – a warning never to leave the safety of the path, to steer clear of bodies of water, a warning against the consequences of misdeeds in life, and a grim reminder that death is only a corpse candle away…

UNTITLED, FROM CROKER'S FAIRY LEGENDS OF IRELAND

"**Cwm Pwcca, or** the Pwcca's Valley, forms part of the deep and romantic glen of the Clydach, which, before the establishment of the iron works of Messrs. Frere and Powell, was one of the most secluded spots in Wales, and therefore well calculated for the haunt of goblins and fairies; but the bustle of a manufactory has now in a great measure scared these beings away, and of late it is very rarely that any of its former inhabitants, the Pwccas, are seen. Such, however, is their attachment to their ancient haunt, that they have not entirely deserted it, as there was lately living near this valley a man who used to assert that he had seen one, and had a narrow escape of losing his life through the maliciousness of the goblin. As he was one night returning home over the mountain from his work, he perceived at some distance before him a light, which seemed to proceed from a candle in a lantern, and upon looking more attentively, he saw what he took to be a human figure carrying it, which he concluded to be one of his neighbours likewise returning from his work. As he perceived that the figure was going the same way with himself, he quickened his pace in order that he might overtake him, and have the benefit of his light to descend the steep and rocky path which led into the valley; but he rather wondered that such a short person as appeared to carry the lantern should be able to walk so fast. However, he redoubled his exertions, determined to come up with him, and although he had some misgivings that he was not going along the usual track, yet he thought that the man with the lantern must know better than himself, and he followed the direction taken by him without further hesitation. Having, by dint of hard walking, overtaken him, he suddenly found himself on the brink of one of the tremendous precipices of Cwm Pwcca, down which another step would have carried him headlong into the roaring torrent beneath. And, to complete his consternation, at the very instant he stopped, the little fellow with the lantern made a spring right across the glen to the opposite side, and there, holding up the light above his head, turned round and uttered with all his might a loud and most malicious laugh, upon which he blew out his candle, and disappeared up the opposite hill."

SATAN PLAYING CARDS

A man was returning home late one night from a friend's house, where he had spent the evening in card playing, and as he was walking along he was joined by a gentleman, whose conversation was very interesting. At last they commenced talking about card playing, and the stranger invited the countryman to try his skill with him, but as it was late, and the man wanted to go home, he declined, but when they were on the bridge his companion again pressed him to have a game on the parapet, and proceeded to take out of his pocket a pack of cards, and at once commenced dealing them out; consequently, the man could not now refuse to comply with the request. With varying success game after game was played, but ultimately the stranger proved himself the more skilful player. Just at this juncture a card fell into the water; and in their excitement both players looked over the bridge after it, and the countryman saw to his horror that his opponent's head, reflected in the water, had on it *two horns*. He immediately turned round to have a careful look at his companion; he, however, did not see him, but in his place was a *ball of fire*, which flashed away from his sight.

SATAN APPEARING IN MANY FORMS TO A MAN WHO TRAVELLED ON SUNDAY

William Davies, Penrhiw, near Aberystwyth, went to England for the harvest, and after having worked there about three weeks, he returned home alone, with all possible haste, as he knew that his father-in-law's fields were by this time ripe for the sickle. He, however, failed to accomplish the journey before Sunday; but he determined to travel on Sunday, and thus reach home on Sunday night to be ready to commence reaping on Monday morning. His conscience, though, would not allow him to be at rest, but he endeavoured to silence its twittings by saying to himself that he had with him no clothes to go to a place of worship. He stealthily, therefore, walked on, feeling very guilty every step he took, and dreading to meet anyone going to chapel or church. By Sunday evening he had reached the hill overlooking Llanfihangel Creuddyn, where he was known, so he determined not to enter the village until after the people had gone to their respective places of worship; he therefore sat down on the hillside and contemplated the scene below. He saw the people leave their houses for the house of God, he heard their songs of praise, and now he thinks he could venture to descend and pass through the village unobserved. Luckily no one saw him going through the village, and now he has entered a barley field, and although still uneasy in mind, he feels somewhat reassured, and steps on quickly. He had not proceeded far in the barley field before he found himself surrounded by a large number of small pigs. He was not much struck by this, though he thought it strange that so many pigs should be allowed to wander about on the Sabbath day. The pigs, however, came up to him, stared at him, grunted, and scampered away. Before he had traversed the barley field he saw approaching him an innumerable number of mice, and these, too, surrounded him, only, however, to stare at him, and then to disappear. By this Davies began to be frightened, and he was almost sorry that he had broken the Sabbath day by travelling with his pack on his back instead of keeping the day holy. He was not now very far from home, and this thought gave him courage and on he went. He had not proceeded any great distance from the spot where the mice had appeared when he saw a large greyhound walking before him on the pathway. He anxiously watched the dog, but suddenly it vanished out of his sight. By this the poor man was thoroughly frightened, and many and truly sincere were his regrets that he had broken the Sabbath; but on he went. He passed through the village of Llanilar without any further fright. He had now gone about three miles from Llanfihangel along the road that goes to Aberystwyth, and he had begun to dispel the fear that had seized him, but to his horror he saw something approach him that made his hair stand on end. He could not at first make it out, but he soon clearly saw that it was a horse that was madly dashing towards him. He had only just time to step on to the ditch, when, horrible to relate, a headless white horse rushed past him. His limbs shook and the perspiration stood out like beads on his forehead. This terrible spectre he saw when close to Tan'rallt, but he dared not turn into the house, as he was travelling on Sunday, so on he went again, and heartily did he wish himself at home. In fear and dread he proceeded on his journey towards Penrhiw. The most direct way from Tan'rallt to Penrhiw was a pathway through the fields, and Davies took this pathway, and now he was in sight of his home, and he hastened towards the boundary fence between Tan'rallt and Penrhiw. He knew that there was a gap in the hedge that he could get through, and for this gap he aimed; he reached it, but further progress was impossible, for in the gap was a lady lying at full length, and immovable, and stopping up the gap entirely. Poor Davies was now more thoroughly terrified than ever. He sprang aside, he screamed, and then he fainted right away. As soon as he recovered consciousness, he, on his knees, and in a loud supplicating voice, prayed for pardon. His mother and father-in-law heard him, and the mother knew the voice and said, "It is my Will; some mishap has overtaken him." They went to him and found he was so weak that he could not move, and they were obliged to carry him home, where he recounted to them his marvellous experience.

SATAN OUTWITTED

There is an incredible tradition connected with this place Ffinant, Trefeglwys. It is said that an old barn stands on the right hand side of the highway. One Sunday morning, as the master was starting to Church, he told one of the servants to keep the crows from a field that had been sown with wheat, in which field the old barn stood. The servant, through some means, collected all the crows into the barn, and shut the door on them. He then followed his master to the Church, who, when he saw the servant there, began to reprove him sharply. But the master, when he heard the strange news, turned his steps homewards, and found to his amazement that the tale was true, and it is said that the barn was filled with crows.

This barn, ever afterwards was called *Crow-barn*, a name it still retains.

It is said that the servant's name was Dafydd Hiraddug, and that he had sold himself to the devil, and that consequently, he was able to perform feats, which in this age are considered incredible. However, it is said that Dafydd was on this occasion more subtle than the old serpent, even according to the agreement which was between them. The contract was that the devil was to have complete possession of Dafydd if his corpse were taken over the side of the bed, or through a door, or if buried in a churchyard, or inside a church. Dafydd had commanded that on his death, the liver and lights were to be taken out of his body and thrown on the dunghill, and notice was to be taken whether a raven or a dove got possession of them; if a raven, then his body was to be taken away by the foot, and not by the side of the bed, and through the wall, and not through the door, and he was to be buried, not in the churchyard nor in the Church but under the Church walls. And the devil, when he saw that by these arrangements he had been duped cried, saying: –

Dafydd Hiraddug, badly bred,
False when living, and false when dead.

THE EJECTMENT OF THE EVIL SPIRIT FROM LLANFOR CHURCH

Llanfor Spirit troubled the neighbourhood of Bala, but he was particularly objectionable and annoying to the inhabitants of Llanfor, for he had taken possession of their Church. At last, the people were determined to get rid of him altogether, but they must procure a mare for this purpose, which they did. A man riding on the mare entered the Church with a friend, to exorcise the Spirit. Ere long this man emerged from the Church with the Devil seated behind him on the pillion. An old woman who saw them cried out, "Duw anwyl! Mochyn yn yr Eglwys" – "Good God! A pig in the Church." On hearing these words the pig became exceedingly fierce, because the silence had been broken, and because God's name had been used, and in his anger he snatched up both the man and the mare, and threw them right over the Church to the other side, and there is a mark to this day on a gravestone of the horse's hoof on the spot where she lit. But the Spirit's anger was all in vain, for he was carried by the mare to the river, and laid in *Llyn-y-Geulan-Goch*, but so much did the poor animal perspire whilst carrying him that, although the distance was only a quarter of a mile, she lost all her hair.

SATAN SEEN LYING RIGHT ACROSS A ROAD

The story related to me was as follows: – Near Pentrevoelas lived a man called John Ty'nllidiart, who was in the habit of taking, yearly, cattle from the uplands in his neighbourhood, to be wintered in the Vale of Clwyd. Once, whilst thus engaged, he saw lying across the road right in front of him and the cattle, and completely blocking up the way, Satan with his head on one wall and his tail on the other, moaning horribly. John, as might be expected, hurried homewards, leaving his charge to take their chance with the Evil One, but long before he came to his house, the odour of brimstone had preceded him, and his wife was only too glad to find that it was her husband that came through the door, for she thought that it was someone else that was approaching.

A MAN CARRIED AWAY BY THE EVIL ONE

W. E., of Ll— M—, was a very bad man; he was a brawler, a fighter, a drunkard. He is said to have spat in the parson's face, and to have struck him, and beaten the parish clerk who interfered. It was believed that he had sold himself to work evil, and many foul deeds he committed, and, what was worse, he gloried in them.

People thought that his end would be a shocking one, and they were not disappointed. One night this reprobate and stubborn character did not return home. The next day a search was made for him, and his dead body was found on the brink of the river. Upon inspecting the ground, it became evident that the deceased had had a desperate struggle with an unknown antagonist, and the battle had commenced some distance above the *ceunant*, or *dingle*, where the body was discovered. It was there seen that the man had planted his heels deep into the ground, as if to resist a superior force, intent upon dragging him down to the river. There were indications that he had lost his footing; but a few yards lower down it was observed that his feet had ploughed the ground, and every step taken from this spot was traceable all down the declivity to the bottom of the ravine, and every yard gave proof that a desperate and prolonged struggle had taken place along the whole course. In one place an oak tree intercepted the way, and it was seen that a bough had its bark peeled off, and evidently the wretched man had taken hold of this bough and did not let go until the bark came off in his hands, for in death he still clutched the bark. The last and most severe struggle took place close to the river, and here the body was dragged underneath the roots of a tree, through a hole not big enough for a child to creep through, and this ended the fight.

Mr Jones stated that what was most remarkable and ominous in connection with this foul work was the fact that, although footprints were seen in the ground, they were all those of the miserable man, for there were no other marks visible. From this fact and the previous evil life of this wretched creature, the people in those parts believed that the fearful struggle had taken place between W. E. and the Evil One, and that he had not been murdered by any man, but that he was taken away by Satan.

SATAN APPEARING TO A YOUNG MAN

A **young man, who** had left Pentrevoelas to live in a farm house called Hafod Elwy, had to go over the hills to Denbigh on business. He started very early, before the cock crew, and as it was winter, his journey over the bleak moorlands was dismal and dreary. When he had proceeded several miles on his journey an unaccountable dread crept over him. He tried to dispel his fear by whistling and by knocking the ground with his walking stick, but all in vain. He stopped, and thought of returning home, but this he could not do, for he was more afraid of the ridicule of his friends than of his own fear, and therefore he proceeded on his journey and reached Pont Brenig, where he stopped awhile, and listened, thinking he might see or hear someone approaching. To his horror, he observed, through the glimmering light of the coming day, a tall gentleman approaching, and by a great exertion he mastered his feelings so far as to enable him to walk towards the stranger, but when within a few yards of him he stood still, for from fright he could not move. He noticed that the gentleman wore grey clothes, and breeches fastened with yellow buckles, on his coat were two rows of buttons like gold, his shoes were low, with bright clasps to them. Strange to say, this gentleman did not pass the terrified man, but stepped into the bog and disappeared from view.

THE GLODDAETH GHOST

I may say that Gloddaeth Wood is a remnant of the primaeval forest that is mentioned by Sir John Wynn, in his *History of the Gwydir Family*, as extending over a large tract of the country. This wood, being undisturbed and in its original wild condition, was the home of foxes and other vermin, for whose destruction the surrounding parishes willingly paid half-a-crown per head. This reward was an inducement to men who had leisure, to trap and hunt these obnoxious animals. Thomas Davies was engaged in this work, and, taking a walk through the wood one day for the purpose of discovering traces of foxes, he came upon a fox's den, and from the marks about the burrow he ascertained that there were young foxes in the hole. This was to him a grand discovery, for, in anticipation, cubs and vixen were already his. Looking about him, he noticed that there was opposite the fox's den a large oak tree with forked branches, and this sight settled his plan of operation. He saw that he could place himself in this tree in such a position that he could see the vixen leave, and return to her den, and, from his knowledge of the habits of the animal, he knew she would commence foraging when darkness and stillness prevailed. He therefore determined to commence the campaign forthwith, and so he went home to make his preparations.

I should say that the sea was close to the wood, and that small craft often came to grief on the coast. I will now proceed with the story.

Davies had taken his seat on a bough opposite the fox's den, when he heard a horrible scream in the direction of the sea, which apparently was that of a man in distress, and the sound uttered was, "Oh, Oh." Thus Davies's attention was divided between the dismal, "Oh" and his fox. But, as the sound was a far way off, he felt disinclined to heed it, for he did not think it incumbent on him to ascertain the cause of that distressing utterance, nor did he think it his duty to go to the relief of a suffering fellow creature. He therefore did not leave his seat on the tree. But the cry of anguish, every now and again, reached his ears, and evidently, it was approaching the tree on which Davies sat. He now listened the more to the awful sounds, which at intervals reverberated through the wood, and he could no longer be mistaken – they were coming in his direction. Nearer and nearer came the dismal "Oh! Oh!" and with its approach, the night became pitch dark, and now the "Oh! Oh! Oh!" was only a few yards off, but nothing could be seen in consequence of the deep darkness. The sounds, however, ceased, but a horrible sight was presented to the frightened man's view. There he saw before him a nude being with eyes burning like fire, and these glittering balls were directed towards him. The awful being was only a dozen yards or so off. And now it crouched, and now it stood erect, but it never for a single instant withdrew its terrible eyes from the miserable man in the tree, who would have fallen to the ground were it not for the protecting boughs. Many times Davies thought that his last moment had come, for it seemed that the owner of those fiery eyes was about to spring upon him. As he did not do so, Davies somewhat regained his self possession, and thought of firing at the horrible being; but his courage failed, and there he sat motionless, not knowing what the end might be. He closed his eyes to avoid that gaze, which seemed to burn into him, but this was a short relief, for he felt constrained to look into those burning orbs; still it was a relief even to close his eyes: and so again and again he closed them, only, however, to open them on those balls of fire. About 4 o'clock in the morning, he heard a cock crow at Penbryn farm, and at the moment his eyes were closed, but at the welcome sound he opened them, and looked for those balls of fire, but, oh! what pleasure, they were no longer before him, for, at the crowing of the cock, they, and the being to whom they belonged, had disappeared.

FFRITH FARM GHOST

It was not known why Ffrith farm was troubled by a Ghost; but when the servants were busily engaged in cheese-making the Spirit would suddenly throw mortar, or filthy matter, into the milk, and thus spoil the curds. The dairy was visited by the Ghost, and there he played havoc with the milk and dishes. He sent the pans, one after the other, around the room, and dashed them to pieces. The terrible doings of the Ghost was a topic of general conversation in those parts. The farmer offered a reward of five pounds to anyone who would lay the Spirit. One Sunday afternoon, about 2 o'clock, an aged priest visited the farm yard, and in the presence of a crowd of spectators exorcised the Ghost, but without effect. In fact, the Ghost waved a woman's bonnet right in the face of the priest. The farmer then sent for Griffiths, an independent minister at Llanarmon, who enticed the Ghost to the barn. Here the Ghost appeared in the form of a lion, but he could not touch Griffiths, because he stood in the centre of a circle, which the lion could not pass over. Griffiths persuaded the Ghost to appear in a less formidable shape, or otherwise he would have nothing to do with him. The Ghost next came in the form of a mastiff, but Griffiths objected even to this appearance; at last, the Ghost appeared as a fly, which was captured by Griffiths and secured in his tobacco box, and carried away. Griffiths acknowledged that this Ghost was the most formidable one that he had ever conquered.

LLANDEGLA SPIRIT

The old Rectory at Llandegla was haunted; the Spirit was very troublesome; no peace was to be got because of it; every night it was at its work. A person of the name of Griffiths, who lived at Graianrhyd, was sent for to lay the Ghost. He came to the Rectory, but the Spirit could not be overcome. It is true Griffiths saw it, but in such a form that he could not approach it; night after night, the Spirit appeared in various forms, but still the conjurer was unable to master it. At last it came to the wise man in the form of a fly, which Griffiths immediately captured, and placed in a small box. This box he buried under a large stone in the river, just below the bridge, near the Llandegla Mills, and there the Spirit is to remain until a certain tree, which grows by the bridge, reaches the height of the parapet, and then, when this takes place, the Spirit shall have power to regain his liberty. To prevent this tree from growing, the school children, even to this day, nip the upper branches, and thus retard its upward growth.

LADY JEFFREY'S SPIRIT

This lady could not rest in her grave because of her misdeeds, and she troubled people dreadfully; at last she was persuaded or enticed to contract her dimensions, and enter into a bottle. She did so, after appearing in a good many hideous forms; but when she got into the bottle, it was corked down securely, and the bottle was cast into the pool underneath the Short bridge, Llanidloes, and there the lady was to remain until the ivy that grew up the buttresses should overgrow the sides of the bridge, and reach the parapet. The ivy was dangerously near the top of the bridge when the writer was a schoolboy, and often did he and his companions crop off its tendrils as they neared the prescribed limits for we were all terribly afraid to release the dreaded lady out of the bottle. In the year 1848, the old bridge was blown up, and a new one built instead of it. A schoolfellow, whom we called Ben, was playing by the aforesaid pool when the bridge was undergoing reconstruction, and he found by the river's side a small bottle, and in the bottle was a little black thing, that was never quiet, but it kept bobbing up and down continually, just as if it wanted to get out. Ben kept the bottle safely for a while, but ere long he was obliged to throw it into the river, for his relations and neighbours came to the conclusion that that was the very bottle that contained Lady Jeffrey's Spirit, and they also surmised that the little black restless thing was nothing less than the lady herself. Ben consequently resigned the bottle and its contents to the pool again, there to undergo a prolonged, but unjust, term of imprisonment.

A GHOST APPEARING TO POINT OUT HIDDEN TREASURES

There is a farm house called Clwchdyrnog in the parish of Llanddeusant, Anglesey, which was said to have been haunted by a Spirit. It seems that no one would summon courage to speak to the Ghost, though it was seen by several parties; but one night, John Hughes, Bodedern, a widower, who visited the house for the purpose of obtaining a second Mrs Hughes from among the servant girls there, spoke to the Ghost. The presence of the Spirit was indicated by a great noise in the room where Hughes and the girl were. In great fright Hughes invoked the Spirit, and asked why he troubled the house. "Have I done any wrong to you?" said he, addressing the Spirit. "No," was the answer. Then he asked if the girl to whom he was paying his attentions was the cause of the Spirit's visit, and again he received the answer, "No." Then Hughes named individually all the inmates of the house in succession, and inquired if they were the cause of the Spirit's visits, and again he was answered in the negative. Then he asked why, since no one in the house had disturbed the Spirit, he came there to disturb the inmates. To this pertinent question the Spirit answered as follows: – "There are treasures hidden on the south side of Ffynnon Wen, which belong to, and are to be given to, the nine months old child in this house: when this is done, I will never disturb this house any more."

The spot occupied by the treasure was minutely described by the Spirit, and Hughes promised to go to the place indicated. The next day, he went to the spot, and digging into the ground, he came upon an iron chest filled with gold, silver, and other valuables, and all these things he faithfully delivered up to the parents of the child to be kept by them for him until he should come of age to take possession of them himself. This they faithfully did, and the Spirit never again came to the house.

THE SPIRIT OF LLYN-NÂD-Y-FORWYN

It is said that a young man was about to marry a young girl, and on the evening before the wedding they were rambling along the water's side together, but the man was false, and loved another better than the woman whom he was about to wed. They were alone in an unfrequented country, and the deceiver pushed the girl into the lake to get rid of her to marry his sweetheart. She lost her life. But ever afterwards her Spirit troubled the neighbourhood, but chiefly the scene of her murder. Sometimes she appeared as a ball of fire, rolling along the river Colwyn, at other times she appeared as a lady dressed in silk, taking a solitary walk along the banks of the river. At other times, groans and shrieks were heard coming out of the river – just such screams as would be uttered by a person who was being murdered. Sometimes a young maiden was seen emerging out of the waters, half naked, with dishevelled hair, that covered her shoulders, and the country resounded with her heart-rending crying as she appeared in the lake. The frequent crying of the Spirit gave to the lake its name, Llyn-Nâd-y-Forwyn.

CYNON'S GHOST

Careg yr Yspryd and Cynon Isaf were at the entrance to the Valley of Llanwddyn, and down this opening, or mouth of the valley, rushed the river – the river that was to be dammed up for the use of Liverpool. The inhabitants of the valley knew the tradition respecting the Spirit, and they much feared its being disturbed. The stone was a large boulder, from fifteen to twenty tons in weight, and it was evident that it was doomed to destruction, for it stood in the River Vyrnwy just where operations were to commence. There was no small stir among the Welsh inhabitants when preparations were made to blast the huge Spirit-stone. English and Irish workmen could not enter into the feeling of the Welsh towards this stone, but they had heard what was said about it. They, however, had no dread of the imprisoned Spirit. In course of time the stone was bored and a load of dynamite inserted, but it was not shattered at the first blast. About four feet square remained intact, and underneath this the Spirit was, if it was anywhere. The men were soon set to work to demolish the stone. The Welshmen expected some catastrophe to follow its destruction, and they were even prepared to see the Spirit bodily emerge from its prison, for, said they, the conditions of its release have been fulfilled – the river had been diverted from its old bed into an artificial channel, to facilitate the removal of this and other stones – and there was no doubt that both conditions had been literally carried out, and consequently the Spirit, if justice ruled, could claim its release. The stone was blasted, and strange to relate, when the smoke had cleared away, the water in a cavity where the stone had been was seen to move; there was no apparent reason why the water should thus be disturbed, unless, indeed, the Spirit was about to appear. The Welsh workmen became alarmed, and moved away from the place, keeping, however, their eyes fixed on the pool. The mystery was soon solved, for a large frog made its appearance, and, sedately sitting on a fragment of the shattered stone, rubbed its eyes with its feet, as if awaking from a long sleep. The question was discussed, "Is it a frog, or the Spirit in the form of a frog; if it is a frog, why was it not killed when the stone was blasted?" And again, "Whoever saw a frog sit up in that fashion and rub the dust out of its eyes? It must be the Spirit." There the workmen stood, at a respectful distance from the frog, who, heedless of the marked attention paid to it, continued sitting up and rubbing its eyes. They would not approach it, for it must be the Spirit, and no one knew what its next movement or form might be. At last, however, the frog was driven away, and the men recommenced their labours. But for nights afterwards people passing the spot heard a noise as of heavy chains being dragged along the ground where the stone once stood.

A SPIRIT LEAVING AND RE-ENTERING THE BODY

A man was in love with two young girls, and they were both in love with him, and they knew that he flirted with them both. It is but natural to suppose that these young ladies did not, being rivals, love each other. It can well be believed that they heartily disliked each other. One evening, according to custom, this young man spent the night with one of his sweethearts, and to all appearance she fell asleep, or was in a trance, for she looked very pale. He noticed her face, and was frightened by its death-like pallor, but he was greatly surprised to see *a bluish flame proceed out of her mouth*, and go towards the door. He followed this light, and saw it take the direction of the house in which his other love lived, and he observed that from that house, too, a like light was travelling, as if to meet the light that he was following. Ere long these lights met each other, and they apparently fought, for they dashed into each other, and flitted up and down, as if engaged in mortal combat. The strife continued for some time, and then the lights separated and departed in the direction of the respective houses where the two young women lived. The man returned to the house of the young woman with whom he was spending the night, following close on the light, which he saw going before him, and which re-entered her body through her mouth; and then she immediately awoke.

A DOCTOR CALLED FROM HIS BED BY A VOICE

Doctor Davies, of Cerrig-y-drudion, had gone to bed and slept, but in the night he heard someone under his bedroom window shout that he was wanted in a farmhouse called Craigeirchan, which was three miles from the doctor's abode, and the way thereto was at all times beset with difficulties, such as opening and shutting the many gates; but of a night the journey to this mountain farm was one that few would think of taking, unless called to do so by urgent business. The doctor did not pay much attention to the first request, but he lay quietly on the bed listening, and almost immediately he heard the same voice requesting him to go at once to Craigeirchan, as he was wanted there. He now got up to the window, but could not see anyone; he therefore re-entered his bed, but for the third time he heard the voice telling him to go to the farm named, and now he opened the window and said that he would follow the messenger forthwith. The doctor got up, went to the stable, saddled the horse, and off he started for a long dismal ride over a wild tract of mountain country; such a journey he had often taken. He was not surprised that he could not see, nor hear, anyone in advance, for he knew that Welsh lads are nimble of foot, and could, by cutting across fields, etc., outstrip a rider. At last he neared the house where he was wanted, and in the distance he saw a light, and by this sign he was convinced that there was sickness in the house. He drove up to the door and entered the abode, to the surprise but great joy of the inmates. To his inquiry after the person who had been sent for him, he was told that no one had left the house, nor had anyone been requested by the family to go to the doctor. But he was told his services were greatly wanted, for the wife was about to become a mother, and the doctor was instrumental in saving both the life of the child and mother.

APPARITIONS OF SPIRITS IN THE PARISH OF ABERYSTRUTH

About the latter end of the sixteenth century and the beginning of the seventeenth, there lived in the Valley of *Ebwy Fawr* one Walter John Harry, belonging to the people called the Quakers, a harmless honest man, and by occupation a Farrier; who went to live at *Ty yn y Fid*, in that Valley, where one Morgan Lewis, a Weaver, had lived before him, and after his death had appeared to some and troubled the house. One night Walter, being in bed with his wife and awake, saw a light come upstairs, and expecting to see the spectre, and being somewhat afraid; though he was naturally a very fearless man, strove to awaken his wife by pinching her, but could not awake her; and seeing the spectre coming with a candle in his hand, and a white woollen cap upon his head, and the dress he always wore; resolved to speak to him, and did when he came near the bed, and said, "Morgan Lewis! Why dost thou walk this earth?" To which the Apparition gravely answered, like one in some distress, that it was because of some bottoms of wool which he had hid in the wall of the house, which he desired him to take away, and then he would trouble them no more. And then Walter said, I charge thee Morgan Lewis in the name of God, that thou trouble my house no more; at which, he vanished away and appeared no more. He was no profane man, nor openly vicious. It is likely the poor man had in an hour of temptation unjustly concealed these things of some value, and was now troubled for it; and chose that these bottoms of wool should be of use to others rather than be of no use; though he neither requested they should be made use of, nor forbid their doing it, but left it to their choice. No doubt but they made use them.

* * *

Long time after the death or removal of Walter John Harry, Thomas Miles Harry came to live at that house: who once coming home by night from Abergavenny, his horse took fright on seeing something, (invisible to Mr. Harry) and ran with him swiftly towards the house. Mr. H. being much terrified, hastened to unsaddle his horse, and on looking towards the other end of the yard, he perceived the appearance of a woman, so prodigiously tall as to be about half as high as the tall beech trees at the other side of the yard; and glad he was of a house to rest himself in.

* * *

Another time, the same person coming home by night from a journey, when near *Ty yn y Llwyn*, saw the resemblance of fire, the west side of the river, on his right hand; and looking towards the Mountain near the rock *Tarren y Trwyn*, on his left hand, all of a sudden, saw the fire near him on one side, and the appearance of a mastiff dog on the other side, at which he was exceedingly terrified. The appearance of a mastiff dog was a most dreadful sight. He called at *Ty yn y Llwyn*, requesting the favour of a person to accompany him home. The man of the house being acquainted with him, sent two of his servants with him home. My thoughts of Mr T. H. M. are, that he was a man of an affable disposition, innocent and harmless, and a respecter of what is good in his later days. His children also; his son and two daughters were godly and religious. He was the grandfather of that eminent and famous preacher of the Gospel Mr. Thomas Lewis, of *Lanharan*, in *Glamorganshire*.

* * *

His son Lewis Thomas, the father of Mr. Thos. Lewis, on his returning home from a journey, and, on passing through a field beyond *Pont Evan Lliwarch Bridge*, on the *Bedwellty* side of the river *Ebwy Fawr*, saw the dreadful resemblance of a man walking on his hands and feet and crossing the path just before him; at which, his hair moved upon his head, his heart panted and beat violently, his flesh trembled, he felt not his clothes about him; felt himself heavy and weak although a strong lively man. He remembered it all his days, and was very ready to declare it, having been much affected with it. [...]

* * *

John ab John, of *Coome Celin*, in the valley of the Church, was travelling very early in the morning, before day, towards *Caerleon* Fair, and, on going up hill on *Milvre Mountain*, he heard a shouting behind him as if it were on *Bryn Mawr* – which is part of the black mountain in Breconshire – and soon after heard the shouting at *Bwlch y Llwyn* on his left hand, nearer to him; upon which, he became oppressed with fear, and heavy in walking; and began to suspect it was no human but a diabolical voice, designed to frighten him; having wondered before what people could be shouting on the mountain so early in the morning. Being come up to the higher part of the mountain, he heard the shouting at *Gilvach* fields on the right – before him, which confirmed his fear: but, being past the *Gilvach* fields, in the way to the cold springs, he heard something coming behind him like the noise of a coach; and what increased his fear the more, was the voice of a woman with the coach which he heard crying *Wow Up*. Now, as he knew that no coach could go that way, and hearing the noise of a coach approaching nearer and nearer , he was certain it must be an evil Spirit following him; he was very much terrified; and fearing he should see some horrid appearance, he walked a short distance from the path and lay down with his face towards the heath, fearing to look about until it had passed him: when it was gone out of hearing he arose; and hearing the birds singing as the day began to break, also seeing some sheep before him, his fear went quite off. [...]

* * *

W.E. of *Hafodafel*, going a journey upon the Beacon Mountain, very early in the morning, passed by the perfect likeness of a Coal Race, where really there was none; there he saw many people very busy; some cutting the coal, some carrying it to fill the sacks, some rising the loads upon the horses' backs, &c. This was an Agency of the Fairies upon his visive faculty, and it was a wonderful extra natural thing, and made a considerable impression upon his mind. He was of undoubted veracity – a great man in the world – and above telling an untruth. The power of Spirits, both good and bad, is very great, not having the weight of bodies to in-cumber and hinder their agility. [...]

* * *

W. L. M. told me, that going upon an errand by night, from the house of Jane Edmund, of *Abertilery*, he heard like the voice of many persons speaking one to the other, at some distance from him; he again listened attentively, then he heard like the falling of a tree, which seemed to break other trees as it fell; he then heard a weak voice – like the voice of a person in pain and misery, which frightened him much, and prevented him proceeding on his journey. Those were Fairies which spoke in his hearing, and they doubtless spoke about his death, and imitated the moan which he made, when some time after he fell from off a tree, which proved his death. This account, previous to his death, he gave me himself. He was a man much alienated from the life of God, though surrounded with the means of knowledge and grace; but there was no cause to question the veracity of his relation.

* * *

The last Apparition of the Fairies in the Parish of *Aberystruth*, was in the fields of the Widow of Mr. Edmund Miles, not long before her death. Two men (one of whom is now an eminent man in his religious life) who were moving hay in one of her fields, the *Bedwellty* side of the river *Ebwy Fawr*, very early in the morning; at which time they saw the chief Servant of the House coming through the field on the other side of the river, toward them, and like a marriage company of people with some bravery, in white aprons to meet him; they met him and passed by, but of whom he seemed to them to take no notice. They asked the servant if he saw the marriage company? He said "No", at the same time they could hardly think any marriage could come that way, and that time of the day. This certainly must have been Fairies, and was partly a presage of Mrs. Miles's death, and partly it may be of the marriage of her daughter, the heiress of the estate after the death of her brother Mr. John Miles, with that servant: the account of the Fairies, resembling a marriage company, could not be kept a secret from Mrs. Miles, which when she heard of it, gave her a deal of uneasiness, as she understood it as a presage of her death, as indeed it was.

More of these kind of accounts may be seen in the geographical and historical account of the Parish of Aberystruth. If so many accounts of Apparitions have been found in one of the parishes in the county of Monmouth, how many may be found in all the Parishes in the County? And how many in all the counties of Wales together? Every reasonable person may easily see. [...]

APPARITIONS OF SPIRITS IN THE PARISH OF BEDWELLTY

From under the hand of the Rev. Mr. Roger Rogers, born and bred in this Parish, I have the following remarkable relation.

A **very remarkable** and odd sight was seen in July, 1760, acknowledged and confessed by several credible eyewitnesses of the same; i.e. by Lewis Thomas Jenkins's two daughters, virtuous and good young women, (their father a good man and a substantial freeholder) his manservant, his maid-servant, Elizabeth David a neighbour and tenant of the said Lewis Thomas, and Edmund Roger a neighbour; who were all making hay in a field called *Y Weirglod Fawr Dafolog*: the first sight they saw was the resemblance of an innumerable flock of sheep, over a hill, called *Cefen Rhychdir*, opposite the place where the spectators stood, about a quarter of a mile distant from them: soon after they saw them go up to a place called *Cefen Rhychdir ucha*, about half a mile distant from them, and then they went out of their sight, as if they vanished in the air: about half an hour before sunset they all saw them again; but all did not see them in the same manner; they saw them in different forms. Two of these persons saw them like sheep, some saw them like greyhounds, some like swine, and some like naked infants: they appeared in the shade of the mountain between them and the sun.

The first sight was as if they rose up out of the earth. This was a notable appearance of the Fairies seen by many credible witnesses. The sons of infidelity are very unreasonable not to believe the testimonies of so many witnesses of the being of Spirits.

APPARITION OF A SPIRIT IN THE PARISH OF LLANHYDDEL

Llanhyddel Mountain was formerly much talked of, and still remembered concerning an Apparition which led many people astray both by day and by night, upon this mountain. The Apparition was the resemblance of a poor old woman, with an ablong four-cornered hat, ash-coloured clothes, her apron thrown a-cross her shoulder, with a pot or wooden Can in her hand, such as poor people carry to fetch milk with, always going be- fore them, sometimes crying out *Wow Up*. Who- ever saw this Apparition, whether by night or in a misty day, though well acquainted with the road, they would be sure to lose their way ; for the road appeared quite different to what it really was ; and so far sometimes the fascination was, that they thought they were going to their journey's end when they were really going the contrary way. Sometimes they heard her cry *Wow Up*, when they did not see her. Sometimes, when they went out by night to fetch coal, water, etc. they would hear the cry very near them, and presently would hear it a-far off, as if it was on the opposite Mountain, in the Parish of Aberystruth, and sometimes passing by their ears. The people have it by tradition, that it was the Spirit of one Juan White, who lived time out of mind in these parts, and was thought to be Witch ; because the Mountain was not haunted with her Apparition until after her death. When people first lost their way, and saw her, they thought it was a real woman which knew the way ; they were glad to see her, and endeavoured to overtake her to enquire about the way ; but they could never over-take her, neither would she ever look back to see them ; so that they never saw her face.

THE FORBIDDEN FOUNTAIN

There was once a boy of twelve years of age who was often sent by his father to tend the sheep on the Frenni fach. Early one morning in June he drove the sheep to their pasture for the day and looked carefully at the top of the Frenni fawr to see which way the morning fog was declining. Young as he was, he was weather-wise, and knew that if the fog declined to the Pembrokeshire side it would be a fine day, whereas if it went to the Cardiganshire side the weather would be foul. The fog was going to the Pembrokeshire side, and the boy, delighted with the prospect of a fine day, was whistling a merry tune and looking idly about him, when he saw at a considerable distance away what seemed to be a party of soldiers busily engaged in some operation, the nature of which he could not make out at first.

"There cannot be any soldiers on the mountain as early as this," he reflected, and going to the top of a little hillock, he perceived that they were too small for soldiers. "I wonder whether they are the Fair Family," he said. He had often heard of them and had seen their rings, but he had never set eyes on the little people themselves. First of all, he thought of running home to tell his father and mother, but reflecting that they might disappear before he returned and that perhaps his parents might even forbid him to come back – for many people were afraid of the Fair Family – he dismissed that idea. After cogitating for a little while he determined to go as near them as he could, and by degrees he arrived within a short distance of the visitors, where he remained for some time observing their motions. The visitors were tiny little people of both sexes, and they were the most handsome people he had ever seen. Some of them were dancing, whirling round and round in a ring with joined hands. Others were chasing one another with surprising swiftness, and others again were galloping about on small white horses. Their dresses varied in colour, some being white and others scarlet. The little men wore red tripled caps and the little women a light headdress, which waved fantastically in the breeze. All were laughing gleefully, and as merry as could be.

Before long they noticed the boy, and, with laughing faces, beckoned him to join them. So he gradually went nearer, till at length he ventured to place one foot in the circle. No sooner had he done so than his ears were charmed with the most melodious music in the world, and he moved his other foot into the circle.

The instant he did this, he found himself, not in a fairy ring on the mountain side, but in a magnificent palace glittering with gold and pearls. Every form of beauty surrounded him, and every variety of pleasure was offered him. He was free to range wherever he pleased, and his every movement was waited on by maidens of matchless loveliness. Instead of the tatws a llaeth (potatoes and butter-milk) and the flummery to which he had hitherto been accustomed, here were the choicest viands, served on silver plates, and instead of small beer, the only kind of intoxicating liquor he had before tasted, here were red and yellow wines of wondrous enjoyableness, brought in golden goblets richly inlaid with gems. There was only one restriction on his freedom: he was not to drink on any consideration from a certain fountain in the garden, in which swam fishes of golden and other colours. Each day new joys were provided for him; new pastimes were invented to charm him and new faces presented themselves, more lovely, if possible, than those he had seen before.

Possessing everything that mortal could desire, the boy still wanted the one thing forbidden. Like Eve in the Garden of Eden, he was undone by curiosity. One day he was near the fountain, gazing at the fishes sporting in the water. There was nobody looking on, and he plunged his hand into the fountain: the fishes all disappeared instantly. He put the water to his mouth: a confused shriek ran through the garden. He drank: the palace and all vanished, and he found himself on the mountain in the very place where he first entered the ring. The sheep were grazing just where he had left them, and the fog on the mountain had scarcely moved. He thought he had been absent for many years, but he had only been away so many minutes.

NED PUW'S FAREWELL

The Tal Clegir Cave runs into a long, bare, steep, rugged hill. About its mouth the grass grows thick and rank, and the briars grew undisturbed, tangling and strangling each other.

In the older time it was dangerous to approach within five paces of the *ogof*. Once upon a time a fox, with a pack of hounds in full cry at his tail, was making straight for the entrance: suddenly he turned right round, with his hair all bristled and fretted like frostwork with terror, and ran back into the middle of the pack as if anything earthly, even an earthly death, was preferable to the unearthly horrors of the cave. He escaped, however, for not a dog would go near him, for his hide was all burnished with green, yellow and blue lights, as it were with a profusion of will-o'-the-wisps.

Another time Elias ap Ifan, who for upwards of twenty years had been a drunkard, happened to stagger just upon the rim of the forbidden space and arrived home as sober as a judge, to the amazement of his family. After this Elias was a changed man.

In the twilight of one misty Hallow Eve a shepherd was returning home accompanied by his dog. When he was about a hundred yards from the cave, he heard a faint burst of melody coming from the rocks above the entrance. In a few minutes a figure well known to him became visible. He had a fiddle at his chest, and his legs were on the caper incessantly.

"Ha, ha," said the shepherd, laughing merrily. "Here's old Ned Puw. I remember him wagering that he would dance all the way down the hill and keep up a tune with his fiddle."

Scarcely had he said this, when he noticed to his horror that Ned had fiddled and capered himself within the fatal five paces. He shouted and shouted to him until the very rocks re-echoed, but Ned Puw seemed perfectly deaf, and fiddled and danced away with all the complacency in the world. The shepherd did not like to abandon him to his fate without making an effort to save him: he ran as near him as he dared, with the intention of pulling him out of the danger zone with his long crook. When he came near him, he saw that by this time Ned's face was as pale as marble, his eyes were staring fixedly and deathfully, and his head was dangling loose and disjointed on his shoulders. He was still fiddling, but his arms seemed to keep the fiddlestick in motion without the least sympathy from their master. Before the shepherd's very eyes he was, as it were, sucked into the cave by some invisible agency, still fiddling and capering, in the same way as the mist is sucked up by the rising sun in summer. The shepherd was transfixed with terror, and he fancied he could count every hair on the back of his dog that crouched and quivered between his legs, as the cold wind howled mournfully, ploughing up first one hair and then another. Some mysterious power seemed to root him to the spot, and it required a strong effort of will to tear himself away and resume his homeward journey.

On Hallow Eve you can, if you have the courage to approach the entrance of the cave, hear the tune Ned Puw is playing. On certain nights in leap-year you can even see him: a star stands opposite the further end of the cave, enabling you to have a view right through it. There is the wretched fiddler scraping and capering away, and there he will be, for all we know, capering and scraping for ever. A musician who went one Hallow Eve to listen to the strains issuing from the cave took down the tune and named it Ned Puw's Farewell.

THE POWER OF ST. TEGLA'S WELL

At the farm of Amnodd Bwll, at the foot of the Little Arenig, there once lived a farmer called Robert Wiliam, his wife Mari Tomos (in those days a woman did not lose her maiden name when she got married; that is only a recent fashion in Wales), and their only child, a boy who was known as Wiliam Robert (a son took his father's surname then as his Christian name). Now Wiliam was subject to fits, and in the summer when he attained the age of twelve his father and mother became terribly anxious about him, because so many signs of death followed one after another. One of the apple trees in the garden burst into blossom long before its time, which is very unlucky. The old cock which had for years behaved as well as any chanticleer in the county took to crowing in the middle of the night, and had to have his head chopped off before he would give up the fatal habit.

Mari Tomos dreamed that she was at a wedding, which of course meant that she would before long attend a funeral. One night a bird flapped its wings against the window of the room in which Robert Wiliam and Mari Tomos slept, and the hearts of the worthy couple sank at the thought that it might have been the Corpse Bird, that weird, featherless bird, with wings of some leathery substance like those of a bat, which occasionally comes from the land of Illusion and Phantasy to beat its wings against the windows of houses which the King of Terrors is about to visit. Another night Robert Wiliam was so frightened that it was hours after his usual time when he crawled home, shaking like an aspen leaf. He was walking home by himself from a fair at Bala, by the side of the River Tryweryn, when he saw in the fading light a repulsive hag, clad in a long black gown trailing on the ground. Her face was deathly pale, with high cheek bones and deep-sunk lack-lustre eyes; she had great black projecting teeth, and a short nose with widely distended nostrils. Her hair was grey and tangled. Her arms were skinny and shrivelled and of great length, out of all proportion to her body. She splashed in the water of the river with her hands, and made a most doleful noise. Robert Wiliam at first could not make out any words, but presently he distinctly heard, "My child, my child, my dear son," after uttering which words the hideous apparition vanished. The thought that he had seen the dreaded Cyhiraeth, and that her cry foreboded the death of his beloved boy, froze the blood in his veins, and the darkness had closed in before he could proceed on his homeward journey.

He had not gone much further when he saw a corpse candle moving before him along the road. It burned with a red flame, from which it was clear that it was not a woman who was doomed (a woman's candle is white), and the candle was small, indicating that a child was to die, for the size of corpse candles varies with the age of those whose death they foretell. This succession of nightly horrors almost paralysed Robert Wiliam, and he reached home more dead than alive.

The next day he went to consult a wise man who lived in Trawsfynydd, to see if there was any hope for his son. The wise man told him that his only chance was to take the boy to St Tegla's Well, in Denbighshire, and instructed him what to do. Robert Wiliam took his son to Llandegla, and the following ceremony was performed. The boy went to the well after sunset, carrying a cock in a basket. First of all he walked round the well thrice, reciting the Lord's Prayer. Then he walked thrice round the church, again repeating the Paternoster. After this he entered the church, crept under the altar, and slept there until break of day, making the Bible his pillow and the communion cloth his coverlet. In the morning he placed sixpence on the altar, and leaving the cock in the church departed home with his father. Great was then the anxiety of Robert Wiliam to know the fate of the bird, for if it did not die in the church there would be no hope of cure. In about a week a messenger came to say that the bird had died, and that consequently the disease which had been transferred to it had died also. Whether this was so or not, it is curious that in spite of the apple tree which bloomed before its time, night-crowing cock, Corpse Bird, Cyhiraeth, and corpse candle, Wiliam Robert completely recovered from his illness and lived to a ripe old age.

STRIKING A CORPSE CANDLE

A clergyman in Carmarthenshire had a son who came home one night very late and found the doors locked against him. Not wishing to disturb his father and mother, and fearing also their reproaches and chidings, he went to the man-servant's bedroom, which was over the stable. He could not awake the man-servant, but while standing over him he saw a small light issue from his nostrils. He followed it out. It went over a foot-bridge which crossed a brook and on to the road which led up to the parish church. After following the corpse candle for some time, the young man, just to see what would happen, struck at it with his stick. It burst into sparks, but afterwards reunited into a flame as before, which stalked on until it finally disappeared in the churchyard.

Not long afterwards the man-servant died: at his funeral the bier broke at the spot where his master's son had struck at the corpse candle, and the coffin fell to the ground.

THE DEVIL'S BRIDGE

One day in the olden time old Megan of Llandunach stood by the side of the River Mynach feeling very sorry for herself.

The Mynach was in flood, and roared down the wooded dingle in five successive falls, tumbling over three hundred feet in less than no time. Just below the place where Megan was standing, there was a great cauldron in which the water whirled, boiled and hissed as if troubled by some evil spirit: from the cauldron the river rushed and swirled down a narrow, deep ravine, and if the old woman had had an eye for the beauties of nature, the sight of the seething pot and the long shadowy cleft would have made her feel joyous rather than sorrowful.

But Megan at this time cared for none of these things, because her one and only cow was on the wrong side of the ravine, and her thoughts were centred on the horned beast which was cropping the green grass carelessly just as if it made no difference what side of the river it was on. How the wrong-headed animal had got there Megan could not guess, and still less did she know how to get it back. As there was no one else to talk to, she talked to herself. "Oh, dear, oh, dear, what shall I do?" she said.

"What is the matter, Megan?" said a voice behind her. She turned round and saw a man cowled like a monk and with a rosary at his belt. She had not heard anyone coming, but the noise of the waters boiling over and through the rocks, she reflected, might easily have drowned the sound of any footsteps. And in any case she was so troubled about her cow that she could not stop to wonder how the stranger had come up.

"I am ruined," said Megan. "There is my one and only cow, the sole support of my old age, on the other side of the river, and I don't know how to get her back again. Oh, dear, oh, dear, I am ruined."

"Don't you worry about that," said the monk, "I'll get her back for you."

"How can you?" asked Megan, greatly surprised.

"I'll tell you," answered the stranger. "It is one of my amusements to build bridges, and if you like I'll throw a bridge across this chasm for you."

"Well, indeed," said the old woman, "nothing would please me better. But how am I to pay you? I am sure you will want a great deal for a job like this, and I am so poor that I have no money to spare, look you, no, indeed."

"I am very easily satisfied," said the monk. "Just let me have the first living thing that crosses the bridge after I have finished it, and I shall be content."

Megan agreed to this, and the monk told her to go back to her cottage and wait there until he should call for her.

Now, Megan was not half such a fool as she looked, and she had noticed, while talking to the kind and obliging stranger, that there was something rather peculiar about his foot. She had a suspicion, too, that his knees were behind instead of being in front, and while she was waiting for the summons she thought so hard that it made her head ache. By the time she was haloed for, she had hit upon a plan. She threw some crusts to her little dog to make him follow her, and took a loaf of bread under her shawl to the river-side.

"There's a bridge for you," said the monk, pointing proudly to a fine span bestriding the yawning chasm. And it really was something to be proud of.

"H'm, yes," said Megan, looking doubtfully at it; "yes, it is a bridge. But is it strong?

"Strong?" said the builder, indignantly. "Of course it is strong."

"Will it hold the weight of this loaf?" asked Megan, bringing the bread out from underneath her shawl.

The monk laughed scornfully. "Hold the weight of this loaf? Throw it on and see. Ha, ha!"

So Megan rolled the loaf right across the bridge, and the little black cur scampered after it.

"Yes, it will do," said Megan, "and, kind sir, my little dog is the first live thing to cross the bridge. You are welcome to him, and I thank you very much for all the trouble you have taken."

"Tut, the silly dog is no good to me," said the stranger, very crossly, and with that he vanished into space. From the smell of brimstone which he had left behind him Megan knew that, as she had suspected, it was the Devil whom she had outwitted.

And this is how the Bad Man's Bridge came to be built.

A GHOSTLY REHEARSAL

While the Manchester and Milford railway was being constructed, many a frugal farmer added to his earnings by boarding and lodging the navvies who were exalting the valleys and making low the hills for the iron rails. Several of these sturdy workers stayed at a farm called Penderlwyngoch.

One evening when they were seated round the fire in the big kitchen smoking and yarning, the farm dogs were heard barking, as they always did when they saw strangers anywhere about. As they continued to bark, the company understood that someone was coming towards the house. By-and-by they heard the sound of footsteps, and the barking of the dogs changed into a melancholy howl. Shortly after the howling ceased, as if the dogs had slunk away. Before many minutes had elapsed the back door opened, and a number of people entered the house: they passed along the passage which divided the dwelling into two parts, and laid a heavy load in the parlour: after this the noise suddenly stopped altogether.

The attention of the smokers would have been arrested by the mere opening of the parlour door. It was no light matter to burst into the musty splendour of the room where the sacred horsehair furniture and the family Bible were kept. There was, besides, something uncanny about the silence of the dogs and the sudden cessation of all noise in the parlour, which disturbed the company assembled in the kitchen. They took a light and proceeded to the parlour to investigate. There was nothing beyond what was always there, nor were there any marks of footsteps either in the room or in the passage. Going outside, they could find no traces of the approach of anyone, but they saw the dogs cowering and shivering with fright in the yard.

On the very next day one of the men who went to see what was the matter in the parlour was killed. His body was carried by his fellow-workmen through the back door and the passage which divided the house into the parlour. Everything occurred as it had been rehearsed the previous night except that the dogs were not frightened by the real corpse.

THE SUPERNATURAL

WITCHES & MYSTICAL BEINGS

This chapter contains a veritable treasure trove of magic and enchantment. Giants who leave their marks upon the landscape, hideous man-eating water monsters and abducted mermaids roam side-by-side with some of Wales's most infamous conjurers and witches. Here is exemplified the complex relationship between folk and magical practitioners, seeking counsel from *dynion hysbys* (cunning men) to protect from witchcraft, such as in Elias Owen's account of the 'Milk That Would Not Churn', while simultaneously seeking the protection of witches from the mischief of fairies, such as in the 'Corwrion Changeling Legend'. An unwitting conjurer is even outed as a fraud in 'A Conjuror's Collusion Exposed', highlighting the myriad of belief structures that existed within Welsh communities.

While the authors of these tales may have injected a degree of artistic flair into these accounts, it is important to remember that many of the characters mentioned within this chapter are based on historic figures, such as the Witches of Llanddona, Ynys Môn, whose tale is told by William Jenkyn Thomas, and whose grisly curse is infamous…

PEDWS FFOWK AND ST ELIAN'S WELL

Pedws Ffowk was for three years afflicted with a complaint which nobody could understand. She was well and yet she was not well: she was sick and yet she was not sick. That is to say, she had no ache or pain, and her appetite was good. But all the time she became thinner and thinner, until at last she was nothing but skin and bone. She went to doctor after doctor, but they could not find out what was the matter with her. She consulted quacks also, but even they did her no good. Finally, she went to a wise man. He, after hearing her story, said, "Someone has put you into St. Elian's Well."

"What do you mean by that?" asked Pedws.

"Someone has gone to the woman who keeps the well," answered the wise man, "and put your name on the register, and thrown a pin into the well, together with a pebble with your initials on it."

"Well, what is the harm of that?" inquired Pedws, who had not heard of the power of the cursing well.

"You are cursed," was the reply, "and unless the curse is removed, you will pine away and die."

"But what am I to do?" said Pedws, now thoroughly frightened.

"You must go to the woman who keeps the well, and pay her to take you out of the well," was the wise man's advice.

Pedws lost no time in going to the guardian of the well, who, for a small fee, agreed to examine her register. Sure enough, the name of Pedws Ffowk was there inscribed, and the date of the entry corresponded with the time when she had begun to waste away. On the payment of another and a larger sum of money the priestess of the fountain agreed to take out of the water the stone on which the initials of Pedws Ffowk were scratched. From that moment flesh began to grow on her bones, and before long her clothes, which had hung upon her like rags upon a scarecrow, were filled out as well as they had ever been. Pedws lived to a good old age, and her greatest trouble was that she never found out which of her best friends had put her into the well.

THE MIGHTY MONSTER AFANG

After the Cymric folk, that is, the people we call Welsh, had come up from Cornwall into their new land, they began to cut down the trees, to build towns, and to have fields and gardens. Soon they made the landscape smile with pleasant homes, rich farms and playing children.

They trained vines and made flowers grow. The young folks made pets of the wild animals' cubs, which their fathers and big brothers brought home from hunting. Old men took rushes and reeds and wove them into cages for songbirds to live in.

While they were draining the swamps and bogs, they drove out the monsters that had made their lair in these wet places. These terrible creatures liked to poison people with their bad breath, and even ate up very little boys and girls when they strayed away from home.

So all the face of the open country between the forests became very pretty to look at. The whole of Cymric land, which then extended from the northern Grampian Hills to Cornwall, and from the Irish Sea, past their big fort, afterward called London, even to the edge of the German Ocean, became a delightful place to live in.

The lowlands and the rivers, in which the tide rose and fell daily, were especially attractive. This was chiefly because of the many bright flowers growing there; while the yellow gorse and the pink heather made the hills look as lovely as a young girl's face. Besides this, the Cymric maidens were the prettiest ever, and the lads were all brave and healthy; while both of these knew how to sing often and well.

Now there was a great monster named the Afang, that lived in a big bog, hidden among the high hills and inside of a dark, rough forest.

This ugly creature had an iron-clad back and a long tail that could wrap itself around a mountain. It had four front legs, with big knees that were bent up like a grasshopper's, but were covered with scales like armour. These were as hard as steel, and bulged out at the thighs. Along its back was a ridge of horns, like spines, and higher than an alligator's. Against such a tough hide, when the hunters shot their darts and hurled their javelins, these weapons fell down to the ground like harmless pins.

On this monster's head were big ears, halfway between those of a jackass and an elephant. Its eyes were as green as leeks, and were round, but scalloped on the edges, like squashes, while they were as big as pumpkins.

The Afang's face was much like a monkey's, or a gorilla's, with long straggling grey hairs around its cheeks like those of a walrus. It always looked as if a napkin, as big as a bath towel, would be necessary to keep its mouth clean. Yet even then, it slobbered a good deal, so that no nice fairy liked to be near the monster.

When the Afang growled, the bushes shook and the oak leaves trembled on the branches, as if a strong wind was blowing.

But after its dinner, when it had swallowed down a man, or two calves, or four sheep, or a fat heifer, or three goats, its body swelled up like a balloon. Then it usually rolled over, lay along the ground, or in the soft mud, and felt very stupid and sleepy, for a long while.

All around its lair lay wagon loads of bones of the creatures, girls, women, men, boys, cows, and occasionally a donkey, which it had devoured.

But when the Afang was ravenously hungry and could not get these animals and when fat girls and careless boys were scarce, it would live on birds, beasts and fishes. Although it was very fond of cows and sheep, yet the wool and hair of these animals stuck in its big teeth; it often felt very miserable and its usually bad temper grew worse.

Then, like a beaver, it would cut down a tree, sharpen it to a point and pick its teeth until its mouth was clean. Yet it seemed all the more hungry and eager for fresh human victims to eat, especially juicy maidens; just as children like cake more than bread.

The Cymric men were not surprised at this, for they knew that girls were very sweet and they almost worshipped women. So they learned to guard their daughters and wives. They saw that to do such things as eating up people was in the nature of the beast, which could never be taught good manners.

But what made them mad beyond measure was the trick which the monster often played upon them by breaking the river banks, and the dykes which with great toil they had built to protect their crops. Then the waters overflowed all their farms, ruined their gardens and spoiled their cow houses and stables.

This sort of mischief the Afang liked to play, especially about the time when the oat and barley crops were ripe and ready to be gathered to make cakes and flummery; that is sour oat-jelly, or pap. So it often happened that the children had to do without their cookies and porridge during the winter. Sometimes the floods rose so high as to wash away the houses and float the cradles. Even those with little babies in them were often seen on the raging waters, and sent dancing on the waves down the river to the sea.

Once in a while, a mother cat and all her kittens were seen mewing for help, or a lady dog howling piteously. Often it happened that both puppies and kittens were drowned.

So, whether for men or mothers, pussies or puppies, the Cymric men thought the time had come to stop this monster's mischief. It was bad enough that people should be eaten up, but to have all their crops ruined and animals drowned, so that they had to go hungry all winter, with only a little fried fish, and no turnips, was too much for human patience. There were too many weeping mothers and sorrowful fathers, and squalling brats and animals whining for something to eat.

Besides, if all the oats were washed away, how could their wives make flummery, without which no Cymric man is ever happy? And where would they get seed for another year's sowing? And if there were no cows, how could the babies or kitties live, or any grown-up persons get buttermilk?

Someone may ask, why did not some brave man shoot the Afang with a poisoned arrow, or drive a spear into him under the arms, where the flesh was tender, or cut off his head with a sharp sword?

The trouble was just here. There were plenty of brave fellows ready to fight the monster, but nothing made of iron could pierce that hide of his. This was like armour, or one of the steel battleships of our day, and the Afang always spat out fire or poison breath down the road up which a man was coming, long before the brave fellow could get near him. Nothing would do but to go up into his lair and drag him out.

But what man or company of men was strong enough to do this, when a dozen giants in a gang, with ropes as thick as a ship's hawser, could hardly tackle the job?

Nevertheless, in what neither man nor giant could do, a pretty maiden might succeed. True, she must be brave also, for how could she know, but if hungry, the Afang might eat her up?

However, one valiant damsel, of great beauty, who had lots of perfumery and plenty of pretty clothes, volunteered to bind the monster in his lair. She said, "I'm not afraid." Her sweetheart was named Gadern, and he was a young and strong hunter. He talked over the matter with her and they two resolved to act together.

Gadern went all over the country, summoning the farmers to bring their ox teams and log chains. Then he set the blacksmiths to work, forging new and especially heavy ones, made of the best native iron from the mines for which Wales is still famous.

Meanwhile, the lovely maiden arrayed herself in her prettiest clothes, dressed her hair in the most enticing way, hanging a white blossom on each side, over her ears, with one flower also at her neck.

When she had perfumed her garments, she sallied forth and up the lake where the big bog and the waters were and where the monster hid himself.

While the maiden was still quite a distance away, the terrible Afang, scenting his visitor from afar, came rushing out of his lair. When very near, he reared his head high in the air, expecting to pounce on her with his iron clad claws and at one swallow make a breakfast of the girl.

But the odours of her perfumes were so sweet that he forgot what he had thought to do. Moreover, when he looked at her, he was so taken with her unusual beauty that he flopped at once on his forefeet. Then he behaved just like a lovelorn beau, when his best girl comes near. He ties his necktie and pulls down his coat and brushes off the collar.

So the Afang began to spruce up. It was real fun to see how a monster behaves when smitten with love for a pretty girl. He had no idea how funny he was.

The girl was not at all afraid, but smoothed the monster's back, stroked and played with its big moustache and tickled its neck until the Afang's throat actually gurgled with a laugh. Pretty soon he guffawed, for he was so delighted.

When he did this, the people down in the valley thought it was thunder, though the sky was clear and blue.

The maiden tickled his chin, and even put up his whiskers in curl papers. Then she stroked his neck, so that his eyes closed. Soon she had gently lulled him to slumber, by singing a cradle song, which her mother had taught her. This she did so softly, and sweetly, that in a few minutes, with its head in her lap, the monster was sound asleep and even began to snore.

Then, quietly, from their hiding places in the bushes, Gadern and his men crawled out. When near the dreaded Afang, they stood up and sneaked forward, very softly on tiptoe. They had wrapped the links of the chain in grass and leaves, so that no clanking was heard. They also held the oxen's yokes, so that nobody or anything could rattle, or make any noise. Slowly but surely they passed the chain over its body, in the middle, besides binding the brute securely between its fore and hind legs.

All this time, the monster slept on, for the girl kept on crooning her melody.

When the forty yoke of oxen were all harnessed together, the drovers cracked all their whips at once, so that it sounded like a clap of thunder and the whole team began to pull together.

Then the Afang woke up with a start.

The sudden jerk roused the monster to wrath, and its bellowing was terrible. It rolled round and round, and dug its four sets of toes, each with three claws, every one as big as a plowshare, into the ground. It tried hard to crawl into its lair, or slip into the lake.

Finding that neither was possible, the Afang looked about for some big tree to wrap its tail around. But all his writhings or plungings were of no use. The drovers plied their whips and the oxen kept on with one long pull together and forward. They strained so hard that one of them dropped its eye out. This formed a pool, and to this day they call it The Pool of the Ox's Eye. It never dries up or overflows, though the water in it rises and falls as regularly as the tides.

For miles over the mountains the sturdy oxen hauled the monster. The pass over which they toiled and strained so hard is still named the Pass of the Oxen's Slope. When going downhill, the work of dragging the Afang was easier.

In a great hole in the ground, big enough to be a pond, they dumped the carcass of the Afang, and soon a little lake was formed. This uncanny bit of water is called "The Lake of the Green Well." It is considered dangerous for man or beast to go too near it. Birds do not like to fly over the surface, and when sheep tumble in, they sink to the bottom at once.

If the bones of the Afang still lie at the bottom, they must have sunk down very deep, for the monster had no more power to get out, or to break the river banks. The farmers no longer cared anything about the creature, and they hardly every think of the old story, except when a sheep is lost.

As for Gadern and his brave and lovely sweetheart, they were married and lived long and happily. Their descendants, in the thirty-seventh generation, are proud of the grand exploit of their ancestors, while all the farmers honour his memory and bless the name of the lovely girl that put the monster asleep.

GIANT TOM AND GIANT BLUBB

Everyone who has read anything of Welsh history – though not of the sort that is written by English folks – knows also that Cornwall is, in soul, a part of Wales. Before the Romans, first, and the Saxons, next, invaded Britain, the Cymric people lived all over the island, south of Scotland.

They were the British people, and nobody ever heard the German name, "Wales", which means a foreign land; or the word "Welsh", which refers to foreigners, until men who were themselves outsiders came into Britain.

Since that time, it has been much the same as when a British Jack Tar, when rambling in Portugal, or China, calls the natives "foreigners", and tells them to "get out of the way".

Ages ago, when the Cymric men, with their wives and little ones rowed over in their coracles, from Gallia, or the Summer Land, to Britain, the Honey Land, they came first to the promontory which we know as Cornwall; that is, the Cornu Galliae, or Walliae, which means Horn or Cape of the new country now called England. Here was a new region, rich in every kind of mineral. Ages before, the Phoenicians had named it Britain or the Land of

Tin. Within the memory of men now living, Cornishmen, that is, the miners of Cornwall, on going to California, discovered gold.

In Cornwall, as part of the Cymric realm, King Arthur found and married Guinevere, his queen. It was in Cornwall, also, that Merlin was hidden. Hear the rhyme:

Marvelous Merlin is wasted away
By a wicked woman, who may she be?
For she hath pent him in a crag
On Cornwall coast.

So it happens that thousands of "English" people in Cornwall are Welsh, by both name or descent, or have translated their names into English form, even while keeping the Welsh meaning. They are also Welsh in traits of character. Just as tens of thousands of Welsh folks, among the first settlers of New England and the American colonies are described in our histories as "English" people.

Now in early Cornwall there were many giants. Some were good but others were bad. One of these, a right fine fellow, was named Tom, and the other, a bad one, Blubb. This giant had had twenty wives, and was awfully cruel. Nobody ever knew what became of the twenty maidens he had married.

Sometimes people called the big fellow, that lived in a castle, Giant Blunderbuss, but Blubb was his name for short. He was much taller than the highest hop pole in Kent. He was made up mostly of head and stomach, for his chief idea in living was to eat. His skull was as big as a hogshead, or a push-ball, or a market wagon loaded with carrots. Indeed, it was strongly suspected by most people that the big bone box set on his shoulders was as hollow inside as a pumpkin, but that a cocoanut would hold all the brains he had. At any rate, during one of his fights with another giant, he had been given an awful thwack from the other giant's club. Then the sound made, which was heard a long distance away, was exactly like that when one pounds on an empty barrel.

Now this Giant Blubb had built a mighty castle between a big hill and a river. Under it were vaults of vast size, filled with treasures of all sorts, gold, silver, jewels and gems. There were cells in which he kept his wives after he had married them. It was the opinion of his neighbours that in every case, soon after the honeymoon was over, he ate them up.

Yet, if even the devil ought to have his due, one should be fair to this human monster, and we are bound to say that Giant Blubb denied these stories as pure gossip. It is certain that such crimes as murder and cannibalism never could be proved against him.

To guard his underground treasures, he had two huge and fierce dogs, supposed to be named Catchem and Tearem. What they were really called by their master was a secret. Yet anyone who had a piece of meat ready to throw to them, and knew their names, which were passwords, could first quiet them. Then he could walk by them and get the treasure.

Besides these dogs, the only living thing left in the castle when the giant went out was the latest Mrs Blubb. Yet she was in constant fear of her life, lest her big husband should sometime make a meal of her. For even she had heard the story that Blubb was a cannibal and looked at all plump women simply as delicacies, exactly as a boy peers into the window of a candy shop.

What made all the country round hate this cruel giant was not wholly on account of his awful appetite. It was because he had ruined the King's High Road. Ever since the time of King

Lud, whose name we read in Ludgate Hill, in London, where His Cymric Majesty had lived, this highway had been free to all. It ran all the way through Cornwall, from Penzance, and thence eastward to London and beyond.

When Giant Blubb wished to enlarge his castle, he had the walls and towers built down to the river's edge. This closed up the big road, so that people had to go far around and up over the hill, or by boat along the river. Such a roundabout way took much time and toil, and was too much trouble for all.

Everybody had to submit to this extortion, until there came along Giant Tom, of whom we shall now tell. His real name was Rolling Stone, for he never stuck long in one place at a job, and cared not a cucumber for money or fine clothes.

This jolly fellow was very good-natured and popular, but often very lazy. His mother talked with him many times, urging him to learn a trade, or in some way make an honest living. She found it very hard to keep anything in her larder, barn, pantry, or cellar, when he was at home. He measured four feet across his shoulders and at every meal he ate what would feed three big men. But as he could do six men's work, when he had a mind to – as often he did – he was always welcome. In fact, he was too popular for his own good.

One day, when ten common fellows were trying their utmost to lift a big long log on a cart, and were unable to do it, Tom came along and told them to stand back. Then he hoisted the tree on to the wain, roped it into place, and told the cartman to drive on. Then they all cheered him, and one of them lifted his Monmouth cap and cried out, "Hurrah for Giant Tom. He's the fellow to whip Giant Blubb."

"He is! He is!" they all cried in chorus.

"Who is this Giant Blubb? Where does he live?" asked Tom, rolling up his sleeves, for he was just spoiling for a row with a fellow of his size.

Then they told the story of how the big bully had ruined the King's Highway by building a great wall and tower across the road, to shut it up, to the grief of many honest men.

"Never mind, boys. I'll attend to his bacon," said Tom. "Leave the matter with me, and don't bother to tell the King about it."

Tom went the next day into town and hired himself out to a beer brewer to drive the wagon. Perhaps he hoped, also, while in this occupation, to keep down his thirst.

He asked the boss to give him the route that led past Giant Blubb's castle, over the old King's Highway.

The master of the brewery saw through Tom's purpose. He winked, and only said:

"Go ahead, my boy. I'll pay you double wages if you will open that road again; but see that Giant Blubb does not get my load of kegs, or that your carcass doesn't count with those of the twenty wives in his vaults and make twenty-one."

Again he winked his eye knowingly to his workmen. Tom drove off. He occupied all the room on the seat of the cart, which two men usually filled and left plenty of room on either side.

Cracking his whip, the new driver kept the four horses on a galloping pace, until very soon he called out, "Whoa," before the frowning high gateway of Giant Blubb.

Tom shouted from the depth of his lungs:

"Open the gate and let me drive through. This is the King's Highway."

The only reply, for a minute, was the barking of the curs. Then a rattling of bolts was heard, and the great gates swung wide open.

"Who are you, you impudent fellow? Go round over the hill, or I'll thrash you," blustered Giant Blubb, in a rage.

"Better save your breath to cool your porridge, you big boaster, and come out and fight," said Tom.

"Fight? You pigmy. I'll just get a switch and whip you as I would a bad boy."

Thereupon Giant Blubb stepped aside into the grove nearby, keeping all the while an eye on his gate, guarded by his two monstrous dogs. He selected an elm tree twenty feet high, tore it up by the roots, pulled off the branches, and peeled it for a whip. This he jerked up and down to make ready for his task of thrashing "the pigmy".

Meanwhile Giant Tom upset the wain, drew out the tongue and took off one of the wheels. Then, as if armed with spear and shield, he advanced to meet Giant Blubb. He whistled like a boy as he went forward.

In a passion of rage, Giant Blubb lifted his elm switch to strike, but Tom warded off the blow with his wheel shield. Then he punched him in the stomach with the wagon tongue, so hard that the big fellow slipped and rolled over in the mud.

Picking himself up, Giant Blubb, now half blind with rage, rushed against Tom, who, this time, made a lunge which planted the cart tongue inside Blubb's bowels, and knocked him over.

But Tom was not a cruel fellow, and had no desire to kill anyone. So he threw down his war tools, and tearing up a yard or two of grassy sod rolled it together, and made a plug of it, as big around as a milk churn. With this, he stopped up the big hole in Giant Blubb's huge body.

But instead of thanking Tom, Giant Blubb rushed at him again. He was in too much of a rage to see anything clearly, while

Tom, perfectly cool, gave the angry monster such a kick, in the place where he kept his dinner, that he rolled over, and Tom gave him another kick. Then the plug of sod fell out of his wound.

As he was bleeding to death, Giant Blubb beckoned to Tom to come up close, for he could only whisper.

"You've beaten me on the square, and I like you. Don't think I killed my twenty wives. They all died naturally. But call the dogs by name, and they will let you pass. Then, in my vaults, you'll find gold, silver, and copper. Make these your own and bury me decently. This is all I ask."

Tom made himself owner of the castle and all its treasures. He opened the King's Highway again. He took care of his aged mother, married the twenty-first wife of Giant Blubb, now a widow, and was always kind to the sick and poor.

Today in Cornwall, they still tell stories of the big fellow who abolished Giant Blubb's tollgate.

Centuries afterward when Christ's gospel came into the land, they restored Giant Tom's tomb and on it were chiselled these words:

The Restorer of Paths to Dwell In.

THE GIANTESS'S APRON-FULL

A huge giant, in company with his wife, travelling towards the island of Mona, with an intention of settling amongst the first inhabitants that had removed there, and having been informed that there was but a narrow channel which divided it from the continent, took up two large stones, one under each arm, to carry with him as a preparatory for making a bridge over this channel, and his lady had her apron filled with small stones for the same purpose; but, meeting a man on this spot with a large parcel of old shoes on his shoulders, the giant asked him how far it was to Mona. The man replied that it was so far that he had worn out those shoes in travelling from Mona to that place. The giant on hearing this dropped down the stones, one on each side of him, where they now stand upright, about a hundred yards or more distant from each other; the space between them was occupied by this Goliath's body. His mistress at the same time opened her apron, and dropped down the contents of it, which formed this heap.

CORWRION CHANGELING LEGEND

Once on a time, in the fourteenth century, the wife of a man at Corwrion had twins, and she complained one day to the witch who lived close by, at Tyddyn y Barcut, that the children were not getting on, but that they were always crying, day and night. "Are you sure that they are your children?" asked the witch, adding that it did not seem to her that they were like hers. "I have my doubts also," said the mother. "I wonder if somebody has changed children with you," said the witch. "I do not know," said the mother. "But why do you not seek to know?" asked the other. "But how am I to go about it?" said the mother. The witch replied, "Go and do something rather strange before their eyes and watch what they will say to one another." "Well I do not know what I should do," said the mother. "Oh," said the other, "take an egg-shell, and proceed to brew beer in it in a chamber aside, and come here to tell me what the children will say about it." She went home and did as the witch had directed her, when the two children lifted their heads out of the cradle to see what she was doing, to watch, and to listen. Then one observed to the other: "I remember seeing an oak having an acorn," to which the other replied, "And I remember seeing a hen having an egg," and one of the two added, "But I do not remember before seeing anybody brew beer in the shell of a hen's egg."

The mother then went to the witch and told her what the twins had said one to the other, and she directed her to go to a small wooden bridge not far off, with one of the strange children under each arm, and there to drop them from the bridge into the river beneath. The mother went back home again and did as she had been directed. When she reached home this time, to her astonishment, she found that her own children had been brought back.

There is one important difference between these two tales. In the latter, the mother drops the children over the bridge into the waters beneath, and then goes home, without noticing whether the poor children had been rescued by the goblins or not, but on reaching her home she found in the cradle her own two children, presumably conveyed there by the Fairies. In the first tale, we are informed that she saw the goblins save their offspring from a watery grave. Subjecting peevish children to such a terrible ordeal as this must have ended often with a tragedy, but even in such cases superstitious mothers could easily persuade themselves that the destroyed infants were undoubtedly the offspring of elfins, and therefore unworthy of their fostering care. The only safeguard to wholesale infanticide was the test applied as to the super-human precociousness, or ordinary intelligence, of the children.

MILK THAT WOULD NOT CHURN

And the Steps Taken to Counteract the Malice of the Witch that Had Cursed the Churn and its Contents

About the year 1815 an old woman, supposed to be a witch, lived at Ffridd Ucha, Llanfrothen, and she got her living by begging. One day she called at Ty Mawr, in the same parish, requesting a charity of milk; but she was refused. The next time they churned, the milk would not turn to butter. They continued their labours for many hours, but at last they were compelled to desist in consequence of the unpleasant odour which proceeded from the churn. The milk was thrown away, and the farmer, John Griffiths, divining that the milk had been witched by the woman who had been begging at their house, went to consult a conjuror, who lived near Pwllheli. This man told him that he was to put a red-hot crowbar into the milk the next time they churned. This was done, and the milk was successfully churned. For several weeks the crowbar served as an antidote, but at last it failed, and again the milk could not be churned, and the unpleasant smell made it again impossible for anyone to stand near the churn. Griffiths, as before, consulted the Pwllheli conjuror, who gave him a charm to place underneath the churn, stating, when he did so, that if it failed, he could render no further assistance. The charm did not act, and a gentleman whom he next consulted advised him to go to Bell, or Bella, the Denbigh witch. Griffiths did so, and to his great surprise he found that Bell could describe the position of his house, and she knew the names of his fields. Her instructions were: gather all the cattle to Gors Goch field, a meadow in front of the house, and then she said that the farmer and a friend were to go to a certain holly tree, and stand out of sight underneath this tree, which to this day stands in the hedge that surrounds the meadow mentioned by Bell. This was to be done by night, and the farmer was told that he should then see the person who had injured him. The instructions were literally carried out. When the cows came to the field they herded together in a frightened manner, and commenced bellowing fearfully. In a very short time, who should enter the field but the suspected woman in evident bodily pain, and Griffiths and his friend heard her uttering some words unintelligible to them, and having done so, she disappeared, and the cattle became quiet, and ever after they had no difficulty in churning the milk of those cows.

A HORSE WITCHED

Pedws Ffoulk, a supposed witch, was going through a field where people were employed at work, and just as she came opposite the horse it fell down, as if it were dead. The workmen ran to the horse to ascertain what was the matter with it, but Pedws went along, not heeding what had occurred. This unfeeling conduct on her part roused the suspicion of the men, and they came to the conclusion that the old woman had witched the horse, and that she was the cause of its illness. They, therefore, determined to run after the woman and bring her back to undo her own evil work. Off they rushed after her, and forced her back to the field, where the horse was still lying on the ground. They there compelled the old creature to say, standing over the horse, these words: "*Duw arno fo*" (God be with him). This she did, and then she was allowed to go on her way. By and by the horse revived, and got upon his feet, and looked as well as ever, but this, it was thought, would not have been the case had not the witch undone her own curse.

HUW LLWYD AND HIS MAGICAL BOOKS

It is said that Huw Llwyd had two daughters; one of an inquisitive turn of mind, like himself, while the other resembled her mother, and cared not for books. On his death bed he called his learned daughter to his side, and directed her to take his books on the dark science, and throw them into a pool, which he named, from the bridge that spanned the river. The girl went to Llyn Pont Rhyd-ddu with the books, and stood on the bridge, watching the whirlpool beneath, but she could not persuade herself to throw them over, and thus destroy her father's precious treasures. So she determined to tell him a falsehood, and say that she had cast them into the river. On her return home her father asked her whether she had thrown the books into the pool, and on receiving an answer in the affirmative, he, inquiring whether she had seen anything strange when the books reached the river, was informed that she had seen nothing. "Then," said he, "you have not complied with my request. I cannot die until the books are thrown into the pool." She took the books a second time to the river, and now, very reluctantly, she hurled them into the pool, and watched their descent. They had not reached the water before two hands appeared, stretched upward, out of the pool, and these hands caught the books before they touched the water and, clutching them carefully, both the books and the hands disappeared beneath the waters. She went home immediately, and again appeared before her father, and in answer to his question, she related what had occurred. "Now," said he, "I know you have thrown them in, and I can now die in peace," which he forthwith did.

A CONJUROR'S COLLUSION EXPOSED

This man's house consisted of but few rooms. Between the kitchen and his study, or consulting room, was a slight partition. He had a servant girl, whom he admitted as a partner in his trade. This girl, when she saw a patient approach the house, which she was able to do, because there was only one approach to it, and only one entrance, informed her master of the fact that someone was coming, and he immediately disappeared, and he placed himself in a position to hear the conversation of the girl with the person who had come to consult him. The servant by questioning the party adroitly obtained that information respecting the case which her master required, and when she had obtained the necessary information, he would appear, and forthwith tell the stranger that he knew hours before, or days ago, that he was to have the visit now paid him, and then he would relate all the particulars which he had himself heard through the partition, to the amazement of the stranger, who was ignorant of this means of communication.

At other times, if a person who wished to consult him came to the house when the conjuror was in the kitchen, he would disappear as before, stating that he was going to consult his books, and then his faithful helper would proceed to extort the necessary information from the visitor. On this, he would reappear and exhibit his wonderful knowledge to the amazed dupe.

On one occasion, though, a knowing one came to the conjuror with his arm in a sling, and forthwith the wise man disappeared, leaving the maid to conduct the necessary preliminary examination, and her visitor minutely described how the accident had occurred, and how he had broken his arm in two places, etc.

All this the conjuror heard, and he came into the room and rehearsed all that he had heard; but the biter was bitten, for the stranger, taking his broken arm out of the sling, in no very polite language accused the conjuror of being an impostor, and pointed out the way in which the collusion had been carried out between him and his maid.

This was an exposure the conjuror had not foreseen!

THE FAIRY OF THE DELL

In olden times fairies were sent to oppose the evil-doings of witches, and to destroy their power. About three hundred years ago a band of fairies, sixty in number, with their queen, called Queen of the Dell, came to Mona to oppose the evil works of a celebrated witch. The fairies settled by a spring, in a valley. After having blessed the spring, or "well", as they called it, they built a bower just above the spring for the queen, placing a throne therein. Near by they built a large bower for themselves to live in.

After that, the queen drew three circles, one within the other, on a nice flat grassy place by the well. When they were comfortably settled, the queen sent the fairies about the country to gather tidings of the people. They went from house to house, and everywhere heard great complaints against an old witch; how she had made some blind, others lame, and deformed others by causing a horn to grow out of their foreheads. When they got back to the well and told the queen, she said:

"I must do something for these old people, and though the witch is very powerful, we must break her power." So the next day the queen fairy sent word to all the bewitched to congregate upon a fixed day at the sacred well, just before noon.

When the day came, several ailing people collected at the well. The queen then placed the patients in pairs in the inner ring, and the sixty fairies in pairs in the middle ring. Each little fairy was three feet and a half high, and carried a small wand in her right hand, and a bunch of fairy flowers – cuckoo's boots, baby's bells, and day's-eyes – in her left hand. Then the queen, who was four feet and a half in height, took the outside ring. On her head was a crown of wild flowers, in her right hand she carried a wand, and in her left a posy of fairy flowers. At a signal from the queen they began marching round the rings, singing in chorus:

"We march round by two and two
The circles of the sacred well
That lies in the dell."

When they had walked twice round the ring singing, the queen took her seat upon the throne, and calling each patient to her, she touched him with her wand and bade him go down to the sacred well and dip his body into the water three times, promising that all his ills should be cured. As each one came forth from the spring he knelt before the queen, and she blessed him, and told him to hurry home and put on dry clothes. So that all were cured of their ills.

II

Now the old witch who had worked all these evils lived near the well in a cottage. She had first learned witchcraft from a book called *The Black Art*, which a gentleman farmer had lent her when a girl. She progressed rapidly with her studies, and being eager to learn more, sold herself to the devil, who made compact with her that she should have full power for seven years, after which she was to become his. He gave her a wand that had the magic power of drawing people to her, and she had a ring on the grass by her house just like the fairy's ring. As the seven years were drawing to a close, and her heart was savage against the farmer who first led her into the paths of evil knowledge, she determined to be revenged. One day, soon after the Fairy of the Dell came to live by the spring, she drew the farmer to her with her wand, and, standing in her ring, she lured him into it. When he crossed the line, she said:

"Cursed be he or she
That crosses my circle to see me,"

and, touching him on the head and back, a horn and a tail grew from the spots touched. He went off in a terrible rage, but she only laughed maliciously. Then, as she heard of the Queen of the Dell's good deeds, she repented of her evil deeds, and begged her neighbour to go to the queen fairy and ask her if she might come and visit her. The queen consented, and the old witch went down and told her everything – of the book, of the magic wand, of the ring, and of all the wicked deeds she had done.

"O, you have been a bad witch," said the queen, "but I will see what I can do; but you must bring me the book and the wand;" and she told the old witch to come on the following day a little before noon. When the witch came the next day with her wand and book, she found the fairies had built a fire in the middle ring. The queen then took her and stood her by the fire, for she could not trust her on the outer circle.

"Now I must have more power," said the queen to the fairies, and she went and sat on the throne, leaving the witch by the fire in the middle ring. After thinking a little, the queen said, "Now I have it," and coming down from her throne muttering, she began walking round the outer circle, waiting for the hour of one o'clock, when all the fairies got into the middle circle and marched round, singing:

"At the hour of one
The cock shall crow one,
Goo! Goo! Goo!
I am here to tell
Of the sacred well
That lies in the dell,
And will conquer hell."

On the second round, they sang:

"At the hour of two
The cock crows two,
Goo! Goo! Goo!
I am here to tell
Of the sacred well
That lies in the dell;
We will conquer hell."

At the last round, they sang:

"At the hour of three
The cock crows three,
Goo! Goo! Goo!

I am here to tell
Of the sacred well
That lies in the dell;
Now I have conquered hell."

Then the queen cast the book and wand into the fire, and immediately the vale was rent by a thundering noise, and numbers of devils came from everywhere, and encircled the outer ring, but they could not pass the ring. Then the fairies began walking round and round, singing their song. When they had finished the song they heard a loud screech from the devils that frightened all the fairies except the queen. She was unmoved, and going to the fire, stirred the ashes with her wand, and saw that the book and wand were burnt, and then she walked thrice round the outer ring by herself, when she turned to the devils, and said:

"I command you to be gone from our earthly home, get to your own abode. I take the power of casting you all from here. Begone! begone! begone!" And all the devils flew up, and there was a mighty clap as of thunder, and the earth trembled, and the sky became overcast, and all the devils burst, and the sky cleared again.

After this the queen put three fairies by the old witch's side, and they constantly dipped their wands in the sacred spring, and touched her head, and she was sorely troubled and converted.

"Bring the mirror," said the queen.

And the fairies brought the mirror and laid it in the middle circle, and they all walked round three times, chanting again the song beginning "At the hour of one." When they had done this the queen stood still, and said:

"Stand and watch to see what you can see."

And as she looked she said:

"The mirror shines unto me
That the witch we can see
Has three devils inside of she."

Immediately the witch had a fit, and the three fairies had a hard job to keep the three devils quiet; indeed, they could not do so, and the queen had to go herself with her wand, for fear the devils should burst the witch asunder, and she said, "Come out three evil spirits, out of thee."

And they came gnashing their teeth, and would have killed all the fairies, but the queen said:

"Begone, begone, begone! you evil spirits, to the place of your abode," and suddenly the sky turned bright as fire, for the evil spirits were trying their spleen against the fairies, but the queen said, "Collect, collect, collect, into one fierce ball," and the fiery sky collected into one ball of fire more dazzling than the sun, so that none could look at it except the queen, who wore a black silk mask to protect her eyes. Suddenly the ball burst with a terrific noise, and the earth trembled.

"Enter into your abode, and never come down to our abode on earth any more," said the queen.

And the witch was herself again, and she and the queen fairy were immediately great friends. The witch, when she came out of the ring, dropped on her knee and asked the queen if she might call her the Lady of the Dell, and how she could serve her.

"We will see about that," said the queen.

"Well, how do you live?" asked the woman who had been a witch.

"Well, I'll tell you," said the queen. "We go at midnight and milk the cows, and we keep the milk, and it never grows less so long as we leave some in the bottom of the vessel; we must not use it all. After milking the cow, we rub the cow's purse and bless it, and she gives double the amount of milk."

"Well, how do you get corn?"

"Well, we were at the mill playing one day, and the miller came in and saw us, and spoke kindly to us, and offered us some flour. 'We never take nothing for nothing,' I said, so I blessed the bin: so in a few minutes the bin was full to the brim with flour, and I said to the miller, 'Now don't you empty the bin, but always leave a peck in it, and for twelve months, no matter how much you use the bin, it will always be full in the morning.' Now I have told you this much, and I will tell further, 'You must love your neighbour, you must love all mankind.' Now here is a purse of gold, go and buy what you want, eggs, bacon, cheese, and get a flagon of wine and use these things freely, giving freely to the aged poor, and if you never finish these things, there will always be as much the next morning as you started with. And I shall make a salve for you, and you must use the water from the sacred well. That will be as a medicine, and people shall come from far and wide to be cured by you, and you shall be loved by all, and you shall be known to the poorest of the poor as Madame Dorothy."

And the woman did as she was told, and she became renowned for her medical skill, especially in childbirth, for her salve eased the pains, and her waters brought milk. By-and-by, she got known all over the island, and rich people came to her from afar, and she always made the rich pay, and the poor were treated free.

Madame Dorothy used to see the queen fairy at times, and one day she asked her, "Shall we meet again?"

"We cannot tell," said the queen, "but I will give you a ring – let me place it on your finger – it is a magic ring worked by fairies. Whenever you seek to know of me, make a ring of your own, and walk round three times and rub the ring; if it turns bright I am alive, but if you see blood I am dead."

"But how can that be? You are much younger than I am."

"Oh, no! We fairies look young to the day of our death; we live to a great age, but die naturally of old age, for we never have any ailments, but still our power fades. Men fade in the flesh and power, but we fade only in power. I am over seventy now."

"But you look to be thirty."

"Well, we will shake hands and part, for I must go elsewhere; as I have no king, I do not stop in one place."

And they shook hands and parted.

ARTHUR IN THE CAVE

Once upon a time a Welshman was walking on London Bridge, staring at the traffic, and wondering why there were so many kites hovering about. He had come to London after many adventures with thieves and highwaymen, which need not be related here, in charge of a herd of black Welsh cattle. He had sold them with much profit, and with jingling gold in his pocket he was going about to see the sights of the city.

He was carrying a hazel staff in his hand, for you must know that a good staff is as necessary to a drover as teeth are to his dog. He stood still to gaze at some wares in a shop (for at that time London Bridge was shops from beginning to end), when he noticed that a man was looking at his stick with a long fixed look.

The man after a while came to him and asked him where he came from. "I come from my own country," said the Welshman, rather surlily, for he could not see what business the man had to ask him such a question.

"Do not take it amiss," said the stranger: "if you will only answer my questions and take my advice, it will be of greater benefit to you than you imagine. Do you remember where you cut that stick?"

The Welshman was still suspicious and said, "What does it matter where I cut it?"

"It matters," said his questioner, "because there is treasure hidden near the spot where you cut that stick. If you remember the place and can conduct me to it, I will put you in possession of great riches."

The Welshman now understood that he had to deal with a sorcerer, and he was greatly perplexed as to what to do. On the one hand, he was tempted by the prospect of wealth; on the other hand, he knew that the sorcerer must have derived his knowledge from devils, and he feared to have anything to do with the powers of darkness. The cunning man strove hard to persuade him, and at length made him promise to show the place where he had cut his hazel staff.

The Welshman and the magician journeyed together to Wales. They went to Craig y Dinas, the Rock of the Fortress, at the head of the Neath Valley, near Pont Nedd Fechan, and the Welshman, pointing to the stock or root of an old hazel, said, "This is where I cut my stick."

"Let us dig," said the sorcerer. They dug until they came to a broad, flat stone. Prising this up, they found some steps leading downwards. They went down the steps and along a narrow passage until they came to a door. "Are you brave," asked the sorcerer, "will you come in with me?"

"I will," said the Welshman, his curiosity getting the better of his fear.

They opened the door, and a great cave opened out before them. There was a faint red light in the cave, and they could see everything. The first thing they came to was a bell. "Do not touch that bell," said the sorcerer, "or it will be all over with us both."

As they went further in, the Welshman saw that the place was not empty. There were soldiers lying down asleep, thousands of them, as far as ever the eye could see. Each one was clad in bright armour, the steel helmet of each was on his head, the shining shield of each was on his arm, the sword of each was near his hand, each had his spear stuck in the ground near him, and each and all were asleep. In the middle of the cave was a great round table at which sat warriors, whose noble features and richly dight armour proclaimed that they were not in the roll of common men.

Each of those, too, had his head bent down in sleep. On a golden throne on the further side of the round table was a King of gigantic stature and august presence. In his hand, held below the hilt, was a mighty sword with scabbard and haft of gold studded with gleaming gems; on his head was a crown set with precious stones which flashed and glinted like so many points of fire. Sleep had set its seal on his eyelids also.

"Are they asleep?" asked the Welshman, hardly believing his own eyes.

"Yes, each and all of them," answered the sorcerer, "but if you touch yonder bell, they will all awake."

"How long have they been asleep?"

"For over a thousand years!"

"Who are they?"

"Arthur's warriors, waiting for the time to come when they shall destroy all the enemies of the Cymry and repossess the Island of Britain, establishing their own King once more at Caer Lleon."

"Who are those sitting at the round table?"

"Those are Arthur's Knights, Owain, the son of Urien; Cai, the son of Cynyr; Gwalchmai, the son of Gwyar; Peredur, the son of Efrawc; Geraint, the son of Erbin; Trystan, the son of March; Bedwyr, the son of Bedrawd; Cilhwch, the son of Celyddon; Edeyrn, the son of Nudd; Cynon, the son of Clydno" – "And on the golden throne?" broke in the Welshman—" is Arthur himself, with his sword Excalibur in his hand," replied the sorcerer.

Impatient by this time at the Welshman's questions, the sorcerer hastened to a great heap of yellow gold on the floor of the cave. He took up as much as he could carry, and bade his companion do the same. "It is time for us to go," he then said, and he led the way towards the door by which they had entered.

But the Welshman was fascinated by the sight of the countless soldiers in their glittering arms, all asleep. "How I should like to see them all awaking!" he said to himself. "I will touch the bell – I *must* see them all arising from their sleep."

When they came to the bell, he struck it until it rang through the whole place. As soon as it rang, lo! the thousands of warriors leapt to their feet and the ground beneath them shook with the sound of the steel arms. And a great voice came from their midst, "Who rang the bell? Has the day come?"

The sorcerer was so frightened that he shook like an aspen leaf. He shouted in answer, "No, the day has not come. Sleep on."

The mighty host was all in motion, and the Welshman's eyes were dazzled as he looked at the bright steel arms which illumined the cave as with the light of myriad flames of fire.

"Arthur," said the voice again, "awake; the bell has rung, the day is breaking. Awake, Arthur the Great."

"No," shouted the sorcerer, "it is still night; sleep on, Arthur the Great."

A sound came from the throne. Arthur was standing, and the jewels in his crown shone like bright stars above the countless throng. His voice was strong and sweet like the sound of many waters, and he said, "My warriors, the day has not come when the Black Eagle and the Golden Eagle shall go to war. It is only a seeker after gold who has rung the bell. Sleep on, my warriors, the morn of Wales has not yet dawned."

A peaceful sound like the distant sigh of the sea came over the cave, and in a trice the soldiers were all asleep again. The sorcerer hurried the Welshman out of the cave, moved the stone back to its place, and vanished.

Many a time did the Welshman try to find the way into the cave again, but though he dug over every inch of the hill, he never found the entrance.

THE CURSE OF PANTANNAS

Long, long ago, at the farm of Pantannas, in Glamorgan, there lived a churlish old husbandman. He hated the Fair Folk who danced on his fields to the light of the moon, and longed to discover some way of ridding his land of them.

Not being able to think of any plan, he went to an old witch and told her of his wish. She made him promise to give her one night's milking on his farm, and then advised him thus:

"Wherever you see a fairy ring in your fields plough it and sow it with corn," she said. "When the fairies find the greensward gone, they will never revisit the spot."

The farmer took her advice. He yoked his oxen and drove his iron ploughshare through every circle in which the fairies had danced at night, and sowed it with corn. The nightly sounds of dance and song ceased, and no fairy was afterwards seen in the fields of Pantannas.

The farmer rejoiced greatly, imagining vain things, until one evening in the spring of the year, when the wheat was green in the fields. The farmer was returning home in the red light of the setting sun, when a tiny little man in a red coat came to him, unsheathed a little sword, and directing the point towards him, said:

Dial a ddaw,	*Vengeance cometh,*
Y mae gerilaw.	*Fast it approacheth.*

After saying this, the mannikin disappeared. The farmer tried to laugh; but there was something in the angry, grim looks of the little man which made him feel very uncomfortable.

Spring, however, turned into summer, and summer into autumn, without anything happening, and the farmer thought that he had been very foolish to fear the threat of the little man in the red coat.

In the autumn, when the corn was golden in the fields and ripe for the sickle, the farmer and his family were one night going to bed. Suddenly they heard a mighty noise, which shook the house as though it would fall. As they trembled with fear, they heard a loud voice saying:

Daw dial. *Vengeance cometh.*

Next morning, no ear or straw was to be seen in the cornfields, only black ashes. The fairies had burnt all the harvest.

The farmer was walking through his fields, gazing ruefully at the destruction wrought by the fairies, when he was met by the same little man as before. Pointing his sword threateningly, the elf said:

Nid yw ond dechrau. *It but beginneth.*

The farmer's face turned as white as milk, and he began to plead for pardon. He was quite willing, he said, to allow the fields where the fairies had been wont to dance and sing to grow again into a greensward.

They could dance in their rings as often as they wished without interference, provided only they would punish him no more.

"No," was the stern reply. "The word of the King has gone forth that he will avenge himself on thee, and no power can recall it."

The farmer burst into tears, and begged so sorrowfully to be forgiven for his fault that the little man at last pitied him and said that he would speak to his lord. "I will come again at the hour of sunset three days hence and bring thee my lord's behest."

When the time came on the third day, the sprite was awaiting the farmer at the appointed spot. "The King's word," he said, "cannot be recalled, and vengeance must come. Still, since thou repentest thee of thy fault and art anxious to atone it, the curse shall not fall in thy time nor in that of thy sons, but will await thy distant posterity."

This promise comforted the farmer. The dark-green circles of grass grew again, the gay elves danced in them, and the sounds of music gladdened the fields as of old. The dread voice came at times, repeating the threat,

Daw dial, *Vengeance will come,*

but the farmer passed away in peaceful old age, and his sons followed him to the churchyard without feeling any effects of the curse pronounced by the King of the fairies.

More than a hundred years after the first warning had been uttered, Madoc, the heir of Pantannas, was betrothed to Teleri, the daughter of the squire of Pen Craig Daf, and the wedding was to take place in a few weeks. It was Christmas-tide, and they made a feast at Pantannas to which Teleri and all her kin were bidden.

The feast sped merrily, and all were seated round the hearth, passing the hours with tale and song. Suddenly, above the noise of the river which flowed outside the house, they seemed to hear a voice saying:

Daeth amser ymddial. *The time for revenge is come.*

A silence fell on the joyous company. They went out and listened if they could hear the voice a second time; but long though they lingered, they could make out no sound except the angry noise of the full river plunging down its rocky bed. They went back into the house; gradually their fears were chased away, and all was as before.

Again, above the sounds of mirth and the noise of the waters as they boiled over the boulders was heard a clear voice:

Daeth yr amser.	*The time is come.*

A dread noise crashed around them, and the house shook to its foundations. As they sat speechless with fear, behold, a shapeless hag appeared at the window. Then one, bolder than the rest, said, "What dost thou, ugly little thing, want here?"

"I have naught to do with thee, chatterer," said the hag. "I had come to tell the doom which awaits this house and that other which hopes to be allied with it, but as thou hast insulted me, the veil which conceals it shall not be lifted by me." With that she vanished, no one knew how or whither.

When she had gone, the voice proclaimed again, more loudly than before:

Daeth amser ymddial.	*The time for vengeance is come.*

Terror and gloom fell upon all. The guests before long parted and went trembling home, and Madoc took his betrothed back to Pen Craig Daf, doing all that a fond lover could to dispel her fears, for she had been struck to the heart with nameless dread.

The hours of darkness succeeded one another wearily, and no Madoc returned to Pantannas. Morning came, but still no Madoc; and his aged parents, already shaken by the vision of the hag and the strange voices which had interrupted their joyous feast, were almost beside themselves with anxiety. As the day wore on, without any sign of Madoc, they sent messengers in all directions to seek news of him, but all they could discover was that he had turned his footsteps homewards after bidding farewell to his betrothed at Pen Craig Daf. All the countryside turned out to find him. With minute care they searched every hill and dale for many miles around, and dragged the depths of every river, but never a trace of him could they find.

When many weeks of unavailing search had gone by the father and mother sought an aged hermit who dwelt in a cave high up the country, and asked him when their lost son would come back to them. He told the lamenting parents that the judgment threatened in olden times by the fairies had overtaken the hapless youth, and bade them hope no more to see him, whether he were alive or dead. It might perhaps come to pass that after generations had gone by he would reappear, but not in their lifetime.

Time rolled on, weeks grew into months and months into years, and gradually all came to believe that the hermit had spoken true. All, that is to say, except one. The gentle maiden, Teleri, never ceased to believe that her beloved was alive and would come again. Every morning when the sun burst open the gates of dawn, she would stand upon the summit of a high rock, looking over the landscape far and near. At even, again, she would be seen at the same spot, seeking some sign of her lover's return until the sun sank behind the battlements of the west. Madoc's father and mother died, and their mortal remains were laid to rest, but Teleri never failed of hope. Year after year she watched until her bright eyes became dim and her chestnut hair was silvered. Worn out with fruitless longing, she died before her time, and they buried her in the graveyard of the old Chapel of the Fan. One by one those who had known Madoc died, and his strange disappearance became only a faint tradition.

Teleri's undying belief that her lover was still alive was, however, true. This is what had happened to him. As he was returning home from Pen Craig Daf, the sounds of the sweetest music he had ever heard in his life came out of a cave in the Raven's Rift, and he stopped to listen. The strains after a while seemed to recede further into the cave, and he stepped inside to hear better. The melody retreated further and further, and Madoc, forgetting everything else, followed it further and further into the recesses of the cavern. After he had been listening for an hour or two, as he thought, the music ceased, and suddenly remembering that after the strange events of the night his parents would be anxious for his return, he retraced his footsteps rapidly to the mouth of the cave. When he issued forth from the hollow, the sun was high in the heavens, and he realized that he had been listening to the music longer than he had at first thought. He hastened towards Pantannas, opened the door and went in. Sitting by the fire was an aged man who asked him, "Who art thou that comest in so boldly?"

A sense of bewilderment came over Madoc. He looked round him. The inside of the house seemed different from what he had been accustomed to. He went to the window and looked out. There appeared to him to be several curious differences in the aspect of the country also. He became dimly conscious that some great change had passed over his life, and answered faintly, "I am Madoc."

"Madoc?" said the aged man. "Madoc? I know thee not. There is no Madoc living in this place, nor have I ever known any man of that name. The only Madoc I have ever heard of was one who, my grandfather said, disappeared suddenly from this place, nobody knew whither, many scores of years ago."

Madoc sank on a chair and wept. The old man's heart went out to him in his grief, and he rose to comfort him. He put his hand on his shoulder, when lo! the weeping figure crumbled into thin dust.

GORONWY TUDOR AND THE WITCHES OF LLANDDONA

Very few men in Anglesey in the olden days dared to cross any of the Witches of Llanddona, and those who were bold enough to do so suffered grievously for their rashness. But Goronwy Tudor, who lived not far from Llanddona, was reckless enough to defy even Bella Fawr, Big Bella, the most famous and most dreaded of all the witches of that uncanny village, and he was not a ha'porth the worse.

Perhaps you do not know the history of the Llanddona witches. Long ago a boat came ashore in Red Wharf Bay without rudder or oars, full of men and women half dead with hunger and thirst. In early days it was the custom to put evil-doers in a boat to drift oarless and rudderless on the sea, and when this boat was swept by wind and waves on the beautiful sands of Llanddona, the good people who then lived there prepared to drive it back into the sea, thinking it was manned by criminals. But the strangers caused a spring of pure water to burst forth on the sands (the well still remains), and this decided their fate. They were allowed to stay and to build cottages. But they did not change their evil natures. The men lived by smuggling, and the women begged and practised witchcraft.

It was impossible to overcome the smugglers in a fray, for each of them carried about with him a black fly tied in a knot of his neckerchief. When their strength failed them in the fight they undid the knots of their cravats, and the flies flew at the eyes of their opponents and blinded them. The women used to visit the farmhouses, and when they asked for a pound of butter, a loaf of bread, some potatoes, eggs, a fowl, part of a pig, or what not, they were not denied, because they cursed those who refused them.

If they attended a fair or market, no one ventured to bid against them for anything.

But Goronwy Tudor was not afraid of them. He had a birthmark above his breast, which is a great protection against witchcraft, and he knew how to break nearly every spell. He had the plant which is called Mary's turnip growing in front of his house: he also nailed horseshoes above every door, and put rings made of the mountain ash under the doorposts, thus making his house and all his farm buildings safe. To make them doubly sure he sprinkled earth from the churchyard in all his rooms, and in his byre, stable and pigsty. When the animals were in the fields, however, he had some difficulty in securing them from harm. One day when he went to fetch his cows from the meadow to be milked he found them sitting like cats before a fire, with their hind legs beneath them. Goronwy took the skin of an adder, burnt it and scattered the ashes over the horns of the cows. They got up at once, and walked off with their usual dignity to the byre.

Another day the milk would not turn into butter, and a very unpleasant smell arose from the churn. Goronwy took a crowbar, heated it red-hot, and put it in the milk. Out jumped a large hare, and ran away through the open door of the dairy. After this the milk was churned into beautiful butter.

Some time after the supply of milk began to decline, and the butter made from it was so bad and evil-smelling that the very dogs would not touch it. The milk became scantier and scantier, until at last it ceased altogether, and the cows gave nothing but blood. Goronwy watched in the fields at night and saw a hare going up to a cow and sucking it. She squirted from her mouth and nostrils the milk she had sucked, and then went on to another cow. She did the same with her and with all the other cows. Goronwy knew that it was old Bella in the form of a hare, and he prepared to stop her evildoing and to punish her. The next night he took his gun, putting into it a silver coin instead of shot (shot cannot penetrate a witch's body), and placed a bit of vervain under the stock. When he saw the hare milking the cows he fired at her. The hare immediately ran off in the direction of Bella's cottage, with Goronwy after her. He was not so fleet of foot as puss, but he managed to keep her in sight, and saw her jumping over the lower half of the door of the house. Going up to the cottage he heard the sound of dreadful groans. When he reached the door he went in. There was no hare to be seen, but old Bella was sitting by the fire with blood streaming from her legs. He was never again troubled by old Bella in the shape of a hare, and by drawing blood from the bewitched kine he broke the spell.

Bella made one more attempt to injure him. She went to the Cold Well and launched at him the great curse of the Witches of Llanddona:

May he wander for ages many,
And at every step, a stile,
At every stile, a fall;
At every fall, a broken bone,
Not the largest nor the least bone,
But the chief neckbone, every time.

Goronwy felt in his bones that he had been cursed. He got some witch's butter that grows on decayed trees and stuck pins in it. When the pain inflicted by the pins penetrated her body, Bella had willy-nilly to appear before him. She was screaming with pain, and Goronwy refused to take the pins which were causing the anguish out of the butter until she said: "Rhad Duw ac ar bopeth ar a feddi – God's blessing on thee and on everything that thou possessest." After this neither Bella nor any of her tribe had any power over Goronwy or his wife, or his man-servant or his maid-servant, or his ox or his ass, or anything that was his.

SIX AND FOUR ARE TEN

A conjuror, on his way to Llanrwst, turned into the tavern at Henllan one evening and called for a glass of beer and some bread and cheese. When he asked for his reckoning, he was charged tenpence – fourpence for the beer and sixpence for the bread and cheese. This charge he considered outrageous, but he did not condescend to dispute it. He determined, however, to have his revenge, and before departing he took a scrap of paper, wrote on it a spell, and put it under the table leg.

The landlord and landlady went to bed early, telling the maid-servant to clear away the things which had been set before the conjuror. No sooner were their heads on the pillow than they heard shouting and jumping downstairs. The maid was shrieking at the top of her voice:

"Six and four are ten,
Count it o'er again,"

and dancing wildly. Surprised and angry, they asked her what was the matter, but the only answer they received was:

"Six and four are ten,
Count it o'er again"

and the girl went on dancing.

The thought now struck the landlord that the dancer had gone out of her mind. He got up and went down to see. The moment he placed his foot in the room he gave a hop, skip and a jump, joined the girl in her mad dance, and with her he shrieked out:

"Six and four are ten,
Count it o'er again."

The noise was doubled, and if the landlady was surprised and angry before, she was now astounded and furious. She shouted to the scandalous couple to cease their noise, but all to no purpose. They bellowed more loudly than before:

"Six and four are ten,
Count it o'er again,"

and danced still more vigorously.

The landlady could stand it no longer: she left her bed and went downstairs. The sight of her husband and maid shamelessly dancing together and yelling:

"Six and four are ten,
Count it o'er again,"

made her wrath overflow, and she determined to put a stop to the proceedings. Seizing a big stick, she bounded into the room, but before she could belabour the heads and shoulders of the two dancers as she had intended, she found herself capering like them and joining in the chorus:

"Six and four are ten,
Count it o'er again."

The uproar was now great indeed, and the neighbours came to see what was the matter. All who ventured into the room joined in the dance and chorus, and soon the room was full of men and women, leaping and frisking and yelling at the tops of their voices:

"Six and four are ten,
Count it o'er again."

Then one of the spectators, more quick-witted than the rest, remembered that he had seen the conjuror leaving the tavern, and at once guessed that he was responsible for this frantic revel. Hurrying after him, he overtook him on the road to Llanrwst, and begged him to release the people from his spell. The conjuror, chuckling at the humour of the punishment he had meted out, consented. "Take," said he, "the piece of paper which is under the table leg and burn it, and they will then stop their row."

The man ran back as fast as he could, rushed to the table and cast the paper into the fire. Immediately the dancing and shouting ceased, and the performers fell down, panting and exhausted after their exertions.

THE CAT WITCHES

Huw Llwyd of Cynfael was the seventh son of a family of sons, and therefore he was a conjuror by nature. He increased his knowledge of the black art by the study of magical books, and he ate eagle's flesh, so that his descendants could for nine generations charm for the shingles. (All they had to do was to spit on the rash and say: "Male eagle, female eagle, I send you over nine seas, and over nine mountains, and over nine acres of waste land, where no dog shall bark and no cow shall low, and no eagle shall higher rise" – which is quite simple.)

One night he was supping at an inn in Pentre Voelas. Four men came in and joined him at supper. Now, by his magical skill, Huw Llwyd knew that they were bandits from Yspytty Ifan, and meant to kill him during the night for his money. He made a horn grow out of the centre of the table, and obliged the robbers to gaze at it. He went to bed, and in the morning when he came down the four men were still staring at the horn, as he knew they would be. He departed, leaving them still looking steadily and earnestly at the horn: they were arrested in this position and cast into prison.

Many robberies used to take place at an inn near Bettws-y-Coed. Travellers who put up there for the night were continually relieved of their money, and they could not tell how. They were certain that no one had entered their rooms, because they were found locked in the morning just as they were the night before. Huw Llwyd was consulted, and he promised to unravel the mystery.

He presented himself at the inn one night, and asked for a night's lodging, saying that he was an officer on his way to Ireland. The inn was kept by two sisters: they were both very comely, and made themselves very agreeable to Huw Llwyd at supper. Not to be outdone, he did his best to entertain them with tales of travel in foreign parts which he had never visited. On retiring for the night he said that it was a habit with him to have lights burning in his room all night, and he was supplied with a sufficient quantity of candles to last until the morning. Huw Llwyd made his arrangements for a night of vigil. He placed his clothes on the floor within easy reach of his bed, and his sword, unsheathed, on the bed close to his hand. He secured the door, got into bed, and feigned to sleep. Before long two cats came stealthily down the chimney. They frisked here and there in the room, but the sleeper lay motionless; they chased each other around the bed, and gambolled and romped, but still the sleeper showed no signs of awaking. At last they approached his clothes and played with them, turning them over and over. Ere long the sleeper (who had been very wide awake the whole time) saw one of the cats putting her paw into the pocket which contained his purse. He struck at the thievish paw like lightning, with his sword. With a hideous howl both cats disappeared up the chimney, and nothing further was seen of them the whole night.

Next morning only one of the sisters appeared at the breakfast table. Huw Llwyd asked where the other was. Receiving the reply that she was ill and could not come down, he expressed his regret, and proceeded to break his fast. The meal over, "I am now going to resume my journey," he said, "but I must say good-bye to your sister, for I greatly enjoyed her company last night." Many excuses were attempted, but he would not be refused, and at last he was admitted to her presence. After sympathizing with her and asking whether he could be of any service, he held out his hand to bid good-bye. The sick lady held out her left hand. "No," said Huw Llwyd laughingly, "I am not going to take your left hand: I have never taken a left hand in my life, and I am not going to begin with yours, white and shapely as it is." Very unwillingly and with evident pain, she put out her right hand. It was swathed in bandages. The mystery was now revealed. The two sisters were witches, and in the form of cats robbed travellers who lodged under their roof: "I have drawn blood from you," said Huw Llwyd, addressing the wounded sister, "and henceforth you will be unable to do any mischief. I will make you equally harmless," he said to the other sister. Seizing her hand, he cut it slightly with a knife, so that the blood came. For the rest of their lives the two sisters were like other women, and no more robberies took place at their inn.

PERGRIN AND THE MERMAIDEN

One fine September afternoon, about the beginning of the eighteenth century, a fisherman of St. Dogmael's, whose name was Pergrin, was rowing in his boat near Pen Cemmes. Looking up at the rocks casually, he thought he saw a maiden in a recess of the cliff. Pergrin was an inquisitive man, and he determined to see what the strange lady was doing. He rowed ashore as quietly as he could, stepped out of his boat and crawled up to a place where he could see into the recess without being seen himself. He espied a lovely maiden – at least, above the waist she was a lovely maiden, but below the waist she was a fish with fins and spreading tail. She was combing her long hair so busily and intently that she had no suspicion that she was being watched, and Pergrin gazed upon her for a long time. During that time his mind was active, and he determined to carry her away. Putting his resolve into action, Pergrin rushed at her, and taking her up in his arms, carried her off to his boat. There he fastened her securely, and turning his boat's nose in the direction of Llandudoch (that is the Welsh for St. Dogmael's), began to ply his oars vigorously. When she realized her situation, being a woman (at least, as far as the waist) she wept, and begged Pergrin to let her go. Pergrin, however, though he answered her very kindly, would not accede to her tearful request, but carried her home and shut her up in a room. He treated her very tenderly, but she refused all meat and drink (she rejected even the best *cawl,* with hundreds of eyes in it), and did nothing but shed tears and beseech Pergrin to release her. A famous man once said that as much pity is to be taken of a woman weeping as of a goose going barefoot, but Pergrin had never heard this saying: it would have made no difference if he had, for he was soft-hearted, and the sight of the beauteous half-woman's eyes becoming red, and her nose swollen with the constant drip of salt water, affected him profoundly. Moreover, as she persistently declined food, she became thin and peakish. To add to his anxiety, a friend of his, who knew far too much to be a pleasant companion, told him what had happened to a man in Conway who caught a mermaid. She prayed him to place her tail at least in the water, but he refused, and she died. Before dying she cursed her captor and the place of her imprisonment. The captor had gone from bad to worse, and had perished miserably: the people of Conway have been so poor ever since, that when a stranger happens to bring a sovereign into that harp-shaped town they have to send across the water to Llansantffraid for change. So when the tearful prisoner at last said to Pergrin, "If thou wilt let me go, Pergrin, I will give thee three shouts in the time of thy greatest need," he accepted her offer. Carrying her down to the strand of the sea, he put her in the water, and she immediately plunged into the depths.

Days and weeks passed without Pergrin seeing her after this. But one fine hot afternoon he was out fishing in his boat, and many of the fishermen were similarly engaged. The sea was calm, and there was hardly a cloud in the sky, so that no one had any thought of danger. Suddenly the mermaiden emerged out of the blue, sunlit water and shouted in a loud voice, "Pergrin, Pergrin, Pergrin, take up thy net, take up thy net, take up thy net." Pergrin instantly obeyed, drew in his net with great haste, and rowed over the bar homewards, amid the jeers of all the others. By the time he had reached the Pwll Cam a dread storm overspread the sea: the wind blew great guns and the waves ran mountain high. Pergrin reached dry land safely, but all the other fishermen, eighteen in number, found watery graves.

THE TALE OF TALIESIN

In times past there lived in Penllyn a man of gentle lineage, named Tegid Voel, and his dwelling was in the midst of the lake Tegid, and his wife was called Caridwen. And there was born to him of his wife a son named Morvran ab Tegid, and also a daughter named Creirwy, the fairest maiden in the world was she; and they had a brother, the most ill-favoured man in the world, Avagddu. Now Caridwen his mother thought that he was not likely to be admitted among men of noble birth, by reason of his ugliness, unless he had some exalted merits or knowledge. For it was in the beginning of Arthur's time and of the Round Table.

So she resolved, according to the arts of the books of the Fferyllt, to boil a cauldron of Inspiration and Science for her son, that his reception might be honourable because of his knowledge of the mysteries of the future state of the world.

Then she began to boil the cauldron, which from the beginning of its boiling might not cease to boil for a year and a day, until three blessed drops were obtained of the grace of Inspiration.

And she put Gwion Bach the son of Gwreang of Llanfair in Caereinion, in Powys, to stir the cauldron, and a blind man named Morda to kindle the fire beneath it, and she charged them that they should not suffer it to cease boiling for the space of a year and a day. And she herself, according to the books of the astronomers, and in planetary hours, gathered every day of all charm-bearing herbs. And one day, towards the end of the year, as Caridwen was culling plants and making incantations, it chanced that three drops of the charmed liquor flew out of the cauldron and fell upon the finger of Gwion Bach. And by reason of their great heat he put his finger to his mouth, and the instant he put those marvel-working drops into his mouth, he foresaw everything that was to come, and perceived that his chief care must be to guard against the wiles of Caridwen, for vast was her skill. And in very great fear he fled towards his own land. And the cauldron burst in two, because all the liquor within it except the three charm-bearing drops was poisonous, so that the horses of Gwyddno Garanhir were poisoned by the water of the stream into which the liquor of the cauldron ran, and the confluence of that stream was called the Poison of the Horses of Gwyddno from that time forth.

Thereupon came in Caridwen and saw all the toil of the whole year lost. And she seized a billet of wood and struck the blind Morda on the head until one of his eyes fell out upon his cheek. And he said, "Wrongfully hast thou disfigured me, for I am innocent. Thy loss was not because of me." "Thou speakest truth," said Caridwen, "it was Gwion Bach who robbed me."

And she went forth after him, running. And he saw her, and changed himself into a hare and fled. But she changed herself into a greyhound and turned him. And he ran towards a river, and became a fish. And she in the form of an otter-bitch chased him under the water, until he was fain to turn himself into a bird of the air. She, as a hawk, followed him and gave him no rest in the sky. And just as she was about to stoop upon him, and he was in fear of death, he espied a heap of winnowed wheat on the floor of a barn, and he dropped among the wheat, and turned himself into one of the grains. Then she transformed herself into a high-crested black hen, and went to the wheat and scratched it with her feet, and found him out and swallowed him. And, as the story says, she bore him nine months, and when she was delivered of him, she could not find it in her heart to kill him, by reason of his beauty. So she wrapped him in a leathern bag, and cast him into the sea to the mercy of God, on the twenty-ninth day of April.

And at that time the weir of Gwyddno was on the strand between Dyvi and Aberystwyth, near to his own castle, and the value of an hundred pounds was taken in that weir every May eve. And in those days Gwyddno had an only son named Elphin, the most hapless of youths, and the most needy. And it grieved his father sore, for he thought that he was born in an evil hour. And by the advice of his council, his father had granted him the drawing of the weir that year, to see if good luck would ever befall him, and to give him something wherewith to begin the world.

And the next day when Elphin went to look, there was nothing in the weir. But as he turned back he perceived the leathern bag upon a pole of the weir. Then said one of the weir-ward unto Elphin, "Thou wast never unlucky until tonight, and now thou hast destroyed the virtues of the weir, which always yielded the value of an hundred pounds every May eve, and tonight there is nothing but this leathern skin within it." "How now," said Elphin, "there may be therein the value of an hundred pounds." Well, they took up the leathern bag, and he who opened it saw the forehead of the boy, and said to Elphin, "Behold a radiant brow!" "Taliesin be he called," said Elphin. *['Taliesin' means 'radiant brow'.]* And he lifted the boy in his arms, and lamenting his mischance, he placed him sorrowfully behind him. And he made his horse amble gently, that before had been trotting, and he carried him as softly as if he had been sitting in the easiest chair in the world. And presently the boy made a Consolation and praise to Elphin, and foretold honour to Elphin; and the Consolation was as you may see:

"Fair Elphin, cease to lament!
Let no one be dissatisfied with his own,
To despair will bring no advantage.
No man sees what supports him;
The prayer of Cynllo will not be in vain;
God will not violate his promise.
Never in Gwyddno's weir
Was there such good luck as this night.
Fair Elphin, dry thy cheeks!
Being too sad will not avail.
Although thou thinkest thou hast no gain,
Too much grief will bring thee no good;
Nor doubt the miracles of the Almighty:
Although I am but little, I am highly gifted.
From seas, and from mountains,
And from the depths of rivers,
God brings wealth to the fortunate man.
Elphin of lively qualities,
Thy resolution is unmanly;

Thou must not be over sorrowful:
Better to trust in God than to forbode ill.
Weak and small as I am,
On the foaming beach of the ocean,
In the day of trouble I shall be
Of more service to thee than three hundred salmon.
Elphin of notable qualities,
Be not displeased at thy misfortune;
Although reclined thus weak in my bag,
There lies a virtue in my tongue.
While I continue thy protector
Thou hast not much to fear;
Remembering the names of the Trinity,
None shall be able to harm thee."

And this was the first poem that Taliesin ever sang, being to console Elphin in his grief for that the produce of the weir was lost, and, what was worse, that all the world would consider that it was through his fault and ill-luck. And then Gwyddno Garanhir [*'Gwyddno Garanhir' instead of 'Elphin ab Gwyddno' is evidently an error of some transcriber of the MS*] asked him what he was, whether man or spirit. Whereupon he sang this tale, and said:

"First, I have been formed a comely person,
In the court of Caridwen I have done penance;
Though little I was seen, placidly received,
I was great on the floor of the place to where I was led;
I have been a prized defence, the sweet muse the cause,
And by law without speech I have been liberated
By a smiling black old hag, when irritated

Dreadful her claim when pursued:
I have fled with vigour, I have fled as a frog,
I have fled in the semblance of a crow, scarcely finding rest;
I have fled vehemently, I have fled as a chain,
I have fled as a roe into an entangled thicket;
I have fled as a wolf cub, I have fled as a wolf in a wilderness,
I have fled as a thrush of portending language;
I have fled as a fox, used to concurrent bounds of quirks;
I have fled as a martin, which did not avail;
I have fled as a squirrel, that vainly hides,
I have fled as a stag's antler, of ruddy course,
I have fled as iron in a glowing fire,
I have fled as a spear-head, of woe to such as has a wish for it;
I have fled as a fierce hull bitterly fighting,
I have fled as a bristly boar seen in a ravine,
I have fled as a white grain of pure wheat,
On the skirt of a hempen sheet entangled,
That seemed of the size of a mare's foal,
That is filling like a ship on the waters;
Into a dark leathern bag I was thrown,
And on a boundless sea I was sent adrift;
Which was to me an omen of being tenderly nursed,
And the Lord God then set me at liberty."

Then came Elphin to the house or court of Gwyddno his father, and Taliesin with him. And Gwyddno asked him if he had had a good haul at the weir, and he told him that he had got that which was better than fish. "What was that?" said Gwyddno. "A bard," answered Elphin. Then said Gwyddno, "Alas, what will he profit thee?" And Taliesin himself replied and said, "He will profit him more than the weir ever profited thee." Asked Gwyddno, "Art thou able to speak, and thou so little?" And Taliesin answered him, "I am better able to speak than thou to question me." "Let me hear what thou canst say," quoth Gwyddno. Then Taliesin sang:

"In water there is a quality endowed with a blessing;
On God it is most just to meditate aright;
To God it is proper to supplicate with seriousness,
Since no obstacle can there be to obtain a reward from him.
Three times have I been born, I know by meditation;
It were miserable for a person not to come and obtain
All the sciences of the world, collected together in my breast,
For I know what has been, what in future will occur.
I will supplicate my Lord that I get refuge in him,
A regard I may obtain in his grace;
The Son of Mary is my trust, great in him is my delight,
For in him is the world continually upholden.
God has been to instruct me and to raise my expectation,
The true Creator of heaven, who affords me protection;
It is rightly intended that the saints should daily pray,
For God, the renovator, will bring them to him."

And forthwith Elphin gave his haul to his wife, and she nursed him tenderly and lovingly. Thenceforward Elphin increased in riches more and more day after day, and in love and favour with the king, and there abode Taliesin until he was thirteen years old, when Elphin son of Gwyddno went by a Christmas invitation to his uncle, Maelgwn Gwynedd, who some time after this held open court at Christmastide in the castle of Dyganwy, for all the number of his lords of both degrees, both spiritual and temporal, with a vast and thronged host of knights and squires. And amongst them there arose a discourse and discussion. And thus was it said.

"Is there in the whole world a king so great as Maelgwn, or one on whom Heaven has bestowed so many spiritual gifts as upon him? First, form, and beauty, and meekness, and strength, besides all the powers of the soul!" And together with these they said that Heaven had given one gift that exceeded all the others, which was the beauty, and comeliness, and grace, and wisdom, and modesty of his queen; whose virtues surpassed those of all the ladies and noble maidens throughout the whole kingdom. And with this they put questions one to another amongst themselves: Who had braver men? Who had fairer or swifter horses or greyhounds? Who had more skilful or wiser bards – than Maelgwn?

Now at that time the bards were in great favour with the exalted of the kingdom; and then none performed the office of those who are now called heralds, unless they were learned men, not only expert in the service of kings and princes, but studious and well versed in the lineage, and arms, and exploits of princes and kings, and in discussions concerning foreign kingdoms, and the ancient things of this kingdom, and chiefly in the annals of the first nobles; and also were prepared always with their answers in various languages, Latin, French, Welsh, and English. And together with this they were great chroniclers, and recorders, and skilful in framing verses, and ready in making englyns in every one of those languages. Now of these there were at that feast within the palace of Maelgwn as many as four-and-twenty, and chief of them all was one named Heinin Vardd.

When they had all made an end of thus praising the king and his gifts, it befell that Elphin spoke in this wise. "Of a truth none but a king may vie with a king; but were he not a king, I would say that my wife was as virtuous as any lady in the kingdom, and also that I have a bard who is more skilful than all the king's bards." In a short space some of his fellows showed the king all the boastings of Elphin; and the king ordered him to be thrown into a strong prison, until he might know the truth as to the virtues of his wife, and the wisdom of his bard.

Now when Elphin had been put in a tower of the castle, with a thick chain about his feet (it is said that it was a silver chain, because he was of royal blood), the king, as the story relates, sent his son Rhun to inquire into the demeanour of Elphin's wife. Now Rhun was the most graceless man in the world, and there was neither wife nor maiden with whom he had held converse, but was evil spoken of. While Rhun went in haste towards Elphin's dwelling, being fully minded to bring disgrace upon his wife, Taliesin told his mistress how that the king had placed his master in durance in prison, and how that Rhun was coming in haste to strive to bring disgrace upon her. Wherefore he caused his mistress to array one of the maids of her kitchen in her apparel; which the noble lady gladly did; and she loaded her hands with the best rings that she and her husband possessed.

In this guise Taliesin caused his mistress to put the maiden to sit at the board in her room at supper, and he made her to seem as her mistress, and the mistress to seem as the maid. And when they were in due time seated at their supper in the manner that has been said, Rhun suddenly arrived at Elphin's dwelling, and was received with joy, for all the servants knew him plainly; and they brought him in haste to the room of their mistress, in the semblance of whom the maid rose up from supper and welcomed him gladly. And afterwards she sat down to supper again the second time, and Rhun with her. Then Rhun began jesting with the maid, who still kept the semblance of her mistress. And verily this story shows that the maiden became so intoxicated, that she fell asleep; and the story relates that it was a powder that Rhun put into the drink, that made her sleep so soundly that she never felt it when he cut from off her hand her little finger, whereupon was the signet ring of Elphin, which he had sent to his wife as a token, a short time before. And Rhun returned to the king with the finger and the ring as a proof, to show that he had cut it from off her hand, without her awaking from her sleep of intemperance.

The king rejoiced greatly at these tidings, and he sent for his councillors, to whom he told the whole story from the beginning. And he caused Elphin to be brought out of his prison, and he chided him because of his boast. And he spake unto Elphin on this wise. "Elphin, be it known to thee beyond a doubt that it is but folly for a man to trust in the virtues of his wife further than he can see her; and that thou mayest be certain of thy wife's vileness, behold her finger, with thy signet ring upon it, which was cut from her hand last night, while she slept the sleep of intoxication." Then thus spake Elphin. "With thy leave, mighty king, I cannot deny my ring, for it is known of many; but verily I assert strongly that the finger around which it is, was never attached to the hand of my wife, for in truth and certainty there are three notable things pertaining to it, none of which ever belonged to any of my wife's fingers. The first of the three is, that it is certain, by your grace's leave, that wheresoever my wife is at this present hour, whether sitting, or standing, or lying down, this ring would never remain upon her thumb, whereas you can plainly see that it was hard to draw it over the joint of the little finger of the hand whence this was cut; the second thing is, that my wife has never let pass one Saturday since I have known her without paring her nails before going to bed, and you can see fully that the nail of this little finger has not been pared for a month. The third is, truly, that the hand whence this finger came was kneading rye dough within three days before the finger was cut therefrom, and I can assure your goodness that my wife has never kneaded rye dough since my wife she has been."

Then the king was mightily wroth with Elphin for so stoutly withstanding him, respecting the goodness of his wife, wherefore he ordered him to his prison a second time, saying that he should not be loosed thence until he had proved the truth of his boast, as well concerning the wisdom of his bard as the virtues of his wife.

In the meantime his wife and Taliesin remained joyful at Elphin's dwelling. And Taliesin showed his mistress how that Elphin was in prison because of them, but he bade her be glad, for that he would go to Maelgwn's court to free his master. Then she asked him in what manner he would set him free. And he answered her:

"A journey will I perform,
And to the gate I will come;
The hall I will enter,
And my song I will sing;
My speech I will pronounce
To silence royal bards,
In presence of their chief,
I will greet to deride,
Upon them I will break
And Elphin I will free.
Should contention arise,
In presence of the prince,
With summons to the bards,
For the sweet flowing song,
And wizards' posing lore
And wisdom of Druids,

In the court of the sons of the Distributor
Some are who did appear
Intent on wily schemes,
By craft and tricking means,
In pangs of affliction
To wrong the innocent,
Let the fools be silent,
As erst in Badon's fight, –
With Arthur of liberal ones
The head, with long red blades;
Through feats of testy men,
And a chief with his foes.
Woe be to them, the fools,
When revenge comes on them.
I Taliesin, chief of bards,
With a sapient Druid's words,
Will set kind Elphin free
From haughty tyrant's bonds.
To their fell and chilling cry,
By the act of a surprising steed,
From the far distant North,
There soon shall be an end.
Let neither grace nor health
Be to Maelgwn Gwynedd,
For this force and this wrong;
And be extremes of ills
And an avenged end
To Rhun and all his race:
Short be his course of life,
Be all his lands laid waste;

And long exile be assigned
To Maelgwn Gwynedd!"

After this he took leave of his mistress, and came at last to the Court of Maelgwn, who was going to sit in his hall and dine in his royal state, as it was the custom in those days for kings and princes to do at every chief feast. And as soon as Taliesin entered the hall, he placed himself in a quiet corner, near the place where the bards and the minstrels were wont to come in doing their service and duty to the king, as is the custom at the high festivals when the bounty is proclaimed. And so, when the bards and the heralds came to cry largess, and to proclaim the power of the king and his strength, at the moment that they passed by the corner wherein he was crouching, Taliesin pouted out his lips after them, and played 'Blerwm, blerwm,' with his finger upon his lips. Neither took they much notice of him as they went by, but proceeded forward till they came before the king, unto whom they made their obeisance with their bodies, as they were wont, without speaking a single word, but pouting out their lips, and making mouths at the king, playing "Blerwm, blerwm," upon their lips with their fingers, as they had seen the boy do elsewhere. This sight caused the king to wonder and to deem within himself that they were drunk with many liquors. Wherefore he commanded one of his lords, who served at the board, to go to them and desire them to collect their wits, and to consider where they stood, and what it was fitting for them to do. And this lord did so gladly. But they ceased not from their folly any more than before. Whereupon he sent to them a second time, and a third, desiring them to go forth from the hall. At the last the king ordered one of his squires to give a blow to the chief of them named Heinin Vardd; and the squire took a broom and struck him on the head, so that he fell back in his seat. Then he arose and went on his knees, and besought leave of the king's grace to show that this their fault was not through want of knowledge, neither through drunkenness, but by the influence of some spirit that was in the hall. And after this Heinin spoke on this wise. "Oh, honourable king, be it known to your grace, that not from the strength of drink, or of too much liquor, are we dumb, without power of speech like drunken men, but through the influence of a spirit that sits in the corner yonder in the form of a child." Forthwith the king commanded the squire to fetch him; and he went to the nook where Taliesin sat, and brought him before the king, who asked him what he was, and whence he came. And he answered the king in verse.

"Primary chief bard am I to Elphin,
And my original country is the region of the summer stars;
Idno and Heinin called me Merddin,
At length every king will call me Taliesin.

I was with my Lord in the highest sphere,
On the fall of Lucifer into the depth of hell
I have borne a banner before Alexander;
I know the names of the stars from north to south;
I have been on the galaxy at the throne of the Distributor;
I was in Canaan when Absalom was slain;
I conveyed the Divine Spirit to the level of the vale of Hebron;
I was in the court of Don before the birth of Gwdion.
I was instructor to Eli and Enoc;
I have been winged by the genius of the splendid crosier;
I have been loquacious prior to being gifted with speech;
I was at the place of the crucifixion of the merciful Son of God;
I have been three periods in the prison of Arianrod;

I have been the chief director of the work of the tower of Nimrod;
I am a wonder whose origin is not known.
I have been in Asia with Noah in the ark,
I have seen the destruction of Sodom and Gomorra;
I have been in India when Roma was built,
I am now come here to the remnant of Troia.

I have been with my Lord in the manger of the ass:
I strengthened Moses through the water of Jordan;
I have been in the firmament with Mary Magdalene;
I have obtained the muse from the cauldron of Caridwen;
I have been bard of the harp to Lleon of Lochlin.
I have been on the White Hill, in the court of Cynvelyn,
For a day and a year in stocks and fetters,
I have suffered hunger for the Son of the Virgin,
I have been fostered in the land of the Deity,
I have been teacher to all intelligences,
I am able to instruct the whole universe.
I shall be until the day of doom on the face of the earth;
And it is not known whether my body is flesh or fish.

Then I was for nine months
In the womb of the hag Caridwen;
I was originally little Gwion,
And at length I am Taliesin."

And when the king and his nobles had heard the song, they wondered much, for they had never heard the like from a boy so young as he. And when the king knew that he was the bard of Elphin, he bade Heinin, his first and wisest bard, to answer

Taliesin and to strive with him. But when he came, he could do no other but play "Blerwm" on his lips; and when he sent for the others of the four-and-twenty bards they all did likewise, and could do no other. And Maelgwn asked the boy Taliesin what was his errand, and he answered him in song.

"Puny bards, I am trying
To secure the prize, if I can;
By a gentle prophetic strain
I am endeavouring to retrieve
The loss I may have suffered;
Complete the attempt I hope,
Since Elphin endures trouble
In the fortress of Teganwy,
On him may there not be laid
Too many chains and fetters;
The Chair of the fortress of Teganwy
Will I again seek;
Strengthened by my muse I am powerful;
Mighty on my part is what I seek,
For three hundred songs and more
Are combined in the spell I sing.
There ought not to stand where I am
Neither stone, neither ring;
And there ought not to be about me
Any bard who may not know
That Elphin the son of Gwyddno
Is in the land of Artro,
Secured by thirteen locks,
For praising his instructor;

And then I Taliesin,
Chief of the bards of the west,
Shall loosen Elphin
Out of a golden fetter."

* * *

"If you be primary bards
To the master of sciences,
Declare ye mysteries
That relate to the inhabitants of the world;
There is a noxious creature,
From the rampart of Satanas,
Which has overcome all
Between the deep and the shallow;
Equally wide are his jaws
As the mountains of the Alps;
Him death will not subdue,
Nor hand or blades;
There is the load of nine hundred wagons
In the hair of his two paws;
There is in his head an eye
Green as the limpid sheet of icicle;
Three springs arise
In the nape of his neck;
Sea-roughs thereon
Swim through it;
There was the dissolution of the oxen
Of Deivrdonwy the water-gifted.
The names of the three springs

From the midst of the ocean;
One generated brine
Which is from the Corina,
To replenish the flood
Over seas disappearing;
The second, without injury
It will fall on us,
When there is rain abroad,
Through the whelming sky;
The third will appear
Through the mountain veins,
Like a flinty banquet,
The work of the King of kings,
You are blundering bards,
In too much solicitude;
You cannot celebrate
The kingdom of the Britons;
And I am Taliesin,
Chief of the bards of the west,
Who will loosen Elphin
Out of the golden fetter."

* * *

"Be silent, then, ye unlucky rhyming bards,
For you cannot judge between truth and falsehood.
If you be primary bards formed by heaven,
Tell your king what his fate will be.
It is I who am a diviner and a leading bard,
And know every passage in the country of your king;

I shall liberate Elphin from the belly of the stony tower;
And will tell your king what will befall him.
A most strange creature will come from the sea marsh of Rhianedd
As a punishment of iniquity on Maelgwn Gwynedd;
His hair, his teeth, and his eyes being as gold,
And this will bring destruction upon Maelgwn Gwynedd."

* * *

"Discover thou what is
The strong creature from before the flood,
Without flesh, without bone,
Without vein, without blood,
Without head, without feet,
It will neither be older nor younger
Than at the beginning;
For fear of a denial,
There are no rude wants
With creatures.
Great God! how the sea whitens
When first it comes!
Great are its gusts
When it comes from the south;
Great are its evaporations
When it strikes on coasts.
It is in the field, it is in the wood,
Without hand, and without foot,
Without signs of old age,
Though it be co-æval
With the five ages or periods

And older still,
Though they be numberless years.
It is also so wide
As the surface of the earth;
And it was not born,
Nor was it seen.
It will cause consternation
Wherever God willeth.
On sea, and on land,
It neither sees, nor is seen.
Its course is devious,
And will not come when desired;
On land and on sea,
It is indispensable.
It is without an equal,
It is four-sided;
It is not confined,
It is incomparable;
It comes from four quarters;
It will not be advised,
It will not be without advice.
It commences its journey
Above the marble rock,
It is sonorous, it is dumb,
It is mild,
It is strong, it is bold,
When it glances over the land,
It is silent, it is vocal,
It is clamorous,
It is the most noisy

On the face of the earth.
It is good, it is bad,
It is extremely injurious.
It is concealed,
Because sight cannot perceive it.
It is noxious, it is beneficial;
It is yonder, it is here;
It will discompose,
But will not repair the injury;
It will not suffer for its doings,
Seeing it is blameless.
It is wet, it is dry,
It frequently comes,
Proceeding from the heat of the sun,
And the coldness of the moon.
The moon is less beneficial,
Inasmuch as her heat is less.
One Being has prepared it,
Out of all creatures,
By a tremendous blast,
To wreak vengeance
On Maelgwn Gwynedd."

And while he was thus singing his verse near the door, there arose a mighty storm of wind, so that the king and all his nobles thought that the castle would fall on their heads. And the king caused them to fetch Elphin in haste from his dungeon, and placed him before Taliesin. And it is said that immediately he sang a verse, so that the chains opened from about his feet.

"I adore the Supreme, Lord of all animation, –
Him that supports the heavens, Ruler of every extreme,
Him that made the water good for all,
Him who has bestowed each gift, and blesses it; –
May abundance of mead be given Maelgwn
of Anglesey, who supplies us,
From his foaming meadhorns, with the choicest pure liquor.
Since bees collect, and do not enjoy,
We have sparkling distilled mead, which is universally praised.
The multitude of creatures which the earth nourishes
God made for man, with a view to enrich him; –
Some are violent, some are mute, he enjoys them,
Some are wild, some are tame; the Lord makes them; –
Part of their produce becomes clothing;
For food and beverage till doom will they continue.
I entreat the Supreme, Sovereign of the region of peace,
To liberate Elphin from banishment,
The man who gave me wine, and ale, and mead,
With large princely steeds, of beautiful appearance;
May he yet give me; and at the end,
May God of his good will grant me, in honour,
A succession of numberless ages, in the retreat of tranquillity.
Elphin, knight of mead, late be thy dissolution!"

And afterwards he sang the ode which is called 'The Excellence of the Bards'.

"What was the first man
Made by the God of heaven;
What the fairest flattering speech

That was prepared by Ieuav;
What meat, what drink,
What roof his shelter;
What the first impression
Of his primary thinking;
What became his clothing;
Who carried on a disguise,
Owing to the wilds of the country,
In the beginning?
Wherefore should a stone be hard;
Why should a thorn be sharp-pointed?
Who is hard like a flint;
Who is salt like brine;
Who sweet like honey;
Who rides on the gale;
Why ridged should be the nose;
Why should a wheel be round;
Why should the tongue be gifted with speech
Rather than another member?
If thy bards, Heinin, be competent,
Let them reply to me, Taliesin."

And after that he sang the address which is called 'The Reproof of the Bards'.

"If thou art a bard completely imbued
With genius not to be controlled,
Be thou not untractable
Within the court of thy king;
Until thy rigmarole shall be known,

Be thou silent, Heinin,
As to the name of thy verse,
And the name of thy vaunting;
And as to the name of thy grandsire
Prior to his being baptized.
And the name of the sphere,
And the name of the element,
And the name of thy language,
And the name of thy region.
Avaunt, ye bards above,
Avaunt, ye bards below!
My beloved is below,
In the fetter of Ariansod
It is certain you know not
How to understand the song I utter,
Nor clearly how to discriminate
Between the truth and what is false;
Puny bards, crows of the district,
Why do you not take to flight?
A bard that will not silence me,
Silence may he not obtain,
Till he goes to be covered
Under gravel and pebbles;
Such as shall listen to me,
May God listen to him."

Then sang he the piece called 'The Spite of the Bards'.

"Minstrels persevere in their false custom,
Immoral ditties are their delight;

Vain and tasteless praise they recite;
Falsehood at all times do they utter;
The innocent persons they ridicule;
Married women they destroy,
Innocent virgins of Mary they corrupt;
As they pass their lives away in vanity,
Poor innocent persons they ridicule;
At night they get drunk, they sleep the day;
In idleness without work they feed themselves;
The Church they hate, and the tavern they frequent;
With thieves and perjured fellows they associate;
At courts they inquire after feasts;
Every senseless word they bring forward;
Every deadly sin they praise;
Every vile course of life they lead;
Through every village, town, and country they stroll;
Concerning the gripe of death they think not;
Neither lodging nor charity do they give;
Indulging in victuals to excess.
Psalms or prayers they do not use,
Tithes or offerings to God they do not pay,
On holidays or Sundays they do not worship;
Vigils or festivals they do not heed.
The birds do fly, the fish do swim,
The bees collect honey, worms do crawl,
Every thing travails to obtain its food,
Except minstrels and lazy useless thieves.

I deride neither song nor minstrelsy,
For they are given by God to lighten thought;

But him who abuses them,
For blaspheming Jesus and his service."

Taliesin having set his master free from prison, and having protected the innocence of his wife, and silenced the bards, so that not one of them dared to say a word, now brought Elphin's wife before them, and showed that she had not one finger wanting. Right glad was Elphin, right glad was Taliesin.

Then he bade Elphin wager the king that he had a horse both better and swifter than the king's horses. And this Elphin did, and the day, and the time, and the place were fixed, and the place was that which at this day is called Morva Rhiannedd: and thither the king went with all his people, and four-and-twenty of the swiftest horses he possessed. And after a long process the course was marked, and the horses were placed for running. Then came Taliesin with four-and-twenty twigs of holly, which he had burnt black, and he caused the youth who was to ride his master's horse to place them in his belt, and he gave him orders to let all the king's horses get before him, and as he should overtake one horse after the other, to take one of the twigs and strike the horse with it over the crupper, and then let that twig fall; and after that to take another twig, and do in like manner to every one of the horses, as he should overtake them, enjoining the horseman strictly to watch when his own horse should stumble, and to throw down his cap on the spot. All these things did the youth fulfil, giving a blow to every one of the king's horses, and throwing down his cap on the spot where his horse stumbled. And to this spot Taliesin brought his master after his horse had won the race. And he caused Elphin to put workmen to dig a hole there; and when they had dug the ground deep enough, they found a large cauldron full of gold. And then said Taliesin, "Elphin, behold a payment and reward unto thee, for having taken me out of the weir, and for having reared me from that time until now." And on this spot stands a pool of water, which is to this time called Pwllbair.

After all this, the king caused Taliesin to be brought before him, and he asked him to recite concerning the creation of man from the beginning; and thereupon he made the poem which is now called 'One of the Four Pillars of Song'.

"The Almighty made,
Down the Hebron vale,
With his plastic hands,
Adam's fair form:

And five hundred years,
Void of any help,
There he remained and lay
Without a soul.

He again did form,
In calm paradise,
From a left-side rib,
Bliss-throbbing Eve.

Seven hours they were
The orchard keeping,
Till Satan brought strife,
With wiles from hell.

Thence were they driven,
Cold and shivering,

To gain their living,
Into this world.

To bring forth with pain
Their sons and daughters,
To have possession
Of Asia's land.

Twice five, ten and eight,
She was self-bearing,
The mixed burden
Of man-woman.

And once, not hidden,
She brought forth Abel,
And Cain the forlorn,
The homicide.

To him and his mate
Was given a spade,
To break up the soil,
Thus to get bread.

The wheat pure and white,
Summer tilth to sow,
Every man to feed,
Till great yule feast.

An angelic hand
From the high Father,

Brought seed for growing
That Eve might sow;

But she then did hide
Of the gift a tenth,
And all did not sow
Of what was dug.

Black rye then was found,
And not pure wheat grain,
To show the mischief
Thus of thieving.

For this thievish act,
It is requisite,
That all men should pay
Tithe unto God.

Of the ruddy wine,
Planted on sunny days,
And on new-moon nights;
And the white wine.

The wheat rich in grain
And red flowing wine
Christ's pure body make,
Son of Alpha.

The wafer is flesh,
The wine is spilt blood,

The Trinity's words
Sanctify them.

The concealed books
From Emmanuel's hand
Were brought by Raphael
As Adam's gift,

When in his old age,
To his chin immersed
In Jordan's water,
Keeping a fast,

Moses did obtain
In Jordan's water,
The aid of the three
Most special rods.

Solomon did obtain
In Babel's tower,
All the sciences
In Asia land.

So did I obtain,
In my bardic books,
All the sciences
Of Europe and Africa.

Their course, their bearing,
Their permitted way,

And their fate I know,
Unto the end.

Oh! what misery,
Through extreme of woe,
Prophecy will show
On Troia's race!

A coiling serpent
Proud and merciless,
On her golden wings,
From Germany.

She will overrun
England and Scotland,
From Lychlyn sea-shore
To the Severn.

Then will the Brython
Be as prisoners,
By strangers swayed,
From Saxony.

Their Lord they will praise,
Their speech they will keep,
Their land they will lose,
Except wild Walia.

Till some change shall come,
After long penance,

When equally rife
The two crimes come.

Britons then shall have
Their land and their crown,
And the stranger swarm
Shall disappear.

All the angel's words,
As to peace and war,
Will be fulfilled
To Britain's race."

He further told the king various prophecies of things that should be in the world, in songs...

The original manuscript breaks off at this point.

A GLOSSARY OF MYTH & FOLKLORE

Aaru Heavenly paradise where the blessed went after death.

Ab Heart or mind.

Abiku (Yoruba) Person predestined to die. Also known as ogbanje.

Absál Nurse to Saláman, who died after their brief love affair.

Achilles The son of Peleus and the sea-nymph Thetis, who distinguished himself in the Trojan War. He was made almost immortal by his mother, who dipped him in the River Styx, and he was invincible except for a portion of his heel which remained out of the water.

Acropolis Citadel in a Greek city.

Adad-Ea Ferryman to Ut-Napishtim, who carried Gilgamesh to visit his ancestor.

Adapa Son of Ea and a wise sage.

Adar God of the sun, who is worshipped primarily in Nippur.

Aditi Sky goddess and mother of the gods.

Adityas Vishnu, children of Aditi, including Indra, Mitra, Rudra, Tvashtar, Varuna and Vishnu.

Aeneas The son of Anchises and the goddess Aphrodite, reared by a nymph. He led the Dardanian troops in the Trojan War. According to legend, he became the founder of Rome.

Aengus Óg Son of Dagda and Boann (a woman said to have given the Boyne river its name), Aengus is the Irish god of love whose stronghold is reputed to have been at New Grange. The famous tale 'Dream of Aengus' tells of how he fell in love with a maiden he had dreamt of. He eventually discovered that she was to be found at the Lake of the Dragon's Mouth in Co. Tipperary, but that she lived every alternate year in the form of a swan. Aengus plunges into the lake, transforming himself also into the shape of a swan. Then the two fly back together to his palace on the Boyne where they live out their days as guardians of would-be lovers.

Aesir Northern gods who made their home in Asgard; there are twelve in number.

Afrásiyáb Son of Poshang, king of Túrán, who led an army against the ruling shah Nauder. Afrásiyáb became ruler of Persia on defeating Nauder.

Afterlife Life after death or paradise, reached only by the process of preserving the body from decay through embalming and preparing it for reincarnation.

Agamemnon A famous King of Mycenae. He married Helen of Sparta's sister Clytemnestra. When Paris abducted Helen, beginning the Trojan War, Menelaus called on Agamemnon to raise the Greek troops. He had to sacrifice his daughter Iphigenia in order to get a fair wind to travel to Troy.

Agastya A rishi (sage). Leads hermits to Rama.

Agemo (Yoruba) A chameleon who aided Olorun in outwitting Olokun, who was angry at him for letting Obatala create life on her lands without her permission. Agemo outwitted Olokun by changing colour, letting her think that he and Olorun were better cloth dyers than she was. She admitted defeat and there was peace between the gods once again.

Aghasur A dragon sent by Kans to destroy Krishna.

Aghríras Son of Poshang and brother of Afrásiyáb, who was killed by his brother.

Agni The god of fire.

Agora Greek marketplace.

Ahura-Mazda Supreme god of the Persians, god of the sky. Similar to the Hindu god Varuna.

Ajax Ajax of Locris was another warrior at Troy. When Troy was captured, he committed the ultimate sacrilege by seizing Cassandra from her sanctuary with the Palladium.

Ajax Ajax the Greater was the bravest, after Achilles, of all warriors at Troy, fighting Hector in single combat and distinguishing himself in the Battle of the Ships. He was not chosen as the bravest warrior and eventually went mad.

Aje (Igbo) Goddess of the earth and the underworld.

Aje (Yoruba) Goddess of the River Niger, daughter of Yemoja.

Akhet Season of the year when the River Nile traditionally flooded.

Akkadian Person of the first Mesopotamian empire, centred in Akkad.

Akwán Diw An evil spirit who appeared as a wild ass in the court of Kai-khosráu. Rustem fought and defeated the demon, presenting its head to Kai-khosráu.

Alba Irish word for Scotland.

Alberich King of the dwarfs.

Alcinous King of the Phaeacians.

Alf-heim Home of the elves, ruled by Frey.

All Hallowmass All Saints' Day.

Allfather Another name for Odin; Yggdrasill was created by Allfather.

Alsvider Steed of the moon (Mani) chariot.

Alsvin Steed of the sun (Sol) chariot.

Amado Outer panelling of a dwelling, usually made of wood.

Ama-no-uzume Goddess of the dawn, meditation and the arts, who showed courage when faced with a giant who scared the other deities, including Ninigi. Also known as Uzume.

Amaterasu Goddess of the sun and daughter of Izanagi after Izanami's death; she became ruler of the High Plains of Heaven on her father's withdrawal from the world. Sister of Tsuki-yomi and Susanoo.

Ambalika Daughter of the king of Benares.

Ambika Daughter of the king of Benares.

Ambrosia Food of the gods.

Amemet Eater of the dead, monster who devoured the souls of the unworthy.

Amen Original creator deity.

Amen-Ra A being created from the fusion of Ra and Osiris. He champions the poor and those in trouble. Similar to the Greek god Zeus.

Ananda Disciple of Buddha.

Anansi One of the most popular African animal myths, Anansi the spider is a clever and shrewd character who outwits his fellow animals to get his own way. He is an entertaining but morally dubious character. Many African countries tell Anansi stories.

Ananta Thousand-headed snake that sprang from Balarama's mouth, Vishnu's attendant, serpent of infinite time.

Andhrímnir Cook at Valhalla.

Andvaranaut Ring of Andvari, the King of the dwarfs.

Angada Son of Vali, one of the monkey host.

Anger-Chamber Room designated for an angry queen.

Angurboda Loki's first wife, and the mother of Hel, Fenris and Jormungander.

Aniruddha Son of Pradyumna.

Anjana Mother of Hanuman.

Anunnaki Great spirits or gods of Earth.

Ansar God of the sky and father of Ea and Anu. Brother-husband to Kishar. Also known as Anshar or Asshur.

Anshumat A mighty chariot fighter.

Anu God of the sky and lord of heaven, son of Ansar and Kishar.

Anubis Guider of souls and ruler of the underworld before Osiris;

he was one of the divinities who brought Osiris back to life. He is portrayed as a canid, African wolf or jackal.

Apep Serpent and emblem of chaos.

Apollo One of the twelve Olympian gods, son of Zeus and Leto. He is attributed with being the god of plague, music, song and prophecy.

Apsaras Dancing girls of Indra's court and heavenly nymphs.

Apsu Primeval domain of fresh water, originally part of Tiawath with whom he mated to have Mummu. The term is also used for the abyss from which creation came.

Aquila The divine eagle.

Arachne A Lydian woman with great skill in weaving. She was challenged in a competition by the jealous Athene who destroyed her work and when she killed herself, turned her into a spider destined to weave until eternity.

Aralu Goddess of the underworld, also known as Eres-ki-Gal. Married to Nergal.

Ares God of War, 'gold-changer of corpses', and the son of Zeus and Hera.

Argonauts Heroes who sailed with Jason on the ship Argo to fetch the golden fleece from Colchis.

Ariki A high chief, a leader, a master, a lord.

Arjuna The third of the Pandavas.

Aroha Affection, love.

Artemis The virgin goddess of the chase, attributed with being the moon goddess and the primitive mother-goddess. She was daughter of Zeus and Leto.

Arundhati The Northern Crown.

Asamanja Son of Sagara.

Asclepius God of healing who often took the form of a snake. He is the son of Apollo by Coronis.

Asgard Home of the gods, at one root of Yggdrasill.

Ashvatthaman Son of Drona.

Ashvins Twin horsemen, sons of the sun, benevolent gods and related to the divine.

Ashwapati Uncle of Bharata and Satrughna.

Asipû Wizard.

Asopus The god of the River Asopus.

Assagai Spear, usually made from hardwood tipped with iron and used in battle.

Astrolabe Instrument for making astronomical measurements.

Asuras Titans, demons, and enemies of the gods possessing magical powers.

Atef crown White crown made up of the Hedjet, the white crown of Upper Egypt, and red feathers.

Atem The first creator-deity, he is also thought to be the finisher of the world. Also known as Tem.

Athene Virgin warrior-goddess, born from the forehead of Zeus when he swallowed his wife Metis. Plays a key role in the travels of Odysseus, and Perseus.

Atlatl Spear-thrower.

Atua A supernatural being, a god.

Atua-toko A small carved stick, the symbol of the god whom it represents. It was stuck in the ground whilst holding incantations to its presiding god.

Augeas King of Elis, one of the Argonauts.

Augsburg Tyr's city.

Avalon Legendary island where Excalibur was created and where Arthur went to recover from his wounds. It is said he will return from Avalon one day to reclaim his kingdom.

Ba Dead person or soul. Also known as ka.

Bairn Little child, also called bairnie.

Balarama Brother of Krishna.

Balder Son of Frigga; his murder causes Ragnarok. Also spelled as Baldur.

Bali Brother of Sugriva and one of the five great monkeys in the Ramayana.

Balor The evil, one-eyed King of the Fomorians and also grandfather of Lugh of the Long Arm. It was prophesied that Balor would one day be slain by his own grandson, so he locked his daughter away on a remote island where he intended that she would never fall pregnant. But Cian, father of Lugh, managed to reach the island disguised as a woman, and Balor's daughter eventually bore him a child. During the second battle of Mag Tured (or Moytura), Balor was killed by Lugh, who slung a stone into his giant eye.

Ban King of Benwick, father of Lancelot and brother of King Bors.

Bannock Flat loaf of bread, typically of oat or barley, usually cooked on a griddle.

Banshee Mythical spirit, usually female, who bears tales of imminent death. They often deliver the news by wailing or keening outside homes. Also known as bean sí.

Bard Traditionally a storyteller, poet or music composer whose work often focused on legends.

Barû Seer.

Basswood Any of several North American linden trees with a soft light-coloured wood.

Bastet Goddess of love, fertility and sex and a solar deity. She is often portrayed with the head of a cat.

Bateta (Yoruba) The first human, created alongside Hanna by the Toad and reshaped into human form by the Moon.

Bau Goddess of humankind and the sick, and known as the 'divine physician'. Daughter of Anu.

Bawn Fortified enclosure surrounding a castle.

Beaver Largest rodent in the United States of America, held in high esteem by the native American people. Although a land mammal, it spends a great deal of time in water and has a dense waterproof fur coat to protect it from harsh weather conditions.

Behula Daughter of Saha.

Bel Name for the god En-lil, the word is also used as a title meaning 'lord'.

Belus Deity who helped form the heavens and earth and created animals and celestial beings. Similar to Zeus in Greek mythology.

Benten Goddess of the sea and one of the Seven Divinities of Luck. Also referred to as the goddess of love, beauty and eloquence and as being the personification of wisdom.

Bere Barley.

Berossus Priest of Bel who wrote a history of Babylon.

Berserker Norse warrior who fights with a frenzied rage.

Bestla Giant mother of Aesir's mortal element.

Bhadra A mighty elephant.

Bhagavati Shiva's wife, also known as Parvati.

Bhagiratha Son of Dilipa.

Bharadhwaja Father of Drona and a hermit.

Bharata One of Dasharatha's four sons.

Bhaumasur A demon, slain by Krishna.

Bhima The second of the Pandavas.

Bhimasha King of Rajagriha and disciple of Buddha.

Bier Frame on which a coffin or dead body is placed before being carried to the grave.

Bifrost Rainbow bridge presided over by Heimdall.

Big-Belly One of Ravana's monsters.

Bilskirnir Thor's palace.

Bodach The term means 'old man'. The Highlanders believed that the Bodach crept down chimneys in order to steal naughty children. In other territories, he was a spirit who warned of death.

Bodkin Large, blunt needle used for threading strips of cloth or tape through cloth; short pointed dagger or blade.

Boer Person of Dutch origin who settled in southern Africa in the late seventeenth century. The term means 'farmer'. Boer people are often called Afrikaners.

Bogle Ghost or phantom; goblin-like creature.

Boliaun Ragwort, a weed with ragged leaves.

Book of the Dead Book for the dead, thought to be written by Thoth, texts from which were written on papyrus and buried with the dead, or carved on the walls of tombs, pyramids or sarcophagi.

Bors King of Gaul and brother of King Ban.

Bothy Small cottage or hut.

Brahma Creator of the world, mythical origin of colour (caste).

Brahmadatta King of Benares.

Brahman Member of the highest Hindu caste, traditionally a priest.

Bran In Scottish legend, Bran is the great hunting hound of Fionn Mac Chumail. In Irish mythology, he is a great hero.

Branstock Giant oak tree in the Volsung's hall; Odin placed a sword in it and challenged the guests of a wedding to withdraw it.

Brave Young warrior of native American descent, sometimes also referred to as a 'buck'.

Bree Thin broth or soup.

Breidablik Balder's palace.

Brigit Scottish saint or spirit associated with the coming of spring.

Brisingamen Freyia's necklace.

Britomartis A Cretan goddess, also known as Dictynna.

Brocéliande Legendary enchanted forest and the supposed burial place of Merlin.

Brokki Dwarf who makes a deal with Loki, and who makes Miolnir, Draupnir and Gulinbursti.

Brollachan A shapeless spirit of unknown origin. One of the most frightening in Scottish mythology, it spoke only two words, 'Myself' and 'Thyself', taking the shape of whatever it sat upon.

Brownie A household spirit or creature which took the form of a small man (usually hideously ugly) who undertakes household chores, and mill or farm work, in exchange for a bowl of milk.

Brugh Borough or town.

Brunhilde A Valkyrie found by Sigurd.

Buddha Founder of buddhism, Gautama, avatar of Vishnu in Hinduism.

Buddhism Buddhism arrived in China in the first century BC via the silk trading route from India and Central Asia. Its founder was Guatama Siddhartha (the Buddha), a religious teacher in northern India. Buddhist doctrine declared that by destroying the causes of all suffering, mankind could attain perfect enlightenment. The religion encouraged a new respect for all living things and brought with it the idea of reincarnation; i.e. that the soul returns to the earth after death in another form, dictated by the individual's behaviour in his previous life. By the fourth century, Buddhism was the dominant religion in China, retaining its powerful influence over the nation until the mid-ninth century.

Buffalo A type of wild ox, once widely scattered over the Great Plains of North America. Also known as a 'bison', the buffalo was an important food source for the Indian tribes and its hide was also used in the construction of tepees and to make clothing. The buffalo was also sometimes revered as a totem animal, i.e. venerated as a direct ancestor of the tribesmen, and its skull used in ceremonial fashion.

Bull of Apis Sacred bull, thought to be the son of Hathor.

Bulu Sacrificial rite.

Bundles, sacred These bundles contained various venerated objects of the tribe, believed to have supernatural powers. Custody or ownership of the bundle was never lightly entered upon, but involved the learning of endless songs and ritual dances.

Bushel Unit of measurement, usually used for agricultural products or food.

Bushi Warrior.

Byre Barn for keeping cattle.

Byrny Coat of mail.

Cacique King or prince.

Cailleach Bheur A witch with a blue face who represents winter. When she is reborn each autumn, snow falls. She is mother of the god of youth (Angus mac Og).

Calabash Gourd from the calabash tree, commonly used as a bottle.

Calchas The seer of Mycenae who accompanied the Greek fleet to Troy. It was his prophecy which stated that Troy would never be taken without the aid of Achilles.

Calpulli Village house, or group or clan of families.

Calumet Ceremonial pipe used by the north American Indians.

Calypso A nymph who lived on the island of Ogygia.

Camaxtli Tlascalan god of war and the chase, similar to Huitzilopochtli.

Camelot King Arthur's castle and centre of his realm.

Caoineag A banshee.

Caravanserai Traveller's inn, traditionally found in Asia or North Africa.

Carle Term for a man, often old; peasant.

Cat A black cat has great mythological significance, is often the bearer of bad luck, a symbol of black magic, and the familiar of a witch. Cats were also the totem for many tribes.

Cath Sith A fairy cat who was believed to be a witch transformed.

Cazi Magical person or influence.

Ceasg A Scottish mermaid with the body of a maiden and the tail of a salmon.

Ceilidh Party.

Cerberus The three-headed dog who guarded the entrance to the Underworld.

Chalchiuhtlicue Goddess of water and the sick or newborn, and wife of Tlaloc. She is often symbolized as a small frog.

Changeling A fairy substitute-child left by fairies in place of a human child they have stolen.

Channa Guatama's charioteer.

Chaos A state from which the universe was created – caused by fire and ice meeting.

Charon The ferryman of the dead who carries souls across the River Styx to Hades.

Charybdis **See** Scylla and Charybdis.

Chicomecohuatl Chief goddess of maize and one of a group of deities called Centeotl, who care for all aspects of agriculture.

Chicomoztoc Legendary mountain and place of origin of the Aztecs. The name means 'seven caves'.

Chinawezi Primordial serpent.

Chinvat Bridge Bridge of the Gatherer, which the souls of the righteous cross to reach Mount Alborz or the world of the dead. Unworthy beings who try to cross Chinvat Bridge fall or are dragged into a place of eternal punishment.

Chitambaram Sacred city of Shiva's dance.

Chrysaor Son of Poseidon and Medusa, born from the severed neck of Medusa when Perseus beheaded her.

Chryseis Daughter of Chryses who was taken by Agamemnon in the battle of Troy.

Chullasubhadda Wife of Buddha-elect (Sumedha).

Chunda A good smith who entertains Buddha.

Churl Mean or unkind person.

Circe An enchantress and the daughter of Helius. She lived on the island of Aeaea with the power to change men to beasts.

Citlalpol The Mexican name for Venus, or the Great Star, and one of the only stars they worshipped. Also known as Tlauizcalpantecutli, or Lord of the Dawn.

Cleobis and Biton Two men of Argos who dragged the wagon carrying their mother, priestess of Hera, from Argos to the sanctuary.

Clio Muse of history and prophecy.

Clytemnestra Daughter of Tyndareus, sister of Helen, who married Agamemnon but deserted him when he sacrificed Iphigenia, their daughter, at the beginning of the Trojan War.

Coatepetl Mythical mountain, known as the 'serpent mountain'.

Coatl Serpent.

Coatlicue Earth mother and celestial goddess, she gave birth to Huitzilopochtli and his sister, Coyolxauhqui, and the moon and stars.

Codex Ancient book, often a list with pages folded into a zigzag pattern.

Confucius (Kong Fuzi) Regarded as China's greatest sage and ethical teacher, Confucius (551–479 BC) was not especially revered during his lifetime and had a small following of some three thousand people. After the Burning of the Books in 213 BC, interest in his philosophies became widespread. Confucius believed that mankind was essentially good, but argued for a highly structured society, presided over by a strong central government which would set the highest moral standards. The individual's sense of duty and obligation, he argued, would play a vital role in maintaining a well-run state.

Coracle Small, round boat, similar to a canoe. Also known as curragh or currach.

Coyolxauhqui Goddess of the moon and sister to Huitzilopochtli, she was decapitated by her brother after trying to kill their mother.

Creel Large basket made of wicker, usually used for fish.

Crodhmara Fairy cattle.

Cronan Musical humming, thought to resemble a cat purring or the drone of bagpipes.

Crow Usually associated with battle and death, but many mythological figures take this form.

Cu Sith A great fairy dog, usually green and oversized.

Cubit Ancient measurement, equal to the approximate length of a forearm.

Cuculain Irish warrior and hero. Also known as Cuchulainn.

Cutty Girl.

Cyclopes One-eyed giants who were imprisoned in Tartarus by Uranus and Cronus, but released by Zeus, for whom they made thunderbolts. Also a tribe of pastoralists who live without laws, and on, whenever possible, human flesh.

Daedalus Descendant of the Athenian King Erechtheus and son of Eupalamus. He killed his nephew and apprentice. Famed for constructing the labyrinth to house the Minotaur, in which he was later imprisoned. He constructed wings for himself and his son to make their escape.

Dagda One of the principal gods of the Tuatha De Danann, the father and chief, the Celtic equivalent of Zeus. He was the god reputed to have led the People of Dana in their successful conquest of the Fir Bolg.

Dagon God of fish and fertility; he is sometimes described as a sea-monster or chthonic god.

Daikoku God of wealth and one of the gods of luck.

Daimyō Powerful lord or magnate.

Daksha The chief Prajapati.

Dana Also known as Danu, a goddess worshipped from antiquity by the Celts and considered to be the ancestor of the Tuatha De Danann.

Danae Daughter of Acrisius, King of Argos. Acrisius trapped her in a cave when he was warned that his grandson would be the cause of his ultimate death. Zeus came to her and Perseus was born.

Danaids The fifty daughters of Danaus of Argos, by ten mothers.

Daoine Sidhe The people of the Hollow Hills, or Otherworld.

Dardanus Son of Zeus and Electra, daughter of Atlas.

Dasharatha A Manu amongst men, King of Koshala, father of Santa.

Deianeira Daughter of Oeneus, who married Heracles after he won her in a battle with the River Achelous.

Deirdre A beautiful woman doomed to cause the deaths of three Irish heroes and bring war to the whole country. After a soothsayer prophesied her fate, Deidre's father hid her away from the world to prevent it. However, fate finds its way and the events come to pass before Deidre eventually commits suicide to remain with her love.

Demeter Goddess of agriculture and nutrition, whose name means earth mother. She is the mother of Persephone.

Demophoon Son of King Celeus of Eleusis, who was nursed by Demeter and then dropped in the fire when she tried to make him immortal.

Dervish Member of a religious order, often Sufi, known for their wild dancing and whirling.

Desire The god of love.

Deva A god other than the supreme God.

Devadatta Buddha's cousin, plots evil against Buddha.

Dhrishtadyumna Twin brother of Draupadi, slays Drona.

Dibarra God of plague. Also a demonic character or evil spirit.

Dik-dik Dwarf antelope native to eastern and southern Africa.

Dilipa Son of Anshumat, father of Bhagiratha.

Dionysus The god of wine, vegetation and the life force, and of ecstasy. He was considered to be outside the Greek pantheon, and generally thought to have begun life as a mortal.

Dioscuri Castor and Polydeuces, the twin sons of Zeus and Leda, who are important deities.

Distaff Tool used when spinning which holds the wool or flax and keeps the fibres from tangling.

Divan Privy council.

Divots Turfs.

Dog The dog is a symbol of humanity, and usually has a role helping the hero of the myth or legend. Fionn's Bran and Grey Dog are two examples of wild beasts transformed to become invaluable servants.

Dōshin Government official.

Dossal Ornamental altar cloth.

Doughty Persistent and brave person.

Dragon Important animal in Japanese culture, symbolizing power, wealth, luck and success.

Draiglin' Hogney Ogre.

Draupadi Daughter of Drupada.

Draupnir Odin's famous ring, fashioned by Brokki.

Drona A Brahma, son of the great sage Bharadwaja.

Druid An ancient order of Celtic priests held in high esteem who flourished in the pre-Christian era. The word 'druid' is derived from an ancient Celtic one meaning 'very knowledgeable'. These individuals were believed to have mystical powers and in ancient Irish literature possess the ability to conjure up magical charms, to create tempests, to curse and debilitate their enemies and to perform as soothsayers to the royal courts.

Drupada King of the Panchalas.

Dryads Nymphs of the trees.

Dun A stronghold or royal abode surrounded by an earthen wall.

Durga Goddess, wife of Shiva.

Durk Knife. Also spelled as dirk.

Duryodhana One of Drona's pupils.

Dvalin Dwarf visited by Loki; also the name for the stag on Yggdrasill.

Dwarfie Stone Prehistoric tomb or boulder.

Dwarfs Fairies and black elves are called dwarfs.

Dwarkanath The Lord of Dwaraka; Krishna.

Dyumatsena King of the Shalwas and father of Satyavan.

Ea God of water, light and wisdom, and one of the creator deities. He brought arts and civilization to humankind. Also known as Oannes and Nudimmud.

Eabani Hero originally created by Aruru to defeat Gilgamesh, the two became friends and destroyed Khumbaba together. He personifies the natural world.

Each Uisge The mythical water-horse which haunts lochs and appears in various forms.

Ebisu One of the gods of luck. He is also the god of labour and fishermen.

Echo A nymph who was punished by Hera for her endless stories told to distract Hera from Zeus's infidelity.

Ector King Arthur's foster father, who raised Arthur to protect him.

Edda Collection of prose and poetic myths and stories from the Norsemen.

Eight Immortals Three of these are reputed to be historical: Han Chung-li, born in Shaanxi, who rose to become a Marshal of the Empire in 21 BC. Chang Kuo-Lao, who lived in the seventh to eighth century AD, and Lü Tung-pin, who was born in AD 755.

Einheriear Odin's guests at Valhalla.

Eisa Loki' daughter.

Ekake (Ibani) Person of great intelligence, which means 'tortoise'. Also known as Mbai (Igbo).

Ekalavya Son of the king of the Nishadas.

Electra Daughter of Agamemnon and Clytemnestra.

Eleusis A town in which the cult of Demeter is centred.

Elf Sigmund is buried by an elf; there are light and dark elves (the latter called dwarfs).

Elokos (Central African) Imps of dwarf-demons who eat human flesh.

Elpenor The youngest of Odysseus's crew who fell from the roof of Circe's house on Aeaea and visited with Odysseus at Hades.

Elysium The home of the blessed dead.

Emain Macha The capital of ancient Ulster.

Emma Dai-o King of hell and judge of the dead.

En-lil God of the lower world, storms and mist, who held sway over the ghostly animistic spirits, which at his bidding might pose as the friends or enemies of men. Also known as Bel.

Eos Goddess of the dawn and sister of the sun and moon.

Erichthonius A child born of the semen spilled when Hephaestus tried to rape Athene on the Acropolis.

Eridu The home of Ea and one of the two major cities of Babylonian civilization.

Erin Term for Ireland, originally spelled Éirinn.

Erirogho Magical mixture made from the ashes of the dead.

Eros God of Love, the son of Aphrodite.

Erpa Hereditary chief.

Erysichthon A Thessalian who cut down a grove sacred to Demeter, who punished him with eternal hunger.

Eshu (Yoruba) God of mischief. He also tests people's characters and controls law enforcement.

Eteocles Son of Oedipus.

Eumaeus Swineherd of Odysseus's family at Ithaca.

Euphemus A son of Poseidon who could walk on water. He sailed with the Argonauts.

Europa Daughter of King Agenor of Tyre, who was taken by Zeus to Crete.

Eurydice A Thracian nymph married to Orpheus.

Excalibur The magical sword given to Arthur by the Lady of the Lake. In some versions of the myths, Excalibur is also the sword that the young Arthur pulls from the stone to become king.

Fabulist Person who composes or tells fables.

Fafnir Shape-changer who kills his father and becomes a dragon to guard the family jewels. Slain by Sigurd.

Fairy The word is derived from 'Fays' which means Fates. They are immortal, with the gift of prophecy and of music, and their role changes according to the origin of the myth. They were often considered to be little people, with enormous propensity for mischief, but they are central to many myths and legends, with important powers.

Faro (Mali, Guinea) God of the sky.

Fates In Greek mythology, daughters of Zeus and Themis, who spin the thread of a mortal's life and cut it when his time is due. Called Norns in Viking mythology.

Fenris A wild wolf, who is the son of Loki. He roams the earth after Ragnarok.

Ferhad Sculptor who fell in love with Shireen, the wife of Khosru, and undertook a seemingly impossible task to clear a passage through the mountain of Beysitoun and join the rivers in return for winning Shireen's hand.

Fialar Red cock of Valhalla.

Fianna/Fenians The word 'fianna' was used in early times to describe young warrior-hunters. These youths evolved under the leadership of Finn Mac Cumaill as a highly skilled band of military men who took up service with various kings throughout Ireland.

Filheim Land of mist, at the end of one of Yggdrasill's roots.

Fingal Another name for Fionn Mac Chumail, used after MacPherson's Ossian in the eighteenth century.

Fionn Mac Chumail Irish and Scottish warrior, with great powers of fairness and wisdom. He is known not for physical strength but for knowledge, sense of justice, generosity and canny instinct. He had two hounds, which were later discovered to be his nephews transformed. He became head of the Fianna, or Féinn, fighting the enemies of Ireland and Scotland. He was the father of Oisin (also called Ossian, or other derivatives), and father or grandfather of Osgar.

Fir Bolg One of the ancient, pre-Gaelic peoples of Ireland who were reputed to have worshipped the god Bulga, meaning god of lighting. They are thought to have colonized Ireland around 1970 BC, after the death of Nemed and to have reigned for a short period of thirty-seven years before their defeat by the Tuatha De Danann.

Fir Chlis Nimble men or merry dancers, who are the souls of fallen angels.

Flitch Side of salted and cured bacon.

Folkvang Freyia's palace.

Fomorians A race of monstrous beings, popularly conceived as sea-pirates with some supernatural characteristics who opposed the earliest settlers in Ireland, including the Nemedians and the Tuatha De Danann.

Frey Comes to Asgard with Freyia as a hostage following the war between the Aesir and the Vanir.

Freyia Comes to Asgard with Frey as a hostage following the war between the Aesir and the Vanir. Goddess of beauty and love.

Frigga Odin's wife and mother of gods; she is goddess of the earth.

Fuath Evil spirits which lived in or near the water.

Fulla Frigga's maidservant.

Furies Creatures born from the blood of Cronus, guarding the greatest sinners of the Underworld. Their power lay in their ability to drive mortals mad. Snakes writhed in their hair and around their waists.

Furoshiki Cloths used to wrap things.

Gae Bolg Cuchulainn alone learned the use of this weapon from the woman-warrior, Scathach and with it he slew his own son Connla and his closest friend, Ferdia. Gae Bolg translates as 'harpoon-like javelin' and the deadly weapon was reported to have been created by Bulga, the god of lighting.

Gaea Goddess of Earth, born from Chaos, and the mother of Uranus and Pontus. Also spelled as Gaia.

Gage Object of value presented to a challenger to symbolize good faith.

Galahad Knight of the Round Table, who took up the search for the Holy Grail. Son of Lancelot, Galahad is considered the purest and most perfect knight.

Galatea Daughter of Nereus and Doris, a sea-nymph loved by Polyphemus, the Cyclops.

Gandhari Mother of Duryodhana.

Gandharvas Demi-gods and musicians.

Gandjharva Musical ministrants of the upper air.

Ganesha Elephant-headed god of scribes and son of Shiva.

Ganges Sacred river personified by the goddess Ganga, wife of Shiva and daughter of the mount Himalaya.

Gareth of Orkney King Arthur's nephew and knight of the Round Table.

Garm Hel's hound.

Garuda King of the birds and mount Vishnu, the divine bird, attendant of Narayana.

Gautama Son of Suddhodana and also known as Siddhartha.

Gawain Nephew of King Arthur and knight of the Round Table, he is best known for his adventure with the Green Knight, who challenges one of Arthur's knights to cut off his head, but only if he agrees to be beheaded in turn in a year and a day, if the Green Knight survives. Gawain beheads the Green Knight, who simply replaces his head. At the appointed time, they meet, and the Green Knight swings his axe but merely nicks Gawain's skin instead of beheading him.

Geisha Performance artist or entertainer, usually female.

Geri Odin's wolf.

Ghommid (Yoruba) Term for mythological creatures such as goblins or ogres.

Giallar Bridge in Filheim.

Giallarhorn Heimdall's trumpet – the final call signifies Ragnarok.

Giants In Greek mythology, a race of beings born from Gaea, grown from the blood that dropped from the castrated Uranus. Usually represent evil in Viking mythology.

Gilgamesh King of Erech, known as a half-human, half-god hero similar to the Greek Heracles, and often listed with the gods. He is the personification of the sun and is protected by the god Shamash, who in some texts is described as his father. He is also portrayed as an evil tyrant at times.

Gillie Someone who works for a Scottish chief, usually as an attendant or servant; guide for fishing or hunting parties.

Gladheim Where the twelve deities of Asgard hold their thrones. Also called Gladsheim.

Gled Bird of prey.

Golden Fleece Fleece of the ram sent by Poseidon to substitute for Phrixus when his father was going to sacrifice him. The Argonauts went in search of the fleece.

Goodman Man of the house.

Goodwife Woman of the house.

Gopis Lovers of the young Krishna and milkmaids.

Gorgon One of the three sisters, including Medusa, whose frightening looks could turn mortals to stone.

Graces Daughters of Aphrodite by Zeus.

Gramercy Expression of surprise or strong feeling.

Great Head The Iroquois Indians believed in the existence of a curious being known as Great Head, a creature with an enormous head poised on slender legs.

Great Spirit The name given to the Creator of all life, as well as the term used to describe the omnipotent force of the Creator existing in every living thing.

Great-Flank One of Ravana's monsters.

Green Knight A knight dressed all in green and with green hair and skin who challenged one of Arthur's knights to strike him a blow with an axe and that, if he survived, he would return to behead the knight in a year and a day. He turned out to be Lord Bertilak and was under an enchantment cast by Morgan le Fay to test Arthur's knights.

Gruagach Mythical creature, often a giant or ogre similar to a wild man of the woods. The term can also refer to other mythical creatures such as brownies or fairies. As a brownie, he is usually dressed in red or green as opposed to the traditional brown. He has great power to enchant the hapless, or to help mortals who are worthy (usually heroes). He often appears to challenge a boy-hero, during his period of education.

Gudea High priest of Lagash, known to be a patron of the arts and a writer himself.

Guebre Religion founded by Zoroaster, the Persian prophet.

Gugumatz Creator god who, with Huracan, formed the sky, earth and everything on it.

Guha King of Nishadha.

Guidewife Woman.

Guinevere Wife of King Arthur; she is often portrayed as a virtuous lady and wife, but is perhaps best known for having a love affair with Lancelot, one of Arthur's friends and knights of the Round Table. Her name is also spelled Guenever.

Gulistan *Rose Garden*, written by the poet Sa'di

Gungnir Odin's spear, made of Yggdrasill wood, and the tip fashioned by Dvalin.

Gylfi A wandering king to whom the Eddas are narrated.

Haab Mayan solar calendar that consisted of eighteen twenty-day months.

Hades One of the three sons of Cronus; brother of Poseidon and Zeus. Hades is King of the Underworld, which is also known as the House of Hades.

Haere-mai Maori phrase meaning 'come here, welcome.'

Haere-mai-ra, me o tatou mate Maori phrase meaning 'come here, that I may sorrow with you.'

Haere-ra Maori phrase meaning 'goodbye, go, farewell.'

Haji Muslim pilgrim who has been to Mecca.

Hakama Traditional Japanese clothing, worn on the bottom half of the body.

Hanuman General of the monkey people.

Harakiri Suicide, usually by cutting or stabbing the abdomen. Also known as seppuku.

Hari-Hara Shiva and Vishnu as one god.

Harmonia Daughter of Ares and Aphrodite, wife of Cadmus.

Hatamoto High-ranking samurai.

Hathor Great cosmic mother and patroness of lovers. She is portrayed as a cow.

Hati The wolf who pursues the sun and moon.

Hatshepsut Second female pharaoh.

Hauberk Armour to protect the neck and shoulders, sometimes a full-length coat of mail.

Hector Eldest son of King Priam who defended Troy from the Greeks. He was killed by Achilles.

Hecuba The second wife of Priam, King of Troy. She was turned into a dog after Troy was lost.

Heimdall White god who guards the Bifrost bridge.

Hel Goddess of death and Loki's daughter. Also known as Hela.

Helen Daughter of Leda and Tyndareus, King of Sparta, and the most beautiful woman in the world. She was responsible for starting the Trojan War.

Heliopolis City in modern-day Cairo, known as the City of the Sun and the central place of worship of Ra. Also known as Anu.

Helius The sun, son of Hyperion and Theia.

Henwife Witch.

Hephaestus or **Hephaistos** The Smith of Heaven.

Hera A Mycenaean palace goddess, married to Zeus.

Heracles An important Greek hero, the son of Zeus and Alcmena. His name means 'Glory of Hera'. He performed twelve labours for King Eurystheus, and later became a god.

Hermes The conductor of souls of the dead to Hades, and god of trickery and of trade. He acts as messenger to the gods.

Hermod Son of Frigga and Odin who travelled to see Hel in order to reclaim Balder for Asgard.

Hero and Leander Hero was a priestess of Aphrodite, loved by Leander, a young man of Abydos. He drowned trying to see her.

Hestia Goddess of the hearth, daughter of Cronus and Rhea.

Hieroglyphs Type of writing that combines symbols and pictures, usually cut into tombs or rocks, or written on papyrus.

Himalaya Great mountain and range, father of Parvati.

Hiordis Wife of Sigmund and mother of Sigurd.

Hoderi A fisher and son of Okuninushi.

Hodur Balder's blind twin; known as the personification of darkness.

Hoenir Also called Vili; produced the first humans with Odin and Loki, and was one of the triad responsible for the creation of the world.

Hōichi the Earless A biwa hōshi, a blind storyteller who played the biwa or lute. Also a priest.

Holger Danske Legendary Viking warrior who is thought to never die. He sleeps until he is needed by his people and then he will rise to protect them.

Homayi Phoenix.

Hoodie Mythical creature which often appears as a crow.

Hoori A hunter and son of Okuninushi.

Horus God of the sky and kinship, son of Isis and Osiris. He captained the boat that carried Ra across the sky. He is depicted with the head of a falcon.

Hotei One of the gods of luck. He also personifies humour and contentment.

Houlet Owl.

Houri Beautiful virgin from paradise.

Hrim-faxi Steed of the night.

Hubris Presumptuous behaviour which causes the wrath of the gods to be brought on to mortals.

Hueytozoztli Festival dedicated to Tlaloc and, at times, Chicomecohuatl or other deities. Also the fourth month of the Aztec calendar.

Hugin Odin's raven.

Huitzilopochtli God of war and the sun, also connected with the summer and crops; one of the principal Aztec deities. He was born a full-grown adult to save his mother, Coatlicue, from the jealousy of his sister, Coyolxauhqui, who tried to kill Coatlicue. The Mars of the Aztec gods. In some origin stories he is one of four offspring of Ometeotl and Omecihuatl.

Hurley A traditional Irish game played with sticks and balls, quite similar to hockey.

Hurons A tribe of Iroquois stock, originally one people with the Iroquois.

Huveane (Pedi, Venda) Creator of humankind, who made a baby from clay into which he breathed life. He is known as the High God or Great God. He is also known as a trickster god.

Hymir Giant who fishes with Thor and is drowned by him.

Iambe Daughter of Pan and Echo, servant to King Celeus of Eleusis and Metaeira.

Icarus Son of Daedalus, who plunged to his death after escaping from the labyrinth.

Ichneumon Mongoose.

Idunn Guardian of the youth-giving apples.

Ifa (Yoruba) God of wisdom and divination. Also the term for a Yoruban religion.

Ife (Yoruba) The place Obatala first arrived on Earth and took for his home.

Igigi Great spirits or gods of Heaven and the sky.

Igraine Wife of the duke of Tintagel, enemy of Uther Pendragon, who marries Uther when her first husband dies. She is King Arthur's mother.

Ile (Yoruba) Goddess of the earth.

Imhetep High priest and wise sage. He is sometimes thought to be the son of Ptah.

Imam Person who leads prayers in a mosque.

Imana (Banyarwanda) Creator or sky god.

In The male principle who, joined with Yo, the female side, brought about creation and the first gods. In and Yo correspond to the Chinese Yang and Yin.

Inari God of rice, fertility, agriculture and, later, the fox god. Inari has both good and evil attributes but is often presented as an evil trickster.

Indra The King of Heaven.

Indrajit Son of Ravana.

Indrasen Daughter of Nala and Damayanti.

Indrasena Son of Nala and Damayanti.

Inundation Annual flooding of the River Nile.

Iphigenia The eldest daughter of Agamemnon and Clytemnestra who was sacrificed to appease Artemis and obtain a fair wind for Troy.

Iris Messenger of the gods who took the form of a rainbow.

Iseult Princess of Ireland and niece of the Morholt. She falls in love with Tristan after consuming a love potion but is forced to marry King Mark of Cornwall.

Ishtar Goddess of love, beauty, justice and war, especially in Ninevah, and earth mother who symbolizes fertility. Married to Tammuz, she is similar to the Greek goddess Aphrodite. Ishtar is sometimes known as Innana or Irnina.

Isis Goddess of the Nile and the moon, sister-wife of Osiris. She and her son, Horus, are sometimes thought of in a similar way to Mary and Jesus. She was one of the most worshipped female

Egyptian deities and was instrumental in returning Osiris to life after he was killed by his brother, Set.

Istakbál Deputation of warriors.

Izanagi Deity and brother-husband to Izanami, who together created the Japanese islands from the Floating Bridge of Heaven. Their offspring populated Japan.

Izanami Deity and sister-wife of Izanagi, creator of Japan. Their children include Amaterasu, Tsuki-yomi and Susanoo.

Jade It was believed that jade emerged from the mountains as a liquid which then solidified after ten thousand years to become a precious hard stone, green in colour. If the correct herbs were added to it, it could return to its liquid state and when swallowed increase the individual's chances of immortality.

Jambavan A noble monkey.

Jason Son of Aeson, King of Iolcus and leader of the voyage of the Argonauts.

Jatayu King of all the eagle-tribes.

Jesseraunt Flexible coat of armour or mail.

Jimmo Legendary first emperor of Japan. He is thought to be descended from Hoori, while other tales claim him to be descended from Amaterasu through her grandson, Ninigi.

Jizo God of little children and the god who calms the troubled sea.

Jord Daughter of Nott; wife of Odin.

Jormunganderr The world serpent; son of Loki. Legends tell that when his tail is removed from his mouth, Ragnarok has arrived.

Jorō Geisha who also worked as a prostitute.

Jotunheim Home of the giants.

Ju Ju tree Deciduous tree that produces edible fruit.

Jurasindhu A rakshasa, father-in-law of Kans.

Jyeshtha Goddess of bad luck.

Ka Life power or soul. Also known as ba.

Kai-káús Son of Kai-kobád. He led an army to invade Mázinderán, home of the demon-sorcerers, after being persuaded by a demon. Known for his ambitious schemes, he later tried to reach Heaven by trapping eagles to fly him there on his throne.

Kaikeyi Mother of Bharata, one of Dasharatha's three wives.

Kai-khosrau Son of Saiawúsh, who killed Afrásiyáb in revenge for the death of his father.

Kai-kobád Descendant of Feridún, he was selected by Zál to lead an army against Afrásiyáb. Their powerful army, led by Zál and Rustem, drove back Afrásiyáb's army, who then agreed to peace.

Kailyard Kitchen garden or small plot, usually used for growing vegetables.

Kali The Black, wife of Shiva.

Kalindi Daughter of the sun, wife of Krishna.

Kaliya A poisonous hydra that lived in the jamna.

Kalki Incarnation of Vishnu yet to come.

Kalnagini Serpent who kills Lakshmindara.

Kal-Purush The Time-man, Bengali name for Orion.

Kaluda A disciple of Buddha.

Kalunga-ngombe (Mbundu) Death, also depicted as the king of the netherworld.

Kama God of desire.

Kamadeva Desire, the god of love.

Kami Spirits, deities or forces of nature.

Kamund Lasso.

Kans King of Mathura, son of Ugrasena and Pavandrekha.

Kanva Father of Shakuntala.

Kappa River goblin with the body of a tortoise and the head of an ape. Kappa love to challenge human beings to single combat.

Karakia Invocation, ceremony, prayer.

Karna Pupil of Drona.

Kaross Blanket or rug, also worn as a traditional garment. It is often made from the skins of animals which have been sewn together.

Kasbu A period of twenty-four hours.

Kashyapa One of Dasharatha's counsellors.

Kauravas or Kurus Sons of Dhritarashtra, pupils of Drona.

Kaushalya Mother of Rama, one of Dasharatha's three wives.

Kay Son of Ector and adopted brother to King Arthur, he becomes one of Arthur's knights of the Round Table.

Keb God of the earth and father of Osiris and Isis, married to Nut. Keb is identified with Kronos, the Greek god of time.

Kehua Spirit, ghost.

Kelpie Another word for each uisge, the water-horse.

Ken Know.

Keres Black-winged demons or daughters of the night.

Keshini Wife of Sagara.

Khalif Leader.

Khara Younger brother of Ravana.

Khepera God who represents the rising sun. He is portrayed as a scarab. Also known as Nebertcher.

Kher-heb Priest and magician who officiated over rituals and ceremonies.

Khnemu God of the source of the Nile and one of the original Egyptian deities. He is thought to be the creator of children and of other gods. He is portrayed as a ram.

Khosru King and husband to Shireen, daughter of Maurice, the Greek Emperor. He was murdered by his own son, who wanted his kingdom and his wife.

Khumbaba Monster and guardian of the goddess Irnina, a form of the goddess Ishtar. Khumbaba is likened to the Greek gorgon.

Kia-ora Welcome, good luck. A greeting.

Kiboko Hippopotamus.

Kikinu Soul.

Kimbanda (Mbundu) Doctor.

Kimono Traditional Japanese clothing, similar to a robe.

King Arthur Legendary king of Britain who plucked the magical sword from the stone, marking him as the heir of Uther Pendragon and 'true king' of Britain. He and his knights of the Round Table defended Britain from the Saxons and had many adventures, including searching for the Holy Grail. Finally wounded in battle, he left Britain for the mythical Avalon, vowing to one day return to reclaim his kingdom.

Kingu Tiawath's husband, a god and warrior who she promised would rule Heaven once he helped her defeat the 'gods of light'. He was killed by Merodach who used his blood to make clay, from which he formed the first humans. In some tales, Kingu is Tiawath's son as well as her consort.

Kinnaras Human birds with musical instruments under their wings.

Kinyamkela (Zaramo) Ghost of a child.

Kirk Church, usually a term for Church of Scotland churches.

Kirtle One-piece garment, similar to a tunic, which was worn by men or women.

Kis Solar deity, usually depicted as an eagle.

Kishar Earth mother and sister-wife to Anshar.

Kist Trunk or large chest.

Kitamba (Mbundu) Chief who made his whole village go into mourning when his head-wife, Queen Muhongo, died. He also pledged that no one should speak or eat until she was returned to him.

Knowe Knoll or hillock.

Kojiki One of two myth-histories of Japan, along with the *Nihon Shoki.*

Ko-no-Hana Goddess of Mount Fuji, princess and wife of Ninigi.

Kore 'Maiden', another name for Persephone.

Kraal Traditional rural African village, usually consisting of huts surrounded by a fence or wall. Also an animal enclosure.

Krishna The Dark one, worshipped as an incarnation of Vishnu.

Kui-see Edible root.

Kumara Son of Shiva and Paravati, slays demon Taraka.

Kumbha-karna Ravana's brother.

Kunti Mother of the Pandavas.

Kura Red. The sacred colour of the Maori.

Kusha or Kusi One of Sita's two sons.

Kvasir Clever warrior and colleague of Odin. He was responsible for finally outwitting Loki.

Kwannon Goddess of mercy.

Labyrinth A prison built at Knossos for the Minotaur by Daedalus.

Lady of the Lake Enchantress who presents Arthur with Excalibur.

Laertes King of Ithaca and father of Odysseus.

Laestrygonians Savage giants encountered by Odysseus on his travels.

Laili In love with Majnun but unable to marry him, she was given to the prince, Ibn Salam, to marry. When he died, she escaped and found Majnun, but they could not be legally married. The couple died of grief and were buried together. Also known as Laila.

Laird Person who owns a significant estate in Scotland.

Lakshmana Brother of Rama and his companion in exile.

Lakshmi Consort of Vishnu and a goddess of beauty and good fortune.

Lakshmindara Son of Chand resurrected by Manasa Devi.

Lancelot Knight of the Round Table. Lancelot was raised by the Lady of the Lake. While he went on many quests, he is perhaps best known for his affair with Guinevere, King Arthur's wife.

Land of Light One of the names for the realm of the fairies. If a piece of metal welded by human hands is put in the doorway to their land, the door cannot close. The door to this realm is only open at night, and usually at a full moon.

Lang syne The days of old.

Lao Tzu (Laozi) The ancient Taoist philosopher thought to have been born in 571 BC, a contemporary of Confucius with whom, it is said, he discussed the tenets of Tao. Lao Tzu was an advocate of simple rural existence and looked to the Yellow Emperor and Shun as models of efficient government. His philosophies were recorded in the Tao Te Ching. Legends surrounding his birth suggest that he emerged from the left-hand side of his mother's body, with white hair and a long white beard, after a confinement lasting eighty years.

Laocoon A Trojan wiseman who predicted that the wooden horse contained Greek soldiers.

Laomedon The King of Troy who hired Apollo and Poseidon to build the impregnable walls of Troy.

Lava Son of Sita.

Leda Daughter of the King of Aetolia, who married Tyndareus. Helen and Clytemnestra were her daughters.

Legba (Dahomey) Youngest offspring of Mawu-Lisa. He was given the gift of all languages. It was through him that humans could converse with the gods.

Leman Lover.

Leprechaun Mythical creature from Irish folk tales who often appears as a mischievous and sometimes drunken old man.

Lethe One of the four rivers of the Underworld, also called the River of Forgetfulness.

Lif The female survivor of Ragnarok.

Lifthrasir The male survivor of Ragnarok.

Lil Demon.

Liongo (Swahili) Warrior and hero.

Lofty mountain Home of Ahura-Mazda.

Logi Utgard-loki's cook.

Loki God of fire and mischief-maker of Asgard; he eventually brings about Ragnarok. Also spelled as Loptur.

Lotus-Eaters A race of people who live a dazed, drugged existence, the result of eating the lotus flower.

Ma'at State of order meaning truth, order or justice. Personified by the goddess Ma'at, who was Thoth's consort.

Macha There are thought to be several different Machas who appear in quite a number of ancient Irish stories. A particularly well-known 'Macha' is the wife of Crunnchu. The story unfolds that after her husband had boasted of her great athletic ability to the King, she was subsequently forced to run against his horses in spite of the fact that she was heavily pregnant. Macha died giving birth to her twin babies and with her dying breath she cursed Ulster for nine generations, proclaiming that it would suffer the weakness of a woman in childbirth in times of great stress. This curse had its most disastrous effect when Medb of Connacht invaded Ulster with her great army.

Machi-bugyō Senior official or magistrate, usually samurai.

Macuilxochitl God of art, dance and games, and the patron of luck in gaming. His name means 'source of flowers' or 'prince of flowers'. Also known as Xochipilli, meaning 'five-flower'.

Madake Weapon used for whipping, made of bamboo.

Maduma Taro tuber.

Mag Muirthemne Cuchulainn's inheritance. A plain extending from River Boyne to the mountain range of Cualgne, close to Emain Macha in Ulster.

Magni Thor's son.

Mahaparshwa One of Ravana's generals.

Maharaksha Son of Khara, slain at Lanka.

Mahasubhadda Wife of Buddha-select (Sumedha).

Majnun Son of a chief, who fell in love with Laili and followed her tribe through the desert, becoming mad with love until they were briefly reunited before dying.

Makaras Mythical fish-reptiles of the sea.

Makoma (Senna) Folk hero who defeated five mighty giants.

Mana Power, authority, prestige, influence, sanctity, luck.

Manasa Devi Goddess of snakes, daughter of Shiva by a mortal woman.

Manasha Goddess of snakes.

Mandavya Daughter of Kushadhwaja.

Man-Devourer One of Ravana's monsters.

Mandodari Wife of Ravana.

Mandrake Poisonous plant from the nightshade family which has hallucinogenic and hypnotic qualities if ingested. Its roots resemble the human form and it has supposedly magical qualities.

Mani The moon.

Manitto Broad term used to describe the supernatural or a potent spirit among the Algonquins, the Iroquois and the Sioux.

Man-Slayer One of Ravana's counsellors.

Manthara Kaikeyi's evil nurse, who plots Rama's ruin.

Mantle Cloak or shawl.

Manu Lawgiver.

Manu Mythical mountain on which the sun sets.

Mara The evil one, tempts Gautama.

Markandeya One of Dasharatha's counsellors.

Mashu Mountain of the Sunset, which lies between Earth and the underworld. Guarded by scorpion-men.

Matali Sakra's charioteer.

Mawu-Lisa (Dahomey) Twin offspring of Nana Baluka. Mawu (female) and Lisa (male) are often joined to form one being. Their own offspring populated the world.

Mbai (Igbo) Person of great intelligence, also known as Ekake (Ibani), which means 'tortoise'.

Medea Witch and priestess of Hecate, daughter of Aeetes and sister of Circe. She helped Jason in his quest for the Golden Fleece.

Medusa One of the three Gorgons whose head had the power to turn onlookers to stone.

Melpomene One of the muses, and mother of the Sirens.

Menaka One of the most beautiful dancers in Heaven.

Menat Amulet, usually worn for protection.

Mendicant Beggar.

Menelaus King of Sparta, brother of Agamemnon. Married Helen and called war against Troy when she eloped with Paris.

Menthu Lord of Thebes and god of war. He is portrayed as a hawk or falcon.

Mere-pounamu A native weapon made of a rare green stone.

Merlin Wizard and advisor to King Arthur. He is thought to be the son of a human female and an incubus (male demon). He brought about Arthur's birth and ascension to king, then acted as his mentor.

Merodach God who battled Tiawath and defeated her by cutting out her heart and dividing her corpse into two pieces. He used these pieces to divide the upper and lower waters once controlled by Tiawath, making a dwelling for the gods of light. He also created humankind. Also known as Marduk.

Merrow Mythical mermaid-like creature, often depicted with an enchanted cap, called a cohuleen driuth, which allows it to travel between land and the depths of the sea. Also known as murúch.

Metaneira Wife of Celeus, King of Eleusis, who hired Demeter in disguise as her nurse.

Metztli Goddess of the moon, her name means 'lady of the night'. Also known as Yohualtictl.

Michabo Also known as Manobozho, or the Great Hare, the principal deity of the Algonquins, maker and preserver of the earth, sun and moon.

Mictlan God of the dead and ruler of the underworld. He was married to Mictecaciuatl and is often represented as a bat. He is also the Aztec lord of Hades. Also known as Mictlantecutli. Mictlan is also the name for the underworld.

Midgard Dwelling place of humans (Earth).

Midsummer A time when fairies dance and claim human victims.

Mihrab Father of Rúdábeh and descendant of Zohák, the serpent-king.

Milesians A group of iron-age invaders led by the sons of Mil, who arrived in Ireland from Spain around 500 BC and overcame the Tuatha De Danann.

Mimir God of the ocean. His head guards a well; reincarnated after Ragnarok.

Minos King of Crete, son of Zeus and Europa. He was considered to have been the ruler of a sea empire.

Minotaur A creature born of the union between Pasiphae and a Cretan Bull.

Minúchihr King who lives to be one hundred and twenty years old. Father of Nauder.

Miolnir *See* Mjolnir.

Mithra God of the sun and light in Iran, protector of truth and guardian of pastures and cattle. Alo known as Mitra in Hindu mythology and Mithras in Roman mythology.

Mixcoatl God of the chase or the hunt. Sometimes depicted as the god of air and thunder, he introduced fire to humankind. His name means 'cloud serpent'.

Mjolnir Hammer belonging to the Norse god of thunder, which is used as a fearsome weapon which always returns to Thor's hand, and as an instrument of consecration.

Mnoatia Forest spirits.

Moccasins One-piece shoes made of soft leather, especially deerskin.

Modi Thor's son.

Moly A magical plant given to Odysseus by Hermes as protection against Circe's powers.

Montezuma Great emperor who consolidated the Aztec Empire.

Mordred Bastard son of King Arthur and Morgawse, Queen of Orkney, who, unknown to Arthur, was his half-sister. Mordred becomes one of King Arthur's knights of the Round Table before betraying and fatally wounding Arthur, causing him to leave Britain for Avalon.

Morgan le Fay Enchantress and half-sister to King Arthur, Morgan was an apprentice of Merlin's. She is generally depicted as benevolent, yet did pit herself against Arthur and his knights on occasion. She escorts Arthur on his final journey to Avalon. Also known as Morgain le Fay.

Morholt, the Knight sent to Cornwall to force King Mark to pay tribute to Ireland. He is killed by Tristan.

Morongoe the brave (Lesotho) Man who was turned into a snake by evil spirits because Tau was jealous that he had married the beautiful Mokete, the chief's daughter. Morongoe was returned to human form after his son, Tsietse, returned him to their family.

Mosima (Bapedi) The underworld or abyss.

Mount Fuji Highest mountain in Japan, on the island of Honshū.

Mount Kunlun This mountain features in many Chinese legends as the home of the great emperors on Earth. It is written in the *Shanghaijing (The Classic of Mountains and Seas)* that this towering structure measured no less than 3300 miles in circumference and 4000 miles in height. It acted both as a central pillar to support the heavens, and as a gateway between Heaven and Earth.

Moving Finger Expression for taking responsibility for one's life and actions, which cannot be undone.

Moytura Translated as the 'Plain of Weeping', Mag Tured, or Moytura, was where the Tuatha De Danann fought two of their most significant battles.

Mua An old-time Polynesian god.

Muezzin Person who performs the Muslim call to prayer.

Mugalana A disciple of Buddha.

Muilearteach The Cailleach Bheur of the water, who appears as a witch or a sea-serpent. On land she grew larger and stronger by fire.

Mul-lil God of Nippur, who took the form of a gazelle.

Muloyi Sorcerer, also called mulaki, murozi, ndozi or ndoki.

Mummu Son of Tiawath and Apsu. He formed a trinity with them to battle the gods. Also known as Moumis. In some tales, Mummu is also Merodach, who eventually destroyed Tiawath.

Munin Odin's raven.

Murile (Chaga) Man who dug up a taro tuber that resembled his baby brother, which turned into a living boy. His mother killed the baby when she saw Murile was starving himself to feed it.

Murtough Mac Erca King who ruled Ireland when many of its people – including his wife and family – were converting to Christianity. He remained a pagan.

Muses Goddesses of poetry and song, daughters of Zeus and Mnemosyne.

Musha Expression, often of surprise.

Muskrat North American beaver-like, amphibious rodent.

Muspell Home of fire, and the fire-giants.

Mwidzilo Taboo which, if broken, can cause death.

Nabu God of writing and wisdom. Also known as Nebo. Thought to be the son of Merodach.

Nahua Ancient Mexicans.

Nakula Pandava twin skilled in horsemanship.

Nala One of the monkey host, son of Vishvakarma.

Nana Baluka (Dahomey) Mother of all creation. She gave birth to an androgynous being with two faces. The female face was Mawu, who controlled the night and lands to the west. The male face was Lisa and he controlled the day and the east.

Nanahuatl Also known as Nanauatzin. Presided over skin diseases and known as Leprous, which in Nahua meant 'divine'.

Nandi Shiva's bull.

Nanna Balder's wife.

Nannar God of the moon and patron of the city of Ur.

Naram-Sin Son or ancestor of Sargon and king of the Four Zones or Quarters of Babylon.

Narcissus Son of the River Cephisus. He fell in love with himself and died as a result.

Narve Son of Loki.

Nataraja Manifestation of Shiva, Lord of the Dance.

Natron Preservative used in embalming, mined from the Natron Valley in Egypt.

Nauder Son of Minúchihr, who became king on his death and was tyrannical and hated until Sám begged him to follow in the footsteps of his ancestors.

Nausicaa Daughter of Alcinous, King of Phaeacia, who fell in love with Odysseus.

Nebuchadnezzar Famous king of Babylon. Also known as Nebuchadrezzar.

Necromancy Communicating with the dead.

Nectar Drink of the gods.

Neith Goddess of hunting, fate and war. Neith is sometimes known as the creator of the universe.

Nemesis Goddess of retribution and daughter of night.

Neoptolemus Son of Achilles and Deidameia, he came to Troy at the end of the war to wear his father's armour. He sacrificed Polyxena at the tomb of Achilles.

Nephthys Goddess of the air, night and the dead. Sister of Isis and sister-wife to Seth, she is also the mother of Anubis.

Nereids Sea-nymphs who are the daughters of Nereus and Doris. Thetis, mother of Achilles, was a Nereid.

Nergal God of death and patron god of Cuthah, which was often known as a burial place. He is also known as the god of fire. Married to Aralu, the goddess of the underworld.

Nestor Wise King of Pylus, who led the ships to Troy with Agamemnon and Menelaus.

Neta Daughter of Shiva, friend of Manasa.

Ngai (Gikuyu) Creator god.

Ngaka (Lesotho) Witch doctor.

Niflheim The underworld. In Norse mythology, ruled over by Hel.

Night Daughter of Norvi.

Nikumbha One of Ravana's generals.

Nila One of the monkey host, son of Agni.

Nin-Girsu God of fertility and war, patron god of Girsu. Also known as Shul-gur.

Ninigi Grandson of Amaterasu, Ninigi came to Earth bringing rice and order to found the Imperial family. He is known as the August Grandchild.

Niord God of the sea; marries Skadi.

Nippur The home of En-lil and one of the two major cities of Babylonian civilization.

Nirig God of war and storms, and son of Bel. Also known as Enu-Restu.

Nirvana Transcendent state and the final goal of Buddhism.

Nis Mythological creature, similar to a brownie or goblin, usually harmless or even friendly, but can be easily offended. They are often associated with Christmas or the winter solstice.

Noatun Niord's home.

Noisy-Throat One of Ravana's counsellors.

Noondah (Zanzibar) Cannibalistic cat which attacked and killed animals and humans.

Norns The fates and protectors of Yggdrasill. Many believe them to be the same as the Valkyries.

Norvi Father of the night.

Nott Goddess of night.

Nsasak bird Small bird who became chief of all small birds after winning a competition to go without food for seven days. The

Nsasak bird beat the Odudu bird by sneaking out of his home to feed.

Nü Wa The Goddess Nü Wa, who in some versions of the Creation myths is the sole creator of mankind, and in other tales is associated with the God Fu Xi, also a great benefactor of the human race. Some accounts represent Fu Xi as the brother of Nü Wa, but others describe the pair as lovers who lie together to create the very first human beings. Fu Xi is also considered to be the first of the Chinese emperors of mythical times who reigned from 2953 to 2838 BC.

Nuada The first king of the Tuatha De Danann in Ireland, who lost an arm in the first battle of Moytura against the Fomorians. He became known as 'Nuada of the Silver Hand' when Diancecht, the great physician of the Tuatha De Danann, replaced his hand with a silver one after the battle.

Nunda (Swahili, East Africa) Slayer that took the form of a cat and grew so big that it consumed everyone in the town except the sultan's wife, who locked herself away. Her son, Mohammed, killed Nunda and cut open its leg, setting free everyone Nunda had eaten.

Nut Goddess of the sky, stars and astronomy. Sister-wife of Keb and mother of Osiris, Isis, Set and Nephthys. She often appears in the form of a cow.

Nyame (Ashanti) God of the sky, who sees and knows everything.

Nymphs Minor female deities associated with particular parts of the land and sea.

Obassi Osaw (Ekoi) Creator god with his twin, Obassi Nsi. Originally, Obassi Osaw ruled the skies while Obassi Nsi ruled the Earth.

Obatala (Yoruba) Creator of humankind. He climbed down a golden chain from the sky to the earth, then a watery abyss, and formed land and humankind. When Olorun heard of his success, he created the sun for Obatala and his creations.

Oberon Fairy king.

Odin Allfather and king of all gods, he is known for travelling the nine worlds in disguise and recognized only by his single eye; dies at Ragnarok.

Oduduwa (Yoruba) Divine king of Ile-Ife, the holy city of Yoruba.

Odur Freyia's husband.

Odysseus Greek hero, son of Laertes and Anticleia, who was renowned for his cunning, the master behind the victory at Troy, and known for his long voyage home.

Oedipus Son of Leius, King of Thebes and Jocasta. Became King of Thebes and married his mother.

Ogdoad Group of eight deities who were formed into four male–female couples who joined to create the gods and the world.

Ogham One of the earliest known forms of Irish writing, originally used to inscribe upright pillar stones.

Oiran Courtesan.

Oisin Also called Ossian (particularly by James Macpherson who wrote a set of Gaelic Romances about this character, supposedly garnered from oral tradition). Ossian was the son of Fionn and Sadbh, and had various brothers, according to different legends. He was a man of great wisdom, became immortal for many centuries, but in the end he became mad.

Ojibwe Another name for the Chippewa, a tribe of Algonquin stock.

Okuninushi Deity and descendant of Susanoo, who married Suseri-hime, Susanoo's daughter, without his consent. Susanoo tried to kill him many times but did not succeed and eventually forgave Okuninushi. He is sometimes thought to be the son or grandson of Susanoo.

Olokun (Yoruba) Most powerful goddess who ruled the seas and marshes. When Obatala created Earth in her domain, other gods began to divide it up between them. Angered at their presumption, she caused a great flood to destroy the land.

Olorun (Yoruba) Supreme god and ruler of the sky. He sees and controls everything, but others, such as Obatala, carry out the work for him. Also known as Olodumare.

Olympia Zeus's home in Elis.

Olympus The highest mountain in Greece and the ancient home of the gods.

Omecihuatl Female half of the first being, combined with Ometeotl. Together they are the lords of duality or lords of the two sexes. Also known as Ometecutli and Omeciuatl or Tonacatecutli and Tonacaciuatl. Their offspring were Xipe Totec, Huitzilopochtli, Quetzalcoatl and Tezcatlipoca.

Ometeotl Male half of the first being, combined with Omecihuatl.

Ometochtli Collective name for the pulque-gods or drink-gods. These gods were often associated with rabbits as they were thought to be senseless creatures.

Onygate Anyway.

Opening the Mouth Ceremony in which mummies or statues were prayed over and anointed with incense before their mouths were opened, allowing them to eat and drink in the afterlife.

Oracle The response of a god or priest to a request for advice – also a prophecy; the place where such advice was sought; the person or thing from whom such advice was sought.

Oranyan (Yoruba) Youngest grandson of King Oduduwa, who later became king himself.

Orestes Son of Agamemnon and Clytemnestra who escaped following Agamemnon's murder to King Strophius. He later returned to Argos to murder his mother and avenge the death of his father.

Orpheus Thracian singer and poet, son of Oeagrus and a Muse. Married Eurydice and when she died tried to retrieve her from the Underworld.

Orunmila (Yoruba) Eldest son of Olorun, he helped Obatala create land and humanity, which he then rescued after Olokun flooded the lands. He has the power to see the future.

Osiris God of fertility, the afterlife and death. Thought to be the first of the pharaohs. He was murdered by his brother, Set, after which he was conjured back to life by Isis, Anubis and others before becoming lord of the afterworld. Married to Isis, who was also his sister.

Otherworld The world of deities and spirits, also known as the Land of Promise, or the Land of Eternal Youth, a place of everlasting life where all earthly dreams come to be fulfilled.

Owuo (Krachi, West Africa) Giant who personifies death. He causes a person to die every time he blinks his eye.

Palamedes Hero of Nauplia, believed to have created part of the ancient Greek alphabet. He tricked Odysseus into joining the fleet setting out for Troy by placing the infant Telemachus in the path of his plough.

Palermo Stone Stone carved with hieroglyphs, which came from the Royal Annals of ancient Egypt and contains a list of the kings of Egypt from the first to the early fifth dynasties.

Palfrey Docile and light horse, often used by women.

Palladium Wooden image of Athene, created by her as a monument to her friend Pallas who she accidentally killed. While in Troy it protected the city from invaders.

Pallas Athene's best friend, whom she killed.

Pan God of Arcadia, half-goat and half-man. Son of Hermes. He is connected with fertility, masturbation and sexual drive. He is also associated with music, particularly his pipes, and with laughter.

Pan Gu Some ancient writers suggest that this God is the offspring of the opposing forces of nature, the yin and the yang. The yin (female) is associated with the cold and darkness of the earth, while the yang (male) is associated with the sun and the warmth of the heavens. 'Pan' means 'shell of an egg' and 'Gu' means 'to secure' or 'to achieve'. Pan Gu came into existence so that he might create order from chaos.

Pandareus Cretan King killed by the gods for stealing the shrine of Zeus.

Pandavas Alternative name for sons of Pandu, pupils of Drona.

Pandora The first woman, created by the gods, to punish man for Prometheus's theft of fire. Her dowry was a box full of powerful evil.

Papyrus Paper-like material made from the pith of the papyrus plant, first manufactured in Egypt. Used as a type of paper as well as for making mats, rope and sandals.

Paramahamsa The supreme swan.

Parashurama Human incarnation of Vishnu, 'Rama with an axe'.

Paris Handsome son of Priam and Hecuba of Troy, who was left for dead on Mount Ida but raised by shepherds. Was reclaimed by his family, then brought them shame and caused the Trojan War by eloping with Helen.

Parsa Holy man. Also known as a zahid.

Parvati Consort of Shiva and daughter of Himalaya.

Passion Wife of desire.

Pavanarekha Wife of Ugrasena, mother of Kans.

Peerie Folk Fairy or little folk.

Pegasus The winged horse born from the severed neck of Medusa.

Peggin Wooden vessel with a handle, often shaped like a tub and used for drinking.

Peleus Father of Achilles. He married Antigone, caused her death, and then became King of Phthia. Saved from death himself by Jason and the Argonauts. Married Thetis, a sea nymph.

Penelope The long-suffering but equally clever wife of Odysseus who managed to keep at bay suitors who longed for Ithaca while Odysseus was at the Trojan War and on his ten-year voyage home.

Pentangle Pentagram or five-pointed star.

Pentecost Christian festival held on the seventh Sunday after Easter. It celebrates the holy spirit descending on the disciples after Jesus's ascension.

Percivale Knight of the Round Table and original seeker of the Holy Grail.

Persephone Daughter of Zeus and Demeter who was raped by Hades and forced to live in the Underworld as his queen for three months of every year.

Perseus Son of Danae, who was made pregnant by Zeus. He fought the Gorgons and brought home the head of Medusa. He eventually founded the city of Mycenae and married Andromeda.

Pesh Kef Spooned blade used in the Opening the Mouth ceremony.

Phaeacia The Kingdom of Alcinous on which Odysseus landed after a shipwreck which claimed the last of his men as he left Calypso's island.

Pharaoh King or ruler of Egypt.

Philoctetes Malian hero, son of Poeas, received Heracles's bow and arrows as a gift when he lit the great hero's pyre on Mount Oeta. He was involved in the last part of the Trojan War, killing Paris.

Philtre Magic potion, usually a love potion.

Pibroch Bagpipe music.

Pintura Native manuscript or painting.

Pipiltin Noble class of the Aztecs.

Pismire Ant.

Piu-piu Short mat made from flax leaves and neatly decorated.

Po Gloom, darkness, the lower world.

Polyphemus A Cyclops, but a son of Poseidon. He fell in love with Galatea, but she spurned him. He was blinded by Odysseus.

Polyxena Daughter of Priam and Hecuba of Troy. She was sacrificed on the grave of Achilles by Neoptolemus.

Pooka Mythical creature with the ability to shapeshift. Often appears as a horse, but also as a bull, dog or in human form, and has the ability to talk. Also known as púca.

Popol Vuh Sacred 'book of counsel' of the Quiché or K'iche' Maya people.

Poseidon God of the sea, and of sweet waters. Also the god of earthquakes. His is brother to Zeus and Hades, who divided the earth between them.

Pradyumna Son of Krishna and Rukmini.

Prahasta (Long-Hand) One of Ravana's generals.

Prajapati Creator of the universe, father of the gods, demons and all creatures, later known as Brahma.

Priam King of Troy, married to Hecuba, who bore him Hector, Paris, Helenus, Cassandra, Polyxena, Deiphobus and Troilus. He was murdered by Neoptolemus.

Pritha Mother of Karna and of the Pandavas.

Prithivi Consort of Dyaus and goddess of the earth.

Proetus King of Argos, son of Abas.

Prometheus A Titan, son of Iapetus and Themus. He was champion of mortal men, which he created from clay. He stole fire from the gods and was universally hated by them.

Prose Edda Collection of Norse myths and poems, thought to have been compiled in the 1200s by Icelandic historian Snorri Sturluson.

Proteus The old man of the sea who watched Poseidon's seals.

Psyche A beautiful nymph who was the secret wife of Eros, against the wishes of his mother Aphrodite, who sent Psyche to perform many tasks in hope of causing her death. She eventually married Eros and was allowed to become partly immortal.

Ptah Creator god and deity of Memphis who was married to Sekhmet. Ptah built the boats to carry the souls of the dead to the afterlife.

Puddock Frog.

Pulque Alcoholic drink made from fermented agave.

Purusha The cosmic man, he was sacrificed and his dismembered body became all the parts of the cosmos, including the four classes of society.

Purvey To provide or supply.

Pushkara Nala's brother.

Pushpaka Rama's chariot.

Putana A rakshasi.

Pygmalion A sculptor who was so lonely he carved a statue of a beautiful woman, and eventually fell in love with it. Aphrodite brought the image to life.

Quauhtli Eagle.

Quern Hand mill used for grinding corn.

Quetzalcoatl Deity and god of wind. He is represented as a feathered or plumed serpent and is usually a wise and benevolent god. Offspring of Ometeotl and Omecihuatl, he is also known as Kukulkan.

Ra God of the sun, ruling male deity of Egypt whose name means 'sole creator'.

Radha The principal mistress of Krishna.

Ragnarok The end of the world.

Rahula Son of Siddhartha and Yashodhara.

Raiden God of thunder. He traditionally has a fierce and demonic appearance.

Rakshasas Demons and devils.

Ram of Mendes Sacred symbol of fatherhood and fertility.

Rama or **Ramachandra** A prince and hero of the Ramayana, worshipped as an incarnation of Vishnu.

Ra-Molo (Lesotho) Father of fire, a chief who ruled by fear. When trying to kill his brother, Tau the lion, he was turned into a monster with the head of a sheep and the body of a snake.

Rangatira Chief, warrior, gentleman.

Regin A blacksmith who educated Sigurd.

Reinga The spirit land, the home of the dead.

Reservations Tracts of land allocated to the native American people by the United States Government with the purpose of bringing the many separate tribes under state control.

Rewati Daughter of Raja, marries Balarama.

Rhadha Wife of Adiratha, a gopi of Brindaban and lover of Krishna.

Rhea Mother of the Olympian gods. Cronus ate each of her children, but she concealed Zeus and gave Cronus a swaddled rock in his place.

Rill Small stream.

Rimu (Chaga) Monster known to feed off human flesh, which sometimes takes the form of a werewolf.

Rishis Sacrificial priests associated with the devas in Swarga.

Rituparna King of Ayodhya.

Rohini The wife of Vasudeva, mother of Balarama and Subhadra, and carer of the young Krishna. Another Rohini is a goddess and consort of Chandra.

Rōnin Samurai whose master had died or fallen out of favour.

Rubáiyát Collection of poems written by Omar Khayyám.

Rúdábeh Wife of Zál and mother of Rustem.

Rudra Lord of Beasts and disease, later evolved into Shiva.

Rukma Rukmini's eldest brother.

Rustem Son of Zál and Rúdábeh, he was a brave and mighty warrior who undertook seven labours to travel to Mázinderán to rescue Kai-káús. Once there, he defeated the White Demon and rescued Kai-káús. He rode the fabled stallion Rakhsh and is also known as Rustam.

Ryō Traditional gold currency.

Sabdh Mother of Ossian, or Oisin.

Sabitu Goddess of the sea.

Sagara King of Ayodhya.

Sahadeva Pandava twin skilled in swordsmanship.

Sahib diwan Lord high treasurer or chief royal executive.

Saiawúsh Son of Kai-káús, who was put through trial by fire when Sudaveh, Kai-káús's wife, told him that Saiawúsh had taken advantage of her. His innocence was proven when the fire did not harm him. He was eventually killed by Afrásiyáb.

Saithe Blessed.

Sajara (Mali) God of rainbows. He takes the form of a multi-coloured serpent.

Sake Japanese rice wine.

Sakuni Cousin of Duryodhana.

Salam Greeting or salutation.

Saláman Son of the Shah of Yunan, who fell in love with Absál, his nurse. She died after they had a brief love affair and he returned to his father.

Salmali tree Cotton tree.

Salmon A symbol of great wisdom, around which many Scottish legends revolve.

Sám Mighty warrior who fought and won many battles. Father of Zál and grandfather to Rustem.

Sambu Son of Krishna.

Sampati Elder brother of Jatayu.

Samurai Noblemen who were part of the military in medieval Japan.

Sanehat Member of the royal bodyguard.

Sango (Yoruba) God of war and thunder.

Sangu (Mozambique) Goddess who protects pregnant women, depicted as a hippopotamus.

Santa Daughter of Dasharatha.

Sarapis Composite deity of Apis and Osiris, sometimes known as Serapis. Thought to be created to unify Greek and Egyptian citizens under the Greek pharaoh Ptolemy.

Sarasvati The tongue of Rama.

Sarcophagus Stone coffin.

Sargon of Akkad Raised by Akki, a husbandman, after being hidden at birth. Sargon became King of Assyria and a great hero. He founded the first library in Babylon. Similar to King Arthur or Perseus.

Sarsar Harsh, whistling wind.

Sasabonsam (Ashanti) Forest ogre.

Sassun Scottish word for England.

Sati Daughter of Daksha and Prasuti, first wife of Shiva.

Satrughna One of Dasharatha's four sons.

Satyavan Truth speaker, husband of Savitri.

Satyavati A fisher-maid, wife of Bhishma's father, Shamtanu.

Satyrs Elemental spirits which took great pleasure in chasing nymphs. They had horns, a hairy body and cloven hooves.

Saumanasa A mighty elephant.

Scamander River running across the Trojan plain, and father of Teucer.

Scarab Dung beetle, often used as a symbol of the immortal human soul and regeneration.

Scylla and Charybdis Scylla was a monster who lived on a rock of the same name in the Straits of Messina, devouring sailors. Charybdis was a whirlpool in the Straits which was supposedly inhabited by the hateful daughter of Poseidon.

Seal Often believed that seals were fallen angels. Many families are descended from seals, some of which had webbed hands or feet. Some seals were the children of sea-kings who had become enchanted (selkies).

Seelie-Court The court of the Fairies, who travelled around their realm. They were usually fair to humans, doling out punishment that was morally sound, but they were quick to avenge insults to fairies.

Segu (Swahili, East Africa) Guide who informs humans where honey can be found.

Sekhmet Solar deity who led the pharaohs in war. She is goddess of healing and was sent by Ra to destroy humanity when people turned against the sun god. She is portrayed with the head of a lion.

Selene Moon-goddess, daughter of Hyperion and Theia. She was seduced by Pan, but loved Endymion.

Selkie Mythical creature which is seal-like when in water but can shed its skin to take on human form when on land.

Seneschal Steward of a royal or noble household.

Sensei Teacher.

Seriyut A disciple of Buddha.

Sessrymnir Freyia's home.

Set God of chaos and evil, brother of Osiris, who killed him by tricking him into getting into a chest, which he then threw in the Nile, before cutting Osiris's body into fourteen separate pieces. Also known as Seth.

Sgeulachd Stories.

Shah Nameh *The Book of Kings* written by Ferdowski, one of the world's longest epic poems, which describes the mythology and history of the Persian Empire.

Shaikh Respected religious man.

Shaivas or Shaivites Worshippers of Shiva.

Shakti Power or wife of a god and Shiva's consort as his feminine aspect.

Shaman Also known as the 'Medicine Men' of Indian tribes, it was the shaman's role to cultivate communication with the spirit world. They were endowed with knowledge of all healing herbs, and learned to diagnose and cure disease. They could foretell the future, find lost property and had power over animals, plants and stones.

Shamash God of the sun and protector of Gilgamesh, the great Babylonian hero. Known as the son of Sin, the moon god, he is also portrayed as a judge of good and evil.

Shamtanu Father of Bhishma.

Shankara A great magician, friend of Chand Sadagar.

Shashti The Sixth, goddess who protects children and women in childbirth.

Sheen Beautiful and enchanted woman who casts a spell on Murtough, King of Ireland, causing him to fall in love with her and cast out his family. He dies at her hands, half burned and half drowned, but she then dies of grief as she returns his love. Sheen is known by many names, including Storm, Sigh and Rough Wind.

Shesh A serpent that takes human birth through Devaki.

Shi-en Fairy dwelling.

Shinto Indigenous religion of Japan, from the pre-sixth century to the present day.

Shireen Married to Khosru. Her beauty meant that she was desired by many, including Khosru's own son by his previous marriage. She killed herself rather than give in to her stepson.

Shitala The Cool One and goddess of smallpox.

Shiva One of the two great gods of post-Vedic Hinduism with Vishnu.

Shogun Military ruler or overlord.

Shoji Sliding door, usually a lattice screen of paper.

Shu God of the air and half of the first divine couple created by Atem. Brother and husband to Tefnut, father to Keb and Nut.

Shubistán Household.

Shudra One of the four fundamental colours (caste).

Shuttle Part of a machine used for spinning cloth, used for passing weft threads between warp threads.

Siddhas Musical ministrants of the upper air.

Sif Thor's wife; known for her beautiful hair.

Sigi Son of Odin.

Sigmund Warrior able to pull the sword from Branstock in the Volsung's hall.

Signy Volsung's daughter.

Sigurd Son of Sigmund, and bearer of his sword. Slays Fafnir the dragon.

Sigyn Loki's faithful wife.

Símúrgh Griffin, an animal with the body of a lion and the head and wings of an eagle. Known to hold great wisdom. Also called a symurgh.

Sin God of the moon, worshipped primarily in Ur.

Sindri Dwarf who worked with Brokki to fashion gifts for the gods; commissioned by Loki.

Sirens Sea nymphs who are half-bird, half-woman, whose song lures hapless sailors to their death.

Sisyphus King of Ephrya and a trickster who outwitted Autolycus. He was one of the greatest sinners in Hades.

Sita Daughter of the earth, adopted by Janaka, wife of Rama.

Skadi Goddess of winter and the wife of Niord for a short time.

Skanda Six-headed son of Shiva and a warrior god.

Skraeling Person native to Canada and Greenland. The name was given to them by Viking settlers and can be translated as 'barbarian'.

Skrymir Giant who battled against Thor.

Sleipnir Odin's steed.

Sluagh The host of the dead, seen fighting in the sky and heard by mortals.

Smote Struck with a heavy blow.

Sohráb Son of Rustem and Tahmineh, Sohráb was slain in battle by his own father, who killed him by mistake.

Sol The sun-maiden.

Soma A god and a drug, the elixir of life.

Somerled Lord of the Isles, and legendary ancestor of the Clan MacDonald.

Soothsayer Someone with the ability to predict or see the future, by the use of magic, special knowledge or intuition. Known as seanagal in Scottish myths.

Squaw North American Indian married woman.

Squint-Eye One of Ramana's monsters.

Squire Shield- or armour-bearer of a knight.

Srutakirti Daughter of Kushadhwaja.

Stirabout Porridge made by stirring oatmeal into boiling milk or water.

Stone Giants A malignant race of stone beings whom the Iroquois believed invaded Indian territory, threatening the Confederation of the Five Nations. These fierce and hostile creatures lived off human flesh and were intent on exterminating the human race.

Stoorworm A great water monster which frequented lochs. When it thrust its great body from the sea, it could engulf islands and whole ships. Its appearance prophesied devastation.

Stot Bullock.

Styx River in Arcadia and one of the four rivers in the Underworld. Charon ferried dead souls across it into Hades, and Achilles was dipped into it to make him immortal.

Subrahmanian Son of Shiva, a mountain deity.

Sugriva The chief of the five great monkeys in the Ramayana.

Sukanya The wife of Chyavana.

Suman Son of Asamanja.

Sumantra A noble Brahman.

Sumati Wife of Sagara.

Sumedha A righteous Brahman who dwelt in the city of Amara.

Sumitra One of Dasharatha's three wives, mother of Lakshmana and Satrughna.

Suniti Mother of Dhruva.

Suparshwa One of Ravana's counsellors.

Supranakha A rakshasi, sister of Ravana.

Surabhi The wish-bestowing cow.

Surcoat Loose robe, traditionally worn over armour.

Surtr Fire-giant who eventually destroys the world at Ragnarok.

Surya God of the sun.

Susanoo God of the storm. He is depicted as a contradictory character with both good and bad characteristics. He was banished from Heaven after trying to kill his sister, Amaterasu.

Sushena A monkey chief.

Svasud Father of summer.

Swarga An Olympian paradise, where all wishes and desires are gratified.

Sweating A ritual customarily associated with spiritual purification and prayer, practised by most tribes throughout North America prior to sacred ceremonies or vision quests. Steam was produced within a 'sweat lodge', a low, dome-shaped hut, by sprinkling water on heated stones.

Syrinx An Arcadian nymph who was the object of Pan's love.

Tablet of Destinies Cuneiform clay tablet on which the fates were written. Tiawath had given this to Kingu, but it was taken by Merodach when he defeated them. The storm god Zu later stole it for himself.

Taiaha A weapon made of wood.

Tailtiu One of the most famous royal residences of ancient Ireland. Possibly also a goddess linked to this site.

Tall One of Ravana's counsellors.

Tammuz Solar deity of Eridu who, with Gishzida, guards the gates of Heaven. Protector of Anu.

Tamsil Example or guidance.

Tangi Funeral, dirge. Assembly to cry over the dead.

Taniwha Sea monster, water spirit.

Tantalus Son of Zeus who told the secrets of the gods to mortals and stole their nectar and ambrosia. He was condemned to eternal torture in Hades, where he was tempted by food and water but allowed to partake of neither.

Taoism Taoism (or Daoism) came into being at roughly the same time as Confucianism, although its tenets were radically different and were largely founded on the philosophies of Lao Tzu (Laozi). While Confucius argued for a system of state discipline, Taoism strongly favoured self-discipline and looked upon nature as the architect of essential laws. A newer form of Taoism evolved after the Burning of the Books, placing great emphasis on spirit worship and pacification of the gods.

Tapu Sacred, supernatural possession of power. Involves spiritual rules and restrictions.

Tara Also known as Temair, the Hill of Tara was the popular seat of the ancient High-Kings of Ireland from the earliest times to the sixth century. Located in Co. Meath, it was also the place where great noblemen and chieftains congregated during wartime, or for significant events.

Tara Sugriva's wife.

Tartarus Dark region, below Hades.

Tau (Lesotho) Brother to Ra-Molo, depicted as a lion.

Taua War party.

Tefnut Goddess of water and rain. Married to Shu, who was also her brother. She, like Sekhmet, is portrayed with the head of a lion. Also known as Tefenet.

Telegonus Son of Odysseus and Circe. He was allegedly responsible for his father's death.

Telemachus Son of Odysseus and Penelope, who was aided by Athene in helping his mother to keep away the suitors in Odysseus's absence.

Temu The evening form of Ra, the Sun God.

Tengu Goblin or gnome, often depicted as bird-like. A powerful fighter with weapons.

Tenochtitlán Capital city of the Aztecs, founded around AD 1350 and the site of the 'Great Temple'. Now Mexico City.

Teo-Amoxtli Divine book.

Teocalli Great temple built in Tenochtitlán, now Mexico City.

Teotleco Festival of the Coming of the Gods; also the twelfth month of the Aztec calendar.

Tepee A conical-shaped dwelling constructed of buffalo hide stretched over lodge-poles. Mostly used by native American tribes living on the plains.

Tepeyollotl God of caves, desert places and earthquakes, whose name means 'heart of the mountain'. He is depicted as a jaguar, often leaping at the sun. Also known as Tepeolotlec.

Tepitoton Household gods.

Tereus King of Daulis who married Procne, daughter of Pandion King of Athens. He fell in love with Philomela, raped her and cut out her tongue.

Tezcatlipoca Supreme deity and Lord of the Smoking Mirror. He was also patron of royalty and warriors. Invented human sacrifice to the gods. Offspring of Ometeotl and Omecihuatl, he is known as the Jupiter of the Aztec gods.

Thalia Muse of pastoral poetry and comedy.

Theia Goddess of many names, and mother of the sun.

Theseus Son of King Aegeus of Athens. A cycle of legends has been woven around his travels and life.

Thetis Chief of the Nereids, loved by both Zeus and Poseidon. They married her to a mortal, Peleus, and their child was Achilles. She tried to make him immortal by dipping him in the River Styx.

Thialfi Thor's servant, taken when his peasant father unwittingly harms Thor's goat.

Thiassi Giant and father of Skadi, he tricked Loki into bringing Idunn to him. Thrymheim is his kingdom.

Thomas the Rhymer Also called 'True Thomas', he was Thomas of Ercledoune, who lived in the thirteenth century. He met with the Queen of Elfland, and visited her country, was given clothes and a tongue that could tell no lie. He was also given the gift of prophecy, and many of his predictions were proven true.

Thor God of thunder and of war (with Tyr). Known for his huge size, and red hair and beard. Carries the hammer Miolnir. Slays Jormungander at Ragnarok.

Thoth God of the moon. Invented the arts and sciences and regulated the seasons. He is portrayed with the head of an ibis or a baboon.

Three-Heads One of Ravana's monsters.

Thrud Thor's daughter.

Thrudheim Thor's realm. Also called Thrudvang.

Thunder-Tooth Leader of the rakshasas at the siege of Lanka.

Tiawath Primeval dark ocean or abyss, Tiawath is also a monster and evil deity of the deep. She took the form of a dragon or sea serpent and battled the gods of light for supremacy over all living beings. She was eventually defeated by Merodach, who used her body to create Heaven and Earth.

Tiglath-Pileser I King of Assyria, who made it a leading power for centuries.

Tiki First man created, a figure carved of wood, or other representation of man.

Tirawa The name given to the Great Creator (**see** Great Spirit) by the Pawnee tribe who believed that four direct paths led from his house in the sky to the four semi-cardinal points: north-east, north-west, south-east and south-west.

Tiresias A Theban who was given the gift of prophecy by Zeus. He was blinded for seeing Athene bathing. He continued to use his prophetic talents after his death, advising Odysseus.

Tirfing Sword made by dwarves which was cursed to kill every time it was drawn, be the cause of three great atrocities, and kill Suaforlami (Odin's grandson), for whom it was made.

Tisamenus Son of Orestes, who inherited the Kingdom of Argos and Sparta.

Titania Queen of the fairies.

Tlaloc God of rain and fertility, so important to the people, because he ensured a good harvest, that the Aztec heaven or paradise was named Tlalocan in his honour.

Tlazolteotl Goddess of ordure, filth and vice. Also known as the earth-goddess or Tlaelquani, meaning 'filth-eater'. She acted as a confessor of sins or wrongdoings.

Tohu-mate Omen of death.

Tohunga A priest; a possessor of supernatural powers.

Toltec Civilization that preceded the Aztecs.

Tomahawk Hatchet with a stone or iron head used in war or hunting.

Tonalamatl Record of the Aztec calendar, which was recorded in books made from bark paper.

Tonalpohualli Aztec calendar composed of twenty thirteen-day weeks called trecenas.

Totec Solar deity known as Our Great Chief.

Totemism System of belief in which people share a relationship with a spirit animal or natural being with whom they interact. Examples include Ea, who is represented by a fish.

Toxilmolpilia The binding up of the years.

Tristan Nephew of King Mark of Cornwall, who travels to Ireland to bring Iseult back to marry his uncle. On the way, he and Iseult consume a love potion and fall madly in love before their story ends tragically.

Triton A sea-god, and son of Poseidon and Amphitrite. He led the Argonauts to the sea from Lake Tritonis.

Trojan War War waged by the Greeks against Troy, in order to reclaim Menelaus's wife Helen, who had eloped with the Trojan prince Paris. Many important heroes took part, and form the basis of many legends and myths.

Troll Unfriendly mythological creature of varying size and strength. Usually dwells in mountainous areas, among rocks or caves.

Truage Tribute or pledge of peace or truth, usually made on payment of a tax.

Tsuki-yomi God of the moon, brother of Amaterasu and Susanoo.

Tuat The other world or land of the dead.

Tupuna Ancestor.

Tvashtar Craftsman of the gods.

Tyndareus King of Sparta, perhaps the son of Perseus's daughter Grogphone. Expelled from Sparta but restored by Heracles. Married Leda and fathered Helen and Clytemnestra, among others.

Tyr Son of Frigga and the god of war (with Thor). Eventually kills Garm at Ragnarok.

Tzompantli Pyramid of Skulls.

Uayeb The five unlucky days of the Mayan calendar, which were believed to be when demons from the underworld could reach Earth. People would often avoid leaving their houses on uayeb days.

Ubaaner Magician, whose name meant 'splitter of stones', who created a wax crocodile that came to life to swallow up the man who was trying to seduce his wife.

Uile Bheist Mythical creature, usually some form of wild beast.

Uisneach A hill formation between Mullingar and Athlone said to mark the centre of Ireland.

uKqili (Zulu) Creator god.

Uller God of winter, whom Skadi eventually marries.

Ulster Cycle Compilation of folk tales and legends telling of the Ulaids, people from the northeast of Ireland, now named Ulster. Also known as the *Uliad Cycle*, it is one of four Irish cycles of mythology.

Unseelie Court An unholy court comprising a kind of fairies, antagonistic to humans. They took the form of a kind of Sluagh, and shot humans and animals with elf-shots.

Urd One of the Norns.

Urien King of Gore, husband of Morgan le Fey and father to Yvain.

Urmila Second daughter of Janaka.

Usha Wife of Aniruddha, daughter of Vanasur.

Ushas Goddess of the dawn.

Utgard-loki King of the giants. Tricked Thor.

Uther Pendragon King of England in sub-Roman Britain; father of King Arthur.

Utixo (Hottentot) Creator god.

Ut-Napishtim Ancestor of Gilgamesh, whom Gilgamesh sought out to discover how to prevent death. Similar to Noah in that he was sent a vision warning him of a great deluge. He built an ark in seven days, filling it with his family, possessions and all kinds of animals.

Uz Deity symbolized by a goat.

Vach Goddess of speech.

Vajrahanu One of Ravana's generals.

Vala Another name for Norns.

Valfreya Another name for Freyia.

Valhalla Odin's hall for the celebrated dead warriors chosen by the Valkyries.

Vali The cruel brother of Sugriva, dethroned by Rama.

Valkyries Odin's attendants, led by Freyia. Chose dead warriors to live at Valhalla. Also spelled as Valkyrs.

Vamadeva One of Dasharatha's priests.

Vanaheim Home of the Vanir.

Vanir Race of gods in conflict with the Aesir; they are gods of the sea and wind.

Varuna Ancient god of the sky and cosmos, later, god of the waters.

Vasishtha One of Dasharatha's priests.

Vassal Person under the protection of a feudal lord.

Vasudev Descendant of Yadu, husband of Rohini and Devaki, father of Krishna.

Vasudeva A name of Narayana or Vishnu.

Vavasor Vassal or tenant of a baron or lord who himself has vassals.

Vedic Mantras, hymns.

Vernandi One of the Norns.

Vichitravirya Bhishma's half-brother.

Vidar Slays Fenris.

Vidura Friend of the Pandavas.

Vigrid The plain where the final battle is held.

Vijaya Karna's bow.

Vikramaditya A king identified with Chandragupta II.

Vintail Moveable front of a helmet.

Virabhadra A demon that sprang from Shiva's lock of hair.

Viradha A fierce rakshasa, seizes Sita, slain by Rama.

Virupaksha The elephant who bears the whole world.

Vishnu The Preserver, Vedic sun-god and one of the two great gods of post-Vedic Hinduism.

Vision Quest A sacred ceremony undergone by Native Americans to establish communication with the spirit set to direct them in life. The quest lasted up to four days and nights and was preceded by a period of solitary fasting and prayer.

Vivasvat The sun.

Vizier High-ranking official or adviser. Also known as vizir or vazir.

Volsung Family of great warriors about whom a great saga was spun.

Vrishadarbha King of Benares.

Vrishasena Son of Karna, slain by Arjuna.

Vyasa Chief of the royal chaplains.

Wairua Spirit, soul.

Wanjiru (Kikuyu) Maiden who was sacrificed by her village to appease the gods and make it rain after years of drought.

Weighing of the heart Procedure carried out after death to assess whether the deceased was free from sin. If the deceased's heart weighed less than the feather of Ma'at, they would join Osiris in the Fields of Peace.

Whare Hut made of fern stems tied together with flax and vines, and roofed in with raupo (reeds).

White Demon Protector of Mázinderán. He prevented Kai-káús and his army from invading.

Withy Thin twig or branch which is very flexible and strong.

Wolverine Large mammal of the musteline family with dark, very thick, water-resistant fur, inhabiting the forests of North America and Eurasia.

Wroth Angry.

Wyrd One of the Norns.

Xanthus & Balius Horses of Achilles, immortal offspring of Zephyrus the west wind. A gift to Achilles's father Peleus.

Xipe Totec High priest and son of Ometeotl and Omecihuatl. Also known as the god of the seasons.

Xiupohualli Solar year, composed of eighteen twenty-day months. Also spelt Xiuhpōhualli.

Yadu A prince of the Lunar dynasty.

Yakshas Same as rakshasas.

Yakunin Government official.

Yama God of Death, king of the dead and son of the sun.

Yamato Take Legendary warrior and prince. Also known as Yamato Takeru.

Yashiki Residence or estate, usually of a daimyō.

Yasoda Wife of Nand.

Yemaya (Yoruba) Wife of Obatala.

Yemoja (Yoruba) Goddess of water and protector of women.

Yggdrasill The World Ash, holding up the Nine Worlds. Does not fall at Ragnarok.

Ymir Giant created from fire and ice; his body created the world.

Yo The female principle who, joined with In, the male side, brought about creation and the first gods. In and Yo correspond to the Chinese Yang and Yin.

Yomi The underworld.

Yudhishthira The eldest of the Pandavas, a great soldier.

Yuki-Onna The Snow-Bride or Lady of the Snow, who represents death.

Yvain Son of Morgan le Fay and knight of the Round Table, who goes on chivalric quests with a lion he rescued from a dragon.

Zahid Holy man.

Zál Son of Sám, who was born with pure white hair. Sám abandoned Zál, who was raised by the Símúrgh, or griffins. Zal became a great warrior, second only to his son, Rustem. Also known as Ním-rúz and Dustán.

Zephyr Gentle breeze.

Zeus King of gods, god of sky, weather, thunder, lightning, home, hearth and hospitality. He plays an important role as the voice of justice, arbitrator between man and gods, and among them. Married to Hera, but lover of dozens of others.

Zohák Serpent-king and figure of evil. Father of Mihrab.

Zu God of the storm, who took the form of a huge bird. Similar to the Persian símúrgh.

Zukin Head covering.

COLLECTOR'S EDITIONS
FLAME TREE
A wide range of new and classic fiction, including short story anthologies, *Collectable Classics*, *Gothic Fantasy* collections and *Epic Tales* of mythology.
•
Available at all good bookstores, and online at *flametreepublishing.com*
FLAME TREE PUBLISHING